PULP
MASTERS

PULP MASTERS

Edited by

ED GORMAN AND
MARTIN H. GREENBERG

CARROLL & GRAF PUBLISHERS, INC.

NEW YORK

First Carroll & Graf edition 2001.

Carroll & Graf Publishers, Inc.
A Division of Avalon Publishing Group
19 West 21st Street
New York, NY 10010-6805

Library of Congress Cataloging-in-Publication Data is available.
ISBN: 0-7867-0873-5

Manufactured in the United States of America

CONTENTS

INTRODUCTION

WHEN I WAS GROWING UP IN THE FORTIES AND FIFTIES, EVERY grocery store, drugstore and dime store sold magazines. You could stand there reading for hours. Especially if you were also interested in comic books.

The most popular magazine titles of the day included *The Saturday Evening Post*, *Collier's*, and *American*.

While they were general interest publications — they ran articles on everything from going to the dentist to biographies of Marilyn Monroe — they also carried, God love 'em, fiction. Short stories to short novels. And in every issue.

In those days, most magazines, believe it or not — felt obliged to carry fiction. We were then, to a much greater degree than we are today, readers of stories. Made-up stories. Campfire tales. F-i-c-t-i-o-n.

In addition to the general interest magazines, there were the pulps.

In the early Fifties, your favorite neighborhood magazine stand was clogged with pulp titles — some in the standard pulp format, others in the new digest size.

Stories of every kind — mystery, romance, western, science fiction, sports, action/adventure, fantasy — there was a pulp for every taste.

A pulp, it seemed, for every writer.

Everybody from Tennessee Williams to Ray Bradbury got his start in the pulps. There was a ritual. You started in the pulps, went on to the slicks (the general interest magazines I cited above) and then on to novels and maybe even Hollywood.

Well after John D. MacDonald got rich and famous writing the Travis McGees, he said he wished the pulp magazines were still around. He would, despite their low pay, still be writing for them, he said, because they offered so much latitude.

And taken together, they certainly did. It was a magazine culture back then. Rex Stout was writing Nero Wolfe short novels. *Cosmopolitan* was running monthly condensed novels by people such as Margaret Millar, Ross Macdonald, Ian Fleming, and John D. himself.

The men's magazines such as *Cavalier* frequently ran long stories and short novels by such major figures as Mickey Spillane and Charles Williams. And everybody from the great Charlotte Armstrong to Mignon Eberhardt could be found in *Good Housekeeping*.

The greatest hard-boiled magazine of all, *Manhunt*, featured every important crime writer of the era, month in and month out. It was a significant showcase for a young Ed McBain and the early careers of Lawrence Block and Donald Westlake.

A magazine culture, indeed.

Few magazines carry fiction today. The short story has gone the way of the black-and-white TV set. The conventional wisdom is that the tube has taken away our desire for short fiction.

But you'd think there'd be room for at least a little fiction in today's general interest magazines.

My partner Marty Greenberg and I thought we'd give you a sampling of what the old days were like when you visited the newsstand and were assaulted by the bright covers of a hundred magazines (literally) that carried fiction of some kind. From *Startling Stories* to the august *Life* (it first published Hemingway's *The Old Man and the Sea*), short fiction was available everywhere.

We've selected an outstanding cross-section of the crime fiction that appeared from the 1930s through the 1970s, in men's magazines and the slicks aimed at women.

Like so many things of my generation, the era of fiction aplenty was a mixed blessing. Yes, there were a lot of bad stories being published. But there were a lot of fine ones, too. And we've selected six of them here from the glory years, to make our point.

Ed Gorman

James M. Cain

THE EMBEZZLER

I've always thought that James M. Cain (1892–1977) was a better writer than either Raymond Chandler or Dashiell Hammett, and that he understood criminality better than either of those gentlemen.

The Postman Always Rings Twice and Double Indemnity have never been rivaled as expressions of sociopathy, nor as "tabloid poetry," as a critic once called Cain's style.

His mainstream novel Mildred Pierce is an amazingly accurate novel about the American working-class, especially on the relationship of a mother and daughter. Even the film version was great, the only Joan Crawford movie I've ever been able to sit through.

While Cain's place is secure in the realm of popular fiction — if not in the hallowed halls of academe — I wish he were more widely appreciated. The last chapter of Double Indemnity is as pure as Baudelarian poetry. And the three chapters leading up to the murder should be studied by anybody interested in the technique of building suspense.

"The Embezzler" is a minor masterpiece, oddly Chekovian in its way (I know that sounds pretentious but that's my judgement), and fascinating as a document of its times. The first time I read it I couldn't read anything else for three days. Every aspect of it is perfectly realized. The love stuff is crushing. Nobody did man-woman better than Cain.

While it's been collected many times over the years, it's been out of print in the United States for some time. Read it and enjoy. It's damned near perfect.

E.G.

1

I FIRST MET HER WHEN SHE CAME OVER TO THE HOUSE ONE night, after calling me on the telephone and asking if she could see me on a matter of business. I had no idea what she wanted, but supposed it was something about the bank. At the time, I was acting cashier at our little Anita Avenue branch, the smallest of the three we've got in Glendale, and the smallest branch we've got, for that matter. In the home office, in Los Angeles, I rate as vice president, but I'd been sent out there to check up on the branch, not on what was wrong with it, but what was right with it. Their ratio of savings deposits to commercial deposits was over twice what we had in any other branch, and the Old Man figured it was time somebody went out there and found out what the trick was, in case they'd invented something the rest of the banking world hadn't heard of.

I found out what the trick was soon enough. It was her husband, a guy named Brent that rated head teller and had charge of the savings department. He'd elected himself little White Father to all those workmen that banked in the branch, and kept after them and made them save until half of them were buying their homes and there wasn't one of them that didn't have a good pile of dough in the bank. It was good for us, and still better for those workmen, but in spite of that I didn't like Brent and I didn't like his way of doing business. I asked him to lunch one day, but he was too busy, and couldn't come. I had to wait till we closed, and then we went to a drugstore while he had a glass of milk, and I tried to get out of him something about how he got those deposits every week, and whether he thought any of his methods could be used by the whole organization. But we got off on the wrong foot, because he thought I really meant to criticize, and it took me half an hour to smooth him down. He was a funny guy, so touchy you could hardly talk to him at all, and with a hymnbook-salesman look to him that made you understand why he regarded his work as a kind of a missionary job among those people that carried their accounts with him. I would say he was around thirty, but he looked older. He was tall and thin, and beginning to get bald, but he walked with a stoop and his face had a gray color that you don't see on a well man. After he drank his milk and ate the two crackers that came with it he took a little tablet out of an envelope he carried in his pocket, dissolved it in his water, and drank it.

But even when he got it through his head I wasn't sharpening an axe for him, he wasn't much help. He kept saying that savings deposits have to be worked up on a personal basis, that the man at the window has to make the depositor feel that he takes an interest in seeing the figures mount up, and more of the same. Once he got a holy look in his eyes, when he said that you can't make the depositor feel that way unless you really feel that way yourself, and for a few seconds he was a little excited, but that died off. It looks all right, as I write it, but it didn't sound good. Of course, a big corporation doesn't like to put things on a personal basis, if it can help it. Institutionalize the bank, but not the man, for the good reason that the man may get an offer somewhere else, and then when he quits he takes all his trade with him. But that wasn't the only reason it didn't sound good. There was something about the guy himself that I just didn't like, and what it was I didn't know, and didn't even have enough interest to find out.

So when his wife called up a couple of weeks later, and asked if she could see me that night, at my home, not at at the bank, I guess I wasn't any sweeter about it than I had to be. In the first place, it looked funny she would want to come to my house, instead of the bank, and in the second place it didn't sound like good news, and in the third place, if she stayed late, it was going to cut me out of the fights down at the Legion Stadium, and I kind of look forward to them. Still, there wasn't much I could say except I would see her, so I did. Sam, my Filipino house boy, was going out, so I fixed a highball tray myself, and figured if she was as pious as he was, that would shock her enough that she would leave early.

It didn't shock her a bit. She was quite a lot younger than he was, I would say around twenty-five, with blue eyes, brown hair, and a shape you couldn't take your eyes off of. She was about medium size, but put together so pretty she looked small. Whether she was really good-looking in the face I don't know, but if she wasn't good-looking, there was something about the way she looked at you that had that thing. Her teeth were big and white, and her lips were just the least little bit thick. They gave her a kind of a heavy, sulky look, but one eyebrow had a kind of twitch to it, so she'd say something and no part of her face would move but that, and yet it meant more than most women could put across with everything they had.

All that kind of hit me in the face at once, because it was the last thing I was expecting. I took her coat, and followed her into the living room. She sat down in front of the fire, picked up a cigarette and tapped it on her nail, and began looking around. When her eye lit on the highball tray she was already lighting her cigarette, but she nodded with the smoke curling up in one eye. "Yes, I think I will."

I laughed, and poured her a drink. It was all that had been said, and yet it got us better acquainted than an hour of talk could have done. She asked me a few questions about myself, mainly if I wasn't the same Dave Bennett that used to play halfback for U.S.C., and when I told her I was. She figured out my age. She was one year off. She said thirty-two, and I'm thirty-three. She said she was twelve years old at the time she saw me go down for a touchdown on an intercepted pass, which put her around twenty-five, what I took her for. She sipped her drink. I put a log of wood on the fire. I wasn't quite so hot about the Legion fights.

When she'd finished her drink she put the glass down, motioned me away when I started to fix her another, and said: "Well."

"Yeah, that awful word."

"I'm afraid I have bad news."

"Which is?"

"Charles is sick."

"He certainly doesn't look well."

"He needs an operation."

"What's the matter with him—if it's mentionable?"

"It's mentionable, even if it's pretty annoying. He has a duodenal ulcer, and he's abused himself so much, or at least his stomach, with this intense way he goes about his work, and refusing to go out to lunch, and everything else that he shouldn't do, that it's got to that point. I mean, it's serious. If he had taken better care of himself, it's something that needn't have amounted to much at all. But he's let it go, and now I'm afraid if something isn't done—well, it's going to be very serious. I might as well say it. I got the report today, on the examination he had. It says if he's not operated on at once, he's going to be dead within a month. He's—verging on a perforation."

"And?"

"This part isn't so easy."

". . . How much?"

"Oh, it isn't a question of money. That's all taken care of. He has a policy, one of these clinical hook-ups that entitles him to everything. It's Charles."

"I don't quite follow you."

"I can't seem to get it through his head that this has to be done. I suppose I could, if I showed him what I've just got from the doctors, but I don't want to frighten him any more than I can help. But he's so wrapped up in his work, he's such a fanatic about it, that he positively refuses to leave it. He has some idea that these people, these workers, are all going to ruin if he isn't there to boss them around, and make them save their money, and pay up their installments on their houses, and I don't know what all. I guess it sounds silly to you. It does to me. But—he won't quit."

"You want me to talk to him?"

"Yes, but that's not quite all. I think, if Charles knew that his work was being done the way he wants it done, and that his job would be there waiting for him when he came out of the hospital, that he'd submit without a great deal of fuss. This is what I've been trying to get around to. Will you let me come in and do Charles' work while he's gone?"

". . . Well—it's pretty complicated work."

"Oh no, it's not. At least not to me. You see, I know every detail of it, as well as he does. I not only know the people, from going around with him while he badgered them into being thrifty, but I used to work in the bank. That's where I met him. And— I'll do it beautifully, really. That is, if you don't object to making it a kind of family affair."

I thought it over a few minutes, or tried to. I went over in my mind the reasons against it, and didn't see any that amounted to anything. In fact, it suited me just as well to have her come in, if Brent really had to go to the hospital, because it would peg the job while he was gone, and I wouldn't have to have a general shake-up, with the other three in the branch moving up a notch, and getting all excited about promotions that probably wouldn't last very long anyway. But I may as well tell the truth. All that went through my mind, but another thing that went through my mind was her. It wasn't going to be a bit unpleasant to have her around for the next few weeks. I liked this dame from the start, and for me anyway, she was plenty easy to look at.

"Why—I think that's all right."

"You mean I get the job?"

"Yeah—sure."

"What a relief. I hate to ask for jobs."

"How about another drink?"

"No, thanks. Well—just a little one."

I fixed her another drink, and we talked about her husband a little more, and I told her how his work had attracted the attention of the home office, and it seemed to please her. But then all of a sudden I popped out: "Who are you, anyway?"

"Why—I thought I told you."

"Yeah, but I want to know more."

"Oh, I'm nobody at all, I'm sorry to say. Let's see, who am I? Born, Princeton, N.J., and not named for a while on account of an argument among relatives. Then when they thought my hair was going to be red they named me Sheila, because it had an Irish sound to it. Then—at the age of ten, taken to California. My father got appointed to the history department of U.C.L.A."

"And who is your father?"

"Henry W. Rollinson—"

"Oh, yes, I've heard of him."

"Ph.D. to you, just Hank to me. And—let's see. High school, valedictorian of the class, tagged for college, wouldn't go. Went out and got myself a job instead. In our little bank. Answered an ad in the paper. Said I was eighteen when I was only sixteen, worked there three years, got a $1 raise every year. Then—Charles got interested, and I married him."

"And, would you kindly explain *that*?"

"It happens, doesn't it?"

"Well, it's none of my business. Skip it."

"You mean we're oddly assorted?"

"Slightly."

"It seems so long ago. Did I mention I was nineteen? At that age you're very susceptible to—what would you call it? Idealism?"

"... Are you still?"

I didn't know I was going to say that, and my voice sounded shaky. She drained her glass and got up.

"Then, let's see. What else is there in my little biography? I have two children, one five, the other three, both girls, and both beautiful. And—I sing alto in the Eurydice Women's Chorus. ... That's all, and now I have to be going."

"Where'd you put your car?"

"I don't drive. I came by bus."

"Then—may I drive you home?"

"I'd certainly be grateful if you would ... By the way, Charles would kill me if he knew I'd come to you. About him, I mean. I'm supposed to be at a picture show. So tomorrow, don't get absent-minded and give me away."

"It's between you and me."

"It sounds underhanded, but he's very peculiar."

I live on Franklin Avenue in Hollywood, and she lived on Mountain Drive, in Glendale. It's about twenty minutes, but when we got in front of her house instead of stopping, I drove on. "I just happened to think; it's awful early for a picture show to let out."

"So it is, isn't it?"

We drove up in the hills. Up to them we had been plenty gabby, but for the rest of the drive we both felt self-conscious and didn't have much to say. When I swung down through Glendale again the Alexander Theatre was just letting out. I set her down on the corner, a little way from her house. She shook hands. "Thanks ever so much."

"Just sell him the idea, and the job's all set."

"... I feel terribly guilty, but—"

"Yes?"

"I've had a grand time."

2

SHE SOLD ME THE IDEA, BUT SHE COULDN'T SELL BRENT, NOT that easy, that is. He squawked, and refused to go to the hospital, or do anything about his ailment at all, except take pills for it. She called me up three or four times about it, and those calls seemed to get longer every night. But one day, when he toppled over at the window, and I had to send him home in a private ambulance, there didn't seem to be much more he could say. They hauled him off to the hospital, and she came in next day to take his place, and things went along just about the way she said they would, with her doing the work fine and the depositors plunking down their money just like they had before.

The first night he was in the hospital I went down there with a basket of fruit, more as an official gift from the bank than on my own account, and she was there, and of course after we left him I offered to take her home. So I took her. It turned out she had arranged that the maid should spend her nights at the house, on account of the children, while he was in the hospital, so we took a ride. Next night I took her down, and waited for her outside, and we took another ride. After they got through taking X-rays they operated, and it went off all right, and by that time she and I had got the habit. I found a newsreel right near the hospital, and while she was with him I'd go in and look at the sports, and then we'd go for a little ride.

I didn't make any passes, she didn't tell me I was different from other guys she'd known, there was nothing like that. We talked about her kids, and the books we'd read, and sometimes she'd remember about my old football days, and some of the things she'd seen me do out there. But mostly we'd just ride along and say nothing, and I couldn't help feeling glad when she'd say the doctors wanted Brent to stay there until he was all healed up. He could have stayed there till Christmas, and I wouldn't have been sore.

The Anita Avenue Branch, I think I told you, is the smallest one we've got, just a little bank building on a corner, with an alley running alongside and a drugstore across the street. It employs six people, the cashier, the head teller, two other tellers, a girl book-keeper, and a guard. George Mason had been cashier, but they transferred him and sent me out there, so I was acting cashier. Sheila was taking Brent's place as head teller. Snelling and Helm were the other two tellers, Miss Church was the bookkeeper, and Adler the guard. Miss Church went in for a lot of apple-polishing with me, or anyway what I took to be apple-polishing. They had to stagger their lunch hours, and she was always insisting that I go out for a full hour at lunch, that she could relieve at any of the windows, that there was no need to hurry back, and more of the same. But I wanted to pull my oar with the rest, so I took a half hour like the rest of them took, and relieved at whatever window needed me, and for a couple of hours I wasn't at my desk at all.

One day Sheila was out, and the others got back a little early, so I went out. They all ate in a little cafe down the street, so I ate there too, and when I got there she was alone at a table. I would have sat down with her, but she didn't look up, and I took a seat a couple of tables away. She was looking out the window, smoking, and pretty soon she doused her cigarette and came over where I was. "You're a little stand-offish today, Mrs. Brent."

"I've been doing a little quiet listening."

"Oh — the two guys in the corner?"

"Do you know who the fat one is?"

"No, I don't."

"That's Bunny Kaiser, the leading furniture man of Glendale. 'She Buys 'Er Stuff from Kaiser'."

"Isn't he putting up a building or something? Seems to me we had a deal on, to handle his bonds."

"He wouldn't sell bonds. It's his building, with his own name chiseled over the door, and he wanted to swing the whole thing himself. But he can't quite make it. The building is up to the first floor now, and he has to make a payment to the contractor. He needs a hundred thousand bucks. Suppose a bright girl got that business for you, would she get a raise?"

"And how would *she* get that business?"

"Sex appeal! Do you think I haven't got it?"

"I didn't say you haven't got it."

"You'd better not."

"Then that's settled."

"And — ?"

"When's this payment on the first floor due?"

"Tomorrow."

"Ouch! That doesn't give us much time to work."

"You let *me* work it, and *I'll* put it over."

"All right, you land that loan, it's a two-dollar raise."

"Two-fifty."

"O.K. — two-fifty."

"I'll be late. At the bank, I mean."

"I'll take your window."

So I went back and took her window. About two o'clock a truck driver came in, cashed a pay check with Helm, then came over to me to make a $10 deposit on savings. I took his book, entered the amount, set the $10 so she could put it with her cash when she came in. You understand: they all have cash boxes, and lock them when they go out, and that cash is checked once a month. But when I took out the card in our own file, the total it showed was $150 less than the amount showing in the passbook.

In a bank, you never let the depositor notice anything. You've got that smile on your face, and everything's jake, and that's fair enough, from his end of it, because the bank is responsible, and what his book shows is what he's got, so he can't lose no matter how you play it. Just the same, under that pasted grin, my lips felt a little cold. I picked up his book again, like there was something else I had to do to it, and blobbed a big smear of ink over it.

"Well, that's nice, isn't it."

"You sure decorated it."

"I tell you what, I'm a little busy just now — will you leave that with me? Next time you come in, I'll have a new one ready for you."

"Anything you say, Cap."

"This one's kind of shopworn, anyway."

"Yeah, getting greasy."

By that time I had a receipt ready for the book, and copied the amount down in his presence, and passed it out to him. He went and I set the book aside. It had taken a little time, and three more depositors were in line behind him. The first two books corresponded with the cards, but the last one showed a $200 difference, more on his book than we had on our card. I hated to do what he had seen me do with the other guy, but I had to have that book. I started to enter the deposit, and once more a big blob of ink went on the page.

"Say, what you need is a new pen."

"What they need is a new teller. To tell you the truth, I'm a little green on this job, just filling in till Mrs. Brent gets back, and I'm hurrying it. If you'll just leave me this book, now —"

"Sure, that's all right."

I wrote the receipt, and signed it, and he went, and I put that book aside. By that time I had a little breathing spell, with nobody at the window, and I checked those books against the cards. Both accounts, on our records, showed withdrawals, running from $25 to $50, that didn't show on the passbooks. Well, brother, it had to show on the passbooks. If a depositor wants to withdraw, he can't do it without his book, because that book's his contract, and we're bound by it, and he can't draw any dough unless we write it right down there, what he took out. I began to feel a little sick at my stomach. I began to think of the shifty way Brent had talked when he explained about working the departments up on a personal basis. I began to think about how he refused to go to the hospital, when any sane man would have been begging for the chance. I began to think of that night call Sheila made on me, and all that talk about Brent's taking things so seriously, and that application she made, to take things over while he was gone.

All that went through my head, but I was still thumbing the cards. My head must have been swimming a little, when I first checked them over, but the second time I ran my eye over those two cards, I noticed little light pencil checks beside each one of those withdrawals. It flashed through my mind that maybe that was his code. He had to have a code, if he was trying to get away with anything. If a depositor didn't have his book, and asked for his balance, he had to be able to tell him. I flipped all the cards over. There were light pencil checks on at least half of them, every one against a withdrawal, none of them against a deposit. I wanted to run those checked amounts off on the adding machine, but I didn't. I was afraid Miss Church would start her apple-polishing again, and offer to do it for me. I flipped the cards over one at a time, slow, and added the amounts in my head. If I was accurate I didn't know. I've got an adding machine mind, and I can do some of those vaudeville stunts without much trouble, but I was too excited to be sure. That didn't matter, that day. I wouldn't be far off. And those little pencil checks, by the time I had turned every card, added up to a little more than eighty-five hundred dollars.

* * *

Just before closing time, around three o'clock, Sheila came in with the fat guy, Bunny Kaiser. I found out why sex appeal had worked, where all our contact men, trying to make a deal for bonds a few months before, had flopped. It was the first time he had ever borrowed a dollar in his life, and he not only hated it, he was so ashamed of it he couldn't even look at me. Her way of making him feel better was not to argue about it at all, but to pat him on the hand, and it was pathetic the way he ate it up. After a while she gave me the sign to beat it, so I went back and got the vault closed, and chased the rest of them out of there as fast as I could. Then we fixed the thing up, I called the main office for O.K.'s, and around four-thirty he left. She stuck out her hand, pretty excited, and I took it. She began trucking around the floor, snapping her fingers and singing some tune while she danced. All of a sudden she stopped, and made motions like she was brushing herself off.

"Well—is there something *on* me?"

". . . No. Why?"

"You've been *looking* at me—for an *hour!*"

"I was—looking at the dress."

"Is there anything the *matter* with it?"

"It's different from what girls generally wear around a bank. It—doesn't look like an office dress."

"I made it myself."

"Then that accounts for it."

3

BROTHER, IF YOU WANT TO FIND OUT HOW MUCH YOU THINK OF a woman, just get the idea she's been playing you for a sucker. I was trembling when I got home, and still trembling when I went up to my room and lay down. I had a mess on my hands, and I knew I had to do something about it. But all I could think of was the way she had taken me for a ride, or I thought she had anyway, and how I had fallen for it, and what a sap I was. My face would feel hot when I thought of those automobile rides, and how I had been too gentlemanly to start anything. Then I would think how she must be laughing at me, and dig my face into the pillow. After a while I got to thinking about tonight. I had a date to take her to the hospital, like I had for the past week, and wondered what I was going to do about that. What I wanted to do was give her a stand-up and never set eyes on her again, but I couldn't. After what she had said at the bank, about me looking at her, she might tumble I was wise if I didn't show up. I wasn't ready for that yet. Whatever I had to do, I wanted my hands free till I had time to think.

So I was waiting, down the street from her house, where we'd been meeting on account of what the neighbors might think if I kept coming to the door, and in a few minutes here she came, and I gave the little tap on the horn and she got in. She didn't say anything about me looking at her, or what had been said. She kept talking about Kaiser, and how we had put over a fine deal, and how there was plenty more business of the same kind that could be had if I'd only let her go out after it. I went along with it, and for the first time since I'd known her, she got just the least little bit flirty. Nothing that meant much, just some stuff about what a team we could make if we really put our minds to it. But it brought me back to what my face had been red about in the afternoon, and when she went in the hospital I was trembling again.

I didn't go to the newsreel that night. I sat in the car for the whole hour she was in there, paying her visit to him, and the longer I sat the sorer I got. I hated that woman when she came out of the hospital, and then, while she was climbing in beside me, an idea hit me between the eyes. If that was her game, how far would she go with me? I watched her light a cigarette, and then felt my mouth go dry and hot. I'd soon find out. Instead of heading for the hills, or the ocean, or any of the places we'd been driving, I headed home.

We went in, and I lit the fire without turning on the living room light. I mumbled something about a drink, and went out in the kitchen. What I really wanted was to see if Sam was in. He wasn't, and that meant he wouldn't be in till one or two o'clock, so that was all right. I fixed the highball tray, and went in the living room with it. She had taken off her hat, and was sitting in front of the fire, or to one side of it. There are two sofas in my living room, both of them half facing the fire, and she was on one of them swinging her foot at the flames. I made two highballs, put them on the low table between the sofas, and sat down beside her. She looked up, took her drink, and began to sip it. I made a crack about how black her eyes looked in the firelight, she said they were blue, but it sounded like she wouldn't mind hearing more. I put my arm around her.

Well, a whole book could be written about how a woman blocks passes when she doesn't mean to play. If she slaps your face she's just a fool, and you might as well go home. If she hands you a lot of stuff that makes *you* feel like a fool, she doesn't know her stuff yet, and you better leave her alone. But if she plays it so you're stopped, and yet nothing much has happened, and you don't feel like a fool, she knows her stuff, and she's all right, and you can stick around and take it as it comes, and you won't wake up next morning wishing that you hadn't. That was what she did. She didn't pull away, she didn't act surprised, she didn't get off any bum gags. But she didn't come to me either, and in a minute or two she leaned forward to pick up her glass, and when she leaned back she wasn't inside of my arm.

I was too sick in my mind though, and too sure I had her sized up right for a trollop, to pay any attention to that, or even figure out what it meant. It went through my mind, just once, that whatever I had to do, down at the bank, I was putting myself in an awful spot, and playing right into her hands, to start something I couldn't stop. But that only made my mouth feel dryer and hotter.

I put my arm around her again, and pulled her to me. She didn't do anything about it at all, one way or the other. I put my cheek against hers, and began to nose around to her mouth. She didn't do anything about that either, but her mouth seemed kind of hard to reach. I put my hand on her cheek, and then deliberately let it slide down to her neck, and unbuttoned the top button of her dress. She took my hand away, buttoned her dress, and reached for her drink again, so when she sat back I didn't have her.

That sip took a long time, and I just sat there, looking at her. When she put the glass down I had my arm around her before she could even lean back. With my other hand I made a swipe, and brushed her dress up clear to where her garters met her girdle. What she did then I don't know, because something happened that I didn't expect. Those legs were so beautiful, and so soft, and warm, that something caught me in the throat, and for about one second I had no idea what was going on. Next thing I knew she was standing in front of the fireplace, looking down at me with a drawn face. "Will you kindly tell me what's got into you tonight?"

"Why—nothing particular."

"Please. I want to know."

"Why, I find you exciting, that's all."

"Is it something I've done?"

"I didn't notice you doing anything."

"Something's come over you, and I don't know what. Ever since I came in the bank today, with Bunny Kaiser, you've been looking at me in a way that's cold, and hard, and ugly. What is it? Is it what I said at lunch, about my having sex appeal?"

"Well, you've got it. We agreed on that."

"Do you know what I think?"

"No, but I'd like to."

"I think that remark of mine, or something, has suddenly wakened you up to the fact that I'm a married woman, that I've been seeing quite a little of you, and that you think it's now up to you to be loyal to the ancient masculine tradition, and try to make me."

"Anyway, I'm trying."

She reached for her drink, changed her mind, lit a cigarette instead. She stood there for a minute, looking into the fire, inhaling the smoke. Then:

"... I don't say it couldn't be done. After all, my home life hasn't been such a waltz dream for the last year or so. It's not so pleasant to sit by your husband while he's coming out of ether, and then have him begin mumbling another woman's name, instead of your own. I guess that's why I've taken rides with you every night. They've been a little breath of something pleasant. Something more than that. Something romantic, and if I pretended they haven't meant a lot to me, I wouldn't be telling the truth. They've been—little moments under the moon. And then today, when I landed Kaiser, and was bringing him in, I was all excited about it, not so much for the business it meant to the bank, which I don't give a damn about, or the two-dollar-and-a-half raise, which I don't give a damn about either, but because it was something you and I had done together, something we'd talk about tonight, and it would be—another moment under the moon, a very bright moon. And then, before I'd been in the bank more than a minute or two, I saw that look in your eye. And tonight, you've been—perfectly horrible. It could have been done, I think. I'm afraid I'm only too human. But not this way. And not any more. Could I borrow your telephone?"

I thought maybe she really wanted the bath, so I took her to the extension in my bedroom. I sat down by the fire quite a while, and waited. It was all swimming around in my head, and it hadn't come out at all like I expected. Down somewhere inside of me, it began to gnaw at me that I had to tell her, I had to come out with the whole thing, when all of a sudden the bell rang. When I opened the door a taxi driver was standing there.

"You called for a cab?"

"No, nobody called."

He fished out a piece of paper and peered at it, when she came downstairs. "I guess that's my cab."

"Oh, you ordered it?"

"Yes. Thanks ever so much. It's been so pleasant."

She was as cold as a dead man's foot, and she was down the walk and gone before I could think of anything to say. I watched her get in the cab, watched it drive off, then closed the door and went back in the living room. When I sat down on the sofa I could still smell her perfume, and her glass was only half drunk. The catch came in my throat again, and I began to curse at myself out loud, even while I was pouring myself a drink.

I had started to find out what she was up to, but all I had found out was that I was nuts about her. I went over and over it till I was dizzy, and nothing she had done, and nothing she had said, proved anything. She might be on the up-and-up, and she might be playing me for a still worse sucker than I had thought she was, a sucker that was going to play her game for her, and not even get anything for it. In the bank, she treated me just like she treated the others, pleasant, polite and pretty. I didn't take her to the hospital any more, and that was how we went along for three or four days.

Then came the day for the monthly check on cash, and I tried to kid myself that was what I had been waiting for, before I did anything about the shortage. So I went around with Helm, and checked them all. They opened their boxes, and Helm counted them up, and I counted his count. She stood there while I was counting hers, with a dead-pan that could mean anything, and of course it checked to the cent. Down in my heart I knew it would. Those false entries had all been made to balance the cash, and as they went back for a couple of years, there wasn't a chance that it would show anything in just one month.

That afternoon when I went home I had it out with myself, and woke up that I wasn't going to do anything about that shortage, that I couldn't do anything about it, until at least I had spoken to her, anyway acted like a white man.

So that night I drove over to Glendale, and parked right on Mountain Drive where I had always parked. I went early, in case she started sooner when she went by bus, and I waited a long time. I waited so long I almost gave up, but then along about half past seven, here she came out of the house, and walking fast. I waited till she was about a hundred feet away, and then I gave that same little tap on the horn I had given before. She started to run, and I had this sick feeling that she was going by without even speaking, so I didn't look. I wouldn't give her that much satisfaction. But before I knew it the door opened and slammed, and there she was on the seat beside me, and she was squeezing my hand, and half whispering:

"I'm so glad you came. So glad."

We didn't say much going in. I went to the newsreel, but what came out on the screen I couldn't tell you. I was going over and over in my mind what I was going to say to her, or at least trying to. But every time when I'd get talking about it, I'd find myself starting off about her home life, and trying to find out if Brent really had taken up with another woman, and more of the same that only meant one thing. It meant I wanted her for myself. And it meant I was trying to make myself believe that she didn't know anything about the shortage, that she had been on the up-and-up all the time, that she really liked me. I went back to the car, and got in, and pretty soon she came out of the hospital, and ran down the steps. Then she stopped, and stood there like she was thinking. Then she started for the car again, but she wasn't running now. She was walking slow. When she got in she leaned back and closed her eyes.

"Dave?"

It was the first time she had ever called me by my first name. I felt my heart jump. "Yes, Sheila?"

"Could we have a fire tonight?"

"I'd love it."

"I've—I've got to talk to you."

So I drove to my house. Sam let us in, but I chased him out. We went in the living room, and once more I didn't turn on the light. She helped me light the fire, and I started into the kitchen to fix something to drink, but she stopped me.

"I don't want anything to drink. Unless you do."

"No. I don't drink much."

"Let's sit down."

She sat on the sofa, where she had been before, and I sat beside her. I didn't try any passes. She looked in the fire a long time, and then she took my arm and pulled it around her. "Am I terrible?"

"No."

"I want it there."

I started to kiss her, but she raised her hand, covered my lips with her fingers, then pushed my face away. She dropped her head on my shoulder, closed her eyes, and didn't speak for a long time. Then: "Dave, there's something I've got to tell you."

"What is it?"

"It's pretty tragic, and it involves the bank, and if you don't want to hear it from me, this way, just say so and I'll go home."

". . . All right. Shoot."

"Charles is short in his accounts."

"How much?"

"A little over nine thousand dollars. Nine one one three point two six, if you want the exact amount. I've been suspecting it. I noticed one or two things. He kept saying I must have made mistakes in my bookkeeping, but tonight I made him admit it."

"Well. That's not so good."

"How bad is it?"

"It's pretty bad."

"Dave, tell me the truth about it. I've got to know. What will they do to him? Will they put him in prison?"

"I'm afraid they will."

"What, actually, does happen?"

"A good bit of what happens is up to the bonding company. If they get tough, he needn't expect much mercy. It's dead open-and-shut. They put him under arrest, have him indicted, and the rest of it's a question of how hard they bear down, and how it hits the court. Sometimes, of course, there are extenuating circumstances—"

"There aren't any. He didn't spend that money on me, or on the children, or on his home. I've kept all expenses within his salary, and I've even managed to save a little for him, every week."

"Yeah, I noticed your account."

"He spent it on another woman."

"I see."

"Does it make any difference if restitution is made?"

"All the difference in the world."

"If so, would he get off completely free?"

"There again, it all depends on the bonding company, and the deal that could be made with them. They might figure they'd make any kind of a deal, to get the money back, but as a rule they're not lenient. They can't be. The way they look at it, every guy that gets away with it means ten guys next year that'll try to get away with it."

"Suppose they never knew it?"

"I don't get you."

"Suppose I could find a way to put the money back, I mean suppose I could get the money, and then found a way to make the records conform, so nobody ever knew there was anything wrong."

"It couldn't be done."

"Oh yes, it could."

"The passbooks would give it away. Sooner or later."

"Not the way I'd do it."

"That—I would have to think about."

"You know what this means to me, don't you?"

"I think so."

"It's not on account of me. Or Charles. I try not to wish ill to anybody, but if he had to pay, it might be what he deserves. It's on account of my two children. Dave, I can't have them spend the rest of their lives knowing their father was a convict, that he'd been in prison. Do you, can you, understand what that means, Dave?"

For the first time since she had begun to talk, I looked at her then. She was still in my arms, but she was turned to me in a strained, tense kind of way, and her eyes looked haunted. I patted her head, and tried to think. But I knew there was one thing I had to do. I had to clear up my end of it. She had come clean with me, and for a while, anyway, I believed in her. I had to come clean with her.

"Sheila?"

"Yes?"

"I've got to tell *you* something."

". . . What is it, Dave?"

"I've known this all along. For at least a week."

"Is that why you were looking at me that day?"

"Yes. It's why I acted that way, that night. I thought you knew it. I thought you had known it, even when you came to me that night, to ask for the job. I thought you were playing me for a sucker, and I wanted to find out how far you'd go, to get me where you wanted me. Well—that clears *that* up."

She was sitting up now, looking at me hard.

"Dave, I *didn't* know it."

"I know you didn't—*now*, I know it."

"I knew about *her*—this woman he's been—going around with. I wondered sometimes where he got the money. But this, I had no idea. Until two or three days ago. Until I began to notice discrepancies in the passbooks."

"Yeah, that's what I noticed."

"And that's why you turned seducer?"

"Yeah. It's not very natural to me, I guess. I didn't fool you any. What I'm trying to say is I don't feel that way about you. I want you every way there is to want somebody, but—I mean it. Do you know what I'm getting at, if anything?"

She nodded, and all of a sudden we were in each other's arms, and I was kissing her, and she was kissing back, and her lips were warm and soft, and once more I had that feeling in my throat, that catch like I wanted to cry or something. We sat there a long time, not saying anything, just holding each other close. We were half-way to her house before we remembered about the shortage and what we were going to do about it. She begged me once more to give her a chance to save her children from the disgrace. I told her I'd have to think it over, but I knew in my heart I was going to do anything she asked me to.

4

"WHERE ARE YOU GOING TO GET THIS MONEY?"

"There's only one place I can possibly get it."

"Which is?"

"My father."

"Has he got that much dough?"

"I don't know. . . . He owns his house. Out in Westwood. He could get something on that. He has a little money. I don't know how much. But for the last few years his only daughter hasn't been any expense. I guess he can get it."

"How's he going to feel about it?"

"He's going to hate it. And if he lets me have it, it won't be on account of Charles. He bears no goodwill to Charles, I can tell you that. And it won't be on account of me. He was pretty bitter when I even considered marrying Charles, and when I actually went and did it—well, we won't go into that. But for his grandchildren's sake, he might. Oh, what a mess. What an awful thing."

It was the next night, and we were sitting in the car, where I had parked on one of the terraces overlooking the ocean. I suppose it was around eight-thirty, as she hadn't stayed at the hospital very long. She sat looking out at the surf, and then suddenly said I might as well drive her over to her father's. I did, and she didn't have much to say. I parked near the house, and she went in, and she stayed a long time. It must have been eleven o'clock when she came out. She got in the car, and then she broke down and cried, and there wasn't much I could do. When she got a little bit under control, I asked, "Well, what luck?"

"Oh, he'll do it, but it was awful."

"If he got sore, you can't blame him much."

"He didn't get sore. He just sat there, and shook his head, and there was no question about whether he'd let me have the money or not. But—Dave, an old man, he's been paying on that house for fifteen years, and last year he got it clear. If he wants to, he can spend his summers in Canada, he and Mamma both. And now—it's all gone, he'll have to start paying all over again, all because of this. And he never said a word."

"What did your mother say?"

"I didn't tell her. I suppose he will, but I couldn't. I waited till she went to bed. That's what kept me so long. Fifteen years, paying regularly every month, and now it's to go, all because Charles fell for a simpleton that isn't worth the powder and shot to blow her to hell."

I didn't sleep very well that night. I kept thinking of the old history professor, and his house, and Sheila, and Brent lying down there in the hospital with a tube in his belly. Up to then I hadn't thought much about him. I didn't like him, and he was washed up with Sheila, and I had just conveniently not thought of him at all. I thought of him now, though, and wondered who the simpleton was that he had fallen for, and whether he was as nuts about her as I was about Sheila. Then I got to wondering whether I thought enough of her to embezzle for her, and that brought me sitting up in bed, staring out the window at the night. I could say I wouldn't, that I had never stolen from anybody, and never would, but here I was already mixed up in it some kind of way. It was a week since I uncovered that shortage, and I hadn't said a word about it to the home office, and I was getting ready to help her cover up.

Something popped in me then, about Brent, I mean, and I quit kidding myself. I did some hard figuring in bed there, and I didn't like it a bit, but I knew what I had to do. Next night, instead of heading for the ocean, I headed for my house again, and pretty soon we were back in front of the fire. I had mixed a drink this time, because at least I felt at peace with myself, and I held her in my arms quite a while before I got to it. Then: "Sheila?"

"Yes?"

"I've had it out with myself."

"Dave, you're not going to turn him in?"

"No, but I've decided there's only one person that can take that rap."

"Who do you mean?"

"Me."

"I don't understand you."

"All right, I drove you over to see your father last night, and he took it pretty hard. Fifteen years, paying on that house, and now it's all got to go, and he don't get anything out of it at all. Why should he pay? I got a house, too, and I do get something out of it."

"What do *you* get out of it?"

"You."

"What are you talking about?"

"I mean I got to cough up that nine thousand bucks."

"You *will* not!"

"Look, let's quit kidding ourselves. All right, Brent stole the dough, he spent it on a cutie, he treated you lousy. He's father of two children that happen also to be your father's grandchildren, and that means your father's got to pay. Well, ain't that great. Here's the only thing that matters about this: Brent's down and out. He's in the shadow of the penitentiary, he's in the hospital recovering from one of the worst operations there is, he's in one hell of a spot. But me — I'm in love with his wife. While he's down, I'm getting ready to take her away from him, the one thing he's got left. O.K., that's not so pretty, but that how I feel about it. But the least I can do is kick in with that dough. So, I'm doing it. So, quit bothering your old man. So, that's all."

"I can't let you do it."

"Why not?"

"If you paid that money, then I'd be bought."

She got up and began to walk around the room. "You've practically said so yourself. You're getting ready to take a man's wife away from him, and you're going to salve your conscience by replacing the money he stole. That's all very well for him, since he doesn't seem to want his wife anyway. But can't you see where it puts me? What can I say to you now? Or what could I say, if I let you put up that money? I can't pay you back. Not in ten years could I make enough to pay you nine thousand dollars. I'm just your — creature."

I watched her as she moved around, touching the furniture

with her hands, not looking at me, and then all of a sudden a hot, wild feeling went through me, and the blood began to pound in my head. I went over and jerked her around, so she was facing me. "Listen, there's not many guys that feel for a woman nine thousand dollars' worth. What's the matter with that? Don't you want to be bought?"

I took her in my arms, and shoved my lips against hers. "Is that so tough?"

She opened her mouth, so our teeth were clicking, and just breathed it: "It's grand, just grand."

She kissed me then, hard. "So it was just a lot of hooey you were handing me?"

"Just hooey, nothing but hooey. Oh, it's so good to be bought. I feel like something in a veil, and a harem skirt—and I just love it."

"Now—we'll put that money back."

"Yes, together."

"We'll start tomorrow."

"Isn't that funny. I'm completely in your power. I'm your slave, and I feel so safe, and know that nothing's going to happen to me, ever."

"That's right. It's a life sentence for you."

"Dave, I've fallen in love."

"Me, too."

5

IF YOU THINK IT'S HARD TO STEAL MONEY FROM A BANK, YOU'RE right. But it's nothing like as hard as it is to put the money back. Maybe I haven't made it quite clear yet what that bird was doing. In the first place, when there's a shortage in a bank, it's always in the savings, because no statements are rendered on them. The commercial depositor, the guy with a checking account, I mean, gets a statement every month. But no statements are rendered to savings depositors. They show up with their passbooks, and plunk their money down, and the deposit is entered in their books, and their books are their statements. They never see the bank's cards, so naturally the thing can go on a long time before it's found out, and when it's found out, it's most likely to be by accident, like this was, because Brent didn't figure on his trip to the hospital.

Well, what Brent had done was fix up a cover for himself with all this stuff about putting it on a personal basis, so no savings depositor that came in the bank would ever deal with anybody but him. That ought to have made George Mason suspicious, but Brent was getting the business in, and you don't quarrel with a guy that's doing good. When he got that part the way he wanted it, with him the only one that ever touched the savings file, and the depositors dealing only with him, he went about it exactly the way they all go about it. He picked accounts where he knew he wouldn't be likely to run into trouble, and if he'd make out a false withdrawal slip, generally for somewhere around fifty bucks. He'd sign the depositor's name to it, just forge it, but he didn't have to be very good at that part, because nobody passed on those signatures but himself. Then he'd put fifty bucks in his pocket, and of course the false withdrawal slip would balance his cash. Our card had to balance too, of course, so he'd enter the withdrawal on that, but beside each false entry he'd make that little light pencil check that I had caught, and that would tell him what the right balance ought to be, in case the depositor made some inquiry.

Well, how were you going to get that money put back, so the daily cash would balance, so the cards would balance, and so the passbooks would balance, and at the same time leave it so nothing would show later, when the auditors came around? It had me stumped, and I don't mind telling you for a while I began to get cold feet. What I wanted to do was report it, as was, let Sheila fork up the dough, without saying where she got it, and let Brent get fired and go look himself up a job. It didn't look like they would do much to him, if the money was put back. But she wouldn't hear of that. She was afraid they might send him up anyway, and then I would be putting up the money all for nothing, her children would have to grow up under the disgrace, and where we would be was nowhere. There wasn't much I could say to that. I figured they would probably let him off, but I couldn't be sure.

It was Sheila that figured out the way. We were riding along one night, just one or two nights after I told her I was going to put up the dough myself, when she began to talk. "The cards, the cash, and the passbooks, is that it?"

"That's all."

"The cards and the cash are easy."

"Oh yeah?"

"That money goes back the same way it came out. Only instead of false withdrawals, I make out false deposits. The cash balances, the posting balances, and the card balances."

"And the passbooks don't balance. Listen. If there's only one passbook—just one—that can tell on us after you're out of there, and I'm out, we're sunk. The only chance we've got is that the thing is never suspected at all—that no question is ever raised. And, what's more, we don't dare make a move till we see every one of the passbooks on those phoney accounts. We think we've got his code, how he ticked his false withdrawals, but we can't be sure, and maybe he didn't tick them all. Unless we can make a clean job of this, I don't touch it. Him going to jail is one thing. All three of us going, and me losing my job and nine thousand bucks—oh no."

"All right then, the passbooks."

"That's it—the passbooks."

"Now when a passbook gets filled up, or there's some mistake on it, what do we do?"

"Give him a new one, don't we?"

"Containing how many entries?"

"One, I suppose. His total as of that date."

"That's right. And that one entry tells no tales. It checks with the card, and there's not one figure to check against all those back entries—withdrawals and deposits and so on, running back for years. All right, then; so far, perfect. Now what do we do with his old book? Regularly, I mean."

"Well—what *do* we do with it?"

"We put it under a punch, the punch that goes through every page and marks it void, and give it back to him."

"And then he's got it—any time an auditor calls for it. Gee, that's a big help."

"But if he doesn't want it?"

"What are you getting at?"

"If he doesn't want it, we destroy it. It's no good to us, is it? And it's not ours, it's his. But he doesn't want it."

"Are you *sure* we destroy it?"

"I've torn up a thousand of them. . . . And that's just what we're going to do now. Between now and the next check on my cash, we're going to get all those books in. First we check totals, to know exactly where we're at. Then the depositor gets a new book that tells no tales."

"Why does he get a new book?"

"He didn't notice it when he brought the old one in, but the stitching is awfully strained, and it's almost falling apart. Or I've accidentally smeared lipstick on it. Or I just think it's time he got one of our nice new books, for luck. So he gets a new book with one entry in it—just his total, that's all. Then I say: 'You don't want this, do you?' And the way I'll say it, that old book seems positively *contaminated*. And then, right in front of his eyes, as though it's the way we do it every day, I'll tear it up, and drop it in the wastebasket."

"Suppose he *does* want it?"

"Then I'll put it under the punch, and give it to him. But somehow that punch is going to make its neat little holes in the exact place where the footings are, and it's going to be impossible for him, or an auditor, or anybody else, to read those figures. I'll punch five or six times, you know, and his book will be like Swiss cheese, more holes than anything else."

"And all the time you're getting those holes in exactly the right place, he's going to be on the other side of the window looking at you, wondering what all the hocus-pocus is about."

"Oh no—it won't take more than a second or two. You see, I've been practicing. I can do it in a jiffy. . . . But he won't want that book back. Trust me. I know how to do it."

There was just a little note of pleading on that, as she said it. I had to think it over. I did think it over, for quite a while, and I began to have the feeling that on her end of it, if that was all, she could put it over all right. But then something else began to bother me. "How many of these doctored accounts are there?"

"Forty-seven."

"And how are you going to get those passbooks in?"

"Well, interest is due on them. I thought I could send out little printed slips,—signed 'per Sheila Brent,' in ink, so they'd be sure to come to me about it,—asking them to bring in their books for interest credits. I never saw anybody that wouldn't bring in his book if it meant a dollar and twenty-two cents. And a printed slip looks perfectly open and above-board, doesn't it?"

"Yeah, a printed slip is about the most harmless, open, and above-board thing there is. But this is what I'm thinking: You send out your printed slips, and within a couple of days all those books come in, and you can't hold them forever. You've got to hand them back—or the new ones they're going to get—or somebody's going to get suspicious. That means the money's got to be put back all at once. That's going to make one awful bulge in your cash. Everybody in the bank is going to wonder at the reason for it, because it's going to show in the posting."

"I've thought of that. I don't have to send out all those slips at once. I can send out four or five a day. And then, even if they do come in bunches—the passbooks I mean—I can issue the new books, right away as the old ones are presented, but make the adjustments on the cards and in my cash little by little—three or four hundred dollars a day. That's not much."

"No, but while that's going on, we're completely defenseless. We've got our chins hanging out and no way in the world of putting up a guard. I mean, while you're holding out those adjustment entries, so you can edge them in gradually, your cash doesn't balance the books. If then something happened—so I had to call for a cash audit on the spot, or if I got called away to the home office for a couple of days, or something happened to you, so you couldn't come to work—then watch that ship go out of water. You may get away with it. But it'll have to be done, everything squared up, before the next check on your cash. That's twenty-one days from now. And at that, a three- or four-hundred dollar bulge in your cash every day is going to look mighty funny. In the bank, I mean."

"I could gag it off. I could say I'm keeping after them, to keep their deposits up, the way Charles always did. I don't think there's any danger. The cash will be there."

So that was how we did it. She had the slips printed, and began mailing them out, three or four at a time. For the first few days' replacement, the cash replacement I mean, I had enough on my own checking account. For the rest, I had to go out and plaster my house. For that I went to the Federal people. It took about a week, and I had to start an outside account, so nobody in the bank would know what I was up to. I took eight thousand bucks, and if you don't think that hurt you never plastered your house. Of course, it would be our luck that when the first of those books came in, she was out to lunch, and I was on the window myself. I took in the book, and receipted for it, but Church was only three or four feet away, running a column on one of the adding machines. She heard what I said to the depositor, and was at my elbow before I even knew how she got there.

"I can do that for you, Mr. Bennett. I'll only be a minute, and there'll be no need for him to leave his book."

"Well—I'd rather Mrs. Brent handled it."

"Oh, *very* well, then."

She switched away then, in a huff, and I could feel the sweat in the palms of my hands. That night I warned Sheila. "That Church can bust it up."

"How?"

"Her damned apple-polishing. She horned in today, wanted to balance that book for me. I had to chase her."

"Leave her to me."

"For God's sake don't let her suspect anything."

"I won't, don't worry."

From then on, we made a kind of a routine out of it. She'd get in three or four books, ask the depositors to leave them with her till next day. She'd make out new cards, and tell me the exact amount she needed, that night. I'd hand her that much in cash. Next day, she'd slip it into her cash box, make out new cards for the depositors, slip them in the file, then make out new passbooks and have them ready when the depositors called. Every day we'd be that much nearer home, both praying that nothing would tip it before we got the whole replacement made. Most days I'd say we plugged about $400 into the cash, one or two days a little more.

One night, maybe a week after we started putting the money back, they had the big dinner dance for the whole organization. I guess about a thousand people were there, in the main ball room of one of the Los Angeles hotels, and it was a pretty nice get-together. They don't make a pep meeting out of it. The Old Man doesn't like that kind of thing. He just has a kind of a family gathering, makes them a little speech, and then the dancing starts, and he stands around watching them enjoy themselves. I guess you've heard of A. R. Ferguson. He's founder of the bank, and the minute you look at him you know he's a big shot. He's not tall, but he's straight and stocky, with a little white moustache that makes him look like some kind of a military man.

Well, we all had to go, of course. I sat at the table with the others from the branch, Miss Church, and Helm, and Snelling, and Snelling's wife, and Sheila. I made it a point not to sit with Sheila. I was afraid to. So after the banquet, when the dancing started, I went over to shake hands with the Old Man. He always treated me fine, just like he treats everybody. He's got that natural courtesy that no little guy ever quite seems capable of. He asked how I was, and then: "How much longer do you think you'll be out there in Glendale? Are you nearly done?"

An icy feeling began to go over me. If he yanked me now, and returned me to the home office, there went all chance of covering that shortage, and God only knew what they would find out, if it was half covered and half not.

"Why, I tell you, Mr. Ferguson, if you can possibly arrange it, I'd like to stay out there till after the first of the month."

". . . So long?"

"Well, I've found some things out there that are well worth making a thorough study of, it seems to me. Fact of the matter, I had thought of writing an article about them in addition to my report. I thought I'd send it to the American Banker, and if I could have a little more time—"

"In that case, take all the time you want."

"I thought it wouldn't hurt us any."

"I only wish more of our officials would write."

"Gives us a little prestige."

"—and makes them *think!*"

My mouth did it all. I was standing behind it, not knowing what was coming out from one minute to the next. I hadn't thought of any article, up to that very second, and I give you one guess how I felt. I felt like a heel, and all the worse on account of the fine way he treated me. We stood there a few minutes, he telling me how he was leaving for Honolulu the next day, but he'd be back within the month, and looked forward to reading what I had to say as soon as he came back. Then he motioned in the direction of the dance floor. "Who's the girl in blue?"

"Mrs. Brent."

"Oh yes. I want to speak to her."

We did some broken-floor dodging, and got over to where Sheila was dancing with Helm. They stopped, and I introduced the Old Man, and he asked how Brent was coming along after the operation, and then cut in on Helm, and danced Sheila off. I wasn't in much of a humor when I met her outside later, and took her home. "What's the matter, Dave?"

"Couldn't quite look the Old Man in the eye, that's all."

"Have you got cold feet?"

"Just feeling the strain."

"If you have got cold feet, and want to quit, there's nothing I can say. Nothing at all."

"All I got to say is I'll be glad when we're clear of that heel, and can kick him out of the bank and out of our lives."

"In two weeks it'll be done."

"How is he?"

"He's leaving the hospital Saturday."

"That's nice."

"He's not coming home yet. The doctor insists that he go up to Arrowhead to get his strength back. He'll be there three or four weeks. He has friends there."

"What have you told him, by the way?"

"Nothing."

"Just nothing?"

"Not one word."

"He had an ulcer, is that what you said?"

"Yes."

"I was reading in a medical magazine the other day what causes it. Do you know what it is?"

"No."

"Worry."

"So?"

"It might help the recuperating process if he knew it was O.K. about the shortage. Lying in a hospital, with a thing like that staring you in the face, that may not be so good. For his health anyway."

"What am I to tell him?"

"Why, I don't know. That you've fixed it up."

"If I tell him I've fixed it up, so nobody is going to know it, he knows I've got some kind of assistance in the bank. That'll terrify him, and I don't know what he's likely to do about it. He may speak to somebody, and the whole thing will come out. And who am I going to say has let me have the money, so I can put it back? You?"

"Do you have to say?"

"No. I don't have to say anything at all, and I'm not going to. The less you're involved in this the better. If he worries, he ought to be used to it by now. It won't hurt that young man to do quite a little suffering over what he's done to me—and to you."

"It's up to you."

"He knows something's cooking, all right, but he doesn't know what. I look forward to seeing his face when I tell him I'm off to—where did you say?"

". . . I said Reno."

"Do you still say Reno?"

"I don't generally change my mind, once it's made up."

"You can, if you want to."

"Shut up."

"I don't want you to."

"Neither do I."

6

WE KEPT PUTTING THE MONEY BACK, AND I KEPT GETTING JIT-terier every day. I kept worrying that something would happen, that maybe the Old Man hadn't left a memo about me, before he went away, and that I'd get a call to report to the home office; that maybe Sheila would get sick and somebody else would have to do her work; that some depositor might think it was funny, the slip he had got to bring his book in, and begin asking about it somewhere.

One day she asked me to drive her home from the bank. By that time I was so nervous I never went anywhere with her in the daytime, and even at night I never met her anywhere that somebody might see us. But she said one of the children was sick, and she wanted a ride in case she had to get stuff from the drugstore that the doctor had ordered, and that anyway nobody was there but the maid and she didn't matter. By that time Brent had gone to the lake, to get his strength back, and she had the house to herself.

So I went. It was the first time I'd ever been in her home, and it was fixed up nice, and smelled like her, and the kids were the sweetest little pair you ever saw. The oldest was named Anna, and the younger was named Charlotte. She was the one that was sick. She was in bed with a cold, and took it like a little soldier. Another time, it would have tickled me to death to sit and watch her boss Sheila around, and watch Sheila wait on her, and take the bossing just like that was how it ought to be. But now I couldn't even keep still that long. When I found out I wasn't needed I ducked, and went home and filled up some more paper with the phoney article I had to have ready for the Old Man when he got back. It was called, "Building a Strong Savings Department."

We got to the last day before the monthly check on cash. Six hundred dollars had to go into her box that day, over and above the regular day's receipts. It was a lot, but it was a Wednesday, the day the factories all around us paid off, and deposits were sure to be heavy, so it looked like we could get away with it. We had all the passbooks in. It had taken some strong-arm work to get the last three we needed, and what she had done was go to those people the night before, like Brent had always done, and ask where they'd been, and why they hadn't put anything on savings. By sitting around a few minutes she managed to get their books, and then I drove her over to my place and we checked it all up. Then I gave her the cash she needed, and it looked like she was set.

But I kept wanting to know how she stood, whether it had all gone through like we hoped. I couldn't catch her eye and I couldn't get a word with her. They were lined up at her window four and five deep all day long, and she didn't go out to lunch. She had sandwiches and milk sent in. On Wednesday they send out two extra tellers from the home office, to help handle the extra business, and every time one of them would go to her for help on something, and she'd have to leave her window for a minute, I'd feel the sweat on the palms of my hands, and lose track of what I was doing. I'm telling you it was a long day.

Along about two-thirty, though, it slacked off, and by five minutes to three there was nobody in there, and at three sharp

Adler, the guard, locked the door. We went on finishing up. The home office tellers got through first, because all they had to do was balance one day's deposits, and around three-thirty they turned in their sheets, asked me to give them a count, and left. I sat at my desk, staring at papers, doing anything to keep from marching around and tip it that I had something on my mind.

About quarter to four there came a tap on the glass, and I didn't look up. There's always that late depositor trying to get in, and if he catches your eye you're sunk. I went right on staring at my papers, but I heard Adler open and then who should be there but Brent, with a grin on his face, a satchel in one hand, and a heavy coat of a sunburn all over him. There was a chorus of "Hey's," and they all went out to shake hands, all except Sheila, and ask him how he was, and when he was coming back to work. He said he'd got home last night, and would be back any time now. There didn't seem to be much I could do but shake hands too, so I gritted my teeth, and did it, but I didn't ask him when he was coming back to work.

Then he said he'd come in for some of his stuff, and on his way back to the lockers he spoke to Sheila, and she spoke, without looking up. Then the rest of them went back to work. "Gee, he sure looks good, don't he?"

"Different from when he left."

"He must have put on twenty pounds."

"They fixed him up all right."

Pretty soon he came out again, closing his grip, and there was some more talk, and he went. They all counted their cash, turned in their sheets, and put their cash boxes into the vault. Helm wheeled the trucks in, with the records on them, and then he went. Snelling went back to set the time lock.

That was when Church started some more of her apple-polishing. She was about as unappetizing a girl as I ever saw. She was thick, and dumpy, with a delivery like she was making a speech all the time. She sounded like a dietician demonstrating a range in a department store basement, and she started in on a wonderful new adding machine that had just come on the market, and didn't I think we ought to have one. I said it sounded good, but I wanted to think it over. So then she said it all over again, and just about when she got going good she gave a little squeal and began pointing at the floor.

Down there was about the evilest-looking thing you ever saw in your life. It was one of these ground spiders you see out here in California, about the size of a tarantula and just about as dangerous. It was about three inches long, I would say, and was walking toward me with a clumsy gait but getting there all the time. I raised my foot to step on it, and she gave another squeal and said if I squashed it she'd die. By that time they were all standing around—Snelling, Sheila and Adler. Snelling said get a piece of paper and throw it out the door, and Sheila said yes, for heaven's sake do something about it quick. Adler took a piece of paper off my desk, and rolled it into a funnel, and then took a pen and pushed the thing into the paper. Then he folded the funnel shut and we all went out and watched him dump the spider into the gutter. Then a cop came along and borrowed the funnel and caught it again and said he was going to take it home to his wife, so they could take pictures of it with their home movie camera.

We went back in the bank, and Snelling and I closed the vault, and he went. Church went. Adler went back for his last tour around before closing. That left me alone with Sheila. I stepped back to where she was by the lockers, looking in the mirror while she put on her hat. "Well?"

"It's all done."

"You put back the cash?"

"To the last cent."

"The cards are all in?"

"It all checks to the last decimal point."

That was what I'd been praying for, for the last month, and yet as soon as I had it, it took me about one fifth of a second to get sore, about Brent.

"Is he driving you home?"

"If so, he didn't mention it."

"Suppose you wait in my car. There's a couple of things I want to talk to you about. It's just across the street."

She went, and Adler changed into his street clothes, and he and I locked up, and I bounced over to the car. I didn't head for her house, I headed for mine, but I didn't wait till we got there before I opened up.

"Why didn't you tell me he was back?"

"Were you interested?"

"Yeah, plenty."

"Well, since you ask me, I didn't know he was back—when I left you last night. He was there waiting for me when I got in. Today, I haven't had one minute to talk to you, or anybody."

"I thought he was due to spend a month up there."

"So did I."

"Then what's he doing back?"

"I haven't the faintest idea. Trying to find out what's going to happen to him, perhaps. Tomorrow, you may recall, you'll check my cash, and he knows it. That may account for why he cut his recuperation short."

"Are you sure he didn't have a date with you, now he's feeling better? To be waiting for you after you said good-night to me?"

"I stayed with the children, if that's what you mean."

I don't know if I believed any of that or not. I think I told you I was nuts about her, and all the money she'd cost me, and all the trouble she'd brought, only seemed to make it worse. The idea that she'd spent a night in the same house with him, and hadn't said anything to me about it, left me with a prickly feeling all over. Since I'd been going around with her, it was the first time that part of it had come up. He'd been in the hospital, and from there he'd gone right up to the lake, so in a way up to then he hadn't seemed real. But he seemed real now, all right, and I was still as sore as a bear when we got to my house, and went in. Sam lit the fire, and she sat down, but I didn't. I kept marching around the room, and she smoked, and watched me.

"All right, this guy's got to be told."

"He will be."

"He's got to be told *everything*."

"Dave, he'll be told, he'll be told everything, and a little more even than you know he's going to be told—when I'm ready to tell him."

"What's the matter with now?"

"I'm not equal to it."

"What's that—a stall?"

"Will you sit down for a moment?"

"All right, I'm sitting."

"Here—beside me."

I moved over beside her, and she took my hand and looked me in the eyes. "Dave, have you forgotten something?"

"Not that I know of."

"I think you have . . . I think you've forgotten that today we finished what we started to do. That, thanks to you, I don't have to lie awake every night staring at the ceiling, wondering whether my father is going to be ruined, my children are going to be ruined—to say nothing of myself. That you've done something for me that was so dangerous to you I hate to think what would have happened if something had gone wrong. It would have wrecked your career, and it's such a nice, promising career. But it wasn't wrong, Dave. It was wonderfully right. It was decenter than any man I know of would have done, would even have thought of doing. And now it's done. There's not one card, one comma, one missing penny to show—and I can sleep, Dave. That's all that matters to me today."

"O.K.—then you're leaving him."

"Of course I am, but—"

"You're leaving him tonight. You're coming in here, with your two kids, and if that bothers you, then I'll move out. We're going over there now, and—"

"We're doing nothing of the kind."

"I'm telling you—"

"And I'm telling *you*! Do you think I'm going over there now, and starting a quarrel that's going to last until three o'clock in the morning and maybe until dawn? That's going to wander all over the earth, from how horribly he says I've treated him to who's going to have the children—the way I feel now? I certainly shall not. When I'm ready, when I know exactly what I'm going to say, when I've got the children safely over to my father's, when it's all planned and I can do it in one terrible half hour—then I'll do it. In the meantime, if he's biting his finger nails, if he's frightened to death over what's going to happen to him—that's perfectly all right with me. A little of that won't hurt him. When it's all done, then I go at once to Reno, if you still want me to, and then my life can go on. . . . Don't you know what I'm trying to tell you, Dave? What you're worried about just couldn't happen. Why—he hasn't even looked at me that way in over a year. Dave, tonight I want to be happy. With you. That's all."

I felt ashamed of myself at that, and took her in my arms, and that catch came in my throat again when she sighed, like some child and relaxed, and closed her eyes.

"Sheila?"

"Yes?"

"We'll celebrate."

"All right."

So we celebrated. She phoned her maid, and said she'd be late, and we went to dinner at a downtown restaurant, and then we drove to a night club on Sunset Boulevard. We didn't talk about Brent, or the shortage, or anything but ourselves, and what we were going to do with our lives together. We stayed till about one o'clock. I didn't think of Brent again till we pulled up near her house, and then this same prickly feeling began to come over me. If she noticed anything she didn't say so. She kissed me goodnight, and I started home.

7

I TURNED IN THE DRIVE, PUT THE CAR AWAY, CLOSED THE GARAGE, and walked around to go in the front way. When I started for the door I heard my name called. Somebody got up from a bench under the trees and walked over. It was Helm. "Sorry to be bothering you this hour of night, Mr. Bennett, but I've got to talk to you."

"Well, come in."

He seemed nervous as I took him inside. I offered him a drink, but he said he didn't want anything. He sat down and lit a cigarette, and acted like he didn't know how to begin. Then: "Have you seen Sheila?"

". . . Why?"

"I saw you drive off with her."

"Yes—I had some business with her. We had dinner together. I—just left her a little while ago."

"Did you see Brent?"

"No. It was late. I didn't go in."

"She say anything about him?"

"I guess so. Now and then . . . What's this about?"

"Did you see him leave the bank? Today?"

"He left before you did."

"Did you see him leave the second time?"

". . . He only came in once."

He kept looking at me, smoking and looking at me. He was a

young fellow, twenty-four or five, I would say, and had only been with us a couple of years. Little by little he was losing his nervousness at talking with me.

". . . He went in there twice."

"He came in once. He rapped on the door, Adler let him in, he stood there talking a few minutes, then he went back to get some stuff out of his locker. Then he left. You were there. Except for the extra tellers, nobody had finished up yet. He must have left fifteen minutes before you did."

"That's right. Then I left. I finished up, put my cash box away, and left. I went over to the drugstore to get myself a malted milk, and was sitting there drinking it when he went in."

"He couldn't have. We were locked, and—"

"He used a key."

". . . When was this?"

"A little after four. Couple of minutes before you all come out with that spider, and dumped it in the gutter."

"So?"

"I didn't see him come out."

"Why didn't you tell me?"

"I haven't seen you. I've been looking for you."

"You saw me drive off with Sheila."

"Yeah, but it hadn't occurred to me, at the time. That cop, after he caught the spider, came in the drugstore to buy some film for his camera. I helped him put the spider in an ice cream container, and punch holes in the top, and I wasn't watching the bank all that time. Later, it just happened to run through my head that I'd seen all the rest of you leave the bank, but I hadn't seen Brent. I kept telling myself to forget it, that I'd got a case of nerves from being around money too much, but then—"

"Yeah? What else?"

"I went to a picture tonight with the Snellings."

"Didn't Snelling see him leave?"

"I didn't say anything to Snelling. I don't know what he saw. But the picture had some Mexican stuff in it, and later, when we went to the Snellings' apartment, I started a bum argument, and got Snelling to call Charlie to settle it. Brent spent some time in Mexico once. That was about twelve o'clock."

"And?"

"The maid answered. Charlie wasn't there."

We looked at each other, and both knew that twelve o'clock was too late for a guy to be out that had just had a bad operation.

"Come on."

"You calling Sheila?"

"We're going to the bank."

The protection service watchman was due on the hour, and we caught him on his two-o'clock round. He took it as a personal insult that we would think anybody could be in the bank without him knowing it, but I made him take us in there just the same, and we went through every part of it. We went upstairs, where the old records were stored, and I looked behind every pile. We went down in the basement and I looked behind every gas furnace. We went all around back of the windows and I looked under every counter. I even looked behind my desk, and under it. That seemed to be all. The watchman went up and punched his clock and we went out on the street again. Helm kind of fingered his chin.

"Well, I guess it was a false alarm."

"Looks like it."

"Sorry."

"It's all right. Report everything."

"Guess there's no use calling Sheila."

"Pretty late, I'm afraid."

What he meant was, we ought to call Sheila, but he wanted me to do it. He was just as suspicious as he ever was, I could tell that from the way he was acting. Only the watchman was sure we were a couple of nuts. We got in the car, and I took him home, and once more he mumbled something about Sheila, but I decided not to hear him. When I let him out I started for home, but as soon as I was out of sight I cut around the block and headed for Mountain Drive.

A light was on, and the screen door opened as soon as I set my foot on the porch. She was still dressed, and it was almost as though she had been expecting me. I followed her in the living room, and spoke low so nobody in the house could hear us, but I didn't waste any time on love and kisses.

"Where's Brent?"

". . . He's in the vault."

She spoke in a whisper, and sank into a chair without looking at me, but every doubt I'd had about her in the beginning, I mean, every hunch that she'd been playing me for a sucker, swept back over me so even looking at her made me tremble. I had to lick my lips a couple of times before I could even talk. "Funny you didn't tell me."

"I didn't know it."

"What do you mean you didn't know it? If you know it now, why didn't you know it then? You trying to tell me he stepped out of there for a couple of minutes, borrowed my telephone, and called you up? He might as well be in a tomb as be in that place, till it opens at eight-thirty this morning."

"Are you done?"

"I'm still asking you why you didn't tell me."

"When I got in, and found he wasn't home, I went out looking for him. Or at any rate, for the car. I went to where he generally parks it — when he's out. It wasn't there. Coming home I had to go by the bank. As I went by, the red light winked, just once."

I don't know if you know how a vault works. There's two switches inside. One lights the overhead stuff that you turn on when somebody wants to get into his safe deposit box, the other works the red light that's always on over the door in the daytime. That's the danger signal, and any employee of the bank always looks to see that it's on whenever he goes inside. When the vault is closed the light's turned off, and I had turned it off myself that afternoon, when I locked the vault with Snelling. At night, all curtains are raised in the bank, so cops, watchman, and any passer-by can see inside. If the red light went on, it would show, but I didn't believe she'd seen it. I didn't believe she'd even been by the bank. "So the red light winked, hey? Funny it wasn't winking when I left there not ten minutes ago."

"I said it winked once. I don't think it was a signal. I think he bumped his shoulder against it, by accident. If he were signaling, he'd keep on winking it, wouldn't he?"

"How'd he get in there?"

"I don't know."

"I think you do know."

"I don't know, but the only way I can think of is that he slipped in there while we were all gathered around, looking at that spider."

"That you conveniently on purpose brought in there."

"Or that he did."

"What's he doing in there?"

"I don't know."

"Come on, come on, quit stalling me!"

She got up and began walking around. "Dave, it's easy to see you think I know all about this. That I know more than I'm telling. That Charles and I are in some kind of plot. I don't know anything I can say. I know a lot I could say if I wasn't—"

She stopped, came to life like some kind of a tiger, and began hammering her fists against the wall.

"—Bought! That was what was wrong! I ought to have cut my heart out, suffered anything rather than let you give me that money! Why did I ever take it? Why didn't I tell you to—"

"Why didn't you do what I begged you to do? Come over here today and let him have it between the eyes—tell him the truth, that you were through, and this was the end of it?"

"Because, God help me, I wanted to be happy!"

"No!... Because, God help you, you knew he wasn't over here! Because you knew he was in that vault, and you were afraid I'd find it out!"

"It isn't true! How can you say that?"

"Do you know what I think? I think you took that money off me, day by day, and that not one penny of it ever found its way into your cash box. And then I think you and he decided on a little phoney hold-up, to cover that shortage, and that that's what he's doing in the vault. And if Helm hadn't got into it, and noticed that Brent didn't come out of the bank the second time he went in, I don't see anything that was to stop you from getting away with it. You knew I didn't dare open my trap about the dough *I* had put up. And if he came out of there masked, and made a quick getaway, I don't know who was going to swear it was him, if it hadn't been for Helm. Now it's in the soup. All right, Mrs. Brent, that vault that don't take any messages till eight-thirty, that works both ways. If he can't get any word to you, you can't get any word to him. Just let him start that little game that looked so good yesterday afternoon, and he's going to get the surprise of his life, and so are you. There'll be a reception committee waiting for him when he comes out of there, and maybe they'll include you in it too."

She looked straight at me the whole time I was talking, and the lamplight caught her eyes, so they shot fire. There was something catlike about her shape anyway, and with her eyes blazing like that, she looked like something out of the jungle. But all of a sudden that woman was gone, and she was crumpled up in front of me, on the sofa, crying in a queer, jerky way. Then I hated myself for what I had said, and had to dig in with my finger nails to keep from crying too.

After a while the phone rang. From what she said, I could tell it was her father, and that he'd been trying to reach her all afternoon and all night. She listened a long time, and when she hung up she lay back and closed her eyes. "He's in there to put the money back."

". . . Where'd he get it?"

"He got it this morning. Yesterday morning. From my father."

"Your father had that much—*ready*?"

"He got it after I talked to him that night. Then when I told him I wouldn't need it, he kept it, in his safe deposit box—just in case. Charles went over there yesterday and said he had to have it—against the check-up on my cash. Papa went down to the Westwood bank with him, and got it out, and gave it to him. He was afraid to call me at the bank. He kept trying to reach me here. The maid left me a note, but it was so late when I got in I didn't call. . . . So, now I pay a price for not telling him. Charles, I mean. For letting him worry."

"I was for telling him, you may remember."

"Yes, I remember."

It was quite a while after that before either of us said anything. All that time my mind was going around like a squirrel cage, trying to reconstruct for myself what was going on in that vault. She must have been doing the same thing, because pretty soon she said, "Dave?"

"Yes?"

"Suppose he *does* put the money back?"

"Then—we're sunk."

"What, actually, will happen?"

"If I find him in there, the least I can do is hold him till I've checked every cent in that vault. I find nine thousand more cash than the books show. All right. What then?"

"You mean the whole thing comes out?"

"On what we've been doing, you can get away with it as long as nobody's got the least suspicion of it. Let a thing like this happen, let them really begin to check, and it'll come out so fast it'll make your head swim."

"And there goes your job?"

"Suppose you were the home office, how would you like it?"

". . . I've brought you nothing but misery, Dave."

"I—asked for it."

"I can understand why you feel bitter."

"I said some things I didn't mean."

"Dave."

"Yes?"

"There's one chance, if you'll take it."

"What's that?"

"Charles."

"I don't get it."

"It may be a blessing, after all, that I told him nothing. He can't be sure what I've done while he's been away—whether I carried his false entries right along, whether I corrected them, and left the cash short—and it does look as though he'd check, before he did anything. He's a wizard at books, you know. And every record he needs is in there. Do you know what I'm getting at, Dave?"

"Not quite."

"You'll have to play dummy's hand, and let him lead."

"I don't want anything to do with him."

"I'd like to wring his neck. But if you just don't force things, if you just act natural, and let me have a few seconds with him, so we'll know just what he *has* done, then—maybe it'll all come out all right. He certainly would be a boob to put the money back when he finds out it's already been put back."

"*Has* it been?"

"Don't you know?"

I took her in my arms then, and for that long was able to forget what was staring us in the face, and I still felt close to her when I left.

8

FOR THE SECOND TIME THAT NIGHT I WENT HOME, AND THIS TIME I turned out all lights, and went upstairs, and took off my clothes, and went to bed. I tried to sleep, and couldn't. It was all running through my mind, and especially what I was going to do when I opened that vault at eight-thirty. How could I act natural about it? If I could guess he was in the vault, Helm must have guessed it. He'd be watching me, waiting for every move, and he'd be doing that even if he didn't have any suspicion of me, which by now he must have, on account of being out that late with Sheila. All that ran through my mind, and after a while I'd figured a way to cover it, by openly saying something to him, and telling him I was going to go along with it, just wait and see what Brent had to say for himself, in case he was really in there. Then I tried once more to go to sleep. But this time it wasn't the play at the vault that was bothering me, it was Sheila. I kept going over and over it, what was said between us, the dirty cracks I had made, how she had taken them, and all the rest of it. Just as day began to break I found myself sitting up in bed. How I knew it I don't know, what I had to go on I haven't any idea, but I knew perfectly well that she was holding out on me, that there was something back of it all that she wasn't telling.

I unhooked the phone and dialed. You don't stay around a bank very long before you know the number of your chief guard. I was calling Dyer, and in a minute or two he answered, pretty sour. "Hello?"

"Dyer?"

"Yeah, who is it?"

"Sorry to wake you up. This is Dave Bennett."

"What do you want?"

"I want some help."

"Well, what the hell is it?"

"I got reason to think there's a man in our vault. Out in the Anita Avenue Branch in Glendale. What he's up to I don't know, but I want you out there when I open up. And I'd like you to bring a couple of men with you."

Up to then he'd been just a sleepy guy that used to be a city detective. Now he snapped out of it like something had hit him. "What do you mean you got reason to think? Who is this guy?"

"I'll give you that part when I see you. Can you meet me by seven o'clock? Is that too early?"

"Whenever you say, Mr. Bennett."

"Then be at my house at seven, and bring your men with you. I'll give you the dope, and I'll tell you how I want you to do it."

He took the address, and I went back to bed.

I went to bed, and lay there trying to figure out what it was I wanted him to do anyway. After a while I had it straightened out. I wanted him close enough to protect the bank, and myself as well, in case Sheila was lying to me, and I wanted him far enough away for her to have those few seconds with Brent, in case she wasn't. I mean, if Brent was really up to something, I wanted him covered every way there was, and by guys that would shoot. But if he came out with a foolish look on his face, and pretended he'd been locked in by mistake, and she found out we could still cover up that book-doctoring, I wanted to leave that open too. I figured on it, and after a while I thought I had it doped out so it would work.

Around six o'clock I got up, bathed, shaved, and dressed. I routed out Sam and had him make me some coffee, and fix up some bacon and eggs. I told him to stand by in case the men that were coming hadn't had any breakfast. Then I went in the living room and began to march around. It was cold. I lit the fire. My head kept spinning around.

Right on the tick of seven the doorbell rang and there they were, Dyer and his two muggs. Dyer's a tall, thin man with a bony face and eyes like gimlets. I'd say he was around fifty. The other two were around my own age, somewhere over thirty, with big shoulders, thick necks, and red faces. They looked exactly like what they were: ex-cops that had got jobs as guards in a bank. One was named Halligan, the other Lewis. They all said yes on breakfast, so we went in the dining-room and Sam made it pretty quick with the service.

I gave it to Dyer, as quick as I could, about Brent being off for a couple of months, with his operation, and how he'd come in yesterday to get his stuff, and Helm had seen him go in the bank a second time, and not come out, and how Sheila had gone out looking for him late at night, and thought she saw the red light flash. I had to tell him that much, to protect myself afterward, because God only knew what was going to come out, and I didn't even feel I was safe on Sheila's end of it. I didn't say anything about the shortage, or Sheila's father, or any of that part. I told what I had to tell, and made it short.

"Now what I figure is, Brent got in there somehow just before we closed it up, maybe just looking around, and that he got locked in there by accident. However, I can't be sure. Maybe— it doesn't seem very likely—he's up to something. So what I'd like you guys to do is be outside, just be where you can see what's going on. If it's all quiet, I'll give you the word, and you can go on home. If anything happens, you're there. Of course, a man spends a night in a vault, he may not feel so good by morning. We may need an ambulance. If so, I'll let you know."

I breathed a little easier. It had sounded all right, and Dyer kept on wolfing down his toast and eggs. When they were gone he put sugar and cream in his coffee, stirred it around, and lit a cigarette. "Well—that's how you got it figured out."

"I imagine I'm not far off."

"All I got to say, you got a trusting disposition."

"What do you make of it?"

"This guy's a regular employee, you say?"

"He's been head teller."

"Then he *couldn't* get locked in by mistake. He couldn't no more do that than a doctor could sew himself up in a man's belly by mistake. Furthermore, you couldn't lock him in by mistake. You take all the usual care, don't you, when you lock a vault?"

"I think so."

"And you done it regular, yesterday?"

"As well as I can recall."

"You looked around in there?"

"Yes, of course."

"And you didn't see nothing?"

"No, certainly not."

"Then he's in there on purpose."

The other two nodded, and looked at me like I must not be very bright.

Dyer went on: "It's possible for a man to hide hisself in a vault. I've thought of it, many a time, how it could be done. You think of a lot of things in my business. Once them trucks are wheeled in, with the records on them, if he once got in without being seen, he could stoop down behind them, and keep quiet, and when you come to close up you wouldn't see him. But not by accident. Never."

I was feeling funny in the stomach. I had to take a tack I didn't like.

"Of course, there's a human element in it. There's nothing in this man's record that gives any ground whatever for thinking he'd pull anything. Fact of the matter, that's what I'm doing in the branch. I was sent out there to study his methods in the savings department. I've been so much impressed by his work that I'm going to write an article about it."

"When did he get in there, do you think?"

"Well, we found a spider. A big one."

"One of them bad dreams with fur all over them?"

"That's it. And we were all gathered around looking at it. And arguing about how to get it out of there. I imagine he was standing there looking at it too. We all went out to throw it in the street, and he must have gone in the vault. Perhaps just looking around. Perhaps to open his box, I don't know. And — was in there when I closed it up."

"That don't hit you funny?"

"Not particularly."

"If you wanted to get everybody in one place in that bank, and everybody looking in one direction, so you could slip in the vault, you couldn't think of nothing better than one of them spiders, could you? Unless it was a rattlesnake."

"That strikes me as a little far-fetched."

"Not if he's just back from the mountains. From Lake Arrowhead, I think you said. That's where they have them spiders. I never seen one around Glendale. If he happened to turn that spider loose the first time he come in, all he had to do was wait till you found it, and he could easy slip in."

"He'd be running an awful risk."

"No risk. Suppose you seen him? He was looking at the spider too, wasn't he? He come in with his key to see what all the fuss was about. Thought maybe there was trouble. . . . Mr. Bennett, I'm telling you, he's not locked in by accident. It couldn't happen."

". . . What would you suggest?"

"I'd suggest that me, and Halligan, and Lewis, are covering that vault with guns when you open the door, and that we take him right in custody and get it out of him what he was doing in there. If he's got dough on him, then we'll know. I'd treat him just like anybody else that hid hisself in a vault. I wouldn't take no chances whatever."

"I can't stand for that."

"Why not?"

For just a split second I didn't know why not. All I knew was that if he was searched, even if he hadn't put his father-in-law's money back in the cash box, they'd find it on him, and a man with nine thousand dollars on him, unaccounted for, stepping out of a bank vault, was going to mean an investigation that was going to ruin me. But if you've got to think fast, you can do it. I acted like he ought to know why not. "Why—morale."

"What do you mean, morale?"

"I can't have those people out there, those other employees, I mean, see that at the first crack out of the box, for no reason whatever, I treat the senior member of the staff like some kind of a bandit. It just wouldn't do."

"I don't agree on that at all."

"Well, put yourself in their place."

"They work for a bank, don't they?"

"They're not criminals."

"Every person that works for a bank is automatically under suspicion from the minute he goes in until he comes out. Ain't nothing personal about it. They're just people that are entrusted with other people's money, and not nothing at all is taken for granted. That's why they're under bond. That's why they're checked all the time—they know it, they want it that way. And if he's got any sense, even when he sees our guns, supposing he is on the up-and-up, and he's in there by mistake, *he* knows it. But he's not on the up-and-up, and you owe it to them other people in there to give them the protection they're entitled to."

"I don't see it that way."

"It's up to you. But I want to be on record, in the presence of Halligan and Lewis, that I warned you. You hear what I say, Mr. Bennett?"

". . . I hear what you say."

My stomach was feeling still worse, but I gave them their orders. They were to take positions outside. They weren't to come in unless they were needed. They were to wait him out.

**

I led, driving over to the bank, and they followed, in Dyer's car. When I went past the bank I touched the horn and Dyer waved at me, so I could catch him in the mirror. They had wanted me to show them the bank, because they were all from the home office and had never been there. A couple of blocks up Anita Avenue I turned the corner and stopped. They pulled in ahead of me and parked. Dyer looked out. "All right. I got it."

I drove on, turned another corner, kept on around the block and parked where I could see the bank. In a minute or two along came Helm, unlocked the door and went in. He's first in, every morning. In about five minutes Snelling drove up, and parked in front of the drugstore. Then Sheila came walking down the street, stopped at Snelling's car, and stood there talking to him.

The curtains on the bank door came down. This was all part of opening the bank, you understand, and didn't have anything to do with the vault. The first man in goes all through the bank. That's in case somebody got in there during the night. They've been known to chop holes in the roof even, to be there waiting with a gun when the vault is opened.

He goes all through the bank, then if everything's O.K. he goes to the front door and lowers the curtains. That's a signal to the man across the street, who's always there by that time. But even that's not all. The man across the street doesn't go in till the first man comes out of the bank, crosses over, and gives the word. That's also in case there's somebody in there with a gun. Maybe he knows all about those curtains. Maybe he tells the first man to go lower the curtains, and be quick about it. But if the first man doesn't come out, as soon as he lowers the curtains, the man across the street knows there's something wrong, and puts in a call, quick.

The curtains were lowered, and Helm came out, and Snelling got out of his car. I climbed out and crossed over. Snelling and Helm went in, and Sheila dropped back with me.

"What are you going to do, Dave?"

"Give him his chance."

"If only he hasn't done something dumb."

"Get to him. Get to him and find out what's what. I'm going to take it as easy as I can. I'm going to stall, listen to what he has

to say, tell him I'll have to ask him to stick around till we check—
and then you get at it. Find out. And let me know."

"Do the others know?"

"No, but Helm's guessed it."

"Do you ever pray?"

"I prayed all I know."

Adler came up then and we went in. I looked at the clock. It
was twenty after eight. Helm and Snelling had their dust cloths,
polishing up their counters. Sheila went back and started to polish
hers. Adler went back to the lockers to put on his uniform. I sat
down at my desk, opened it, and took out some papers. They
were the same papers I'd been stalling with the afternoon before.
It seemed a long time ago, but I began stalling with them again.
Don't ask me what they were. I don't know yet.

My phone rang. It was Church. She said she wasn't feeling
well, and would it be all right if she didn't come in today? I said
yeah, perfectly all right. She said she hated to miss a day, but she
was afraid if she didn't take care of herself she'd really get sick. I
said certainly, she ought to take care of herself. She said she
certainly hoped I hadn't forgotten about the adding machine, that
it was a wonderful value for the money, and would probably pay
for itself in a year by what it would save. I said I hadn't forgotten
it. She said it all over again about how bad she felt, and I said
get well, that was the main thing. She hung up. I looked at the
clock. It was twenty-five after eight.

Helm stepped over, and gave my desk a wipe with his cloth. As
he leaned down he said: "There's a guy in front of the drugstore
I don't like the looks of, and two more down the street."

I looked over. Dyer was there, reading a paper.

"Yeah, I know. I sent for them."

"O.K."

"Have you said anything, Helm? To the others?"

"No sir, I haven't."

"I'd rather you didn't."

"No use starting anything, just on a hunch."

"That's it. I'll help you open the vault."

"Yes, sir."

"See the front door is open."

"I'll open it now."

At last the clock said eight-thirty, and the time lock clicked off. Adler came in from the lockers, strapping his belt on over his uniform. Snelling spoke to Helm, and went over to the vault. It takes two men to open a vault, even after the time lock goes off, one to each combination. I opened the second drawer of my desk, took out the automatic that was in there, threw off the catch, slipped it in my coat pocket, and went back there.

"I'll do that, Snelling."

"Oh, that's all right, Mr. Bennett. Helm and I have it down to a fine art. We've got so we can even do it to music."

"I'll try it, just once."

"O.K.—you spin and I'll whistle."

He grinned at Sheila, and began to whistle. He was hoping I'd forgotten the combination, and would have to ask help, and then he'd have a laugh on the boss. Helm looked at me, and I nodded. He spun his dial, I spun mine. I swung the door open.

At first, for one wild second, I thought there was nobody in there at all. I snapped on the switch, and couldn't see anything. By then my eye caught bright marks on the steel panels of the compartments that hold the safe deposit boxes. Then I saw the trucks had all been switched. They're steel frames, about four feet high, that hold the records. They run on rubber wheels, and when they're loaded they're plenty heavy. When they were put in there, they were all crosswise of the door. Now they were end to it, one jammed up against the other, and not three feet away from me. I dropped my hand in my gun pocket, and opened my mouth to call, and right that second the near truck hit me.

It hit me in the pit of the stomach. He must have been crouched behind it, like a runner, braced against the rear shelves and watching the time lock for the exact second we'd be in there. I went over backwards, still trying to get out the gun. The truck was right over me, like it had been shot out of a cannon. A roller went over my leg, and then I could see it crashing down on top of me.

I must have gone out for a split second when it hit my head, because the next thing I knew screams were ringing in my ears, and then I could see Adler and Snelling, against the wall, their hands over their heads.

But that wasn't the main thing I saw. It was this madman, this maniac, in front of the vault, waving an automatic, yelling that it was a stick-up, to put them up and keep them up, that whoever moved was going to be killed. If he had hoped to get away with it without being recognized, I can't say he didn't have a chance. He was dressed different from the way he was the day before. He must have brought the stuff in the grip. He had on a sweat shirt that made him look three times as big as he really was, a pair of rough pants and rough shoes, a black silk handkerchief over the lower part of his face, a felt hat pulled down over his eyes—and this horrible voice.

He was yelling, and the screaming was coming from Sheila. She seemed to be behind me, and was telling him to cut it out. I couldn't see Helm. The truck was on top of me, and I couldn't see anything clear, on account of the wallop on my head. Brent was standing right over me.

Then, right back of his head, a chip fell out of the wall. I didn't hear any shot at all, but he must have, because Dyer fired, from the street, right through the glass window. Brent turned, toward the street, and I saw Adler grab at his holster. I doubled up my legs and drove against the truck, straight at Brent. It missed him, and crashed against the wall, right beside Adler. Brent wheeled and fired. Adler fired. I fired. Brent fired again. Then he made one leap, and heaved the grip, that he had in his other hand, straight through the glass at the rear of the bank. You understand: the bank is on a corner, and on two sides there's glass. There's glass on half the third side too, at the rear, facing the parking lot. It was through that window that he heaved the grip. The glass broke with a crash, and left a hole the size of a door. He went right through it.

I jumped up, and dived after him, through the hole. I could hear Dyer and his two men coming up the street behind me, shooting as they came. They hadn't come in the bank at all. At the first yelp that Sheila let out they began shooting through the glass.

He was just grabbing up the grip as I got there and leveled his gun right at me. I dropped to the ground and shot. He shot. There was a volley of shots from Dyer and Halligan and Lewis. He ran about five steps, and jumped into a car. It was a blue sedan, the door was open and it was already moving when he landed on it. It shot ahead, straight across the parking lot and over to Grove Street. I raised my gun to shoot at the tires. Two kids came around the corner carrying school books. They stopped and blinked. I didn't fire. The car was gone.

I turned around and stepped back through the hole in the glass. The place was full of smoke, from the shooting. Sheila, Helm, and Snelling were stooped down, around Adler. He was lying a little to one side of the vault, and a drop of blood was trickling down back of his ear. It was the look on their faces that told me. Adler was dead.

9

I STARTED FOR THE TELEPHONE. IT WAS ON MY DESK, AT THE front of the bank, and my legs felt queer as I walked along toward it, back of the windows. Dyer was there ahead of me. He came through the brass gate, from the other side and reached for it.

"I'm using that for a second, Dyer."

He didn't answer, and didn't look at me, just picked up the phone and started to dial. So far as he was concerned, I was the heel that was responsible for it all, by not doing what he said, and he was letting me know it. I felt that way about it too, but I wasn't taking anything off him. I grabbed him by the neck of his coat and jerked him back on his heels.

"Didn't you hear what I said?"

His face got white, and he stood there beside me, his nostrils fanning and his little gray eyes drawn down to points. I broke his connection and dialed the home office. When they came in I asked for Lou Frazier. His title is vice president, same as mine, but he's special assistant to the Old Man, and with the Old Man in Honolulu, he was in charge. His secretary said he wasn't there, but then she said wait a minute, he's just come in. She put him on.

"Lou?"

"Yeah?"

"Dave Bennett, in Glendale."

"What is it, Dave?"

"We've had some trouble. You better get out. And bring some money. There'll be a run."

"What kind of trouble?"

"Stick-up. Guard killed. I think we're cleaned."

"O.K. — how much do you need?"

"Twenty thousand, to start. If we need more, you can send for it later. And step on it."

"On my way."

While I was talking, the sirens were screeching, and now the place was full of cops. Outside, an ambulance was pulling in, and about five hundred people standing around, with more coming by the second. When I hung up, a drop of blood ran off the end of my nose on the blotter, and then it began to patter down in a stream. I put my hand to my head. My hair was all sticky and wet, and when I looked, my fingers were full of blood. I tried to think what caused it, then remembered the truck falling on me.

"Dyer?"

". . . Yes sir."

"Mr. Frazier is on his way out. He's bringing money to meet all demands. You're to stay here with Halligan and Lewis, and keep order, and hold yourself ready for anything he tells you. Let the police take care of Adler."

"They're taking him out now."

I looked, and two of them, with the ambulance crew, were carrying him out. They were going the front way. Halligan had opened the door. Lewis and five or six cops were already outside, keeping the people back. They put him in the ambulance. Helm started out there, but I called him.

"Get in the vault, check it up."

"We've been in. Snelling and I."

"What did he get?"

"He got it all. Forty-four thousand, cash. And that's not all. He got in the boxes. He left the little boxes alone. He went in the others with a chisel, the ones that had big valuables and securities in them, and he took it all from them, too. He knew which ones."

"Mr. Frazier is on his way out with cash for the depositors. As soon as that's under way, make a list of all the riffled boxes, get the box holders on the phone if you can, send them wires otherwise, and get them in here."

"I'll start on it now."

The ambulance crew came in, and started over toward me. I waved them away, and they went off with Adler. Sheila came over to me.

"Mr. Kaiser wants to speak to you."

He was right behind her, Bunny Kaiser, the guy she had brought in for the $100,000 loan the afternoon I had found the shortage. I was just opening my mouth to tell him that all demands would be met, that he could take his turn with the other depositors as soon as we opened, when he motioned to the windows. Every window on one side was full of breaks and bullet holes, and the back window had the big hole in it where Brent had thrown his grip through it.

"Mr. Bennett, I just wanted to say, I've got my glaziers at work now, they're just starting on the plate glass windows for my building, they've got plenty of stock, and if you want, I'll send them over and they can get you fixed up here. Them breaks don't look so good."

"That would help, Mr. Kaiser."

"Right away."

"And—thanks."

I stuck out my left hand, the one that wasn't covered with blood, and he took it. I must have been pretty rung up. For just that long it seemed to me I loved him more than anybody on earth. At a time like that, what it means to you, one kind word.

The glaziers were already ripping out the broken glass when Lou Frazier got there. He had a box of cash, four extra tellers, and one uniformed guard, all he could get into his car. He came over, and I gave it to him quick, what he needed to know. He stepped out on the sidewalk with his cash box, held it up, and made a speech:

"All demands will be met. In five minutes the windows will open, all depositors kindly fall in line, the tellers will identify you, and positively nobody but depositors will be admitted!"

He had Snelling with him, and Snelling began to pick depositors out of the crowd, and the cops and the new guard formed them in line, out on the sidewalk. He came in the bank again, and his tellers set the upset truck on its wheels again, and rolled the others out, and they and Helm started to get things ready to pay. Dyer was inside by now. Lou went over to him, and jerked his thumb toward me.

"Get him out of here."

It was the first it had dawned on me that I must be an awful-looking thing, sitting there at my desk in the front of the bank, with blood all over me. Dyer came over and called another ambulance. Sheila took her handkerchief and started to wipe off my face. It was full of blood in a second. She took my own handkerchief out of my pocket, and did the best she could with it. From the way Lou looked away every time his eye fell on me, I figured she only made it worse.

Lou opened the doors, and forty or fifty depositors filed in. "Savings depositors on this side, please have your passbooks ready."

He split them up to four windows. There was a little wait, and then those at the head of the line began to get their money. Four or five went out, counting bills. Two or three that had been in line saw we were paying, and dropped out. A guy counting bills stopped, then fell in at the end of the line, to put his money back in.

The run was over.

My head began to go around, and I felt sick to my stomach. Next thing I knew, there was an ambulance siren, and then a doctor in a white coat was standing in front of me, with two orderlies beside him. "Think you can go, or you going to need a little help?"

"Oh, I can go."

"Better lean on me."

I leaned on him, and I must have looked pretty terrible, because Sheila turned away from me, and started to cry. It was the first she had broken down since it happened, and she couldn't fight it back. Her shoulders kept jerking and the doctor motioned to one of the orderlies.

"Guess we better take her along too."

"Guess we better."

* * *

They rode us in together, she on one stretcher, me on the other, the doctor riding backwards, between us. As we went he worked on my cut. He kept swabbing at it, and I could feel the sting of the antiseptic. But I wasn't thinking about that. Once out of the bank, Sheila broke down completely, and it was terrible to hear the sound in her voice, as the sobs came out of her. The doctors talked to her a little, but kept on working on me. It was a swell ride.

10

IT WAS THE SAME OLD HOSPITAL AGAIN, AND THEY LIFTED HER out, and wheeled her away somewhere, and then they took me out. They wheeled me in an elevator, and we went up, and they wheeled me out of the elevator to a room, and then two more doctors came and looked at me. One of them was an older man, and he didn't seem to be an intern. "Well, Mr. Bennett, you've got a bad head."

"Sew it up, it'll be all right."

"I'm putting you under an anaesthetic, for that."

"No anaesthetic, I've got things to do."

"Do you want to bear that scar the rest of your life?"

"What are you talking about, scar?"

"I'm telling you, you've got a bad head. Now if—"

"O.K.—but get at it."

He went, and an orderly came in and started to undress me, but I stopped him and made him call my house. When he had Sam on the line I talked, and told him to drop everything and get in there with another suit of clothes, a clean shirt, fresh necktie, and everything else clean. Then I slipped out of the rest of my clothes, and they put a hospital shirt on me, and a nurse came in and jabbed me with a hypodermic, and they took me up to the operating room. A doctor put a mask over my face and told me to breathe in a natural manner, and that was the last I knew for a while.

When I came out of it I was back in the room again, and the nurse was sitting there, and my head was all wrapped in bandages. They hadn't used ether, they had used some other stuff, so in about five minutes I was myself again, though I felt pretty sick. I asked for a paper. She had one on her lap, reading it, and handed it over. It was an early edition, and the robbery was smeared all over the front page, with Brent's picture, and Adler's picture, and my picture, one of my old football pictures. There was no trace of Brent yet, it said, but the preliminary estimate of what he got was put at $90,000. That included $44,000 from the bank, and around $46,000 taken from the private safe deposit boxes. The story made me the hero. I knew he was in the vault, it said, and although I brought guards with me, I insisted on being the first man in the vault, and suffered a serious head injury as a result. Adler got killed on the first exchange of shots, after I opened fire. He left a wife and one child, and the funeral would probably be held tomorrow.

There was a description of Brent's sedan, and the license number. Dyer had got that, as the car drove off, and it checked with the plates issued in Brent's name. There was quite a lot about the fact that the car was moving when he jumped aboard, and how that proved he had accomplices. There was nothing about Sheila, except that she had been taken to the hospital for nervous collapse, and nothing about the shortage at all. The nurse got up and came over to feed me some ice. "Well, how does it feel to be a hero?"

"Feels great."

"You had quite a time out there."

"Yeah, quite a time."

Pretty soon Sam got there with my clothes, and I told him to stand by. Then two detectives came in and began asking questions. I told them as little as I could, but I had to tell them about Helm, and Sheila seeing the red light, and how I'd gone against Dyer's advice, and what happened at the bank. They dug in pretty hard, but I stalled as well as I could, and after a while they went.

Sam went out and got a later edition of the afternoon paper. They had a bigger layout now on the pictures. Brent's picture was still three columns, but my picture and Adler's picture were smaller, and in an inset there was a picture of Sheila. It said police had a talk with her, at the hospital, and that she was unable to give any clue as to why Brent had committed the crime, or as to his whereabouts. Then, at the end, it said: "It was intimated, however, that Mrs. Brent will be questioned further."

At that I hopped out of bed. The nurse jumped up and tried to stop me, but I knew I had to get away from where cops could get at me, anyway until the thing broke enough that I knew what I was going to do.

"What are you doing, Mr. Bennett?"

"I'm going home."

"But you can't! You're to stay until—"

"I said I'm going home. Now if you want to stick around and watch me dress, that's O.K. by me, but if you're a nice girl, now is the time to beat it out in the hall."

While I was dressing they all tried to stop me, the nurse and the intern, and the head nurse, but I had Sam pitch the bloody clothes into the suitcase he had brought, and in about five minutes we were off. At the desk downstairs I wrote a check for my bill, and asked the woman how was Mrs. Brent.

"Oh, she'll be all right, but of course it was a terrible shock to her."

"She still here?"

"Well, they're questioning her, you know."

"Who?"

"The police. . . . If you ask me, she'll be held."

"You mean—arrested?"

"Apparently she knows something."

"Oh, I see."

"Don't say I told you."

"I won't, of course."

Sam had a taxi by then, and we got in. I had the driver go out to Glendale, and pull up beside my car, where I had left it on Anita Avenue. I had Sam take the wheel, and told him to drive around and keep on driving. He took Foothill, and went on up past San Fernando somewhere, I didn't pay any attention where.

Going past the bank, I saw the glass was all in place, and a goldleafer was inside, putting on the lettering. I couldn't see who was in there. Late in the afternoon we came back through Los Angeles, and I bought a paper. My picture was gone now, and so was Adler's, and Brent's was smaller. Sheila's was four columns wide, and in an inset was a picture of her father, Dr. Henry W. Rollinson, of U.C.L.A. The headline stretched clear across the page, and called it a "cover-up robbery." I didn't bother to read any more. If Dr. Rollinson had told his story, the whole thing was in the soup.

Sam drove me home then, and fixed me something to eat. I went in the living room and lay down, expecting cops, and wondered what I was going to tell them.

Around eight o'clock the doorbell rang, and I answered myself. But it wasn't cops, it was Lou Frazier. He came in and I had Sam fix him a drink. He seemed to need it. I lay down on the sofa again, and held on to my head. It didn't ache, and I felt all right, but I was getting ready. I wanted an excuse not to talk any more than I had to. After he got part of his drink down he started in.

"You seen the afternoon papers?"

"Just the headlines."

"The guy was short in his accounts."

"Looks like it."

"She was in on it."

"Who?"

"The wife. That sexy-looking thing known as Sheila. She doctored the books for him. We just locked up a half hour ago. I've just come from there. Well boy, it's a crime what that dame got away with. That system in the savings department, all that stuff you went out there to make a report on — that was nothing but a cover. The laugh's on you, Bennett. Now you got a real article for the American Banker."

"I doubt if she was in on it."

"I know she was in on it."

"If she was, why did she let him go to her father for the dough to cover up the shortage? Looks to me like that was putting it on a little too thick."

"O.K. — it's taken me all afternoon to figure that one out, and I had to question the father pretty sharp. He's plenty bitter against Brent. All right, take it from their point of view, hers and Brent's. They were short on the accounts, and they figured on a phoney hold-up that would cover their deficit, so nobody would even know there *had* been a shortage. The first thing to do was get the books in shape, and I'm telling you she made a slick job of that. She didn't leave a trace, and if it wasn't for her father, we'd never have known how much they were short. All right, she's got to get those books in shape, and do it before your next check on her cash. That was the tough part, they were up against time, but she was equal to it, I'll say that for her. All right, now she brings a spider in, and he slips in the vault and hides there. But they couldn't be sure what was going to happen next morning, could they? He might get away with it clean, with that handkerchief over his face nobody could identify him, and then later she could call the old man up and say please don't say anything, she'll explain to him later, that Charles is horribly upset, and when the cops go to his house, sure enough he is. He's in bed, still recovering from his operation, and all this and that—but no money anywhere around, and nothing to connect him with it.

"But look: they figure maybe he don't get away with it. Maybe he gets caught, and then what? All the money's there, isn't it? He's got five doctors to swear he's off his nut anyway, on account of illness—and he gets off light. With luck, he even gets a suspended sentence, and the only one that's out is her old man. She shuts him up, and they're not much worse off than they were before. Well, thanks to a guy named Helm it all went sour. None of it broke like they expected—he got away, but everybody knew who he was, and Adler got killed. So now he's wanted for murder—*and* robbery, and she's held for the same."

"Is she held?"

"You bet your sweet life she's held. She doesn't know it yet—she's down at that hospital, with a little dope in her arm to quiet her after the awful experience she had, but there's a cop outside the door right now, and tomorrow when she wakes up maybe she won't look quite so sexy."

I lay there with my eyes shut, wondering what I was going to do, but by that time my head was numb, so I didn't feel anything any more. After a while I heard myself speak to him. "Lou?"

"Yeah?"

"I knew about that shortage."

"... You mean you suspected it?"

"I knew—"

"You mean you suspected it!"

He fairly screamed it at me. When I opened my eyes he was standing in front of me, his eyes almost popping out of their sockets, his face all twisted and white. Lou is a pretty good-looking guy, big and thickset, with brown eyes and a golf tan all over him, but now he looked like some kind of a wild man.

"If you knew about it, and didn't report it, *there goes our bond! Don't you get it, Bennett? There goes our bond!"*

It was the first I had even thought of the bond. I could see it, though, the second he began to scream, that little line in fine type on the bond. We don't make our people give individual bond. We carry a group bond on them, ourselves, and that line reads: ". . . The assured shall report to the Corporation any shortage, embezzlement, defalcation, or theft on the part of any of their employees, within twenty-four hours of the time such shortage, embezzlement, defalcation, or theft shall be known to them, or to their officers, and failure to report such shortage, embezzlement, defalcation, or theft shall be deemed ground for the cancellation of this bond, and the release of the Corporation from liability for such shortage, embezzlement, defalcation, or shortage." I felt my lips go cold, and the sweat stand out on the palms of my hands, but I went on:

"You're accusing a woman of crimes I know damned well she didn't commit, and bond or no bond, I'm telling you—"

"You're not telling me anything, get that right now!"

He grabbed his hat and ran for the door. "And listen: If you know what's good for you, you're not telling anybody else either! If that comes out, there goes our fidelity bond and our burglary bond—we won't get a cent from the bonding company, we're hooked for the whole ninety thousand bucks, and—God, ninety thousand bucks! Ninety thousand bucks!"

He went, and I looked at my watch. It was nine o'clock. I called up a florist, and had them send flowers to Adler's funeral. Then I went upstairs and went to bed, and stared at the ceiling trying to get through my head what I had to face in the morning.

11

DON'T ASK ME ABOUT THE NEXT THREE DAYS. THEY WERE THE
worst I ever spent in my life. First I went in to the Hall of Justice
and talked to Mr. Gaudenzi, the assistant district attorney that
was on the case. He listened to me, and took notes, and then
things began to hit me.

First I was summoned to appear before the Grand Jury, to tell
what I had to say there. I had to waive immunity for that, and
boy, if you think it's fun to have those babies tearing at your
throat, you try it once. There's no judge to help you, no lawyer
to object to questions that make you look like a fool, nothing but
you, the district attorney, the stenographer, and them. They kept
me in there two hours. I squirmed and sweated and tried to get
out of admitting why I put up the money for Sheila, but after a
while they had it. I admitted I had asked her to divorce Brent
and marry me, and that was all they wanted to know. I was hardly
home before a long wire from Lou Frazier was delivered, telling
me the bonding company had filed notice they denied liability
for the money that was gone, and relieving me of duty until further notice. He would have fired me, if he could, but that had
to wait till the Old Man got back from Honolulu, as I was an
officer of the company, and couldn't be fired until the Old Man
laid it before the directors.

But the worst was the newspapers. The story had been doing
pretty well until I got in it, I mean it was on the front page, with
pictures and all kinds of stuff about clues to Brent's whereabouts,
one hot tip putting him in Mexico, another in Phoenix, and still
another in Del Monte, where an auto court man said he'd registered the night of the robbery. But when they had my stuff, they
went hog wild with it. That gave it a love interest, and what they
did to me was just plain murder. They called it the Loot Triangle,
and went over to old Dr. Rollinson's, where Sheila's children
were staying, and got pictures of them, and of him, and stole at
least a dozen of her, and they ran every picture of me they could
dig out of their files, and I cursed the day I ever posed in a
bathing suit while I was in college, with a co-ed skinning the cat
on each arm, in an "Adonis" picture for some football publicity.

And what I got for all that hell was that the day before I appeared before them, the Grand Jury indicted Sheila for alteration

of a corporation's records, for embezzlement, and for accessory to robbery with a deadly weapon. The only thing they didn't indict her for was murder, and why they hadn't done that I couldn't understand. So it all went for nothing. I'd nailed myself to the cross, brought all my federal mortgage notes to prove I'd put up the money, and that she couldn't have had anything to do with it, and she got indicted just the same. I got so I didn't have the heart to put my face outside the house, except when a newspaper man showed up, and then I'd go out to take a poke at him, if I could. I sat home and listened to the short wave radio, tuned to the police broadcasts, wondering if I could pick up something that would mean they were closing in on Brent. That, and the news broadcasts. On of them said Sheila's bail had been set at $7,500, and that her father had put it up, and that she'd been released. It wouldn't have done any good for me to have gone down to put up bail. I'd given her all I had, already.

That day I got in the car and took a ride, just to keep from going nuts. Coming back I drove by the bank and peeped in. Snelling was at my desk. Church was at Sheila's window. Helm was at Snelling's place, and there were two tellers I'd never seen before.

When I tuned in on the news, after supper that night, for the first time there was some sign the story was slackening off. The guy said Brent hadn't been caught yet, but there was no more stuff about me, or about Sheila. I relaxed a little, but then after a while something else began to bore into me. Where was Brent? If she was out on bail, was she meeting him? I'd done all I could to clear her, but that didn't mean I was sure she was innocent, or felt any different about her than I had before. The idea that she might be meeting him somewhere, that she had played me for a sucker that way, right from the start, set me to tramping around that living room once more, and I tried to tell myself to forget it, to forget her, to wipe the whole thing off the slate and be done with it, and I couldn't. Around eight-thirty I did something I guess I'm not proud of. I got in the car, drove over there, and parked down the street about half a block, to see what I could see.

There was a light on, and I sat there a long time. You'd be surprised what went on, the newspaper reporters that rang the bell, and got kicked out, the cars that drove by, and slowed down so fat women could rubber in there, the peeping that was going on from upstairs windows of houses. After a while the light went off. The door opened, and Sheila came out. She started down the street, toward me. I felt if she saw me there I'd die of shame. I dropped down behind the wheel, and bent over on one side so I couldn't be seen from the pavement, and held my breath. I could hear her footsteps coming on, quick, like she was in a hurry to get somewhere. They went right on by the car, without stopping, but through the window, almost in a whisper, I heard her say: "You're being watched."

I knew in a flash then, why she hadn't been indicted for murder. If they'd done that, she wouldn't have been entitled to bail. They indicted her, but they left it so she could get out, and then they began doing the same thing I'd been doing: watching her, to see if she'd make some break that would lead them to Brent.

Next day I made up my mind I had to see her. But now to see her was tough. If they were watching her that close, they'd probably tapped in on her phone, and any wire I sent her would be read before she got it, that was a cinch. I figured on it a while, and then I went down in the kitchen to see Sam. "You got a basket here?"

"Yes sir, a big market basket."

"O.K., I tell you what you do. Put a couple of loaves of bread in it, put on your white coat, and get on over to this address on Mountain Drive. Go in the back way, knock, ask for Mrs. Brent. Make sure you're talking to her, and that nobody else is around. Tell her I want to see her, and will she meet me tonight at seven o'clock, at the same place she used to meet me downtown, after she came from the hospital. Tell her I'll be waiting in the car."

"Yes sir, seven o'clock."

"You got that all straight?"

"I have, sir."

"There's cops all around the house. If you're stopped, tell them nothing, and if possible, don't let them know who you are."

"Just leave it to me."

* * *

I took an hour that night shaking anybody that might be following me. I drove up to Saugus, and coming in to San Fernando
I shoved up to ninety, and I knew nobody was back of me, because I could see everything behind. At San Fernando I cut
over to Van Nuys, and drove in to the hospital from there. It
was one minute after seven when I pulled in to the curb, but I
hadn't even stopped rolling before the door opened and she
jumped in. I kept right on.

"You're being followed."

"I think not. I shook them."

"I couldn't. I think my taxi driver had his instructions before
he came to the house. They're about two hundred yards behind."

"I don't see anything."

"They're there."

We drove on, me trying to think what I wanted to say. But it
was she that started it.

"Dave?"

"Yes?"

"We may never see each other again, after tonight. I think I'd
better begin. You've—been on my mind, quite a lot. Among
other things."

"All right, begin."

"I've done you a great wrong."

"I didn't say so."

"You didn't have to. I felt everything you were thinking in that
terrible ride that morning in the ambulance. I've done you a great
wrong, and I've done myself a great wrong. I forgot one thing a
woman can never forget. I didn't forget it. But I—closed my eyes
to it."

"Yeah, and what was that?"

"That a woman must come to a man, as they say in court, with
clean hands. In some countries, she has to bring more than that.
Something in her hand, something on her back, something on
the ox cart—a dowry. In this country we waive that, but we don't
waive the clean hands. I couldn't give you them. If I was going
to come to you, I had to come with encumbrances, terrible encumbrances. I had to be bought."

"I suggested that."

"Dave, it can't be done. I've asked you to pay a price for me that no man can pay. I've cost you a shocking amount of money, I've cost you your career, I've cost you your good name. On account of me you've been pilloried in the newspapers, you've endured torture. You've stood by me beautifully, you did everything you could for me, before that awful morning and since—but I'm not worth it. No woman can be, and no woman has a right to think she is. Very well, then, you don't have to stand by me any longer. You can consider yourself released, and if it lies in my power, I'll make up to you what I've cost you. The career, the notoriety, I can't do anything about. The money, God willing, some day I shall repay you. I guess that's what I wanted to say. I guess that's all I wanted to say. That—and good-bye."

I thought that over for five or ten miles. It was no time for lolly-gagging. She had said what she meant and I had to say what I meant. And I wasn't kidding myself that a lot of it wasn't true. The whole mess, from the time we had started doctoring those books, and putting the money back, I had just hated, and they weren't love scenes, those nights when we were getting ready for the next day's skulduggery. They were nervous sessions, and she never looked quite so pretty going home as she had coming over. But it still wasn't what was on my mind. If I could be sure she was on the up-and-up with me, I'd still feel she was worth it, and I'd still stand by her, if she needed me and wanted me. I made up my mind I was going to hit it on the nose. "Sheila?"

"Yes, Dave."

"I did feel that way in the ambulance."

"There's no need to tell me."

"Partly on account of what you've been talking about, maybe. There's no use kidding ourselves. It was one awful morning, and we've both had awful mornings since. But that wasn't the main thing."

". . . What was the main thing?"

"I wasn't sure, I haven't been sure from the beginning, and I'm not sure now, that you haven't been two-timing me."

"What are you talking about? Two-timing you with whom?"

"Brent."

"With *Charles?* Are you crazy?"

"No, I'm not crazy. All right, now you get it. I've known from the beginning, and I'm perfectly sure of it now, that you know more about this than you've been telling, that you've held out on me, that you've held out on the cops. All right, now you can put it on the line. Were you in on this thing with Brent or not?"

"Dave, how can you ask such a thing?"

"Do you know where he is?"

". . . Yes."

"That's all I want to know."

I said it mechanically, because to tell you the truth I'd about decided she was on the up-and-up all the way down the line, and when she said that it hit me between the eyes like a fist. I could feel my breath trembling as we drove along, and I could feel her looking at me too. Then she began to speak in a hard, strained voice, like she was forcing herself to talk, and measuring everything she said.

"I know where he is, and I've known a lot more about him than I ever told you. Before that morning, I didn't tell you because I didn't want to wash a lot of dirty linen, even before you. Since that morning I haven't told anybody because—*I want him to escape!*"

"Oh, you do!"

"I pulled you into it, when I discovered that shortage, for the reason I told you. So my children wouldn't grow up knowing their father was in prison. I'm shielding Charles now, I'm holding out on you, as you put it, because if I don't, they're going to grow up knowing their father was executed for murder. I won't have it! I don't care if the bank loses ninety thousand dollars, or a million dollars, I don't care if your career is ruined—I might as well tell you the truth, Dave—*if there's any way I can prevent it my children are not going to have their lives blighted by that horrible disgrace.*"

That cleared it up at last. And then something came over me. I knew we were going through the same old thing again, that I'd be helping her cover up something, that I wasn't going to have any more of that. If she and I were to go on, it had to be a clean slate between us, and I felt myself tighten. "So far as I'm concerned, I won't have that."

"I'm not asking you to."

"And not because of what you said about me. I'm not asking you to put me ahead of your children, or anything ahead of your children."

"I couldn't, even if you did ask me."

"It's because the game is up, and you may as well learn that your children aren't any better than anybody else."

"I'm sorry. To me they are."

"They'll learn, before they die, that they've got to play the cards God dealt them, and you'll learn it too, if I know anything about it. What you're doing, you're ruining other lives, to say nothing of your own life, and doing wrong, too—to save them. O.K., play it your own way. But that lets me out."

"Then it's good-bye?"

"I guess it is."

"It's what I've been trying to tell you."

She was crying now, and she took my hand and gave it a little jerky shake. I loved her more than I'd ever loved her, and I wanted to stop, and put my arms around her, and start all over again, but I didn't. I knew it wouldn't get us anywhere at all, and I kept right on driving. We'd got to the beach by then, by way of Pico Boulevard, and I ran up through Santa Monica to Wilshire, then turned back to take her home. We were done, and I could feel it that she had called the turn. We'd never see each other again.

How far we'd got I don't know, but we were somewhere coming in toward Westwood. She had quieted down, and was leaning against the window with her eyes closed, when all of a sudden she sat up and turned up the radio. I had got so I kept it in short wave all the time now, and it was turned low, so you could hardly hear it, but it was on. A cop's voice was just finishing an order, and then it was repeated: "Car No. forty-two, Car No. forty-two . . . Proceed to No. six eight two five Sanborn Avenue, Westwood, at once. . . . Two children missing from home of Dr. Henry W. Rollinson . . ."

I stepped on it hard, but she grabbed me.

"Stop!"

"I'm taking you there!"

"Stop! I said stop—will you please stop!"

I couldn't make any sense out of it, but I pulled over and we skidded to a stop. She jumped out. I jumped out. "Will you kindly tell me what we're stopping here for? They're your kids, don't you get it—?"

But she was on the curb, waving back the way we had come. Just then a pair of headlights snapped on. I hadn't seen any car, but it dawned on me this must be that car that had been following us. She kept on waving, then started to run toward it. At that, the car came up. A couple of detectives were inside. She didn't even wait till she stopped before she screamed: "Did you get that call?"

"What call?"

"The Westwood call, about the children?"

"Baby, that was for car forty-two."

"Will you wipe that grin off your face and listen to me? Those are my children. They've been taken by my husband, and it means he's getting ready to skip, to wherever he's going—"

She never even finished. Those cops hopped out and she gave it to them as fast as she could. She said he'd be sure to stop at his hideout before he blew, that they were to follow us there, that we'd lead the way if they'd only stop talking and hurry. But the cops had a different idea. They knew by now it was a question of time, so they split the cars up. One of them went ahead in the police car, after she gave him the address, the other took the wheel of my car, and we jumped in on the back seat. Boy, if you think you can drive, you ought to try it once with a pair of cops. We went through Westwood with everything wide open, it wasn't five minutes before we were in Hollywood, and we just kept on going. We didn't stop for any kind of a light, and I don't think we were under eighty the whole trip.

All the time she kept holding onto my hand and praying: "Oh God, if we're only in time! If we're only in time!"

12

WE PULLED UP IN FRONT OF A LITTLE WHITE APARTMENT HOUSE in Glendale. Sheila jumped out, and the cops and myself were right beside her. She whispered for us to keep quiet. Then she stepped on the grass, went around to the side of the house and looked up. A light was on in one window. Then she went back to the garage. It was open, and she peeped in. Then she came

back to the front and went inside, still motioning to us to keep
quiet. We followed her, and she went up to the second floor. She
tiptoed to the third door on the right, stood there a minute, and
listened. She tiptoed back to where we were. The cops had their
guns out by now. Then she marched right up to the door, her
heels clicking on the floor, and rapped. It opened right away, and
a woman was standing there. She had a cigarette in one hand
and her hat and coat on, like she was getting ready to go out. I
had to look twice to make sure I wasn't seeing things. It was
Church.

"Where are my children?"

"Well, Sheila, how should I know—?"

Sheila grabbed her and jerked her out into the hall. "Where
are my children, I said?"

"They're all right. He just wanted to see them a minute
before he—"

She stopped when one of the cops walked up behind her,
stepped through the open door with his gun ready, and went
inside. The other cop stayed in the hall, right beside Sheila and
Church, his gun in his hand, listening. After a minute or two the
cop that went in came to the door and motioned us inside. Sheila
and Church went in, then I went in, then the other cop stepped
inside, but stood where he could cover the hall. It was a one-
room furnished apartment, with a dining alcove to one side, and
a bathroom. All doors were open, even the closet door, where the
cop had opened them, ready to shoot if he had to. In the middle
of the floor were a couple of suitcases strapped up tight. The cop
that went in first walked over to Church.

"All right, Fats, spit it out."

"I don't even know what you're talking about."

"Where are those kids?"

"How should I know—?"

"You want that puss mashed in?"

". . . He's bringing them here."

"When?"

"Now. He ought to be here by now."

"What for?"

"To take with us. We were going to blow."

"He using a car?"

"He's using his car."

"O.K. — open them suitcases."
"I have no key. He — "
"I said open them."

She stooped down and began to unstrap the suitcases. The cop poked her behind with the gun.

"Come on, step on it, step on it!"

When she had them unstrapped, she took keys from her hand-bag and unlocked them. The cop kicked them open. Then he whistled. From the larger of the two suitcases money began tumbling out on the floor, some of it in bundles, with rubber bands around it, some of it with the paper wrappers still on, showing the amounts. That was the new money we had in the vault, stuff that had never even been touched. Church began to curse at Sheila.

"It's all there, and now you've got what you want, haven't you? You think I didn't know what you were doing? You think I didn't see you fixing those cards up so you could send him up when they found that shortage? All right, he beat you to it, and he took your old man for a ride too — that sanctimonious old fool! But you haven't got him yet, and you haven't got those brats! I'll — "

She made a dive for the door, but the cop was standing there and threw her back. Then he spoke to the other one, the one that was stooped down, fingering the money. "Jake!"

"Yeah?"

"He'll be here for that dough. You better put in a call. No use taking chances. We need more men."

"God, I never seen that much dough."

He stepped over to the phone and lifted the receiver to dial. Just then, from outside, I heard a car horn give a kind of a rattle, like they give when they're tapped three or four times quick. Church heard it too, and opened her mouth to scream. That scream never came out. Sheila leaped at her, caught her throat with one hand and covered her mouth with the other. She turned her head around to the cops.

"Go on, hurry up, he's out there."

The cops dived out and piled down the stairs, and I was right after them. They no sooner reached the door than there was a shot, from a car parked out front, right behind my car. One cop ducked behind a big urn beside the door, the other ran behind a tree. But I didn't duck behind any urn and I didn't run behind any tree. The car was moving now, and I meant to get that guy if it was the last thing I did on earth. I ran off to the right, across the apartment house lawn and the lawn next to it and the lawn next to that, as hard as I could. There was no way he could turn. If he was going to get away, he had to pass me. I got to a car that was parked about fifty feet up the street, and crouched down in front of it, right on the front bumper, so that the car was between him and me. He was in second now, and giving her the gun, but I jumped and caught the door handle.

What happened in the next ten seconds I'm not sure I know myself. The speed of the car threw me back, so I lost my grip on the door handle, and I hit my head on the fender. I was still wearing a bandage, from the other cut, so that wasn't so good. But I caught the rear door handle, and hung on. All that happened quicker than I can tell it, but being thrown back that way, I guess that's what saved me. He must have thought I was still up front, because inside the car he began to shoot, and I saw holes appear in the front door, one by one. I had some crazy idea I had to count them, so I'd know when he'd shot his shells out. I saw three holes, one right after the other. But then I woke up that there were more shots than holes, that some of those shots were coming from behind. That meant the cops had got in it again. I was right in the line of fire, and I wanted to drop off and lay in the street, but I held on. Then these screams began coming from the back seat, and I remembered the kids. I yelled at the cops that the children were back there, but just then the car slacked and gave a yaw to the left, and we went crashing into the curb and stopped.

I got up, opened the front door, and jumped aside, quick. There was no need to jump. He was lying curled up on the front seat, with his head hanging down, and all over the upholstery was blood. But what I saw, when one of the cops ran up and opened the rear door was just pitiful. The oldest of the kids, Anna, was down on the floor moaning, and her sister, the little three-year-old, Charlotte, was up on the seat, screaming to her father to look at Anna, that Anna was hurt.

Her father wasn't saying anything.

It seemed funny that the cop, the one that had treated Church so rough, could be so swell when it came to a couple of children. He kept calling them Sissy, and got the little one calmed down in just about a minute, and the other one too, the one that was shot. The other cop ran back to the apartment house, to phone for help, and to collar Church before she could run off with that dough, and he caught her just as she was beating it out the door. This one stayed right with the car, and he no sooner got the children quiet than he had Sheila on his hands, and about five hundred people that began collecting from every place there was.

Sheila was like a wild woman, but she didn't have a chance with that cop. He wouldn't let her touch Anna, and he wouldn't let Anna be moved till the doctors moved her. There on the floor of the car was where she was going to stay, he said, and nothing that Sheila said could change him. I figured he was right, and put my arms around her, and tried to get her quiet, and in a minute or two I felt her stiffen and knew she was going to do everything she could to keep herself under control.

The ambulances got there at last, and they put Brent in one, and the little girl in the other, and Sheila rode in with her. I took little Charlotte in my car. As she left me Sheila touched my arm.

"More hospitals."

"You've had a dose."

"But this—Dave!"

It was one in the morning before they got through in the operating room, and long before that the nurses put little Charlotte to bed. From what she said to me on the way in, and what the cops and I were able to piece together, it wasn't one of the cop's shots that had hit Anna at all.

What happened was that the kids were asleep on the back seat, both of them, when Brent pulled up in front of the apartment house, and didn't know a thing till he started to shoot through the door at me. Then the oldest one jumped up and spoke to her father. When he didn't answer she stood up and tried to talk to him on his left side, back of where he was trying to shoot and drive at the same time. That must have been when he turned and let the cops have it over his shoulder. Except that instead of getting the cops, he got his own child.

When it was all over I took Sheila home. I didn't take her to

Glendale. I took her to her father's house in Westwood. She had
phoned him what had happened and they were waiting for her.
She looked like a ghost of herself, and leaned against the window
with her eyes closed. "Did they tell you about Brent?"

She opened her eyes.

". . . No. How is he?"

"He won't be executed for murder."

"You mean—?"

"He died. On the table."

She closed her eyes again, and didn't speak for a while, and
when she did it was a dull, lifeless way.

"Charles was all right, a fine man—until he met Church. I
don't know what effect she had on him. He went completely
insane about her, and then he began to go bad. What he did, I
mean at the bank that morning, wasn't his think-up, it was hers."

"But why, will you tell me that?"

"To get back at me. At my father. At the world. At everything.
You noticed what she said to me? With her that meant an ob-
session that I was set to ruin Charles, and if I was, then they
would strike first, that's all. Charles was completely under her,
and she's bad. Really, I'm not sure she's quite sane."

"What a looking thing to call a sweetie."

"I think that was part of the hold she had on him. He wasn't
a very masculine man. With me, I think he felt on the defensive,
though certainly I never gave him any reason to. But with her,
with that colorless, dietician nature that she had—I think he felt
like a man. I mean, she excited him. Because she is such a frump,
she gave him something I could never give him."

"I begin to get it now."

"Isn't that funny? He was my husband, and I don't care whether
he's alive or dead—I simply don't care. All I can think of is that
little thing down there—"

"What do the doctors say?"

"They don't know. It's entirely her constitution and how it
develops. It was through her abdomen, and there were eleven
perforations, and there'll be peritonitis, and maybe other
complications—and they can't even know what's going to happen for two or three days yet. And the loss of blood was
frightful."

"They'll give her transfusions."

"She had one, while they were operating. That was what they were waiting for. They didn't dare start till the donor arrived."

"If blood's what it takes, I've got plenty."

She started to cry, and caught my arm. "Even blood, Dave? Is there anything you haven't given me?"

"Forget it."

"Dave?"

"Yes?"

"If I'd played the cards that God dealt me, it wouldn't have happened. That's the awful part. If I'm to be punished—all right, it's what I deserve. But if only the punishment—*doesn't fall on her!*"

13

THE NEWSPAPERS GAVE SHEILA A BREAK, I'LL SAY THAT FOR THEM, once the cops exonerated her. They played the story up big, but they made her the heroine of it, and I can't complain of what they said about me, except I'd rather they hadn't said anything. Church took a plea and got sent over to Tehachapi for a while. She even admitted she was the one that brought in the spider. All the money was there, so Dr. Rollinson got his stake back, and the bonding company had nothing to pay, which kind of eased off what had been keeping me awake nights.

But that wasn't what Sheila and I had to worry about. It was that poor kid down there in the hospital, and that was just awful. The doctors knew what was coming, all right. For two or three days she went along and you'd have thought she was doing fine, except that her temperature kept rising a little bit at a time, and her eyes kept getting brighter and her cheeks redder. Then the peritonitis broke, and broke plenty. For two weeks her temperature stayed up around a hundred and four, and then when it seemed she had that licked, pneumonia set in. She was in oxygen three days, and when she came out of it she was so weak you couldn't believe she could live at all. Then, at last, she began to get better.

All that time I took Sheila in there twice a day, and we'd sit and watch the chart, and in between we'd talk about what we were going to do with our lives. I had no idea. The mess over the bond was all cleared up, but I hadn't been told to come back to work, and I didn't expect to be. And after the way my name had been plastered on the front pages all over the country I didn't know where I could get a job, or whether I could get a job. I knew a little about banking, but in banking the first thing you've got to have is a good name.

Then one night we were sitting there, Sheila and myself, with the two kids on the bed, looking at a picture book, when the door opened, and the Old Man walked in. It was the first time we had seen him since the night he danced with Sheila, just before he sailed for Honolulu. He had a box of flowers, and handed them to Sheila with a bow. "Just dropped in to see how the little girl is getting along."

Sheila took the flowers and turned away quickly to hide how she felt, then rang for the nurse and sent them out to be put in water. Then she introduced him to the children, and he sat on the bed and kidded along with them, and they let him look at the pictures in the picture book. The flowers came back, and Sheila caught her breath, and they were jumbo chrysanthemums all right. She thanked him for them, and he said they came from his own garden in Beverly. The nurse went and the kids kind of quieted down again, and Sheila went over to him, and sat down beside him on the bed, and took his hand. "You think this is a surprise, don't you?"

"Well, I can do better."

He dug in his pocket and fished up a couple of little dolls. The kids went nuts over them, and that was the end of talk for about five minutes. But Sheila was still hanging onto the Old Man's hand, and went on: "It's no surprise at all. I've been expecting you."

"Oh, you have."

"I saw you were back."

"I got back yesterday."

"I knew you'd come."

The Old Man looked at me and grinned. "I must have done pretty well in that dance. I must have uncorked a pretty good rhumba."

"I'd say you did all right."

Sheila laughed, and kissed his hand, and got up and moved into a chair. He moved into a chair too, and looked at his chrysanthemums and said, "Well, when you like somebody you have to bring her flowers."

"And when you like somebody, you know they'll do it."

He sat there a minute, and then he said, "I think you two are about the silliest pair of fools I ever knew. Just about the silliest."

"We think so too."

"But not a pair of crooks . . . I read a little about it, in Honolulu, and when I got back I went into it from beginning to end, thoroughly. If I'd been here, I'd have let you have it right in the neck, just exactly where Lou Frazier let you have it, and I haven't one word of criticism to offer for what he did. But I wasn't here. I was away, I'm glad to say. Now that I'm back I can't find it in me to hold it against you. It was against all rules, all prudence, but it wasn't morally wrong. And—it was silly. But all of us, I suppose, are silly now and then. Even I feel the impulse—especially when dancing the rhumba."

He stopped, and let his fingertips touch in front of his eyes, and stared through them for a minute or so. Then he went on:

"But—the official family is the official family, and while Frazier isn't quite as sore as he was, he's not exactly friendly, even yet. I don't think there's anything for you in the home office for some little time yet, Bennett—at any rate, until this blows over a little. However, I've about decided to open a branch in Honolulu. How would you like to take charge of *that?*"

Brother, does a cat like liver?

So Honolulu's where we are now, all five of us, Sheila, and myself, and Anna, and Charlotte, and Arthur, a little number you haven't heard about yet, that arrived about a year after we got here, and that was named after the Old Man. They're out there on the beach now, and I can see them from where I'm writing on the veranda, and my wife looks kind of pretty in a bathing suit, if anybody happens to ask you. The Old Man was on a few weeks ago, and told us that Frazier's been moved east, and any time I want to go back, it's all clear, and he'll find a spot for me.

But I don't know. I like it here, and Sheila likes it here, and the kids like it here, and the branch is doing fine. And another thing: I'm not so sure I want to make it too handy for Sheila and the Old Man to dance the rhumba.

Donald E. Westlake

ORDO

Donald E. Westlake (1933–) has written well in every sub-genre of crime fiction. His career has been first-rate all the way. You can't define him beyond that.

His first novels were Hammett-style hardboiled and while they were critical successes, his comic novels — The Busy Body, The Spy in the Ointment, God Save the Mark — brought him popular success, especially in Hollywood.

His career as Richard Stark, pseudonym for his popular series about professional thief Parker, made him into a world-wide cult figure. While Point Blank, the movie version of the first Parker novel, The Hunter, is a masterpiece and Lee Marvin was brilliant, I've always felt that Robert Duvall in the adaptation of The Outfit gave a more complex and powerful performance as Parker.

There was a long lay-off between Stark novels, Westlake didn't bring him back until a few years ago. I think the three latest are the best in the series, except maybe for the early (1966) The Seventh, which I re-read in 1999. I'm not sure if it's the "perfect" crime novel but it'll do until another contender comes along. A stunning piece of writing, from the first sentence to the last.

Westlake, in my opinion, has written two mainstream masterpieces, Adios, Scheherazade and The Ax, the former a hilariously forlorn novel about the business of writing dirty books (this was back in the early 1960s when "dirty" meant "naughty") and the latter, a stinging novel that deals with contemporary America far more believably and incisively than the literary novels that have walked the same turf.

Here, then, Donald Westlake, for my money the best crime novelist of his generation.

E.G.

1

MY NAME IS ORDO TUPIKOS, AND I WAS BORN IN NORTH FLAT Wyoming on November 9th, 1936. My father was part Greek and part Swede and part American Indian, while my mother was half Irish and half Italian. Both had been born in this country, so I am one hundred percent American.

My father, whose first name was Samos, joined the United States Navy on February 17th, 1942, and he was drowned in the Coral Sea on May 15th, 1943. At that time we were living in West Bowl, Oklahoma, my mother and my two sisters and my brother and I, and on October 12th of that year my mother married a man named Eustace St. Claude, who claimed to be half Spanish and half French but who later turned out to be half Negro and half Mexican and passing for white. After the divorce, my mother moved the family to San Itari, California. She never remarried, but she did maintain a long-term relationship with an air conditioner repairman named Smith, whose background I don't know.

On July 12th, 1955, I followed my father's footsteps by joining the United States Navy. I was married for the first time in San Diego, California on March 11th, 1958, when I was twenty-one, to a girl named Estelle Anlic, whose background was German and Welsh and Polish. She put on the wedding license that she was nineteen, having told me the same, but when her mother found us in September of the same year it turned out she was only sixteen. Her mother arranged the annulment, and it looked as though I might be in some trouble, but the Navy transferred me to a ship and that was the end of that.

By the time I left the Navy, on June 17, 1959, my mother and my half brother, Jacques St. Claude, had moved from California to Deep Mine, Pennsylvania, following the air conditioner repairman named Smith, who had moved back east at his father's death in order to take over the family hardware store. Neither Smith nor Jacques was happy to have me around, and I'd by then lost touch with my two sisters and my brother, so in September of that year I moved to Old Coral, Florida, where I worked as a carpenter (non-union) and where, on January 7th, 1960, I married my second wife, Sally Fowler, who was older than me and employed as a waitress in a diner on the highway toward Fort Lauderdale.

Sally, however, was not happy tied to one man, and so we were divorced on April 12th, 1960, just three months after the marriage. I did some drinking and trouble-making around that time, and lost my job, and a Night Court judge suggested I might be better off if I rejoined the Navy, which I did on November 4th, 1960, five days before my twenty-fourth birthday.

From then on, my life settled down. I became a career man in the Navy, got into no more marriages, and except for my annual Christmas letter from my mother in Pennsylvania I had no more dealings with the past. Until October 7th, 1974, when an event occurred that knocked me right over.

I was assigned at that time to a Naval Repair Station near New London, Connecticut, and my rank was Seaman First Class. It was good weather for October in that latitude, sunny, clean air, not very cold, and some of us took our afternoon break out on the main dock. Norm and Stan and Pat and I were sitting in one group, on some stacks of two by fours, Norm and Stan talking football and Pat reading one of his magazines and me looking out over Long Island Sound. Then Pat looked up from his magazine and said, "Hey, Orry."

I turned my head and looked at him. My eyes were half-blinded from looking at the sun reflected off the water. I said, "What?"

"You never said you were married to Dawn Devayne."

Dawn Devayne was a movie star. I'd seen a couple of her movies, and once or twice I saw her talking on television. I said, "Sure."

He gave me a dirty grin and said, "You shouldn't of let that go, boy."

With Pat, you play along with the joke and then go do something else, because otherwise he won't give you any peace. So I grinned back at him and said, "I guess I shouldn't," and then I turned to look some more at the water.

But this time he didn't quit. Instead, he raised his voice and he said, "Goddamit, Orry, it's right here in this goddam magazine."

I faced him again. I said, "Come on, Pat."

By now, Norm and Stan were listening too, and Norm said, "What's in the magazine, Pat?"

Pat said, "That Orry was married to Dawn Devayne."

Norm and Stan both grinned, and Stan said, "Oh *that*."

"Goddamit!" Pat jumped to his feet and stormed over and shoved the magazine in Stan's face. "You look at that!" he shouted. "You just look at that!"

I saw Stan look, and start to frown, and I couldn't figure out what was going on. Had they set this up ahead of time? But not Stan; Norm sometimes went along with Pat's gags, but Stan always brushed them away like mosquitoes. And now Stan frowned at the magazine, and he said, "Son of a bitch."

"Now, look," I said, "a joke's a joke."

But nobody was acting like it was a joke. Norm was looking over Stan's shoulder, and he too was frowning. And Stan, shaking his head, looked at me and said, "Why try to hide it, for Christ's sake? Brother, if *I'd* been married to Dawn Devayne, I'd tell the world about it."

"But I wasn't," I said. "I swear to God, I never was."

Norm said, "How many guys you know named Ordo Tupikos?"

"It's a mistake," I said. "It's got to be a mistake."

Norm seemed to be reading aloud from the magazine. He said, "Married in San Diego, California, in 1958, to a sailor named Ordo Tu—"

"Wait a minute," I said. "I was married then to, uh, Estelle—"

"Anlic," Pat said, and nodded his head at me. "Estelle Anlic, right?"

I stared at him. I said, "How'd you know that name?"

"Because that's Dawn Devayne, dummy! That's her real name!" Pat grabbed the magazine out of Norm's hands and rushed over to jab it at me. "Is that you, or isn't it?"

There was a small black-and-white photo on the page, surrounded by printing. I hadn't seen that picture in years.

It was Estelle and me, on our wedding day, a picture taken outside City Hall by a street photographer. There I was in my whites—you don't wear winter blues in San Diego—and there was Estelle. She was wearing her big shapeless black sweater and that tight tight gray skirt down to below her knees that I liked in those days. We were both squinting in the sunlight, and Estelle's short dark hair was in little curls all around her head.

"That's not Dawn Devayne," I said. "Dawn Devayne has blonde hair."

Pat said something scornful about people dyeing their hair, but I didn't listen. I'd seen the words under the picture and I was reading them. They said: "Dawn and her first husband, Navy man Ordo Tupikos. Mama had the marriage annulled six months later."

Norm and Stan had both come over with Pat, and now Stan looked at me and said, "You didn't even know it."

"I never saw her again." I made a kind of movement with the magazine, and I said, "When her mother took her away. The Navy put me on a ship, I never saw her after that."

Norm said, "Well, I'll be a son of a bitch."

Pat laughed, slapping himself on the hip. He said: "You're married to a movie star!"

I got to my feet and went between them and walked away along the dock toward the repair sheds. The guys shouted after me, wanting to know where I was going, and Pat yelled, "That's my magazine!"

"I'll bring it back," I said. "I want to borrow it." I don't know if they heard.

I went to the Admin Building and into the head and closed myself in a stall and sat on the toilet and started in to read about Dawn Devayne.

The magazine was called *True Man*, and the picture on the cover was a foreign sports car with a girl lying on the hood. Down the left side of the cover was lettering that read:

WILL THE
ENERGY CRISIS
KILL LE MANS?
✳ ✳ ✳ ✳ ✳ ✳ ✳ ✳ ✳ ✳

DAWN DEVAYNE:
THE WORLD'S NEXT
SEX GODDESS
✳ ✳ ✳ ✳ ✳ ✳ ✳ ✳ ✳ ✳

WHAT SLOPE?
CONFESSIONS OF A
GIRL SKI BUM

Inside the magazine, the article was titled, *Is Dawn Devayne
The World's New Sex Queen?* by Abbie Lancaster. And under the
title in smaller letters was another question, with an answer:
"Where did all the bombshells go? Dawn Devayne is ready to
burst on the scene."

Then the article didn't start out to be about Dawn Devayne at
all, but about all the movie stars that had ever been considered
big sex symbols, like Jean Harlow and Marilyn Monroe and Rita
Hayworth and Jayne Mansfield. Then it said there hadn't been
any major sex star for a long time, which was probably because
of Women's Lib and television and X-rated movies and looser
sexual codes. "You don't need a fantasy bedwarmer," the article
said, "if you've got a real-life bedwarmer of your own."

Then the article said there were a bunch of movie stars who
were all set to take the crown as the next sex queen if the job
ever opened up again. It mentioned Raquel Welch and Ann-
Margret and Goldie Hawn and Julie Christie. But then it said
Dawn Devayne was the likeliest of them all to make it, because
she had that wonderful indescribable quality of being all things
to all men.

Then there was a biography. It said Dawn Devayne was born
Estelle Anlic in Big Meadow, Nebraska on May 19th, 1942, and
her father died in the Korean conflict in 1955, and she and her
mother moved to Los Angeles in 1956 because her mother had
joined a religious cult that was based in Los Angeles. It said her
mother was a bus driver in that period, and Dawn Devayne grew
up without supervision and hung around with boys a lot. It didn't
exactly say she was the neighborhood lay, but it almost said it.

Then it came to me. It said Dawn Devayne ran away from
home a lot of times in her teens, and one time when she was
sixteen she ran away to San Diego and married me until her
mother took her home again and turned her over to the juvenile
authorities, who put her in a kind of reformatory for wayward
girls. It called me a "stock figure." What it said was:

". . . a sailor named Ordo Tupikos, a stock figure, the San Diego sailor in every sex star's childhood."

I didn't much care for that, but what I was mostly interested
in was where Estelle Anlic became Dawn Devayne, so I kept
reading. The article said that after the reformatory Estelle got a
job as a carhop in a drive-in restaurant in Los Angeles, and it was

there she got her first crack at movie stardom, when an associate producer with Farber International Pictures met her and got her a small role in a B-movie called *Tramp Killer*. She played a prostitute who was murdered. That was in 1960, when she was eighteen. There was a black-and-white still photo from that movie, showing her cowering back from a man with a meat cleaver, and she still looked like Estelle Anlic then, except her hair was dyed platinum blonde. Her stage name for that movie was Honey White.

Then nothing more happened in the movies for a while, and Estelle went to San Francisco and was a cashier in a movie theater. The article quoted her as saying, "When 'Tramp Killer' came through, I sold tickets to myself." She had other jobs too for the next three years, and then when she was twenty-one, in 1963, a man named Les Moore, who was the director of *Tramp Killer*, met her at a party in San Francisco and remembered her and told her to come back to Los Angeles and he would give her a big part in the movie he was just starting to work on.

(The article then had a paragraph in parentheses that said Les Moore had become a very important new director in the three years since *Tramp Killer*, which had only been his second feature, and that the movie he wanted Dawn Devayne to come back to Los Angeles for was *Bubbletop*, the first of the zany comedies that had made Les Moore the Preston Sturges of the sixties.)

So Dawn Devayne—or Estelle, because her name wasn't Dawn Devayne yet and she'd quit calling herself Honey White— went back to Los Angeles and Les Moore introduced her to a star-making agent named Byron Cartwright, who signed her to exclusive representation and who changed her name to Dawn Devayne. And *Bubbletop* went on to become a smash hit and Dawn Devayne got rave notices, and she'd been a movie star ever since, with fifteen movies in the last eleven years, and her price for one movie now was seven hundred fifty thousand dollars. The article said she was one of the very few stars who had never had a box-office flop.

About her private life, the article said she was "between marriages." I thought that would mean she was engaged to somebody, but so far as I could see from the rest of the article she wasn't. So I guess that's just a phrase they use for people like movie stars when they aren't married.

Anyway, the marriages she was between were numbers four and five. After me in 1958, her next marriage was in 1963, to a movie star named Rick Tandem. Then in 1964 there was a fight in a nightclub where a producer named Josh Weinstein knocked Rick Tandem down and Rick Tandem later sued for divorce and said John Weinstein had come between him and Dawn Devayne. The article didn't quite say that Rick Tandem was in reality queer, but it got the point across.

Then marriage number three, in 1966, was to another movie actor, Ken Forrest, who was an older man, a contemporary of Gable and Tracy who was still making movies but wasn't quite the power he used to be. That marriage ended in 1968 when Forrest shot himself on a yacht off the coast of Spain; Dawn Devayne was in London making a picture when it happened.

And the fourth marriage, in 1970, was to a Dallas businessman with interests in computers and airlines and oil. His name was Ralph Chucklin, and that marriage had ended with a quiet divorce in 1973. "Dawn is dating now," the article said, "but no one in particular tops her list. 'I'm still looking for the right guy,' she says."

Then the article got to talking about her age, and the person who wrote the article raised the question as to whether a thirty-two year old woman was young enough to still make it as the next Sex Goddess of the World. "Dawn is more beautiful every year," the article said, and then it went back to all the business about Women's Lib and television and X-rated movies and looser sexual codes, and it said the next Superstar Sex Symbol wasn't likely to be another girl-child type like the ones before, but would be more of an adult woman, who could bring brains and experience to sex. "Far from the dumb blondes of yesteryear," the article said, "Dawn Devayne is a bright blonde, who combines with good old-fashioned lust the more modern feminine virtues of intelligence and independence. A Jane Fonda who doesn't nag." And the article finished by saying maybe the changed social conditions meant there wouldn't be any more Blonde Bombshells or Sexpot Movie Queens, which would make the world a colder and a drabber place, but the writer sure hoped there would be more, and the best bet right now to bring sex back to the world was Dawn Devayne.

There were photographs with the article, full page color pic-

tures of Dawn Devayne with her clothes off, and when I finished
reading I sat there on the toilet a while longer looking at the
pictures and trying to remember Estelle. Nothing. The face, the
eyes, the smile, all different. The stomach and legs were different.
Even the nipples didn't remind me of Estelle Anlic's nipples.

There's something wrong, I thought. I wondered if maybe this
Dawn Devayne woman had a criminal record or was wanted for
murder somewhere or something like that, and she'd just paid
Estelle money to borrow her life story. Was that possible?

It sure didn't seem possible that *this* sexy woman was Estelle.
I know it was sixteen years, but how much can one person
change? I sat studying the pictures until I noticed I was beginning
to get an erection, so I left the head and went back to work.

All I could think about, the next three days, was Dawn Devayne.
I was once married to her, married to a sexy movie star. Me. I
just couldn't get used to the idea.

And the other guys didn't help. Norm and Stan and Pat spread
the word, and pretty soon all the guys were coming around, even
some of the younger officers, talking and grinning and winking
and all that. Nobody came right out with the direct question, but
what they really wanted to know was what it was like to be in
bed with Dawn Devayne.

And what could I tell them? I didn't *know* what it was like to
be in bed with Dawn Devayne. I knew what it was like to be in
bed with Estelle Anlic—or anyway I had a kind of vague memory,
after sixteen years—but that wasn't what they wanted to know,
and anyway I didn't feel like telling them. She was a teenage girl,
sixteen (though she told me nineteen), and I was twenty-one, and
neither of us was exactly a genius about sex, but we had fun. I
remember she had very very soft arms and she liked to have her
arms around my neck, and she laughed with her mouth wide
open, and she always drowned her french fries in so much
ketchup I used to tell her I had to eat them with ice tongs and
one time in bed she finally admitted she didn't know what ice
tongs were and she cried because she was sure she was stupid,
and we had sex that time in order for me to tell her (a) she wasn't
stupid, and (b) I loved her anyway even though she was stupid,
and that's the one time in particular I have any memory of at all,

which is mostly because that was the time I learned I could control myself and hold back ejaculation almost as long as I wanted, almost forever. We were both learning about things then, we were both just puppies rolling in a basket of wool, but the guys didn't want to hear anything like that, it would just depress them. And I didn't want to tell them about it either. Their favorite sex story was one that Pat used to tell about being in bed with a girl with a candle in her ass. That's what they really wanted me to tell them, that Dawn Devayne had a candle in her ass.

But even though I couldn't tell them any stories that would satisfy them, they kept coming around, they kept on and on with the same subject, they couldn't seem to let it go. It fascinated them, and every time they saw me they got reminded and fascinated all over again. In fact, a couple of the guys started calling me "Devayne," as though that was going to be my new nickname, until one time I picked up a wrench and patted it into my other palm and went over to the guy and said:

"My name is Orry."

He looked surprised, and a little scared. He said:

"Sure. Sure, I know that."

I said:

"Let me hear you say it."

He said:

"Jeez, Orry, it was just a — "

"Okay, then," I said, and went back over to where I was working, and that was the last I heard of that.

But it wasn't the last I heard of Dawn Devayne. For instance, I was more or less going then with a woman in New London named Fran Skiburg, who was divorced from an Army career man and had custody of the three children. She was part Norwegian and part Belgian and her husband had been almost all German. Fran and I would go to the movies sometimes, or she'd cook me a meal, but it wasn't serious. Mostly, we didn't even go to bed together. But then somebody told her about Dawn Devayne, and the next time I saw Fran she was a different person. She kept grinning and winking all through dinner, and she hustled the kids to bed earlier than usual, and then sort of crowded me into the living room. She liked me to rub her feet sometimes, because she was standing all day at the bank, so I sat on the sofa and she kicked off her slippers and while I rubbed her feet she kept opening and closing her knees and giggling at me.

Well, I was looking up her skirt anyway, so I slid my hand up from her feet, and the next thing we were rolling around on the wall-to-wall carpet together. She was absolutely all over me, nervous and jumpy and full of loud laughter, all the time wanting to change position or do this and that. Up till then, my one complaint about Fran was that she'd just lie there; now all of a sudden she was acting like the star of an X-movie.

I couldn't figure it out, until after it was all finished and I was lying there on the carpet on my back, breathing like a diver with the bends. Then Fran, with this big wild-eyed smile, came looming over me, scratching my chest with her fingernails and saying, "What would you like to do to me? What do you *really* want to do to me?"

This was *after.* I panted at her for a second, and then I said, "What?"

And she said, "What would you do to me if I was Dawn Devayne?"

Then I understood. I sat up and said. "Who told you that?"

"What would you do? Come on, Orry, let's do something!"

"Do what? We just did everything!"

"There's *lots* more! There's *lots* more!" Then she leaned down close to my ear, where I couldn't see her face, and whispered, "You don't want me to have to *say* it."

I don't know if she had anything special in mind, but I don't think so. I think she was just excited in general, and wanted something different to happen. Anyway, I pushed her off and got to my feet and said, "I don't know anything about any Dawn Devayne or any kind of crazy sex stuff. That's no way to act."

She sat there on the green carpet with her legs curled to the side, looking something like the nude pictures in Pat's magazines except whiter and a little heavier, and she stared up at me without saying anything at all. Her mouth was open because she was looking upward so her expression seemed to be mainly surprised. I felt grumpy. I sat down on the sofa and put on my underpants.

And all at once Fran jumped up and grabbed half her clothes and ran out of the room. I finished getting dressed, and sat on the sofa a little longer, and then went out to the kitchen and ate a bowl of raisin bran. When Fran still didn't come back, I went to her bedroom and looked in through the open door, and she wasn't there. I said, "Fran?"

No answer.

The bathroom door was closed, so I knocked on it, but nothing happened. I turned the knob and the door was locked. I said, "Fran?"

A mumble sounded from in there.

"Fran? You all right?"

"Go away."

"What?"

"Go *away!*"

That was the last she said. I tried talking to her through the door, and I tried to get her to come out, and I tried to find out what the problem was, but she wouldn't say anything else. There wasn't any sound of crying or anything, she was just sitting in there by herself. After a while I said, "I have to get back to the base, Fran."

She didn't say anything to that, either. I said it once or twice more, and said some other things, and then I left and went back to the base.

I was shaving the next morning when I suddenly remembered that picture, the one in the magazine of Estelle and me on our wedding day. We were squinting there in the sunlight, the both of us, and now I was squinting again because the light bulb over the mirror was too bright. Shaving, I looked at myself, looked at my nose and my eyes and my ears, and here I was. I was still here. The same guy. Same short haircut, same eyebrows, same chin.

The same guy.

What did Fran want from me, anyway? Just because it turns out I used to be married to somebody famous, all of a sudden I'm supposed to be different? I'm not any different, I'm the same guy I always was. People don't just change, they have ways that they are, and that's what they are. That's who they are, that's what you mean by personality. The way a person is.

Then I thought: Estelle changed.

That's right. Estelle Anlic is Dawn Devayne now. She's

changed, she's somebody else. There isn't any—she isn't—there isn't any Estelle Anlic any more, nowhere on the face of the earth.

But it isn't the same as if she died, because her *memories* are still there inside Dawn Devayne, she'd remember being the girl with the mother that drove the bus, and she'd remember marrying the sailor in San Diego in 1958, and even in that article I'd read there'd been a part where she was remembering being Estelle Anlic and working as a movie cashier in San Francisco. But still she was changed, she was somebody else now, she was different. Like a wooden house turning itself into a brick house. How could she . . . how could anybody do that? How could *anybody* do that?

Then I thought: Estelle Anlic is Dawn Devayne now, but I'm still me. Ordo Tupikos, the same guy. But if she was—If I'm—

It was hard even to figure out the question. If she was that back then, and if she's this now, and if I was *that*. . . .

I kept on shaving. More and more of my face came out from behind the white cream, and it was the same face. Getting older, a little older every minute, but not—

Not different.

I finished shaving. I looked at that face, and then I scrubbed it with hot water and dried it on a towel. And after mess I went to Headquarters office and put in for leave. Twenty-two days, all I had saved up.

2

THE FIRST PLACE I WENT WAS NEW YORK, ON THE BUS, WHERE I looked in a magazine they have there called *Cue* that tells you what movies are playing all over the city. A Dawn Devayne movie called "The Captain's Pearls" was showing in a theater on West 86th Street, which was forty-six blocks uptown from the bus terminal, so I walked up there and sat through the second half of a western with Charles Bronson and then "The Captain's Pearls" came on.

The story was about an airline captain with two girl friends both named Pearl, one of them in Paris and one in New York. Dawn Devayne played the one in New York, and the advertising agency she works for opens an office in Paris and she goes there to head it, and the Paris girl friend is a model who gets hired by

Dawn Devayne for a commercial for the captain's airline, and then the captain had to keep the two girls from finding out he's going out with both of them. It was a comedy.

This movie was made in 1967, which was only nine years after I was married to Estelle, so I should have been able to recognize her, but she just wasn't there. I stared and stared and stared at that woman on the screen, and the only person she reminded me of was Dawn Devayne. I mean, from before I knew who she was. But there wasn't anything of Estelle there. Not the voice, not the walk, not the smile, not anything.

But sexy. I saw what that article writer meant, because if you looked at Dawn Devayne your first thought was she'd be terrific in bed. And then you'd decide she'd also be terrific otherwise, to talk with or take a trip together or whatever it was. And then you'd realize since she was so all-around terrific she wouldn't have to settle for anybody but an all-around terrific guy, which would leave you out, so you'd naturally idolize her. I mean, you'd want it without any idea in your head that you could ever get it.

I was thinking all that, and then I thought. *But I've had it!* And then I tried to put together arms-around-neck ice-tongs-stupid Estelle Anlic with this terrific female creature on the screen here, and I just couldn't do it. I mean, not even with a fantasy. If I had a fantasy about going to bed with Dawn Devayne, not even in my fantasy did I see myself in bed with Estelle.

After the movie I walked back downtown toward the bus terminal, because I'd left my duffel bag in a locker there. It was only around four-thirty in the afternoon, but down around 42nd Street the whores were already out, strolling on the sidewalks and standing in the doorways of shoe stores. The sight of a Navy uniform really agitates a whore, and half a dozen of them called out to me as I walked along, but I didn't answer.

Then one of them stepped out from a doorway and stood right in my path and said, "Hello, sailor. You off a ship?"

I started to walk around her, but then I stopped dead and stared, and I said, "You look like Dawn Devayne!"

She grinned and ducked her head, looking pleased with herself. "You really think so, sailor?"

She did. She was wearing a blonde wig like Dawn Devayne's hair style, and her eyes and mouth were made up like Dawn

Devayne, and she'd even fixed her eyebrows to look like Dawn Devayne's eyebrows.

Only at a second look none of it worked. The wig didn't look like real hair, and the make-up was too heavy, and the eyebrows looked like little false moustaches. And down inside all that phony stuff she was Puerto Rican or Cuban or something like that. It was all like a Halloween costume.

She was poking a finger at my arm, looking up at me sort of slantwise in imitation of a Dawn Devayne movement I'd just seen in *The Captain's Pearls.* "Come on, sailor," she said. "Wanna fuck a movie star?"

"No," I said. It was all too creepy. "No no," I said, and went around her and hurried on down the street.

And she shouted after me, "You been on that ship too long! What you want is Robert Redford!"

This was my first time in Los Angeles since 1963, when the Gulf of Tonkin incident got me transferred from a ship in the Mediterranean to a ship in the Pacific. They'd flown me with a bunch of other guys from Naples to Washington, then by surface transportation to Chicago and by air to Los Angeles and Honolulu, where I met my ship. I'd had a two-day layover in Los Angeles, and now I remembered thinking then about looking up Estelle. But I didn't do it, mostly because five years had already gone by since I'd last seen her, and also because her mother might start making trouble again if she caught me there.

The funny thing is, that was the year Estelle first became Dawn Devayne, in the movie called *Bubbletop.* Now I wondered what might have happened if I'd actually found her back then, got in touch somehow. I'd never seen *Bubbletop,* so I didn't know if by 1963 she was already this new person, this Dawn Devayne, if she'd already changed so completely that Estelle Anlic couldn't be found in there any more. If I'd met her that time, would something new have started? Would my whole life have been shifted, would I now be somebody in the movie business instead of being a sailor? I tried to see myself as that movie person; who would I be, what would I be like? Would I be *different?*

But there weren't any answers for questions like that. A person

is who he is, and he can't guess who he would be if he was
somebody else. The question doesn't even make sense. But I
guess it's just impossible to think at all about movie stars without
some fantasy or other creeping in.

My plane for Los Angeles left New York a little after seven P.M.
and took five hours to get across the country, but because of the
time zone differences it was only a little after nine at night when
I landed, and still not ten o'clock when the taxi let me off at a
motel on Cahuenga Boulevard, pretty much on the line separat-
ing Hollywood from Burbank. The taxi cost almost twenty dollars
from the airport, which was kind of frightening. I'd taken two
thousand dollars out of my savings, leaving just over three thousand in the account, and I was spending the money pretty fast.

The cabdriver was a leathery old guy who buzzed along the freeways like it was a stock car race, all the time telling me how much
better the city had been before the freeways were built. Most people pronounce Los Angeles as though the middle is "angel," but he
was one of those who pronounce it as though the middle is "angle."
"Los Ang-gleez," he kept saying, and one time he said, "I'm a sight
you won't see all that much. I'm your native son."

"Born here?"

"Nope. Come out in forty-eight."

The motel had a large neon sign out front and very small rooms in
a low stucco building in back. It was impossible to tell what color the
stucco was because green and yellow and orange and blue floodlights were aimed at it from fixtures stuck into the ivy border, but in
the morning the color turned out to be a sort of dirty cream shade.

My room had pale blue walls and a heavy maroon bedspread
and a paper ribbon around the toilet seat saying it had been
sanitized. I unpacked my duffel and turned on the television set,
but I was too restless to stay cooped up in that room forever. Also,
I decided I was hungry. So I changed into civvies and went out
and walked down Highland to Hollywood Boulevard, where I ate
something in a fast-food place. It was like New York in that neighborhood, only skimpier. For some reason Los Angeles looks older
than New York. It looks like an old old Pueblo Indian village
with neon added to it by real estate people. New York doesn't
look any older than Europe, but Los Angeles looks as old as sand.
It looks like a place that almost had a Golden Age, a long long
time ago, but nothing happened and now it's too late.

After I ate I walked around for half an hour, and then I went back to the motel and all of a sudden I was very sleepy. I had the television on, and the light, and I still wore all my clothes except my shoes, but I fell asleep anyway, lying on top of the bedspread, and when I woke up the TV was hissing and it was nearly four in the morning. I was very thirsty, and nervous for some reason. Lonely, I felt lonely. I drank water, and went out to the street again, and after a while I found an all-night super-market called Hughes. I took a cart and went up and down the aisles.

There were some people in there, not many. I noticed something about them. They were all dressed up in suede and fancy denim, like people at a terrific party in some movie, but they were buying the cheapest of everything. Their baskets were filled as though by gnarled men and women wearing shabby pants or faded kerchiefs, but the men were all young and tanned and wearing platform shoes, and the women were all made up with false eyelashes and different-colored fingernails. Also, some of them had food stamps in their hands.

Another thing. When these people pushed their carts down the aisles they stood very straight and were sure of themselves and on top of the world, but when they lowered their heads to take something off a shelf they looked very worried.

Another thing. Every one of them was alone. They went up and down the aisles, pushing their carts past one another—from up above, they must have looked like pieces in a labyrinth game—and they never looked at one another, never smiled at one another. They were just alone in there, and from up front came the clatter of the cash register.

After a while I didn't want to be in that place any more. I bought shaving cream and a can of soda and an orange, and walked back to the motel and went to bed.

There wasn't anybody in the phone book named Byron Cartwright, who was the famous agent who had changed Estelle's name to Dawn Devayne and then guided her to stardom. In the motel office they had the five different Los Angeles phone books, and he wasn't in any of them. He also wasn't in the yellow pages under "Theatrical Agencies." Finally I found a listing for something called the Screen Actors' Guild, and I called, and spoke to a girl who said, "Byron Cartwright? He's with GLA."

"I'm sorry?"

"GLA," she repeated, and hung up.

So I went back to the phone books, hoping to find something called GLA. The day clerk, a sunken-cheeked faded-eyed man of about forty with thinning yellow hair and very tanned arms, said, "You seem to be having a lot of trouble."

"I'm looking for an actor's agent," I told him.

His expression lit up a bit. "Oh, yeah? Which one?"

"Byron Cartwright."

He was impressed. "Pretty good," he said. "He's with GLA now, right?"

"That's right. Do you know him?"

"Don't I wish I did." This time he was rueful. His face seemed to jump from expression to expression with nothing in between, as though I were seeing a series of photographs instead of a person.

"I'm trying to find the phone number," I said.

I must have seemed helpless, because his next expression showed the easy superiority of the insider. "Look under Global-Lipkin," he told me.

Global-Lipkin. I looked, among "Theatrical Agencies," and there it was: Global-Lipkin Associates. You could tell immediately it was an important organization; the phone number ended in three zeroes. "Thank you," I said.

His face now showed slightly belligerent doubt. He said, "They send for you?"

"Send for me? No."

The face was shut; rejection and disapproval. Shaking his head he said, "Forget it."

Apparently he thought I was a struggling actor. Not wanting to go through a long explanation, I just shrugged and said, "Well, I'll try it," and went back to the phone booth.

A receptionist answered. When I asked for Byron Cartwright she put me through to a secretary, who said, "Who's calling, please?"

"Ordo Tupikos."

"And the subject, Mr. Tupikos?"

"Dawn Devayne."

"One moment, please."

I waited a while, and then she came back and said, "Mr. Tupikos, could you tell me who you're with?"

"With? I'm sorry, I . . ."

"Which firm."

"Oh. I'm not with any firm, I'm in the Navy."

"In the Navy."

"Yes. I used to be—" But she'd gone away again.

Another wait, and then she was back. "Mr. Tupikos, is this official Navy business?"

"No," I said. "I used to be married to Dawn Devayne."

There was a little silence, and then she said, "Married?"

"Yes. In San Diego."

"One moment, please."

This was a longer wait, and when she came back she said, "Mr. Tupikos, is this a legal matter?"

"No, I just want to see Estelle again."

"I beg your pardon?"

"Dawn Devayne. She was named Estelle when I married her."

A male voice suddenly said, "All right, Donna, I'll take it."

"Yes, sir," and there was a click.

The male voice said, "You're Ordo Tupikos?"

"Yes, sir," I said. It wasn't sensible to call him "sir," but the girl had just done it, and in any event he had an authoritative officer-like sound in his voice, and it just slipped out.

He said, "I suppose you can prove your identity."

That surprised me. "Of course," I said "I still look the same."

I still look the same.

"And what is it you want?"

"To see Estelle. Dawn. Miss Devayne."

"You told my secretary you were with the Navy."

"I'm *in* the Navy."

"You're due to retire pretty soon, aren't you?"

"Two years," I said.

"Let me be blunt, Mr. Tupikos," he said. "Are you looking for money?"

"Money?" I couldn't think what he was talking about. (Later, going over it in my mind, I realized what he'd been afraid of, but just at that moment I was bewildered.) "Money for what?" I asked him.

He didn't answer. Instead, he said, "Then why show up like this, after all these years?"

"There was something in a magazine. A friend showed it to me."

"Yes?"

"Well, it surprised me, that's all."

"*What* surprised you?"

"About Estelle turning into Dawn Devayne."

There was a very short silence. But it wasn't an ordinary empty silence, it was a kind of slammed-shut silence, a startled silence. Then he said, "You mean you didn't know? You just found out?"

"It was some surprise," I said.

He gave out with a long laugh, turning his head away from the phone so it wouldn't hurt my ears. But I could still hear it. Then he said, "God damn, Mr. Tupikos, that's a new one."

I had nothing to say to that.

"All right," he said. "Where are you?"

I told him the name of the motel.

"I'll get back to you," he said. "Some time today."

"Thank you," I said.

The phone booth was out in front of the motel, and I had to go back through the office to get to the inner courtyard and my room. When I walked into the office the day clerk motioned to me. "Come here." His expression now portrayed pride.

I went over and he handed me a large black-and-white photograph; what they call a glossy. The blacks in it were very dark and solid, which made it a little bit hard to make out what was going on, but the picture seemed to have been taken in a parking garage. Two people were in the foreground. I couldn't swear to it, but it looked as though Ernest Borgnine was strangling the day clerk.

"Whadaya think of that?"

I didn't know what I thought of it. But when people hand you a picture — their wife, their girl friend, their children, their dog, their new house, their boat, their garden — what you say is *very nice*. I handed the picture back. "Very nice," I said.

***

Everybody knows about the movie stars' names being embedded in the sidewalks of Hollywood Boulevard, but it's always strange when you see it. There are the squares of pavement, and on every square is a gold outline of a five-pointed star, and in every other star there is the name of a movie star. Every year, fewer of those names mean anything. The idea of the names is immortality, but what they're really about is death.

I took a walk for a while after talking to Byron Cartwright, and I walked along two or three blocks of Hollywood Boulevard with some family group behind me that had a child with a loud piercing voice, and the child kept wanting to know who people were:

"Daddy, who's Vilma Banky?"

"Daddy, who's Charles Farrell?"

"Daddy, who's Dolores Costello?"

"Daddy, who's Conrad Nagel?"

The father's answers were never loud enough for me to hear, but what could he have said? "She was a movie star." "He used to be in silent movies, a long time ago." Or maybe, "I don't know. Emil Jannings? I don't know."

I didn't look back, so I have no idea what the family looked like, or even if the child was a boy or a girl, but pretty soon I hated listening to them, so I turned in at a fast-food place to have a hamburger and onion rings and a Coke. I sat at one of the red formica tables to eat, and at the table across the plastic partition from me was another family—father, mother, son, daughter—and the daughter was saying, "Why did they put those names there anyway?"

"Just to be nice," the mother said.

The son said, "Because they're buried there."

The daughter stared at him, not knowing if that was true or not. Then she said, "They are not!"

"Sure they are," the son said. "They bury them standing up, so they can all fit. And they all wear the clothes from their most famous movie. Like their cowboy hats and the long gowns and their Civil War Army uniforms."

The father, chuckling, said, "And their white telephones?"

The son gave his father a hesitant smile and a head-shake, saying, "I don't get it."

"That's okay," the father said. He grinned and ruffled the son's hair, but I could see he was irritated. He was older, so his memory stretched back farther, so his jokes wouldn't always mean anything to his son, whose memories had started later—and would probably end later. The son had reminded his father that the father would some day die.

After I ate I didn't feel like walking on the stars' names any more. I went up to the next parallel street, which is called Yucca, and took that over to Highland Avenue and then on back to the motel.

When I walked into the office the day clerk said, "Got a message for you." His expression was tough and secretive, like a character in a spy movie. The hotel clerk in a spy movie who is really a part of the spy organization; this is the point where he tells the hero that the Gestapo is in his room.

"A message?"

"From GLA," he said. His face flipped to the next expression, like a digital clock moving on to the next number. This one showed make-believe comic envy used to hide real envy. I wondered if he really did feel envy or if he was just practicing being an actor by pretending to show envy. No; pretending to *hide* envy. Maybe he himself was actually feeling envy but was hiding it by pretending to be someone who was showing envy by trying to hide it. That was too confusing to think about; it made me dizzy, like looking too long off the fantail of a ship at the swirls of water directly beneath the stern. Layers and layers of twisting white foam with bottomless black underneath; but then it all organizes itself into swinging straight white lines of wake.

I said, "What did they want?"

"They'll send a car for you at three o'clock." Flip, friendliness, conspiracy. "You could do me a favor."

"I could?"

From under the counter he took out a tan manila envelope, then halfway withdrew from it another gloss photograph; I couldn't see the subject. "This," he said and slid the photo back into the envelope. Twisting the red string on the two little round closure tabs of the envelope, he said, "Just leave it in the office, you know. Just leave it some place where they can see it."

"Oh," I said. "All right." And I took the envelope.

***

The car was a black Cadillac limousine with a uniformed chauffeur who held the door for me and called me, "sir." It didn't seem to matter to him that he was picking me up at a kind of seedy motel, or that I was wearing clothes that were somewhat shabby and out of date. (I wear civvies so seldom that I almost never pay any attention to what clothing I own or what condition it's in.)

I had never been in a limousine before, with or without a chauffeur. In fact, this was the first time in my life I'd ever ridden in a Cadillac. I spent the first few blocks just looking at the interior of the car, noticing that I had my own radio in the back, and power windows, and that there were separate air conditioner controls on both sides of the rear seat.

There were grooves for a glass partition between front and rear, but the glass was lowered out of sight, and when we'd driven down Highland and made a right turn onto Hollywood Boulevard, going past Grauman's Chinese theater, the chauffeur suddenly said, "You a writer?"

"What? Me? No."

"Oh," he said. "I always try to figure out what people are. They're fascinating, you know? People."

"I'm in the Navy," I said.

"That right? I did two in the Army myself."

"Ah," I said.

He nodded. He'd look at me in the rear-view mirror from time to time while he was talking. He said, "Then I pushed a hack around Houston for six years, but I figured the hell with it, you know? Who needs it. Come out here in sixty-seven, never went back."

"I guess it's all right out here."

"No place like it," he said.

I didn't have an answer for that, and he didn't seem to have anything else to say, so I opened the day clerk's envelope and looked at the photograph he wanted me to leave in Byron Cartwright's office.

Actually it was four photographs on one eight-by-ten sheet of glossy paper, showing the day clerk in four poses, with different clothing in each one. Four different characters, I guess. In the upper left, he was wearing a light plaid jacket and a pale turtleneck sweater and a medium-shade cloth cap, and he had a cigarette in the corner of his mouth and he was squinting; looking mean and tough. In the upper right he was wearing a tuxedo, and he had a big smile on his face. His head was turned toward the camera, but his body was half-twisted away and he was holding a top hat out to the side, as though he were singing a song and was about to march off-stage at the end of the music. In the bottom left, he was wearing a cowboy hat and a bandana around his neck and a plaid shirt, and he had a kind of comical-foolish expression on his face, as though somebody had just made a joke and he wasn't sure he'd understood the point. And in the bottom right he was wearing a dark suit and white shirt and pale tie, and he was leaning forward a little and smiling in a friendly way directly at the camera. I guess that was supposed to be him in his natural state, but it actually looked less like him than any of the others.

The whole back of the photograph was filled with printing. His name was at the top (MAURY DEE) and underneath was a listing of all the movies he'd been in and all the play productions, with the character he performed in each one. Down at the bottom were three or four quotes from critics about how good he was.

The driver turned left on Fairfax and went down past Selma to Sunset Boulevard, and then turned right. Then he said, "The best thing about this job is the people."

"Is that right?" I put Maury Dee's photograph away and twisted the red string around the closure tabs.

"And I'll tell you something," said the driver. "The bigger they are, the nicer they are. You'd be amazed, some of the people been sitting right where you are right now."

"I bet."

"But you know who's the best of them all? I mean, just a nice regular person, not stuck up at all."

"Who's that?"

"Dawn Devayne," he said. "She's always got a good word for you, she'll take a joke, she's just terrific."

"That's nice," I said.

"Terrific." He shook his head. "Always remembers your name. 'Hi, Harry,' she says. 'How you doing?' Just a terrific person."

"I guess she must be all right," I said.

"Terrific," he said, and turned the car in at one of the taller buildings just before the Beverly Hills line. We drove down into the basement parking garage and the driver stopped next to a bank of elevators. He hopped out and opened my door for me, and when I got out he said, "Eleventh floor."

"Thanks, Harry," I said.

3

ALL YOU COULD SEE WAS ARTIFICIAL PLANTS. I STEPPED OUT OF the elevator and there were great pots all over the place on the green rug, all with plastic plants in them with huge dark-green leaves. Beyond them, quite a ways back, expanses of plate glass showed the white sky.

I moved forward, not sure what to do next, and then I saw the receptionist's desk. With the white sky behind her, she was very hard to find. I went over to her and said, "Excuse me."

She'd been writing something on a long form, and now she looked up with a friendly smile and said, "May I help you?"

"I'm supposed to see Byron Cartwright."

"Name, please?"

"Ordo Tupikos."

She used her telephone, sounding very chipper, and then she smiled at me again, saying, "He'll be out in a minute. If you'll have a seat?"

There were easy chairs in among the plastic plants. I thanked her and went off to sit down, picking up a newspaper from a white formica table beside the chair. It was called *The Hollywood Reporter*, and it was magazine size and printed on glossy paper. I read all the short items about people signing to do this or that, and I read a nightclub review of somebody whose name I didn't recognize, and then a girl came along and said, "Mr. Tupikos?"

"Yes?"

"I'm Mr. Cartwright's secretary. Would you come with me?"

I put the paper down and followed her away from the plants and down a long hall with tan walls and brown carpet. We passed offices on both sides of the hall; about half were occupied, and most of the people were on the phone.

I suddenly realized I'd forgotten the day clerk's photograph. I'd left it behind in the envelope on the table with *The Hollywood Reporter*.

Well, that actually was what he'd asked me to do; leave it in the office. Maybe on the way back I should take it out of the envelope.

The girl stopped, gesturing at a door on the left. "Through here, Mr. Tupikos."

Byron Cartwright was standing in the middle of the room. He had a big heavy chest and brown leathery skin and yellow-white hair brushed straight back over his balding head. He was dressed in different shades of pale blue, and there was a white line of smoke rising from a long cigar in an ashtray on the desk behind him. The room was large and so was everything in it; massive desk, long black sofa, huge windows showing the white sky, with the city of Los Angeles down the slope on the flat land to the south, pastel colors glittering in the haze: pink, peach, coral.

Byron Cartwright strode toward me, hand outstretched. He was laughing, as though remembering a wonderful time we'd once shared together. Laughter made erosion lines crisscrossing all over his face. "Well, hello, Orry," he said. "Glad to see you." He took my hand, and patted my arm with his other hand, saying, "That's right, isn't it? Orry?"

"That's right."

"Everybody calls me By. Come in, sit down."

I was already in. We sat together on the long sofa. He crossed one leg over the other, half-turning in my direction, his arm stretched out toward me along the sofa back. He had what looked like a class ring on one finger, with a dark red stone. He said, "You know where I got it from? The name 'Orry'? From Dawn." There was something almost religious about the way he said the name. It reminded me of when Jehovah's Witnesses pass out their literature; they always smile and say, "Here's good news!"

I said, "You told her about me?"

"Phoned her the first chance I got. She's on location now. You could've knocked her over with a feather, Orry. I could hear it in her voice."

"It's been a long time," I said. I wasn't sure what this conversation was about, and I was sorry to hear Dawn Devayne was "on location." It sounded as though I might not be able to get to see her.

"Sixteen years," Byron Cartwright said, and he had that reverential sound in his voice again, with the same happiness around his mouth and eyes. "Your little girl has come a long way, Orry."

"I guess so."

"It's just amazing that you never knew. Didn't any reporters ever come around, any magazine writers?"

"I never knew anything," I told him. "When the fellows told me about it, I didn't believe them. Then they showed me the magazine."

"Well, it's just astonishing." But he didn't seem to imply that I might be a liar. He kept smiling at me, and shaking his head with his astonishment.

"It sure was astonishing to me," I said.

He nodded, letting me know he understood completely. "So the first thing you thought," he said, "you had to see her again, just had to say hello. Am I right?"

"Not to begin with." It was hard talking when looking directly at him, because his face was so full of smiling eagerness. I leaned forward a little, resting my elbows on my knees, and looked across the room. There was a huge full-color blown-up photograph of a horse taking up most of the opposite wall. I said, looking at the horse, "At first I just thought it was eerie. Of course, nice for Estelle. Or Dawn, I guess. Nice for her, I was glad things worked out for her. But for me it was really strange."

"In what way *strange*, Orry?" This time he sounded like a chaplain, sympathetic and understanding.

"It took me a while to figure that out." I chanced looking at him again, and he had just a small smile going now, he looked expectant and receptive. It was easier to face him with that expression. I said, "There was a picture of Estelle and me in the magazine, from our wedding day."

"Got it!" He bounded up from the sofa and hurried over to the desk. I became aware then that most of the knick-knacks and things around on the desk and the tables and everywhere had some connection with golf; small statues of golfers, a gold golf ball on a gold tee, things like that.

Byron Cartwright came back with a small photo in a frame.

He handed it to me, smiling, then sat down again and said, "That's the one, right?"

"Yes," I said, looking at it. Then I turned my face toward him, not so much to see him as to let him see me. "You can recognize me from that picture."

"I know that," he said. "I was noticing that, Orry, you're remarkable. You haven't aged a bit. I'd hate to see a picture of *me* taken sixteen years ago."

"I'm not talking about getting older," I said. "I'm talking about getting *different*. I'm not different."

"I believe you're right." He moved the class-ring hand to pat my knee, then put it back on the sofa. "Dawn told me a little about you, Orry," he said. "She told me you were the gentlest man she'd ever met. She told me she's thought about you often, she's always hoped you found happiness somewhere. I believe you're still the same good man you were then."

"The same." I pointed at Estelle in the photo. "But that isn't Dawn Devayne."

"Ha ha," he said. "I'll have to go along with you there."

I looked at him again. "How did that happen? How do people chance, or not change?"

"Big questions, Orry." If a smile can be serious, his smile had turned serious. But still friendly.

"I kept thinking about it," I said. I almost told him about Fran then, and the changes all around me, but at the last second I decided not to. "So I came out to talk to her about it," I said. And then, because I suddenly realized this could be a brush-off, that Byron Cartwright might have the job of smiling at me and being friendly and telling me I wasn't going to be allowed to see Estelle, I added to that, "If she wants to see me."

"She does, Orry," he said. "Of course she does." And he acted surprised. But I could see he was *acting* surprised.

I said, "You were supposed to find out if I'd changed or not, weren't you? If I was going to be a pest or something."

Grinning, he said, "She told me you weren't stupid, Orry. But you could have been an impostor, you know, maybe some maniac or something. Dawn *wants* to see you, if you're still the Orry she used to know."

"That's the problem."

He laughed hugely, as though I'd said a joke. "She's filming up in Stockton today," he said, "but she'll be flying back when they're done. She wants you to go out to the house, and she'll meet you there."

"Her house?"

"Well, naturally." Chuckling at me, he got to his feet, saying, "You'll be driven out there now, unless you have other plans."

"No, nothing." I also stood.

"I'll phone down for the car. You came in through the parking area?"

"Yes."

"Just go straight back down. The car will be by the elevators."

"Thank you."

We shook hands again, at his prompting, and this time he held my hand in both of his and gazed at me. The religious feeling was there once more, this time as though he were an evangelist and I a cripple he was determined would walk. Total sincerity filled his eyes and his smile. "She's my little girl now, too, Orry," he said.

The envelope containing the day clerk's pictures was gone from the table out front.

"Hello, Harry," I said. He was holding the door open for me.

He gave me a kind of roguish grin, and waggled a finger at me. "You didn't tell me you were pals with Dawn Devayne."

"It was a long story," I said.

"Good thing I didn't have anything bad to say, huh?" And I could see that inside his joking he was very upset.

I didn't know what to answer. I gave him an apologetic smile and got into the car and he shut the door behind me. It wasn't until we were out on Sunset driving across the line into Beverly Hills, that I decided what to say: "I don't really know Dawn Devayne," I told him. "I haven't seen her for sixteen years. I wasn't trying to be smart with you or anything."

"Sixteen years, huh?" That seemed to make things better. Lifting his head to look at me in the rear-view mirror, he said, "Old high school pals?"

I might as well tell him the truth; he'd probably find out sooner or later anyway. "I was married to her."

The eyes in the rear-view mirror got sharper, and then fuzzier, and then he looked out at Sunset Boulevard and shifted position so I could no longer see his face in the mirror. I don't suppose he disbelieved me. I guess he didn't know what attitude to take. He didn't know what to think about me, or about what I'd told him, or about anything. He didn't say another word the whole trip.

The house was in Bel Air, way up in the hills at the very end of a curving steep street with almost no houses on it. What residences I did see were very spread out and expensive-looking, though mostly only one story high, and tucked away in folds and dimples of the slope, above or below the road. Many had flat roofs with white stones sprinkled on top for decoration. Like pound cake with confectioner's sugar on it.

At the end of the street was a driveway with a No Trespassing sign. Great huge plants surrounded the entrance to the driveway; they reminded me of the plants in Byron Cartwright's outer office, except that these were real. But the leaves were so big and shiny and green that the real ones looked just as fake as the plastic ones.

The driveway curved upward to the right and then came to a closed chain-link gate. The driver stopped next to a small box mounted on a pipe beside the driveway, and pushed a button on the box. After a minute a metallic voice spoke from the box, and the driver responded, and then the gate swung open and we drove on up, still through this forest of plastic-like plants, until we suddenly came out on a flat place where there was a white stucco house with many windows. The center section was two stories high, with tall white pillars out front, but the wings angling back on both sides were only one story, with flat roofs. These side sections were bent back at acute angles, so that they really did look like wings, so that the taller middle section would be the body of the bird. Either that, or the central part could be thought of as a ship, with the side sections as the wake.

The driver stopped before the main entrance, hopped out, and opened the door for me. "Thanks, Harry," I said.

Something about me—my eyes, my stance, something—made him soften in his attitude. He nodded as I got out, and almost smiled, and said, "Good luck."

The Filipino who let me in said his name was Wang, "Miss Dawn told me you were coming," he said. "She said you should swim."
"She did?"
"This way. No luggage? This way."
The inside was supposed to look like a Spanish mission, or maybe an old ranch house. There were shiny dark wood floors, and rough plaster walls painted white, and exposed dark beams in the ceiling, and many rough chandeliers of wood or brass, some with amber glass.
Wang led me through different rooms into a corridor in the right wing, and down the corridor to a large room at the end with bluish-green drapes hanging ceiling-to-floor on two walls, making a great L of underwater cloth through which light seemed to shimmer. A king size bed with a blue spread took up very little of the room, which had a lot of throw rugs here and there on the dark-stained random-plank floor. Wang went to one of the dressers—there were three, two with mirrors—and opened a drawer full of clothing. "Swim suit," he said. "Change of linen. Everything." Going to one of two doors in the end wall, he opened it and waved at the jackets and coats and slacks in the closet there. "Everything." He tugged the sleeve of a white terrycloth robe hanging inside the door. "Very nice robe."
"Everything's fine," I said.
"Here." He shut the closet door, opened the other one, flicked a light switch. "Bathroom," he said. "Everything here."
"Fine. Thank you."
He wasn't finished. Back by the entrance, he demonstrated the different light switches, then pointed to a lever sticking horizontally out from the wall, and raised a finger to get my complete attention. "Now this," he said. He pushed the lever down, and the drapes on the two walls silently slid open, moving from the two ends toward the right angle where the walls met.
Beyond the drapes were walls of sliding glass doors, and beyond the glass doors were two separate views. The view to the right,

out the end wall, was of a neat clipped lawn sweeping out to a border of those lush green plants. The view straight ahead, of the section enclosed by the three sides of the house, was of a large oval swimming pool, with big urns and statues around it, and with a small narrow white structure on the fourth side, consisting mostly of doors; a cabana, probably, changing rooms for guests who weren't staying in rooms like this.

Wang showed me that the drapes opened when the lever was pushed down, and closed when it was pulled up. He demonstrated several times; back and forth ran the drapes, indecisively. Then he said, "You swim."

"All right."

"Miss Dawn say she be back, seven o'clock."

The digital clock on one of the dressers read three fifty-two. "All right," I said, and Wang grinned at me and left.

It was a heated pool. When I finally came out and slipped into the terrycloth robe I felt very rested and comfortable. In the room I found a small bottle of white wine, and a glass, and half a dozen different cheeses on a plate under a glass dome. I had some cheese and wine, and then I shaved, and then I looked at the clothing here.

There was a lot of it, but in all different sizes, so I really didn't have that much to choose from. Still, I found a pair of soft gray slacks, and a kind of ivory shirt with full sleeves, and a black jacket in a sort of Edwardian style, and in the mirror I almost didn't recognize myself. I looked taller, and thinner, and successful. I picked up the wine glass and stood in front of the mirror and watched myself drink. All right, I thought. Not bad at all.

I went out by the pool and walked around, wearing the clothes and carrying the wine glass. Part of the area was in late afternoon sun and part in shade. I strolled this way and that, admiring my reflections in the glass doors all around, and trying not to smile too much. I wondered if Wang was watching, and what he thought about me. I wondered if there were other servants around the place, and what kind of job it was to be a servant for a famous movie star. Like being assigned to an Admiral, I supposed. I was once on a ship with a guy who'd been an Admiral's servant for three years, and he said it was terrific duty, the best in the world.

He lost his job because he started sleeping with some other officer's wife. He always claimed he'd kept strictly away from the Admiral's family and friends, but there was this Lieutenant Commander who lived in the same area near Arlington, Virginia, and whose wife kept trying to suck up to the Admiral's wife. That's how Tony met her, one time when she came over and the Admiral's wife wasn't there. According to Tony it wasn't his fault there was trouble; it was just that the Lieutenant Commander's wife kept making things so obvious, hanging around all the time, honking horns at him, calling him on the phone in the Admiral's house. "So they kicked me out," he said. (Tony wasn't very popular with the guys on the ship, which probably wasn't fair, but we couldn't help it. The rest of us had been assigned here as a normal thing, but he'd been sent to this ship as a *punishment*. If this was punishment duty, what did that say about the rest of us? Nobody particularly wanted to think about that, so Tony was generally avoided.)

Anyway, he did always claim that the job of servant to the brass was the best duty in the world, and I suppose it is. Except for *being* the brass, of course, which is probably even better duty, except who thinks that way?

After a while I went back into the room, and the digital clock said six twenty-four. I looked at myself in the mirror one more time, and all of a sudden it occurred to me I was looking at Dawn Devayne's clothes. Not my clothes. She'd come home, she wouldn't see somebody looking terrific, she'd see somebody wearing *her* clothes.

No. I changed into my own things, and went back to the living room by the main entrance. There were long low soft sofas there, in brown corduroy. I sat on one, and read more *Hollywood Reporters*, and pretty soon Wang came and asked me if I wanted a drink.

I did.

She arrived at twenty after seven, with a bunch of people. It later turned out there were only five, but at first it seemed like hundreds. To me, anyway. I didn't give them separate existences then; they were just a bunch of laughing, hand-waving, talking people surrounding a beautiful woman named Dawn Devayne.

Dawn Devayne. No question. The clear, bright, level gray eyes. The skin as smooth as a lion's coat. Those slightly sunken cheeks. (Estelle had round cheeks.) The look of intelligence, sexiness, recklessness. Of course that was Dawn Devayne; I'd seen her in the movies.

I got to my feet, looking through the wide arched doorway from the living room to the entrance hall, where they were clustered around her. That group all bunched there made me realize Dawn Devayne already had her own full life, as much as she wanted. What was I doing here? Did I think I could wedge myself into Dawn Devayne's life? How? And why?

"Wang!" she yelled. "God damn it, Wang, bring me liquor! I've been kissing a faggot all day!" Then she turned, and over someone's shoulder, past someone else's laugh, she caught a glimpse of me beyond the doorway, and she put an expression on her face that I remembered from movies; quizzical-amused. She said something, quietly, that I couldn't hear, but from the way her lips moved I thought it was just my own name: "Orry." Then she nodded at two things that were being said to her, stepped through the people as though they were grouped statues, and came through the doorway with her hand out for shaking and her mouth widely smiling. "Orry," she said. "God damn, Orry, if you don't bring it back."

Her hand was strong when I took it; I could feel the bones, as though I were holding a small wild bird in my palm. "Hello . . ." I said, stumbling because I didn't know what name to use. I couldn't call her Estelle, and I couldn't call her Dawn, and I wouldn't call her Miss Devayne.

"We'll talk later on," she said, squeezing my hand, then turned to the others, who had followed her. "This is Orry," she said. "An old friend of mine." And said the names of everybody else.

Wang arrived then, and while he took drink orders Dawn Devayne looked at me, frowning slightly at my clothing, saying, "Didn't Wang give you a room?"

"Yes. Down at the end there."

Her glance at my clothes was a bit puzzled, but then her expression cleared and she grinned at me, saying, "Yes, Orry. I'm beginning to remember you now."

"I don't remember you at all," I told her. Which was true. So far, Estelle Anlic had made no appearance in this room.

She still didn't. Dawn Devayne laughed, patting my arm, saying, "We'll talk later, after this crowd goes." She turned half away:
"Wang! Get over here." Back to me: "What are you drinking?"

I tried not to drink too much, not wanting to make a fool of
myself. Though Dawn Devayne had spoken about the others as
though they would leave at any instant, in fact they stayed on for
an hour or more, mostly gossiping about absent people involved
in the movie they were currently making. Then we all got into
two cars and drove down to Beverly Hills for dinner at a Chinese
restaurant. I rode in the same car with Dawn Devayne, a tan-
colored Mercedes Benz with the license plate WIPPER, but I
didn't sit beside her. I rode in back with a grim-faced moustached
man named Frank, whose job I didn't yet know, while Dawn
Devayne sat beside the driver, a tall and skinny, leathery-faced,
sly-smiling man named Rod, who I remembered as having played
the airline pilot in the *The Captain's Pearls,* and who was apparently Dawn Devayne's co-star again this time. The other three
people, an actor named Wally and an unidentified man called
Bobo and a heavyset girl named June, followed us in Wally's
black Porsche, which also had a special license plate; BIG JR.
  Phone-calling had been done before we'd left the house, and
four more people joined us at the restaurant; Frank's plump wife,
a tough-looking blonde girl for Wally, a grinning hippie-type guy
in blue denim for June, and a willowy young man in a black
jumpsuit for Rod. I realized Rod must be the faggot Dawn Devayne had been kissing all day, and the fact of his homosexuality
startled me a lot less than what she had shouted in his presence.
  The eleven of us filled an alcove at the rear of the restaurant.
Eleven people can't possibly be quiet; we made our presence felt.
There was a party atmosphere, and I saw other patrons glancing
our way with envy. We were, after all, quite obviously having a
wonderful time. Not only that, but at least two of us were famous.
But perhaps in Beverly Hills there's more sophistication about
movie fame than in most other places; no one came by the table
in search of autographs.
  As for the party atmosphere, that was more apparent than real.
Dawn Devayne and Rod and Wally and June's hippie-type friend
did a lot of loud talking, mostly anecdotes about the movie world

or the record business, to which June's friend belonged, but the rest of us were no more than audience. We laughed at the right moments, and otherwise sat silent, eating one platter of Chinese food after another. Rounds of drinks kept being ordered, but I let them pile up in front of me—four glasses, eventually—while I drank tea.

Rod drove us back home. Again Dawn Devayne sat up front with him, while I shared the back seat with Rod's friend, who was called Dennis. In the dark, wearing his black jumpsuit and with his pale-skinned hands and face and wispy yellow hair, Dennis was startling to look at, almost unearthly. And when he touched the back of my hand with a fingertip, his skin was so cold that I automatically flinched away.

He ignored that; maybe people always flinched when he touched them. "I know who you are," he said, and his small head floating there had a smile on it that was very sweet and innocent, as though he were on his way to his First Communion. *My God,* I thought, *you'd last six hours on a ship. They'd shove what was left in a canvas bag.*

I said, "You do?"

"Orry," he said. "That's not a common name."

"No, I guess it isn't."

"You were in the Navy."

"I still am."

"You were married to Dawn."

"That's right," I said.

He turned his sweet smile and his wide eyes toward the two heads up front. They were talking seriously together now, Dawn Devayne and Rod, about some disagreement they were having with the director, and what they should do about it tomorrow.

Dennis, staring and smiling so hard that it was as though he wanted to burrow into their ears and live inside their brains, said, "It must have been wonderful. To know her at the very beginning of her career. If only I'd met Rod, all those years ago." When he looked at me again, his eyes were luminous. Maybe he was crying. "I keep everything that's ever written about him," he said. "I have dozens of scrapbooks, dozens. That's how I know about *you.*"

"Ah."

"Do you keep scrapbooks?"

"About what?" Then I understood. "Oh, you mean Dawn Devayne."

"You don't? I'll *never* be blasé about Rod. Never."

In the house Dawn Devayne held my forearm and said, "Orry,
I'm bushed. I'm sorry, baby, I can't talk tonight. Come along with
me tomorrow, all right? We'll have some time together."

"All right." I was disappointed, but she did look tired. Also, my
own body was still more on East Coast time, three hours later; I
wouldn't mind sleeping, after such a long day. I don't know why
it is, but emotions are exhausting.

"I'm going to swim for five minutes," she said, "and then hit
the sack. We get up at seven around here. You ready for that?"

"I will be." And I smiled at her. God knows she wasn't Estelle,
but I felt just the same as though I knew her. We were old friends
in some other way, entirely different and apart from reality. I
suspected that was a form of human contact she had learned to
develop, as a means of dealing with all the faces a movie star has
to meet. It wasn't the real thing, but that didn't matter. It was a
friendly falseness, a fakery that made life smoother.

I watched her swim. She was naked, and she spent as much time
diving as she did swimming, and it was the same nude body that
had excited me so much in the magazine pictures, and yet my
sexual feelings were thwarted, imprisoned. Maybe it was because
I was being a peeping tom and felt ashamed of myself. Or maybe
it was because, in accepting the counterfeit friendship of Dawn
Devayne, I had lessened the existence of Estelle Anlic just that
much more, and I felt guilty about *that*. Whatever it was, for as
long as I looked at her I kept feeling the lust rise, and then become strangled, and then rise, and then become strangled.

I should have stopped looking, of course, but I couldn't. The
most I could do was close my eyes from time to time and argue
with myself. But I couldn't leave, I had to stay kneeling at a corner
of the darkened room, with one edge of the drapes pulled back
just far enough to peek out, during the ten minutes that Dawn

Devayne spent moving, diving, swimming, the green-white underwater lights and yellow surrounding lanterns glinting and flashing off the wet sheen slickness of her flesh. Drops of water caught in her hair made tiny flashing round rainbows. Her legs were long, her body strong and sleek, a tanned thoroughbred, graceful and self-contained.

When at last she put on a white robe and walked away, I awkwardly stood, padded across the room by the dim light filtering through the drapes, and slid into the cool bed. A few seconds later, as though waiting for me to settle, the pool lights went off.

4

I MUST HAVE GONE TO SLEEP ALMOST AT ONCE, THOUGH I'D BEEN sure I would stay awake for hours. But the pool lights ceased to shine on the blue-green drapes, darkness and silence drifted down like a collapsing tent—four white numerals floating in the black said 11:42, then 11:43—and I closed my eyes and slept.

To awake in the same darkness, with the white numbers reading 12:12 and some fuss taking place at the edge of my consciousness. I didn't know where I was, I didn't know what that pair of twelves meant, and I couldn't understand the rustling and whooshing going on. In my bewilderment I thought I was assigned to a ship again, and we were in a storm; but the double twelve made no sense.

Then one of the twelves became thirteen, and I remembered where I was, and I understood that someone was at the glass doors leading to the pool, making a racket. Then Dawn Devayne's voice, loud and rather exasperated, said, "Orry?"

"Yes?"

"Open these damn drapes, will you?"

At the Chinese restaurant there had been a red-jacketed young man who parked the cars. He leaped into every car that came along, and whipped it away with practiced skill, as though he'd been driving *that* car all his life. At some point he must have had a first car, of course, the car in which he'd learned to drive and with which he'd gotten his first license, but if some customer of the restaurant were to drive up in that car today would the young man recognize it? Would it feel *different* to him? Since his driving technique was already perfect with any car, what special familiarity would he be able to display? It could not be by skill that he would show his particular relationship with this car; possibly it would be with a breakdown of skill, a tiny reminiscent awkwardness.

Dawn Devayne was wonderful in bed. It's true, she was what men thought she would be, she was agile and quick and lustful and friendly and funny and demanding and responsive and exhausting and exhilarating and plunging and utterly skillful. Her skill produced in me responses of invention I hadn't known I possessed. Fran Skiburg was right; there *are* other things to do. I did things with Dawn Devayne that I'd never done before, that it had never occurred to me to do but that now came spontaneously into my mind. For instance, I followed with the tip of my tongue all the creases of her body; the curving borders of her rump, the line at the inside of each elbow, the arcs below her breasts. She laughed and hugged me and gave me a great deal of pleasure, and not once did I think of Estelle Anlic, who was not there.

We'd turned the lights on for our meeting, and when she kissed my shoulder and leaned away to turn them off again the digital clock read 2:02. In the dark she kissed my mouth, bending over me, and whispered, "Welcome back, Orry."

"Mmm." I said nothing more, partly because I was tired and partly because I still hadn't fixed on a name to call her.

She rolled away, adjusting her head on the pillow next to me, settling down with a pleasant sigh, and when next I opened my eyes vague daylight pressed grayly at the drapes and the clock read 6:03, and Dawn Devayne was asleep on her back beside me, tousled but beautiful, one hand, palm up, with curled fingers, on the pillow by her ear.

How did Estelle look asleep? She was becoming harder to remember. We had lived together in off-base quarters, a two-room apartment with a used bed. Sunlight never entered the bedroom, where the sheets and clothing and the very air itself were always just slightly damp. Estelle would curl against me in her sleep, and at times I would awake to find her arm across my chest. A memory returned; Estelle once told me she'd slept with a toy panda in her childhood, and at times she would call me Panda. I hadn't thought of that in years. Panda.

Dawn Devayne's eyes opened. They focused on me at once, and she smiled, saying, "Don't frown, Orry, Dawn is here." Then she looked startled, stared toward the drapes, and cried, "My God, dawn *is* here! What time is it?"

"Six oh six," I read.

"Oh." She relaxed a little, but said, "I have to get back to my room." Then she looked at me with another of her private smiles and said, "Orry, do you know you're terrific in bed?"

"No," I said. "But you are."

"A workman is as good as his tools," she said, grinning, and reached under the covers for me. "And you've been practicing."

"So have you."

She laughed, pulling me closer, with easy ownership. "Time for a quickie," she said.

We swam together naked in the pool while the sun came up. ("If Wang *does* look," she'd answered me, "I'll blind him.") Then at last she climbed out of the pool, wet, glistening gold and orange in the fresh sunlight, saying, "Time to face the new day, baby."

"All right." I followed her up to the blue tiles.

"Orry."

"Yes?"

"Take a look in the closet," she said. "See if there's something that fits you. Wang can have your other stuff cleaned."

I knew she was laughing at me, but in a friendly way. And the problem of what to call her was solved. "Thanks, Dawn," I said. "I will."

"See you at breakfast."

I wore the gray slacks, but neither the full-sleeved shirt nor the Edwardian jacket seemed right for me, so I found instead a green shirt and a gray pullover sweater. "That's fine," Dawn said, with neutral disinterest.

A limousine took us to Burbank Airport, over the hills and

across the stucco floor of the San Fernando Valley, a place that looks like an over-exposed photograph. Dawn asked me questions as we rode together, and I told her about my marriage to Sally Fowler and my years in the Navy, and even a little about Fran Skiburg, though not the part where Fran got so excited about me having once been married to Dawn Devayne. There were spaces of silence as we rode, and I could have asked her my question several times, but there didn't seem to be any way to phrase it. I tried different practice sentences in my head, but none of them were right:

"Why aren't you Estelle Anlic any more, when I'm still Orry Tupikos?" No. That sounded as though I was blaming her for something.

"Who would I be, if I wasn't me?" No. That wasn't even the right question.

"How do you stop being the person you are and become somebody entirely different? What's it like?" No. That was like a panel-show question on television, and anyway not exactly what I was trying for.

Dawn herself gave me a chance to open the subject, when she asked me what I figured to do after I retired from the Navy two years from now, but all I said was, "I haven't thought about it very much. Maybe I'll just travel around a while, and find some place, and settle down."

"Will you marry Fran?"

"That might be an idea."

At Burbank Airport we got on a private plane with the two actors, Rod and Wally, and the grim-faced man named Frank and the heavyset quiet man called Bobo, all of whom I'd met last night. Listening to conversations during the flight, I finally worked it out that Frank was a photographer whose job it was to take pictures while the movie was being made; the "stills man," he was called. Bobo's job was harder to describe; he seemed to be somewhere between servant and bodyguard, and mostly he just sat and smiled at everybody and looked alert but not very bright.

We flew from Burbank to Stockton, where another limousine took us to the movie location, which was an imitation Louisiana bayou in the San Joaquin River delta. The rest of the movie people, who were staying in nearby motels and not commuting home every night, were already there, and most of the morning was spent with the crew endlessly preparing things—setting up reflectors to catch sunlight, laying a track for the camera to roll along, moving potted plants this way and that along the water's edge—while Dawn and Rod argued for hours with the director, a fat man with pasty jowls and an amused-angry expression and a habit of constantly taking off and putting back on his old black cardigan sweater. His name was Harvey, and when I was introduced to him he nodded without looking at me and said, "Ted, they really *are* putting that fucking dock the wrong place," and a short man with a moustache went away to do something about it.

The argument, with Dawn and Rod on one side and Harvey on the other, wasn't like anything I'd ever seen in my life. When the people I've known get into an argument, they either settle it pretty soon or they get violent; the men hit and the women throw things. Dawn and Rod and Harvey almost immediately got to the point where hitting and throwing would start, except it never happened. Dawn Devayne stood with her feet apart and her hands on her hips, as though leaning into a strong wind, and made firm logical statements of her point of view, salted with insults; for instance, "The motivation throughout the whole story, you cocksucker, is for my character to feel protective toward Jenny." Rod's style, on the other hand, was heavy sarcasm: "Since it's a *given* that you have the sensitivity of a storm drain, Harvey, why not simply accept the fact that Dawn and I have thought this over very carefully." Harvey, with his angry-amused smile, always looked as though he was either just about to say something horribly insulting or would suddenly start pounding the other two with a piece of wood, and his *manner* was very insulting-patronizing-hostile, but in fact he merely kept saying things like, "Well, I think we'll simply all be much happier if we do it my way."

Unless there's a fist fight, the person who remains the calmest usually wins most arguments, so I knew from the beginning Harvey would win this one, but it went on for hours anyway, and when it ended (Harvey won, and Dawn and Rod both sulked) they only had time before lunch to shoot one small scene with Dawn and Wally on the riverbank. It was just a scene where Dawn said, "I don't think they'll ever come back, Billy." They shot it eight times, with the camera in three different positions, and then we all had a buffet lunch brought out from Stockton by a catering service.

Dawn's dressing room was a small motor home, where she took a nap by herself after lunch, while I walked around looking at everything. Another part of the Dawn-Wally scene was shot, with just Wally visible in the picture, talking to an empty spot in space where Dawn was supposed to be, and then they set up a more complicated scene involving Dawn and Rod and some other people getting into a boat and rowing away. Dawn woke up while the crew was still preparing that one, and she and Rod groused together about Harvey, but when they went out to shoot the scene everybody was polite to everybody else, and then the day was over, and we flew back to Los Angeles.

There was a huge gift-wrapped package in the front hall at Dawn's house. It was about the size and shape of a door, all wrapped up in colorful paper and miles of ribbon and a big red bow, and a card hung from the bow reading, "Love to Dawn and Orry, from By."

Dawn frowned and said, "What's that asshole up to now?"

Rod and Wally and Frank and Bobo had come in with us, and Wally said, "It's an aircraft carrier. By gave you an aircraft carrier."

"For God's sake, open it," Rod said.

"I'm afraid to," Dawn told him. She tried to make that sound like a joke, but I could see she really was afraid to open it. I later learned that Byron Cartwright's sentimentalism was famous for causing embarrassment, but I don't think even Dawn suspected what he had chosen to send us. I know I didn't.

Finally it was Wally and Rod who pulled off the bow and the ribbon and the paper, and inside was the wedding day picture, Estelle and me in San Diego, squinting in the sunlight. The picture had been blown up to be slightly bigger than life, and it was in a wooden frame with a piece of glass in front of it, and here were these two stiff uncomfortable figures in grainy gray, staring out of some horrible painful prison of the past. Usually this picture was perfectly ordinary, neither wonderful nor awful, but blown up to life size—larger than life—it became a kind of cruelty.

124 Donald E. Westlake

Everybody stared at it. Wally said, "What the hell is *that?*"

They hadn't recognized that earlier me. Dawn wouldn't have been recognizable anyway, of course, but expanding the original photo had strained the rough quality of the negative beyond its capacity, so that I myself might not have guessed at first the white blob face was mine.

After the first shock of staring at the picture, I turned to look at Dawn, to see her with a face of stone, glaring—with hatred? rage? revulsion? bitterness? resentment?—at her own image in the photograph. She turned her head, flashed me a look of irritation that I'd been watching her, and without a word strode out of the room.

Rod, with the eager look of the born gossip, said, "I don't know what's going on here, but it looks to *me* like By's done it again."

Wally was still frowning at the picture. "What *is* that?" he said. "Who *are* those people?"

"Orry? Isn't that you?"

It was the voice of Frank, the stills man, the professional photographer, who had backed away from the giant picture, across the hall and through the doorway into the next room, until he was distant enough to see it clear. Head cocked to one side, eyes half closed, he was standing against the back of a sofa in there, studying the picture.

At first I didn't say anything. Wally turned to frown at Frank, then at me, then at the picture, then at me again. "You? That's you?"

Rod and Bob were moving toward Frank, squinting over their shoulders at the picture as they went. I said to Wally, "Yes. It's me."

"That girl is familiar," Frank said.

I felt obscurely that Dawn would want to be protected, though I didn't see how it was going to be possible. "That's my wife," I said. "Or, she *was* my wife. That was our wedding day."

Rob and Bobo were now standing next to Frank, gazing at the picture, and Wally was moving back to join them. I was like a stage performer, and they were my audience, and the picture was used in my act. Frank said, "I know that girl. What's her name?"

Rod suddenly said, "Wait a minute, *I* know that picture! That's Dawn!"

"Yes," I said, but before I could say anything else—explain, apologize, defend—Wang came in to say, "Miss Dawn say, everybody out."

Rod, nodding at the picture and ignoring Wang, said thoughtfully, "Byron Cartwright, the avalanche that walks like a man."

Wang said to me, "You, too. Miss Dawn say, go away, eat dinner, come back."

"All right," I said.

We were joined by Frank's wife and Wally's girl and Rod's friend Dennis in an Italian restaurant that looked like something from a silent movie about Biblical times. Bronze-colored plaster statues, lots of columns, heavily-framed paintings of Roman emperors on the walls. The food was covered with too much tomato sauce.

My story was amazing but short, and when I was done Rod and Wally told stories for the rest of dinner about other disastrous gestures made by Byron Cartwright in the past. He was everyone's warmhearted uncle, except that his instincts were constantly betrayed by his inability to think through the effect of his activities. As as a businessman he was considered one of the best (toughest, coldest, coolest) in his very tough business, but away from the office his affection toward his clients and other acquaintances led him to one horrible misjudgment after another.

(These acts of Byron Cartwright's were not simple goofs like sending flowers to a hay-fever victim. As with the picture to Dawn and me, each story took about five minutes to explain the characters and relationships involved, the nuances that turned Byron Cartwright's offerings into Molotov cocktails, and while some of the errors were funny, most of them produced only groans among the listeners at the table. It was Wally who finally summed it up, saying, "Most mutations don't work, and By is simply one more proof of it. You can't have an agent with a heart of gold, it isn't a viable combination.")

After dinner, Rod drove me back to Dawn's house, with Dennis a silent worshipper vibrating behind us on the back seat. As we neared the house, Rod said, "May I give you a piece of advice, Orry?"

"Sure."

"You haven't known Dawn for a long time, and she's probably changed a lot."

"Yes, she has."

"I don't think she'll ever mention that picture again," Rod told me, "and I don't think you ought to bring it up either."

"You may be right."

"If it's still there, have Wang get rid of it. If you want it yourself, tell Wang to ship it off to your home. But don't show it to Dawn, don't ask her about it. Just deal with Wang."

"Thank you," I said. "I agree with you."

We reached the house, and Rod stopped in front of the door. "Good luck," he said.

I didn't immediately leave the car. I said, "Do you mind if I ask you a question?"

"Go ahead."

"You saw how different Dawn used to be, when she was Estelle Anlic. And if you remember the picture, I haven't changed very much."

"Hardly at all. The Navy must agree with you."

"The reason I came out here," I said, "was because I had a question in my mind about that. I wanted to know how a person could change so completely into somebody different. Somebody with different looks, a different personality, a whole different kind of life. I mean, when I married Estelle, she wasn't anybody who could even *hope* to be a movie star."

Rod seemed both amused and in some hidden way upset by the question. He said, "You want to know how she did it?"

"I suppose. Not exactly. Something like that."

"She decided to," he said. He had a crinkly, masculine, self-confident smile, but at the same time he had another expression going behind the smile, an expression that told me the smile was a fake, a mask. The inner expression was also smiling, but it was more intelligent, and more truly friendly. He said, using that inner expression, "Why did you ask *me* that question, Orry?"

It was, of course, because I believed he'd somehow done the same sort of thing as Dawn, that somewhere there existed photos of him in some unimaginable other person. But it would sound like an insult to say that, and I said nothing, floundering around for an alternate answer.

He nodded. "You're right," he said.

"Then how?" I asked him. "She decided to be somebody else. How is it possible to *do* that?"

He shrugged and grinned, friendly and amiable but not really able to describe colors to a blind man. "You find somebody you'd rather be," he said. "It really is as simple as that, Orry."

I knew he was wrong. There was truth in the idea that people like Dawn and himself had found somebody else they'd rather be, but it surely couldn't be as simple as that. Everybody has fantasies, but not everybody throws away the real self and lives in the fantasy.

Still, it would have been both rude and useless to press him, so I said, "Thank you," and got out of the car.

"Hold the door," he said. Then he patted the front seat, as though calling a dog, and said, "Dennis, come on up."

And Dennis, a nervous high-bred afghan hound in his fawn-colored jumpsuit, clambered gratefully into the front seat.

I was about to shut the door when Rod leaned over Dennis and said, "One more little piece of advice, Orry."

"Yes?"

"Don't ask Dawn that question."

"Oh," I said.

The picture was gone from the front hallway. My luggage from the motel was in my room, and Dawn was naked in the pool, her slender long intricate body golden-green in the underwater lights. I opened the drapes and stepped out to the tepid California air and said, "Shall I join you in there?"

"Hey, baby," she called, treading water, grinning at me, sunny and untroubled. "Come on in, the water's fine."

5

THE REST OF THE DAYS THAT WEEK WERE ALL THE SAME, EXCEPT that no more unfortunate presents came from Byron Cartwright. Dawn and I got up early every morning, flew to Stockton, she worked in the movie and napped—alone—after lunch, we flew back to Los Angeles, and then there'd be dinner in a restaurant with several other people, a shifting cast that usually included

Rod and Wally and Dennis, plus others, sometimes strangers and sometimes known to me. Then Dawn and I would go back to the house and swim and go to bed and play with one another's bodies until we slept. The sex was wonderful, and endlessly various, but afterwards it never seemed real. I would look at Dawn during the daytime, and I would remember this or that specific thing we had done together the night before, and it wasn't as though I'd actually done it with *her*. It was more as though I'd dreamed it, or fantasized it.

Maybe that was partly because we always slept in the guest room, in what had become my bed. Dawn never took me to her own bed, or even brought me into her private bedroom. Until the second week I was there, I was never actually in that wing of the house.

On the Thursday evening we stayed longer in Stockton, to see the film shot the day before. Movie companies when they're filming generally show the previous day's work every evening, which some people call the *dailies* and some call the *rushes*. Its purpose is to give the director and performers and other people involved a chance to see how they're doing, and also so the film editor and director can begin discussing the way the pieces of film will be organized together to make the movie. Dawn normally stayed away from the rushes, but on Thursday evening they would be viewing the sequence that she and Rod had argued about with Harvey, so the whole group of us stayed and watched.

I supposed movie people get so they can tell from the rushes whether things are working right or not, but when I look at half a dozen strips of film each recording the same action sequence or lines of dialogue, over and over and over, all I get is bored. Nevertheless, I could sense when the lights came up in the screening room that almost everybody now believed Harvey to have been right all along. Rod wouldn't come right out and admit it, but it was clear his objections were no longer important to him. Dawn, on the other hand, had some sort of emotional commitment to her position, and all she had to say afterwards was, grumpily, "Well, I suppose the picture will survive, despite that." And off she stomped, me in her wake.

Still, by the time we reached the plane to go back to Los Angeles, she was in a cheerful mood again. Bad temper never lasted long with her.

* * *

Friday afternoon there were technical problems of some sort, delaying the shooting, so after Dawn's nap she and I sat in the parlor of her dressing room and talked together about the past. It was one of those conversations full of sentences beginning, "Do you remember when—?" We talked about troubles we'd had with the landlord, about the time we snuck into a movie theater when we didn't have any money, things like that. She didn't seem to have any particular attitude about these memories, neither nostalgia nor revulsion; they were simply interesting anecdotes out of our shared history.

But they led me finally, despite Rod's advice, to ask her the question that had brought me out here. "You've changed an awful lot since then," I said. "How did you do that?"

She frowned at me, apparently not understanding. "What do you mean, changed?"

"Changed. Different. Somebody else."

"I'm not somebody else," she said. Now she looked and sounded annoyed, as though somebody were pestering her with stupidities. "I dyed my hair, that's all. I learned about makeup, I learned how to dress."

"Personality," I said. "Emotions. Everything about you is different."

"It is not." Her annoyance was making her almost petulant. "People change when they grow older, that's all. It's been sixteen years, Orry."

"I'm still the same."

"Yes, you are," she said. "You still plod along with those flat feet of yours."

"I suppose I do," I said.

Abruptly she shifted, shaking her head and softening her expression and saying, "I'm sorry, Orry, you didn't deserve that. You're right, you are the same man. You were wonderful then, and you're wonderful now."

"I think the flat feet was more like the truth," I said because that is what I think.

But she shook her head, saying, "No. I loved living with you, Orry, I loved being your wife. That was the first time in my life I ever relaxed. You know what you taught me?"

"Taught you?"

"That I didn't have to just run all the time, in a panic. That I could slow down, and look around."

I wanted to ask her if that was when she realized she could become somebody else, but I understood by now that Rod had been right, it wasn't something I could ask her directly, so I changed the subject. But I remembered what the magazine article had said about me being a "stock figure, the San Diego sailor in every sex star's childhood," and I wondered if what Dawn had just said was really true, if being with me had in some way started the change that turned Estelle Anlic into Dawn Devayne. Plodding with my flat feet? Most of the Estelle Anlics in the world marry flat-footed Orry Tupikoses; what had been different with us?

Saturday we drove to Palm Springs, to the home of a famous comedian named Lennie Hacker, for a party. There were about two hundred people there, many of them famous, and maybe thirty of them staying on as house guests for the rest of the weekend. Lennie Hacker had his own movie theater on his land, and we all watched one of his movies plus some silent comedies. That was in the afternoon. In the evening, different guests who were professional entertainers performed, singing, dancing, playing the piano, telling jokes. It was too big a party for anybody to notice one face more or less, so I didn't have to explain myself to anybody. (There was only one bad moment, at the beginning, when I was introduced to the host. Lennie Hacker was a short round man with sparkly black eyes and a built-in grin on his face, and when he shook my hand he said, "Hiya, sailor." I thought that was meant to be some kind of insult joke, but later on I heard him say the same thing to different other people, so it was just a way he had of saying hello.)

I'd never been to a party like this—a famous composer sat at the piano, singing his own songs and interrupting himself to make put-down gags about the lyrics—and I just walked around with a drink in my hand, looking at everything, enjoying being a spectator. (I was wearing the Edwardian jacket and the full-sleeved shirt, no longer self-conscious about my appearance.) Dawn and I crossed one another's paths from time to time, but we didn't stay together; she had lots of friends she wanted to spend time with.

As for me, I had very few conversations. Rod and Dennis were there, and I had a few words with Rod about the silent comedies we'd seen, and I also made small talk with a few other people I'd met at different restaurant dinners over the last week. At one point, when I was standing in a corner watching two television comedians trade insult jokes in front of an audience of twenty or thirty other guests, Lennie Hacker came over to me and said, "Listen."

"Yes?"

"You look like an intelligent fella," he said. He looked out at the crowd of his guests, and made a sweeping gesture to include them all. "Tell me," he said, "who the fuck *are* all these people?"

"Movie stars," I said.

"Yeah?" He studied them, skeptical but interested. "They look like a bunch a bums," he said. "See ya." And he drifted away.

A little later I ran into Byron Cartwright, who beamed at me and took my hand in both of his and said, "How *are* you, Orry?"

"Fine," I said.

"Listen, Orry," he said. He kept my hand in one of his, and put his other arm around my shoulders, turning me a bit away from the room and the party, making ours a private conversation. "I've wanted to have a *good* talk with you," he said.

"You have?"

"I'm sorry about that picture." He looked at me with a pained smile. "The way Dawn talked about you, I thought she'd *like* that reminder."

I didn't know what to say. "I guess so," I told him.

"But things are good between *you* two, aren't they? No trouble there."

"No, we're fine."

"That's good, that's good." He thumped my back, and finally released my hand. "You two look good together, Orry," he said. "You did way back then, and you do now."

"Well, *she* looks good."

"The two of you," he insisted. "Together. When's your leave up, Orry? When do you have to go back to the Navy?"

"In two weeks."

"Do you want me to fix it?"

"Fix it?"

"We could get you an early release," he said. "Get you out of the Navy."

"I've only got two years before I collect my pension."

"We could probably work something out," he told me. "Make some arrangement with the Navy. Believe me, Orry, I know people who know people."

I said, "But I couldn't go on living at Dawn's house."

"Orry," he said, chuckling at me and patting my arm. "You were her first love, Orry. You're her man. Look how she took you right in again, the minute you showed up. Look how well you're getting along. In some little corner of that girl, Orry, you've always been her husband. She left the others, but she was taken away from you."

I stared at him. "*Marry* her? Dawn Devayne? Mr. Cartwright, I don't—"

"By. Call me By. And think about it, Orry. Will you do that? Just think about it."

There was no question in the Hacker household about our belonging together, Dawn and me. We'd been initially shown by a uniformed maid to a bedroom we were to share on the second floor, overlooking Hacker's private three-hole golf course, and by one o'clock in the morning I was ready to return to it and go to sleep, although the party was still going strong. I found Dawn with a group of people singing show tunes around the piano, and I told her, "I'm going to sleep now."

"Stick around five minutes, we'll go up together."

I did—it's surprising how many old lyrics we all remember, the words to songs we no longer know we know—and then we found our way to the right bedroom, used the private bath next door, and went to bed. When I reached for Dawn, though, she laughed and said, "You must be kidding."

I was. I realized I was too sleepy to have any true interest in sex, that I'd started only out of a sense of obligation, that I'd felt it was my duty to perform at this point. "You're right," I said. "See you in the morning."

"You're a good old boy, Orry," she said, and kissed my chin, and rolled away, and I guess we both went right to sleep.

When I woke up it was still dark, but light of some sort was glittering faintly outside the window, and there were distant voices. I'd lived with Dawn Devayne less than a week, but already I was used to the rounded shapes of her asleep beside me, and already I missed the numerals of the digital clock shimmering white in the darkness. I didn't know what time it was, but it had to be very late.

I got up from bed and looked out the window, and the illumination came from floodlights over the golf course. Lennie Hacker and some of his male guests were playing golf out there. I recognized Byron Cartwright among them. Lennie Hacker's distinctive nasal voice said something, and the others laughed, and somebody drove a white ball high up out of the light, briefly out of existence before it suddenly bounced, small and white and clear, on the clipped grass of the green.

The men moved as a group, accompanied by a servant driving a golf cart filled with bags and clubs. A portable bar was mounted on the back of the cart, and they were all having drinks from it, but no one appeared drunk, or sloppy, or tired. None of them were particularly young, but none of them were in any way old.

The golf course made a wobbly triangle around an artificial pond, with the first tee and the third green forming the angle nearest the house. As the players moved away toward the first green, I looked beyond the lit triangle, seeing only black darkness, but sensing the other Palm Springs estates around us, and then the great circle of desert around that. Desert. These men—*some* men—had come out to this desert and by force of will had converted it into a royal domain. "To live like kings." That's a cliché, but here it was the truth. In high school I read that the ancient Roman emperors had ordered snow carted down from the mountain peaks to cool their palaces in summer. It has always been the prerogative of kings to make a comfortable toy of their environment. Here, where a hundred years ago they would have broiled and starved and died grindingly of thirst, these men strolled on clipped green grass under floodlights, laughing together and reaching for their drinks from the back of a golf cart.

If I married Dawn Devayne—

I shook my head, and closed my eyes, and then turned away from the window to look at the mound of her asleep in the bed.

It was a good thing I'd been warned about Byron Cartwright's sentimental errors, or I might actually have started dreaming about such impossibilities, and wound up a character in another Byron Cartwright horror story: "And the poor fellow actually proposed to her!" If an Indian who had grubbed his lean and careful existence from this desert a hundred years ago were to return here now, how could he set up his tent? How could he take up his life again? He's never been *here*. I was married to Estelle Anlic once, a long time ago. I was never married to Dawn Devayne.

6

AFTER THE WEEKEND, WE WENT BACK TO THE OLD ROUTINE UNTIL Wednesday evening, when, on the plane back to Los Angeles, Dawn said, "We won't be going out to dinner tonight."

"No?"

"My mother's coming over, with her husband."

I felt a sudden nervousness. "Oh," I said.

She laughed at my expression. "Don't worry, she won't even remember you."

"She won't?"

"And if she does, she won't care. I'm not sixteen any more."

Nevertheless, it seemed to me that Dawn was also nervous, and when we got to the house she immediately started finding fault with Wang and the other servants. These servants, a staff of four or five, I almost never saw—except for the cook at breakfast—but now they were abruptly visible, cleaning, carrying things, being yelled at for no particular reason. Dawn had said her mother would arrive at eight, so I went off to my own room with today's *Hollywood Reporter*—I was getting so I recognized some of the names in the stories there—until the digital clock read 7:55. Then I went out to the living room, got a drink from Wang, and sat there waiting. Dawn was out of both sight and hearing now, probably changing her clothes.

They came in about ten after eight, two short leathery-skinned people in pastel clothing that looked all wrong. Dawn's mother had on a fuzzy pink sweater of the kind worn by young women twenty years ago, with a stiff-looking skirt and jacket in checks of pale green and white. Her shoes were white and she carried a white patent leather purse with a brass clasp. None of the parts went together, though it was understandable that they would all belong in the same wardrobe. She looked like a blind person who'd been dressed by an indifferent volunteer.

Her husband, as short as she was but considerably thinner, was dressed more consistently, in white casual shoes, pale blue slacks, white plastic belt, and white and blue short-sleeved shirt. He had a seamed and bony face, the tendons stood out on his neck, and his elbows looked like the kind of bone soothsayers once used to tell the future. With his thin black hair slicked to the side over his browned scalp, and his habit of leaning slightly forward from the waist at all times, and his surprisingly bright pale blue eyes, he looked like a finalist in some Senior Citizens' golf tournament.

I stood up when the doorbell rang, and moved tentatively forward as Wang let them both in, but I was saved from introducing (explaining) myself by Dawn's sudden arrival from the opposite direction. Striding forward in a swirl of floor-length white skirt, she held both arms straight out from the shoulder and cried, "Mother! Leo! Delighted!"

All I could do was stare. She had redone herself from top to bottom, had changed her hair, covered herself with necklaces and bracelets and rings, made up her face differently, dressed herself in a white ballgown I'd never seen before, and she was coming forward with such patently false joy that I could hardly believe I'd ever watched her do a *good* job of acting. I was suddenly reminded of that whore back in New York, and I realized that now Dawn herself was pretending to be Dawn Devayne. Some imitation Dawn Devayne, utterly impregnable and larger than life, had been wrapped around the original, and the astonishing thing was, the real Dawn Devayne was just as bad at imitating Dawn Devayne as that whore had been.

I don't mean to say that finally I saw Estelle again, tucked away inside those layers of Dawn, as I had seen the Hispanic hidden inside the whore. It was Dawn Devayne, the one I had come to know over the last week, who was inside this masquerade.

But now Dawn was introducing me, saying, "Mother, this is a friend of mine called Orry. Orry, this is my mother, Mrs. Hettick, and her husband Leo."

Leo gave me a firm if bony handclasp, and a nod of his pointed jaw. "Good to know you," he said.

Dawn's mother gave me a sharp look. Inside her mismatched vacation clothing and her plump body and her expensive beauty shop hair treatment she was some kind of scrawny bird. She said, "You in pictures?"

"No, I'm not."

"Seen you someplace."

"Come along, everybody," Dawn said, swirling and swinging her arms so all her jewelry jangled, "we'll sit out by the pool for a while."

I didn't think there was anything wrong with the evening except that Dawn was so tense all the time. Her mother, whom I'd never met before except when she was yelling at me, did a lot of talking about arguments she'd had with different people in stores — "So then *I* said, so then *she* said . . ." — but she wasn't terrible about it, and she did have an amusing way of phrasing herself sometimes. Leo Hettick, who sat to my right in the formal dining room where we had our formal dinner, was an old Navy man as it turned out, who'd done a full thirty years and got out in 1972, so he and I talked about different tours we'd spent, ships we'd been on, what we thought of different ports and things like that. Meantime, Dawn mostly listened to her mother, pretending the things she said were funnier than they were.

What started the fight was when Mrs. Hettick turned to me, over the parfait and coffee, and said, "You gonna be number five?"

I had to pretend I didn't know what she was talking about. "I beg pardon?"

"You're living here, aren't you?"

"I'm a houseguest," I said. "For a couple of weeks."

"I know that kind of houseguest," she said. "I've seen a lot of them."

Dawn said, "Mother, eat your parfait." Her tension had suddenly closed down in from all that sprightliness, had become very tightly knotted and quiet.

Her mother ignored her. Watching me with her quick bird eyes she said, "You can't be worse than any of the others. The first one was a child molester, you know, and the second was a faggot."

"Stop, Mother," Dawn said.

"The third was impotent," her mother said. "He couldn't get it up if the flag went by. What do you think *of that?*"

"I don't think people should talk about other people's marriages," I said.

Leo Hettick said, "Edna, let it go now."

"You stay out of this Leo," she told him, and turned back to say to me, "The whole world talks about my daughter's marriages, why shouldn't I? If you *are* number five, you'll find your picture in newspapers you wouldn't use to wrap fish."

"I don't think I read those papers," I said.

"No, but my mother does," Dawn said. Some deep bitterness had twisted her face into someone I'd never seen before. "My mother has the instincts of a pig," she said. "Show her some mud and she can't wait to start rooting in it."

"Being *your* mother, I get plenty of mud to root in."

I said, "I was the first husband, Mrs. Hettick, and I always thought *you* were the child molester."

"Oh, Orry," Dawn said; not angry but sad, as though I'd just made some terrible mistake that we both would suffer for.

Slowly, delightedly, as though receiving an unexpected extra dessert, Mrs. Hettick turned to stare at me, considering me, observing me. Slowly she nodded, slowly she said, "By God, you are, aren't you? That filthy sailor."

"You treated your daughter badly, Mrs. Hettick. If you'd ever—"

But she didn't care what I had to say. Turning back to her daughter, crowing, she said, "You running through the whole lot again? A triumphant return tour! Let me know when you dig up Ken Forrest, will you? At least he'll be stiff this time."

Leo Hettick said, "That's just about enough, Edna."

His wife glared at him. "What do *you* know about it?"

"I know when you're being impolite, Edna," he said. "If you remember, you made me a promise, some little time ago."

She sat there, glaring at him with a sullen stare, her body looking more than ever at odds with her clothing; the fuzzy pink sweater, most of all, seeming like some unfunny joke. While the Hetticks looked at one another, deciding who was in charge, I found myself remembering that magazine's description of me as "a stock figure," and of course here was another stock figure, the quarrelsome mother of the movie star. I thought of myself as something other than, or more than, a stock figure; was Mrs. Hettick also more than she seemed? What did it mean that she had broken up her daughter's first marriage, to a sailor, and later had married a sailor herself, and wore clothing dating from the time of her daughter's marriage? What promise had she made her husband, "some little time ago"? Was *he* a stock figure? The feisty old man telling stories on the porch of the old folks' home; all the rest of us were simply characters in one of his reminiscences.

Maybe that was the truth, and he was the hero of the story after all. He was certainly the one who decided how this evening would end; he won the battle of wills with his wife, while Dawn and I both sat out of the picture, having no influence, having no part to play until Edna Hettick's face finally softened, she gave a quick awkward nod, and she said, "You're right, Leo. I get carried away." She even apologized to her daughter, to some extent, turning to Dawn and saying, "I guess I live in the past too much."

"Well, it's over and forgotten," Dawn said, and invented a smile.

After they left—not late—the smile at last fell like a dead thing from Dawn's mouth. "I have a headache," she said, not looking at me. "I don't feel like swimming tonight, I'm going to bed."

Her own bed, she meant. I went off to my room, and left the drapes partway open, and didn't go to sleep till very late, but she never came by.

It was ten forty-three by the digital clock when I awoke. I put on the white robe and wandered through the house, and found Wang in the kitchen. Nodding at me with his usual polite smile, he said, "Breakfast?"

"Is Dawn up yet?"

"Gone to work."

I couldn't understand that. Last night she'd been upset, and of course she'd wanted to be alone for a while. But why ignore me this morning? I had breakfast, and then I settled down with magazines and the television set, and waited for the evening.

***

By nine o'clock I understood she wasn't coming home. It had been a long long day, an empty day, but at least I'd been able to tell myself it would eventually end, Dawn would come home around seven and everything would be the same again. Now it was nine o'clock, she wasn't here, I knew she wouldn't be here tonight at all, and I didn't know what to do.

I thought of all the people I'd met in the last week and a half, Dawn's friends, and the only ones I might talk to at all were Byron Cartwright or Rod, but even if I did talk to one of them what would I say? "Dawn and her mother had a little argument, and Dawn didn't sleep with me, and she left alone this morning and hasn't come back." Rod, I was certain, would simply advise me to sit tight, wait, do nothing. As for Byron Cartwright, this was a situation tailor-made for him to do the wrong thing. So I talked to no one, I stayed where I was, I watched more television, read more magazines, and I waited for Dawn.

The next day, driven more by boredom than anything else, I finally explored that other wing of the house. Dawn's bedroom, directly across the pool from mine, was all done in pinks and golds, with a thick white rug on the floor. Several awkward paintings of white clapboard houses in rural settings were on the walls. They weren't signed, and I never found out who'd done them.

But a more interesting room was also over there, down a short side corridor. A small cluttered attic-like place, it was filled with luggage and old pieces of furniture and mounds of clothing. Leaning with its face to the wall was the blown-up photograph, unharmed, and atop a ratty bureau in the farthest corner slumped a small brown stuffed animal; a panda? The room had a damp smell — it reminded me of our old apartment in San Diego — and I didn't like being in there, so I went back once more to the television set.

People on game shows are very emotional.

Saturday morning I finally admitted to myself that Dawn was staying away only because I was still there. I'd been alone now for three days, except for Wang and the silent anonymous other

servants—from time to time the phone would ring, but it was
Wang's right to answer it, and he always assured me afterward it
was nothing, nothing, unimportant—and all I'd done was sit
around and think, and try to ignore the truth, and by Saturday
morning I couldn't hide it from myself any more.

Dawn would not come back until I had given up and left. She
couldn't throw me out of her house, but she couldn't face me
either, not now or ever again. I belonged in the room with the
photograph and the panda and the old clothing, the furniture,
the bits and pieces of Estelle Anlic.

I knew the answer now to the question I'd brought out here.
In order to create a new person to be, you have to hate the old
person enough to kill it. Estelle *was* Dawn, and Dawn was happy.

She had dealt with my sudden reappearance out of the past by
forcing me also to accept Dawn Devayne, to put this new person
in Estelle's place in my memory, so that once more Estelle would
cease to exist.

But the mother remained outside control, with her dirty knowledge; in front of her, Estelle was only pretending to be Dawn
Devayne. After Wednesday night, Dawn must believe her mother
had re-created Estelle also in my mind, turned Dawn back into
Estelle in my eyes. No wonder she couldn't be in my presence
any longer.

I put the borrowed clothes away and packed my bag and asked
Wang to call a taxi. There wasn't anybody to say goodbye to.

Back on the base a week early, I explained part of the situation
to the Commander and applied for a transfer, and got it. I told
Fran everything—almost everything—and she moved to Norfolk
to be near me at my new post (where my history with Dawn
Devayne never came to light), and when I retired this year we
were married.

I don't go to Dawn Devayne movies. I also don't do those
things with Fran that I'd first done with Dawn. I don't have any
reason not to, it's just I don't feel that way any more. And Fran's
vehemence for new sexual activity was only a temporary thing
anyway; she very quickly cooled back down to what she had been
before. We get along very well.

Sometimes I have a dream. In the dream, I'm walking on Hollywood Boulevard, on the stars' names, and I stop at one point, and look down, and the name in the pavement is ESTELLE ANLIC. I just stand there. That's the dream. Later, when I wake up, I understand there isn't any Estelle Anlic any more; she's buried out there, on Hollywood Boulevard, underneath her name, standing up, squinting in the San Diego sun.

Lawrence Block

STAG PARTY GIRL

Lawrence Block (1938-) writes the best sentences in the business, that business being crime fiction. No tortured self-conscious arty stuff, either. Just pure, graceful, skilled writing of a very high order.

No matter what he writes—the dark Scudder private-eye novels; the spunky Bernie Rhodenbarrs about the kind of thief even a mom could love; or his latest creation, John Keller the hitman, an existential figure full of quirks and kindnesses rare in his profession—no matter what he's telling us, he always makes it sweet to read. He's just so damned nimble and graceful and acute with his language.

By now, his story is pretty well-known. Wrote a lot of erotica in the late Fifties and early Sixties, all the while writing his early crime paperback originals and stories for magazines of every kind. Started becoming a name in crime fiction in the Seventies, really broke out in the Nineties and is now poised, one would think, for superstardom.

Block has always reminded me of a very intelligent fighter. He knows what he's good at and sticks to his own fight, unmoved by popular fads and critical fancies. He writes about women as well as any male writer I've ever read (though since I'm a guy, I may just be saying that he perceives women the same way I do) and he deals with subjects as Oprah-ready as alcoholism and failed fatherhood realistically, yet without resorting to weepiness.

One senses in him sometimes a frustrated mainstream writer. He's always pushing against the restrictions of form and yet never failing to give the reader what he came there for in the first place. No easy trick, believe me.

For some reason, I've always hated the word "wordsmith" (probably because it's popular among pretentious young advertising copywriters who don't want to admit that they're writing hymns to beer and dish soap) but that's what Block is. A singer of songs, a teller of tales, a bedazzler.

I read three of his erotic novels recently and I'll tell you something. They're better written (and we're talking 1958–1961) than half the contemporary novels I read today. He was pushing against form even back then, creating real people and real problems, and doing so in a simple, powerful voice that stays with you a hell of a long time. Here's an early Lawrence Block private-eye novelette.

E.G.

HAROLD MERRIMAN PUSHED HIS CHAIR BACK AND STOOD UP, drink in hand. "Gentlemen," he said solemnly, "to all the wives we love so well. May they continue to belong to us body and soul." He paused theatrically. "And to their husbands—may they never find out!"

There was scattered laughter, most of it lost in the general hubbub. I had a glass of cognac on the table in front of me. I took a sip and looked at Mark Donahue. If he was nervous, it didn't show. He looked like any man who was getting married in the morning—which is nervous enough, I suppose. He didn't look like someone threatened with murder.

Phil Abeles—short, intense, brittle-voiced—stood. He started to read a sheaf of fake telegrams. "Mark," he intoned, "don't panic—marriage is the best life for a man. Signed, Tommy Manville" . . . He read more telegrams. Some funny, some mildly obscene, some dull.

We were in an upstairs dining room at McGraw's, a venerable steakhouse in the East Forties. About a dozen of us. There was Mark Donahue, literally getting married in the morning, Sunday, tying the nuptial knot at 10:30. Also Harold Merriman, Phil Abeles, Ray Powell, Joe Conn, Jack Harris and a few others whose names I couldn't remember, all fellow wage slaves with Donahue at Darcy & Bates, one of Madison Avenue's rising young ad agencies.

And there was me. Ed London, private cop, the man at the party who didn't belong. I was just a hired hand. It was my job to get Donahue to the church on time, and alive.

On Wednesday, Mark Donahue had come to my apartment. He cabbed over on a long lunch hour that coincided with the time

I rolled out of bed. We sat in my living room. I was rumpled and ugly in a moth-eaten bathrobe. He was fresh and trim in a Tripler suit and expensive shoes. I drowned my sorrows with coffee while he told me his problems.

"I think I need a bodyguard," he said.

In the storybooks and the movies, I show him the door at this point. I explain belligerently that I don't do divorce or bodyguard work or handle corporation investigations—that I only rescue stacked blondes and play modern-day Robin Hood. That's in the storybooks. I don't play that way. I have an apartment in an East Side brownstone and I eat in good restaurants and drink expensive cognac. If you can pay my fee, friend, you can buy me.

I asked him what it was all about.

"I'm getting married Sunday morning," he said.

"Congratulations."

"Thanks." He looked at the floor. "I'm marrying a . . . a very fine girl. Her name is Lynn Farwell."

I waited.

"There was another girl I . . . used to see. A model, more or less. Karen Price."

"And?"

"She doesn't want me to get married."

"So?"

He fumbled for a cigarette. "She's been calling me," he said. "I was . . . well, fairly deeply involved with her. I never planned to marry her. I'm sure she knew that."

"But you were sleeping with her?"

"That's right."

"And now you're marrying someone else."

He sighed at me. "It's not as though I ruined the girl," he said. "She's . . . well, not a tramp, exactly, but close to it. She's been around, London."

"So what's the problem?"

"I've been getting phone calls from her. Unpleasant ones, I'm afraid. She's told me that I'm not going to marry Lynn. That she'll see me dead first."

"And you think she'll try to kill you?"

"I don't know."

"That kind of threat is common, you know. It doesn't usually lead to murder."

He nodded hurriedly. "I know that," he said, "I'm not terribly afraid she'll kill me. I just want to make sure she doesn't throw a monkey wrench into the wedding. Lynn comes from an excellent family. Long Island, society, money. Her parents wouldn't appreciate a scene."

"Probably not."

He forced a little laugh. "And there's always a chance that she really may try to kill me," he said. "I'd like to avoid that." I told him it was an understandable desire. "So I want a bodyguard. From now until the wedding. Four days. Will you take the job?"

I told him my fee ran a hundred a day plus expenses. This didn't faze him. He gave me $300 for a retainer, and I had a client and he had a bodyguard.

From then on I stuck to him like perspiration.

Saturday, a little after noon, he got a phone call. We were playing two-handed pinochle in his living room. He was winning. The phone rang and he answered it. I only heard his end of the conversation. He went a little white and sputtered; then he stood for a long moment with the phone in his hand, and finally slammed the receiver on the hook and turned to me.

"Karen," he said, ashen. "She's going to kill me."

I didn't say anything. I watched the color come back into his face, saw the horror recede. He came up smiling. "I'm not really scared," he said.

"Good."

"Nothing's going to happen," he added. "Maybe it's her idea of a joke . . . maybe she's just being bitchy. But nothing's going to happen."

He didn't entirely believe it. But I had to give him credit.

I don't know who invented the bachelor dinner, or why he bothered. I've been to a few of them. Dirty jokes, dirty movies, dirty toasts, a line-up with a local whore — maybe I would appreciate them if I were married. But for a bachelor who makes out there is nothing duller than a bachelor dinner.

This one was par for the course. The steaks were good and there was a lot to drink, which was definitely on the plus side. The men busy making asses of themselves were not friends of mine, and that was also on the plus side — it kept me from getting embarrassed for them. But the jokes were still unfunny and the voices too drunkenly loud.

I looked at my watch. "Eleven-thirty," I said to Donahue. "How much longer do you think this'll go on?"

"Maybe half an hour."

"And then 10 hours until the wedding. Your ordeal's just about over, Mark."

"And you can relax and spend your fee."

"Uh-huh."

"I'm glad I hired you," he said. "You haven't had to do anything, but I'm glad anyway." He grinned. "I carry life insurance, too. But that doesn't mean I'm going to die. And you've even been good company, Ed. Thanks."

I started to search for an appropriate answer. Phil Abeles saved me. He was standing up again, pounding on the table with his fist and shouting for everyone to be quiet. They let him shout for a while, then quieted down.

"And now the grand finale," Phil announced wickedly. "The part I knew you've all been waiting for."

"The part Mark's been waiting for," someone said lewdly.

"Mark better watch this," someone else added. "He has to learn about women so that Lynn isn't disappointed."

More feeble lines, one after the other. Phil Abeles pounded for order again and got it. "Lights," he shouted.

The lights went out. The private dining room looked like a blackout in a coal mine.

"Music!"

Somewhere, a record played went on. The record was *Stripper*, played by David Rose's orchestra.

"Action!"

A spotlight illuminated the pair of doors at the far end of the room. The doors opened. Two bored waiters wheeled in a large table on rollers. There was a cardboard cake on top of the table and, obviously, a girl inside the cake. Somebody made a joke about Mark cutting himself a piece. Someone else said they wanted to put a piece of this particular wedding cake under their pillow. "On the pillow would be better," a voice corrected.

The two bored waiters wheeled the cake into position and left.

The doors closed. The spotlight stayed on the cake and the stripper music swelled.

There were two or three more lame jokes. Then the chatter died. Everyone seemed to be watching the cake. The music grew louder, deeper, fuller. The record stopped suddenly and another—the Mendelsohn's *Wedding March*—took its place.

Someone shouted, "Here comes the bride!"

And she leaped out of the cake like a nymph from the sea.

She was naked and beautiful. She sprang through the paper cake, arms wide, face filled with a lipstick smile. Her breasts were full and firm and her nipples had been reddened with lipstick.

Then, just as everyone was breathlessly silent, just as her arms spread and her lips parted and her eyes widened slightly, the whole room exploded like Hiroshima. We found out later that it was only a .38. It sounded more like a howitzer.

She clapped both hands to a spot between her breasts. Blood spurted forth like a flower opening. She gave a small gasp, swayed forward, then dipped backward and fell.

Lights went on. I raced forward. Her head was touching the floor and her legs were propped on what remained of the paper cake. Her eyes were open. But she was horribly dead.

And then I heard Mark Donahue next to me, his voice shrill. "Oh, no!" he murmured. ". . . It's Karen, it's Karen!"

I felt for a pulse; there was no point to it. There was a bullet in her heart.

Karen Price was dead.

2

LIEUTENANT JERRY GUNTHER GOT THE CALL. HE BROUGHT A clutch of Homicide men who went around measuring things, studying the position of the body, shooting off a hell of a lot of flashbulbs and taking statements. Jerry piloted me into a corner and started pumping.

I gave him the whole story, starting with Wednesday and ending with Saturday. He let me go all the way through once, then went over everything two or three times.

"Your client Donahue doesn't look too good," he said.

"You think he killed the girl?"

"That's the way it reads."

I shook my head. "Wrong customer."

"Why?"

"Hell, he hired me to keep the girl off his neck. If he was going to shoot a hole in her, why would he want a detective along for company?"

"To make the alibi stand up, Ed. To make us reason just the way you're reasoning now. How do you know he was scared of the girl?"

"Because he said so. But—"

"But he got a phone call?" Jerry smiled. "For all you know it was a wrong number. Or the call had been staged. You only heard his end of it. Remember?"

"I saw his face when he took a good look at the dead girl," I said. "Mark Donahue was one surprised hombre, Jerry. He didn't know who she was."

"Or else he's a good actor."

"Not that good. I can't believe it."

He let that one pass. "Let's go back to the shooting," he said. "Were you watching him when the gun went off?"

"No."

"What were you watching?"

"The girl," I said. "And quit grinning, you fathead."

His grin spread. "You old lecher. All right, you can't alibi him for the shooting. And you can't prove he was afraid of the girl. This is the way I make it, Ed. He was afraid of her, but not afraid she would kill him. He was afraid of something else. Call it blackmail, maybe. He's getting set to make a good marriage to a rich doll and he's got a mistress hanging around his neck. Say the rich girl doesn't know about the mistress. Say the mistress wants hush money."

"Go on."

"Your Donahue finds out the Price doll is going to come out of the cake."

"They kept it a secret from him, Jerry."

"Sometimes people find out secrets. The Price kid could have told him herself. It might have been her idea of a joke. Say he finds out. He packs a gun—"

"He didn't have a gun."

"How do you know, Ed?"

I couldn't answer that one. He might have had a gun. He might have tucked it into a pocket while he was getting dressed. I didn't believe it, but I couldn't disprove it either.

Jerry Gunther was thorough. He didn't have to be thorough to turn up the gun. It was under a table in the middle of the room. The lab boys checked it for prints. None. It was a .38 police positive with five bullets left in it. The bullets didn't have any prints on them, either.

"Donahue shot her, wiped the gun and threw it on the floor," Jerry said.

"Anybody else could have done the same thing," I interjected.

"Uh-huh. Sure."

He grilled Phil Abeles, the man who had hired Karen Price to come out of the cake. Abeles was also the greenest, sickest man in the world at that particular moment.

Gunther asked him how he got hold of the girl. "I never knew anything about her," Abeles insisted. "I didn't even know her last name."

"How'd you find her?"

"A guy gave me her name."

"What guy?"

"I forget. Some guy gave me her name and her number. When I . . . when we set up the dinner, the stag, we thought we would have a wedding cake with a girl jumping out of it. We thought it would be so . . . so corny that it might be cute. You know?"

No one said anything. Abeles was sweating up a storm. The dinner had been his show and it had not turned out as he had planned it, and he looked as though he wanted to go somewhere quiet and die.

"So I asked around to find out where to get a girl," he went on. "Honest, I asked a dozen guys, two dozen. I don't know how many. I asked everybody in this room except Mark. I asked half the guys on Madison Avenue. Someone gave me a number, told me to call it and ask for Karen. So I did. She said she'd jump out of the cake for $100 and I said that was fine."

"You didn't know anything about her?"

"Not a thing."

"You didn't know she was Donahue's mistress?"

"Oh, brother," he said. "You have to be kidding."

We told him we weren't kidding. He got greener. "Maybe that made it a better joke," I suggested. "to have Mark's girl jump out of the cake the night before he married someone else. Was that it?"

"Hell, no!"

Jerry grilled everyone in the place. No one admitted knowing Karen Price, or realized that she had been involved with Mark Donahue. No one admitted anything. Most of the men were married. They were barely willing to admit that they were alive. Some of them were almost as green as Phil Abeles.

They wanted to go home. That was all they wanted. They kept mentioning how nice it would be if their names didn't get into the papers. Some of them tried a little genteel bribery. Jerry was tactful enough to pretend he didn't know what they were talking about. He was an honest cop. He didn't do favors and didn't take gifts.

By 1:30, he had sent them all home. The lab boys were still making chalk marks but there wasn't much point to it. According to their measurements and calculations of the bullet's trajectory, and a few other scientific bits and pieces, they managed to prove conclusively that Karen Price had been shot by someone in Mc-Graw's private dining room.

And that was all they could prove.

Four of us rode down to headquarters at Centre Street. Mark Donahue sat in front, silent. Jerry Gunther sat on his right. A beardless cop named Ryan, Jerry's driver, had the wheel. I occupied the back seat all alone.

At Fourteenth Street Mark broke his silence. "This is a nightmare. I didn't kill Karen. Why in God's name would I kill her?"

Nobody had an answer for him. A few blocks further he said, "I suppose I'll be railroaded now. I suppose you'll lock me up and throw the key away."

Gunther told him, "We don't railroad people. We couldn't if we wanted to. We don't have enough of a case yet. But right now you look like a pretty good suspect. Figure it out for yourself."

"But—"

"I have to lock you up, Donahue. You can't talk me out of it. Ed can't talk me out of it. Nobody can."

"I'm supposed to get married tomorrow."

"I'm afraid that's out."

The car moved south. For a while nobody had anything to say.

A few blocks before police headquarters Mark told me he wanted me to stay on the case.

"You'll be wasting your money," I told him. "The police will work things out better than I can. They have the manpower and the authority. I'll just be costing you a hundred a day and getting you nothing in return."

"Are you trying to talk yourself out of a fee?"

"He's an ethical bastard," Jerry put in. "In his own way, of course."

"I want you working for me, Ed."

"Why?"

He waited a minute, organizing his thoughts. "Look," he sighed, "do you think I killed Karen?"

"No."

"Honestly?"

"Honestly."

"Well, that's one reason I want you in my corner. Maybe the police are fair in these things. I don't know anything about it. But they'll be looking for things that'll nail me. They have to— it's their job. From where they sit I'm the killer." He paused, as if the thought stunned him a little. "But you'll be looking for something that will help me. Maybe you can find someone who was looking at me when the gun went off. Maybe you can figure out who did pull that trigger and why. I know I'll feel better if you're working for me."

"Don't expect anything."

"I don't."

"I'll do what I can," I told him.

Before I caught a cab from headquarters to my apartment, I told Mark to call his lawyer. He wouldn't be able to get out on bail because there is no bail in first-degree murder cases; but a lawyer could do a lot of helpful things for him. Lynn Farwell's family had to be told that there wasn't going to be a wedding.

I don't envy anyone who has to call a mother or father at 3

A.M. and explain that their daughter's wedding, set for 10:30 that very morning, must be postponed because the potential bridegroom has been arrested for murder.

I sat back in the cab with an unlit pipe in my mouth and a lot of aimless thoughts rumbling around in my head. Nothing made much sense yet. Perhaps nothing ever would. It was that kind of a deal.

3

MORNING WAS NOISY, UGLY AND SEVERAL HOURS PREMATURE. A sharp, persistent ringing stabbed my brain into a semiconscious state. I cursed and groped for the alarm clock . . . turned it off. The buzzing continued. I reached for the phone, lifted the receiver to my ear, and listened to a dial tone. The buzzing continued. I cursed even more vehemently and stumbled out of bed. I found a bathrobe and groped into it. I splashed cold water on my face and blinked at myself in the mirror. I looked as bad as I felt.

The doorbell kept ringing. I didn't want to answer it, but that seemed the only way to make it stop ringing. I listened to my bones creak on the way to the door. I turned the knob, opened the door and blinked at the blonde who was standing there. She blinked back at me.

"Mister," she said. "You look terrible."

She didn't. Even at that ghastly hour she looked like a toothpaste ad. Her hair was blonde silk and her eyes were blue jewels and her skin was creamed perfection. With a thinner body and a more severe mouth she could have been a *Vogue* model. But the body was just too bountiful for the fashion magazines. The breasts were a perfect 38, high and large, the waist trim, the hips a curved invitation.

"You're Ed London?"

I nodded foolishly.

"I'm Lynn Farwell."

She didn't have to tell me. She looked exactly like what my client had said he was going to marry, except a little better. Everything about her stated emphatically that she was from Long Island's North Shore, that she had gone to an expensive finishing

school and a ritzy college, that her family had half the money in
the world.

"May I come in?"

"You got me out of bed," I grumbled.

"I'm sorry. I wanted to talk to you."

"Could you sort of go somewhere and come back in about 10
minutes? I'd like to get human."

"I don't really have any place to go. May I just sit in your living
room, or something? I'll be quiet."

There are a pair of matching overstuffed leather chairs in my
living room, the kind they have in British men's clubs. She curled
up and got lost in one of them. I left her there and ducked back
into the bedroom. I showered, shaved, dressed. When I came out
again the world was a somewhat better place. I smelled coffee.

"I put up a pot of java," she smiled. "Hope you don't mind."

"I couldn't mind less," I said. We waited while the coffee
dripped through, I poured out two cups, and we both drank it
black.

"I haven't seen Mark," she said. "His lawyer called. I suppose
you know all about it, of course."

"More or less."

"I'll be seeing Mark later this afternoon, I suppose. We were
supposed to be getting married in—" she looked at her watch "—
a little over an hour."

She seemed unperturbed. There were no tears, not in her eyes
and not in her voice. She asked me if I was still working for
Donahue. I nodded.

"He didn't kill that girl," she said.

"I don't think he did."

"I'm sure. Of all the ridiculous things . . . Why did he hire you,
Ed?"

I thought a moment and decided to tell her the truth. She
probably knew it anyway. Besides, there was no point in sparing
her the knowledge that her fiance had a mistress somewhere
along the line. That should be the least of her worries, compared
to a murder rap.

It was. She greeted the news with a half-smile and shook her
head sadly. "Now why on earth would they think she could black-

mail him?" Lynn Farwell demanded. "I don't care who he slept with . . . Policemen are asinine."

I didn't say anything. She sipped her coffee, stretched a little in the chair, crossed one leg over the other. She had very nice legs.

We both lit cigarettes. She blew out a cloud of smoke and looked at me through it, her blue eyes narrowing. "Ed," she said, "how long do you think it'll be before he's cleared?"

"It's impossible to say, Miss Farwell."

"Lynn."

"Lynn. It could take a day or a month."

She nodded thoughtfully. "He has to be cleared as quickly as possible. That's the most important thing. There can't be any scandal, Ed. Oh, a little dirt is bearable. But nothing serious, nothing permanent."

Something didn't sound right. She didn't care who he slept with, but no scandal could touch them—this was vitally important to her. She sounded like anything but a loving bride-to-be.

She read my mind. "I don't sound madly in love, do I?"

"Not particularly."

She smiled kittenishly. "I'd like more coffee, Ed . . ."

I got more for both of us.

Then she said, "Mark and I don't love each other, Ed."

I grunted noncommittally.

"We like each other, though. I'm fond of Mark, and he's fond of me. That's all that matters, really."

"Is it?"

She nodded positively. Finishing schools and high-toned colleges produce girls with the courage of their convictions. "It's enough," she said. "Love's a poor foundation for marriage in the long run. People who love are too . . . too vulnerable. Mark and I are perfect for each other. We'll both be getting something out of this marriage."

"What will Mark get?"

"A rich wife. A proper connection with an important family. That's what he wants."

"And you?"

"A repectable marriage to a promising young man."

"If that's all you want—"

"It's all I want," she said. "Mark is good company. He's bright, socially acceptable, ambitious enough to be stimulating. He'll make a good husband and a good father. I'm happy."

She yawned again and her body uncoiled in the chair. The movement drew her breasts into sharp relief against the front of her sweater. This was supposed to be accidental. I know better.

"Besides," she said, her voice just slightly husky, "he's not at all bad in bed."

I wanted to slap her well-bred face. The lips were slightly parted now, her eyes a little less than half lidded. The operative term, I think, is *provocative*. She knew damned well what she was doing with the coy posing and the sex talk and all the rest. She had the equipment to carry it off, too. But it was a horrible hour on a horrible Sunday morning, and her fiance was also my client, and he was sitting in a cell, booked on suspicion of homicide.

So I neither took her to bed nor slapped her face. I let the remark die in the stuffy air and finished my second cup of coffee. There was a rack of pipes on the table next to my chair. I selected a sandblast Barling and stuffed some tobacco into it. I lit it and smoked.

"Ed?"

I looked at her.

"I didn't mean to sound cheap."

"Forget it."

"All right." A pause. "Ed, you'll find a way to clear Mark, won't you?"

"I'll try."

"If there's any way I can help—"

"I'll let you know."

She gave me her phone number and address. She was living with her parents.

Then she paused at the door and turned enough to let me look at her lovely young body in profile. "If there's anything you want," she said softly, "be sure to let me know."

It was an ordinary enough line. But I had the feeling that it covered a lot of ground.

At 11:30 I picked up my car at the garage around the corner from my apartment.

The car is a Chevy convertible, an old one that dates from the pre-fin era. I left the top up. The air had an edge to it. I took the East Side Drive downtown and pulled up across the street from headquarters at noon.

They let me see Mark Donahue. He was wearing the same expensive suit but it didn't hang right now. It looked as though it had been slept in, which figured. He needed a shave and his eyes had red rims. I didn't ask him how he had slept. I could tell.

"Hello," he said.

"Getting along all right?"

"I suppose so." He swallowed. "They asked me questions most of the night. No rubber hose, though. That's something."

"Sure," I said. "Mind some more questions?"

"Go ahead."

"When did you start seeing Karen Price?"

"Four, five months ago."

"When did you stop?"

"About a month ago."

"Why?"

"Because I was practically married to Lynn."

"Who knew you were sleeping with Karen?"

"No one I know of."

"Anybody at the stag last night?"

"I don't think so."

More questions. When had she started phoning him? About two weeks ago, maybe a little longer than that. Was she in love with him? He hadn't thought so, no, and that was why the phone calls were such a shock to him at first. As far as he was concerned, it was just a mutual sex arrangement with no emotional involvement on either side. He took her to shows, bought her presents, gave her occasional small loans with the understanding that they weren't to be repaid. He wasn't exactly keeping her and she wasn't exactly going to bed in return for the money. It was just a convenient arrangement.

Everything, it seemed, was just a convenient arrangement. He and Karen Price had had a convenient shack-up. He and Lynn Farwell were planning a convenient marriage.

But someone had put a bullet in Karen's pretty chest. People don't do that because it's convenient. They usually have more emotional reasons.

More questions. Where did Karen live? He gave me an address in the Village, not too very far from his own apartment. Who were her friends? He knew one, her roommate, Ceil Gorski. Where did she work? He wasn't too clear.

"My lawyer's trying to get them to reduce the charge," he said. "So that I can get out on bail. You think he'll manage it?"

"He might."

"I hope so," he said. His face went serious, then brightened again. "This is a hell of a place to spend a wedding night," he smiled. "Funny—when I was trying to pick the right hotel, I never thought of a jail."

4

IT WAS ONLY A FEW BLOCKS FROM MARK DONAHUE'S CELL TO THE building where Karen Price had lived . . . a great deal further in terms of dollars and cents. She had an apartment in a red-brick five-story building on Sullivan Street, just below Bleecker.

The girl who opened the door was blonde, like Lynn Farwell. But her dark roots showed and her eyebrows were dark brown. If her mouth and eyes relaxed she would have been pretty. They didn't.

"You just better not be another cop," she said.

"I'm afraid I am. But not city. Private."

The door started to close. I made like a brush salesman and tucked a foot in it. She glared at me.

"Private cops, I don't have to see," she said. "Get the hell out, will you?"

"I just want to talk to you."

"The feeling isn't mutual. Look—"

"It won't take long."

"You son of a bitch," she said. But she opened the door and let me inside. We walked through the kitchen to the living room. There was a couch there. She sat on it. I took a chair.

"Who are you anyway?" she said.

"My name's Ed London."

"Who you working for?"

"Mark Donahue."

"The one who killed her?"

"I don't think he did," I said. "What I'm trying to find out, Miss Gorski, is who did."

She got to her feet and started walking around the room. There was nothing deliberately sexy about her walk. She was hard, tough. She lived in a cheap apartment on a bad block. She bleached her hair, and her hairdresser wasn't the only one who knew for sure. She could have—but didn't—come across as a slut.

There was something honest and forthright about her, if not necessarily wholesome. She was a big blonde with a hot body and a hard face. There are worse things than that.

"What do you want to know, London?"

"About Karen."

"What is there to know? You want a biography? She came from Indiana because she wanted to be a success. A singer, an actress, a model, something. She wasn't too clear on just what. She tried, she flopped. She woke up one day knowing she wasn't going to make it. It happens."

I didn't say anything.

"So she could go back to Indiana or she could stay in the city. Only she couldn't go back to Indiana. You give in to enough men, you drink enough drinks and do enough things, then you can't go back to Indiana. What's left?"

She lit a cigarette. "Karen could have been a whore. But she wasn't. She never put a price tag on it. She spread it around, sure. Look, she was in New York and she was used to a certain kind of life and a certain kind of people, and she had to manage that life and those people into enough money to stay alive on, and she had one commodity to trade. She had sex. But she wasn't a whore." She paused. "There's a difference."

"All right."

"Well, dammit, what else do you want to know?"

"Who was she sleeping with besides Donahue?"

"She didn't say and I didn't ask. And she never kept a diary."

"She ever have men up here?"

"No."

"She talk much about Donahue?"

"No." She leaned over, stubbed out a cigarette. Her breasts loomed before my face like fruit. But it wasn't purposeful sexiness. She didn't play that way.

"I've got to get out of here," she said. "I don't feel like talking any more."

"If you could just—"

"I couldn't just." She looked away. "In 15 minutes I have to be uptown on the West Side. A guy there wants to take some pictures of me naked. He pays for my time, Mr. London. I'm a working girl."

"Are you working tonight?"

"Huh?"

"I asked if—"

"I heard you. What's the pitch?"

"I'd like to take you out to dinner."

"Why?"

"I'd like to talk to you."

"I'm not going to tell you anything I don't feel like telling you, London."

"I know that, Miss Gorski."

"And a dinner doesn't buy my company in bed, either. In case that's the idea."

"It isn't. I'm not all that hard up, Miss Gorski."

She was suddenly smiling. The smile softened her face all over and cut her age a good three years. Before she had been attractive. Now she was genuinely pretty.

"You give as good as you take."

"I try to."

"Is eight o-clock too late? I just got done with lunch a little while ago."

"Eight's fine," I said. "I'll see you."

I left. I walked the half block to my car and sat behind the wheel for a few seconds and thought about two girls I had met that day. Both blondes, one born that way, one self-made. One of them had poise, breeding and money, good diction and flawless bearing—and she added up to a tramp. The other was a tramp, in an amateurish sort of way, and she talked tough and dropped an occasional final consonant. Yet she was the one who managed to retain a certain degree of dignity. Of the two, Ceil Gorski was more the lady.

At 3:30 I was up in Westchester County. The sky was bluer, the air fresher and the houses more costly. I pulled up in front of a $35,000 split-level, walked up a flagstone path and leaned on a doorbell.

The little boy who answered it had red hair, freckles and a chipped tooth. He was too cute to be snotty, but this didn't stop him.

He asked me who I was. I told him to get his father. He asked me why. I told him that if he didn't get his father I would twist his arm off. He wasn't sure whether or not to believe me, but I was obviously the first person who had ever talked to him this way. He took off in a hurry and a few seconds later Phil Abeles came to the door.

"Oh, London," he said. "Hello. Say, what did you tell the kid?"

"Nothing."

"Your face must have scared him." Abeles' eyes darted around. "You want to talk about what happened last night, I suppose."

"That's right."

"I'd just as soon talk somewhere else," he said. "Wait a minute, will you?"

I waited while he went to tell his wife that somebody from the office had driven up, that it was important, and that he'd be back in an hour. He came out and we went to my car.

"There's a quiet bar two blocks down and three over," he said, then added: "Let me check something. The way I've got it, you're a private detective working for Mark. Is that right?"

"Yes."

"Okay," he said. "I'd like to help the guy out. I don't know very much, but there are things I can talk about to you that I'd just as soon not tell the police. Nothing illegal. Just . . . Well, you can figure it out."

I could figure it out. That was the main reason why I had agreed to stay on the case for Donahue. People do not like to talk to the police if they can avoid it.

If Phil Abeles was going to talk at all about Karen Price,

he would prefer me as a listening post to Lieutenant Jerry Gunther.

"Here's the place," he said. I pulled up next to the chosen bar, a log-cabin arrangement.

Abeles had J & B with water and I ordered a pony of Courvoisier.

"I told that homicide lieutenant I didn't know anything about the Price girl," he said. "That wasn't true."

"Go on."

He hesitated, but just a moment. "I didn't know she had anything going with Donahue," he said. "Nobody ever thought of Karen in one-man terms. She slept around."

"I gathered that."

"It's a funny thing," he said. "A girl, not exactly a whore but not convent-bred either, can tend to pass around in a certain group of men. Karen was like that. She went for ad men. I think at one time or another she was intimate with half of Madison Avenue."

Speaks well of the dead, I thought. "For anyone in particular?" I asked.

"It's hard to say. Probably for most of the fellows who were at the dinner last night. For Ray Powell—but that's nothing new; he's one of those bachelors who gets to everything in a skirt sooner or later. But for the married ones, too."

"For you?"

"That's a hell of a question."

"Forget it. You already answered it."

He grinned sourly, "Yes"—he lapsed into flippant Madison Avenue talk—"the Price was right." He sipped his drink, then continued. "Not recently, and not often. Two or three times over two months ago. You won't blackmail me now, will you?"

"I don't play that way." I thought a minute. "Would Karen Price have tried a little subtle blackmail?"

"I don't think so. She played pretty fair."

"Was she the type to fall in love with somebody like Donahue?"

Abeles scratched his head. "The story I heard," he said. "Something to the effect that she was calling him, threatening him, trying to head off his marriage."

I nodded. "That's why he hired me."

"It doesn't make much sense."

"No?"

"No. It doesn't fit in with what I know about Karen. She wasn't the torch-bearer type. And she was hardly making a steady thing with Mark, either. I may not have known he was sleeping with her, but I knew damn well that a lot of other guys had been making with her lately."

"Could she have been shaking him down?"

He shrugged. "I told you," he said. "It doesn't sound like her. But who knows? She might have gotten into financial trouble. It happens. Perhaps she'd try to milk somebody for a little money." He pursed his lips. "But why should she blackmail Mark, for heaven's sake? If she blackmailed a bachelor he could always tell her to go to hell. You'd think she would work that on a married man, not a bachelor."

"I know."

He started to laugh then. "But not me," he said. "Believe me, London. She didn't blackmail me and I didn't kill her."

I got a list from him of all the men at the dinner. In addition to Donahue and myself, there had been eight men present, all of them from Darcy & Bates. Four—Abeles, Jack Harris, Harold Merriman and Joe Conn—were married. One—Ray Powell—was the bachelor and stud-about-town of the group, almost a compulsive Don Juan, according to Abeles. Another, Fred Klein, had a wife waiting out a residency requirement in Reno.

The remaining two wouldn't have much to do with girls like Karen Price. Lloyd Travers and Kenneth Bream were as queer as rectangular eggs.

I drove Abeles back to his house. Before I let him off he told me again not to waste time suspecting him.

"One thing you might remember," I said. "*Somebody* in that room shot Karen Price. Either Mark or one of the eight of you . . . I don't think it was Mark." I paused. "That means there's a murderer in your office, Abeles!"

5

IT WAS LATE ENOUGH IN THE DAY TO CALL LIEUTENANT GUNTHER. I tried him at home first. His wife answered, told me he was at the station. I tried him there and caught him.

"Nice hours you work, Jerry."

"Well, I didn't have anything else on today. So I came on down. You know how it is . . . Say, I got news for you, Ed."

"About Donahue?"

"Yes. We let him go."

"He's clear?"

"No, not clear." Jerry grunted. "We could have held him but there was no point, Ed. He's not clear, not by a mile. But we ran a check on the Price kid and learned she's been sleeping with two parties—Democrats and Republicans. Practically everyone at the stag. So there's nothing that makes your boy look too much more suspicious than the others."

"I found out the same thing this afternoon."

"Ed, I wasn't too crazy about letting him get away. Donahue still looks like the killer from where I sit. He hired you because the girl was giving him trouble. She wasn't giving anybody else trouble. He looks like the closest thing to a suspect around."

"Then why release him?"

I could picture Jerry's shrug. "Well, there was pressure," he said. "The guy got himself an expensive lawyer and the lawyer was getting ready to pull a couple of strings. That's not all, of course. Donahue isn't a criminal type, Ed. He's not going to run far. We let him go, figuring we won't have much trouble picking him up again."

"Maybe you won't have to."

"You get anything yet, Ed?"

"Not much," I said. "Just enough to figure out that everything's mixed up."

"I already knew that."

"Uh-huh. But the more I hunt around, the more loose ends I find. I'm glad you boys let my client loose. I'm going to see if I can get hold of him."

"Bye," Jerry said, clicking off.

I took time to get a pipe going, then dialed Mark Donahue's number. The phone rang eight times before I gave up. I decided he must be out on Long Island with Lynn Farwell. I was halfway through the complicated process of prying a number out of the information operator when I decided not to bother. Donahue had my number. He could reach me when he got the chance.

Then I closed my eyes, gritted my teeth and tried to think straight.

It wasn't easy. So far I had managed one little trick—I had succeeded in convincing myself that Donahue had not killed the girl. But this wasn't much cause for celebration. When you're working for someone, it's easy to get yourself to thinking that your client is on the side of the angels.

First of all, the girl. Karen Price. According to all and sundry, she was something of a tramp. According to her roommate she didn't put a price tag on it—but she didn't keep it under lock and key, either. She had wound up in bed with most of the heterosexual ad men on Madison Avenue. Donahue, a member of this clan, had been sleeping with her.

This didn't mean she was in love with him, or carrying a flaming torch, or singing blues, or issuing dire threats concerning his upcoming marriage. According to everyone who knew Karen, there was no reason for her to give a whoop in hell whether he got married, turned queer, became an astronaut or joined the Foreign Legion.

But Donahue said he had received threatening calls from her. That left two possibilities. One: Donahue was lying. Two: Donahue was telling the truth.

If he was lying, why in hell had he hired me as a bodyguard? And if he had some other reason to want the girl dead, he wouldn't need me along for fun and games. Hell, if he hadn't gone through the business of hiring me, no one could have tagged him as the prime suspect in the shooting. He would just be another person at the bachelor dinner, another former playmate of Karen's with no more motive to kill her than anyone else at the party.

I gave up the brainwork and concentrated on harmless if time-consuming games. I sat at my desk and drew up a list of the eight men who had been at the dinner. I listed the four married men, the Don Juan, the incipient divorcé and, just for the sake of completion, Lloyd and Kenneth. I worked on my silly little list for over an hour, creating mythical motives for each man.

It made an interesting mental exercise, although it didn't seem to be of much value.

6

THE ALHAMBRA IS A SYRIAN RESTAURANT ON WEST 27TH STREET, an Arabian oasis in a desert of Greek night clubs. Off the beaten track, it doesn't advertise, and the sign announcing its presence is almost invisible. You have to know the Alhambra is there in order to find it.

The owner and maitre d' is a little man whom the customers call Kamil. His name is Louis, his parents brought him to America before his eyes were open, and one of his brothers is a full professor at Columbia, but he liked to put on an act. When I brought Ceil Gorski into the place around 8:30, he smiled hugely at me and bowed halfway to the floor.

"*Salaam alekhim*," he said solemnly. "My pleasure, Mist' London."

"*Alekhim salaam*," I intoned, glancing over at Ceil while Louis showed us to a table.

Our waiter brought a bottle of very sweet white wine to go with the entree.

"I was bitchy before. I'm sorry about it."

"Forget it."

"Ed—"

I looked at her. She was worth looking at in a pale green dress which she filled to perfection.

"You want to ask me some questions," she said, "don't you?"

"Well—"

"I don't mind, Ed."

I gave her a brief rundown on the way things seemed to shape up at that point.

"Let me try some names on you," I suggested. "Maybe you can tell me whether Karen mentioned them."

"You can try."

I ran through the eight jokers who had been at the stag. A few sounded vaguely familiar to her, but one of them, Ray Powell, turned out to be someone Ceil knew personally.

"A chaser," she said. "A very plush East Side apartment and an appetite for women that never lets up. He used to see Karen now and then, but there couldn't have been anything serious."

"You know him—very well?"

"Yes." She colored suddenly. She was not the sort you expected to blush. "If you mean intimately, no. He asked often enough. I wasn't interested." She lowered her eyes. "I don't sleep around that much," she said. "Karen—well, she came to New York with stars in her eyes, and when the stars dimmed and died, she went a little crazy, I suppose. I wasn't that ambitious and didn't fall as hard. I have some fairly farout ways of earning a living, Ed, but most nights I sleep alone."

She was one hell of a girl. She was hard and soft, a cynic and a romantic at the same time. She hadn't gone to college, hadn't finished high school, but somewhere along the way she had acquired a veneer of sophistication that reflected more concrete knowledge than a diploma.

"Poor Karen," she said. "Poor Karen."

I didn't say anything. She sat somberly for a moment, then tossed her head so that her bleached blonde mane rippled like a wheat field in the wind. "I'm getting morbid as hell," she said. "You'd better take me home, Ed."

We climbed three flights of stairs. I stood next to her while she rummaged through her purse. She came up with a key and turned to face me before opening the door. "Ed," she said softly, "if I asked you, would you just come in for a few drinks? Could it be that much of an invitation and no more?"

"Yes."

"I hate to sound like—"

"I understand."

We went inside. She turned on lamps in the living room and we sat on the couch.

* * *

She started talking about the modeling session she'd gone
through that afternoon. "The money was good," she said, "but I
had to work for it. He took three or four rolls of film. Slightly
advanced cheesecake, Ed. Nudes, underwear stuff. He'll print the
best pictures and they'll wind up for sale in the dirty little stores
on 42nd Street."

"With the face retouched?"

She laughed. "He won't bother. Nobody's going to look at the
face, Ed."

"I would."

"Would you?"

"Yes."

"And not the body?"

"That too."

She looked at me for a long moment. There was something
electric in the air. I could feel the sweet animal heat of her. She
was right next to me. I could reach out and touch her, could take
her in my arms and press her close. The bedroom wasn't far away.
And she would be good, very good.

Two drinks later, I got up and walked to the door. She followed
me. I stopped at the doorway, started to say something, changed
my mind. We said goodnight and I started down the stairs.

If she had been just any girl—actress, secretary, college girl or
waitress—then it would have ended differently. It would have
ended in her bedroom, in warmth and hunger and fury. But she
was not just any girl. She was a halfway tramp, a little tarnished,
a little soiled, a little battered around the edges. And so I could
not make that pass at her, could not maneuver from couch to
bed.

I didn't want to go back to my apartment. It would be lonely
there. I drove to a Third Avenue bar where they pour good drinks.

Somewhere between two and three I left the bar and looked
around for the Chevy. By the time I found it I decided to leave
it there and take a cab. I had had too little sleep the night before
and too much to drink this night, and things were beginning to
go a little out of focus. The way I felt, they looked better that
way. But I didn't much feel like bouncing the car off a telephone

pole or gunning down some equally stoned pedestrian. I flagged
a cab and left the driving to him.

He had to tell me three times that we were in front of my
building before it got through to me. I shook myself awake, paid
him, and wended my way into the brownstone and up a flight of
stairs.

Then I blinked a few times.

There was something on my doormat, something that hadn't been
there when I left.

It was blonde, well-bred and glassy-eyed. It had an empty wine
bottle in one hand and its mouth was smiling lustily. It got to its
feet and swayed there, then pitched forward slightly. I caught it
and it burrowed its head against my chest.

"You keep late hours," it said.

It was very soft and very warm. It rubbed its hips against me
and purred like a kitten. I growled like a randy old tomcat.

"I've been waiting for you," it said. "I've been wanting to go to
bed. Take me to bed, Ed London."

Its name, in case you haven't guessed, was Lynn Farwell.

We were a pair of iron filings and my bed was a magnet. I
opened the door and we hurried inside. I closed the door and slid
the bolt. We moved quickly through the living room and along a
hall to the bedroom. Along the way we discarded clothing.

She left her skirt on my couch, her sweater on one of my
leather chairs. Her bra and slip and shoes landed in various spots
on the hall floor. In the bedroom she got rid of her stockings and
garter belt and panties. She was naked and beautiful and hungry
. . . and there was no time to waste on words.

Her body welcomed me. Her breasts, firm little cones of happiness, quivered against me. Her thighs enveloped me in the lust-
heat of desire. Her face twisted in a blind agony of need.

We were both pretty well stoned. This didn't matter. We could
never have done better sober. There was a beginning, bittersweet
and almost painful. There was a middle, fast and furious, a
scherzo movement in a symphony of fire. And there was an ending, gasping, spent, two bodies washed up on a lonely barren
beach.

At the end she used words that girls are not supposed to learn in the schools she had attended. She screamed them out in a frenzy of completion, a song of obscenity offered as a coda.

And afterward, when the rhythm was gone and only the glow remained, she talked. "I needed that," she told me. "Needed it badly. But you could tell that, couldn't you?"

"Yes."

"You're good, Ed." She caressed me. "Very good."

"Sure. I win blue ribbons."

"Was I good?"

I told her she was fine.

"Mmmmm," she said.

7

I ROLLED OUT OF BED JUST AS THE NOON WHISTLES STARTED GO-ing off all over town. Lynn was gone. I listened to bells from a nearby church ring 12 times; then I showered, shaved and swallowed aspirin. Lynn had left. Living proof of indiscretions makes bad company on the morning after.

I caught a cab, and the driver and I prowled Third Avenue for my car. It was still there. I drove it back to the garage and tucked it away. Then I called Donahue, but hung up before the phone had a chance to ring. Not that I expected to reach him anyway, since calling him on the phone didn't seem to produce much in the way of concrete results. But I didn't feel like talking to him just then.

A few hours ago I had been busy coupling with his bride-to-be. It seemed an unlikely prelude to a conversation.

Darcy & Bates wasn't really on Madison Avenue. It was around the corner on 48th Street, a suite of offices on the fourteenth floor of a 22 story building. I got out of the elevator and stood before a reception desk.

"Phil Abeles," I said.

"May I ask your name?"

"Go right ahead," I smiled. She looked unhappily snowed. "Ed

London," I finally said. She smiled gratefully and pressed one of 20 buttons and spoke softly into a tube.

"If you'll have a seat, Mr. London," she said.

I didn't have a seat. I stood instead and loaded up a pipe. I finished lighting it as Abeles emerged from an office and came over to meet me. He motioned for me to follow him. We went into his air-cooled office and he closed the door.

"What's up, Ed?"

"I'm not sure," I said. "I want some help." I drew on the pipe. "I'll need a private office for an hour or two," I told him. "And I want to see all of the men who were at Mark Donahue's bachelor dinner. One at a time."

"All of us?" He grinned. "Even Lloyd and Kenneth?"

"I suppose we can pass them for the time being. Just you and the other five then. Can you arrange it?"

He nodded with a fair amount of enthusiasm. "You can use this office," he said. "And everybody's around today, so you won't have any trouble on that score. Who do you want to see first?"

"I might as well start with you, Phil."

I talked with him for 10 minutes. But I had already pumped him dry the day before. Still, he gave me a little information on some of the others I would be seeing. Before, I had tried to ask him about his own relationship with Karen Price. Although that tack had been fairly effective, it didn't look like the best way to come up with something concrete. Instead, I asked him about the other men. If I worked on all of them that way, I just might turn up an answer or two.

Abeles more or less crossed Fred Klein off the suspect list, if nothing else. Klein, whose wife was in Reno, had tentatively made the coulda-dunnit sheet on the chance that Karen was threatening to give his wife information that would boost her alimony, or something of the sort. Abeles knocked the theory to pieces with the information that Klein's wife had money of her own, that she wasn't looking for alimony, and that a pair of expensive lawyers had already worked out all the details of the divorce agreement.

I asked Phil Abeles which of the married men he knew definitely had contact at one time or another with Karen Price. This was the sort of information a man is supposed to keep to himself, but the mores of Madison Avenue tend to foster subtle backstabbing. Abeles told me he knew for certain that Karen had been intimate with Harold Merriman, and he was almost sure about Joe Conn as well.

After Abeles left, I knocked the dottel out of my pipe and filled it again. I lit it, and as I shook out the match, I looked up at Harold Merriman.

A pudgy man with a bald spot and bushy eyebrows, 40 or 45, somewhat older than the rest of the crew. He sat down across the desk from me and narrowed his eyes. "Phil said you wanted to see me," he said. "What's the trouble?"

"Just routine," I smiled. "I need a little information. You knew Karen Price before the shooting, didn't you?"

"Well, I knew who she was."

Sure, I thought. But I let it pass and played him the way I had planned. I asked him who in the office had had anything to do with the dead girl. He hemmed and hawed a little, then told me that Phil Abeles had taken her out for dinner once or twice and that Jack Harris was supposed to have had her along on a business trip to Miami one week end. Strictly in a secretarial capacity, no doubt.

"And you?"

"Oh, no," Merriman said. "I'd met her, of course, but that was as far as it went."

"Really?"

The hesitation was admission enough. "Listen," he stammered, "all right, I . . . saw her a few times. It was nothing serious and it wasn't very recent. London—"

I waited.

"Keep it a secret, will you?" He forced a grin. "Write it off as a symptom of the foolish forties. She was available and I was ready to play around a little. I'd just as soon it didn't get out. Nobody around here knows, and I'd like to keep it that way." He hesitated again. "My wife knows. I was so damn ashamed of myself that I told her. But I wouldn't want the boys in the office to know."

I didn't tell him that they already knew, and that they had passed the information on to me.

Ray Powell came in grinning. He was a bachelor, and this made a difference. "Hello, London," he said. "I made it with the girl, if that's what you want to know."

"I heard rumors."

"I don't keep secrets," he said. He sprawled in the chair across from me and crossed one leg over the other. It was a relief to talk to someone other than a reticent, guilt-ridden adulterer.

He certainly looked like a Don Juan. He was 28, tall, dark and handsome, with wavy black hair and piercing brown eyes. A little prettier and he might have passed for a gigolo. But there was a slight hardness about his features that prevented this.

"You're working for Mark," he said.

"That's right."

He sighed. "Well, I'd like to see him wind up innocent, but from where I sit, it's hard to see it that way. He's a funny guy, London. He wants to have his cake and eat it, too. He wanted a marriage and he wanted a playmate. With the girl he was marrying, you wouldn't think he'd worry about playing around. Ever meet Lynn?"

"I've met her."

"Then you know what I mean."

I nodded. "Was she one of your conquests?"

"Lynn?" He laughed easily. "Not that girl. She's the pure type, London. The one-man woman. Mark found himself a sweet girl there. Why he bothered with Karen is beyond me."

I switched the subject to the married men in the office. With Powell, I didn't try to find out which of them had been intimate with Karen Price, since it seemed fairly obvious they all had. Instead I tried to ascertain which of them could be in trouble as a result of an affair with the girl.

I learned a few things. Jack Harris was immune to blackmail — his wife knew he cheated on her regularly and had schooled herself to ignore such indiscretions just as long as he returned to her after each rough passage through the turbulent waters of adultery.

Harold Merriman was sufficiently well-off financially so that he could pay a blackmailer indefinitely rather than quiet her by murder; besides, Merriman had already told me that his wife knew, and I was more or less prepared to believe him.

Both Abeles and Joe Conn were possibilities. Conn looked best of all. He wasn't doing very well in advertising but he could hold his job indefinitely—he had married a girl whose family ran one of Darcy and Bates' major accounts. Conn had no money of his own, and no talent to hold a job if his wife wised up and left him.

Of course, there was always the question of how valid Ray Powell's impressions were. *Lynn? She's the pure type. The one-man woman.*

That didn't sound much like the drunken blonde who had turned up on my doormat the night before.

Jack Harris revealed nothing new, merely reinforced what I had managed to pick up elsewhere along the line. I talked to him for 15 minutes or so. He left, and Joe Conn came into the room.

He wasn't happy. "They said you wanted to see me," he muttered. "We'll have to make it short, London. I've got a pile of work this afternoon and my nerves are jumping all over the place as it is."

The part about the nerves was something he didn't have to tell me. He didn't sit still, just paced back and forth like a lion in a cage before chow time.

I could play it slow and easy or fast and hard, looking to shock and jar. If he was the one who killed her, his nervousness now gave me an edge. I decided to press it.

I got up, walked over to Conn. A short stocky man, crew cut, no tie. "When did you start sleeping with Karen?" I snapped.

He spun around wide-eyed. "You're crazy!"

"Don't play games," I told him. "The whole office knows you were bedding her."

I watched him. His hands curled into fists at his sides. His eyes narrowed and his nostrils flared.

"What is this, London?"

"Your wife doesn't know about Karen, does she?"

"Damn you." He moved toward me. "How much, you bastard? A private detective," he snickered. "Sure you are. You're a damn blackmailer, London. How much?"

"Just how much did Karen ask for?" I said. "Enough to make you kill her?"

He answered with a left hook that managed to find the point of my chin and send me crashing back against the wall. There was a split second of blackness. Then he was coming at me again, fists ready, and I spun aside, ducked and planted a fist of my own in his gut. He grunted and threw a right at me. I took it on the shoulder and tried his belly again. It was softer this time. He wheezed and folded up. I hit him in the face and just managed to pull the punch at the last minute. It didn't knock him out— only spilled him on the seat of his tweed pants.

"You've got a good punch, London."

"So do you," I said. My jaw still ached.

"You ever do any boxing?"

"No."

"I did," he said. "In the Navy. I still try to keep in shape. If I hadn't been so angry I'd have taken you."

"Maybe."

"But I got mad," he said. "Irish temper, I guess. Are you trying to shake me down?"

"No."

"You don't honestly think I killed Karen, do you?"

"Did you?"

"God, no."

I didn't say anything.

"You think I killed her," he said hollowly. "You must be insane. I'm no killer, London."

"Of course. You're a meek little man."

"You mean just now? I lost my temper."

"Sure."

"Oh, hell," he said. "I never killed her. You got me mad. I don't like shakedowns and I don't like being called a murderer. That's all, damn you."

I called Jerry Gunther from a pay phone in the lobby. "Two things," I told the lieutenant. "First I think I've got a hotter prospect for you than Donahue. A man named Joe Conn, one of the boys at the stag. I tried shaking him up a little and he cracked wide open, tried to beat my brains in. He's got a good motive, too."

"Ed, listen—"

"That's the first thing," I said. "The other is that I've been trying to get in touch with my client for the past too-many hours and can't reach him. Did you have him picked up again?"

There was a long pause. All at once the air in the phone booth felt much too close. Something was wrong.

"I saw Donahue half an hour ago," Jerry said. "I'm afraid he killed that girl, Ed."

"He confessed?" I couldn't believe it.

"He confessed . . . in a way."

"I don't get it."

A short sigh. "It happened yesterday," Jerry said. "I can't give you the time until we get the medical examiner's report, but the guess is that it was just after we let him go. He sat down at his typewriter and dashed off a three-line confession. Then he stuck a gun in his mouth and made a mess. The lab boys are still there trying to scrape his brains off the ceiling. Ed?"

"What?"

"You didn't say anything . . . I didn't know if you were still on the line. Look, everybody guesses wrong some of the time."

"This was more than a guess. I was sure."

"Well, listen, I'm on my way to Donahue's place again. If you want to take a run over there you can have a look for yourself. I don't know what good it's going to do—"

"I'll meet you there," I said.

8

THE LAB CREW LEFT SHORTLY AFTER WE ARRIVED. "JUST A FOR-mality for the inquest," Jerry Gunther said. "That's all."

"You're sure it's suicide, then?"

"Stop dreaming, Ed. What else?"

What else? All that was left in the world of Mark Donahue was sprawled in a chair at a desk. There was a typewriter in front of him and a gun on the floor beside him. The gun was just where it would have dropped after a suicide shot of that nature. There were no little inconsistencies.

The suicide note in the typewriter was slightly incoherent. It read: *It has to end now. I can't help what I did but there is no way out any more. God forgive me and God help me. I am sorry.*

"You can go if you want, Ed. I'll stick around until they send a truck for the body. But—"

"Run over the timetable, will you?"

"From when to when?"

"From when you released him to when he died."

Jerry shrugged. "Why? You can't read it any way but suicide, can you?"

"I don't know. Give me a rundown."

"Let's see," he said. "You called around five, right?"

"Around then. Five or 5:30."

"We let him go around three. There's your timetable, Ed. We let him out around three, he came back here, thought about things for a while, then wrote that note and killed himself. That checks with the rough estimate we've got of the time of death. You narrow it down—you did call him after I spoke to you, didn't you?"

"Yes. No answer."

"He must have been dead by that time; probably killed himself within an hour after he got here."

"How did he seem when you released him?"

"Happy to be out, I thought at the time. But he didn't show much emotion one way or the other. You know how it is with a person who's getting ready to knock himself off. All the problems and emotions are kept bottled up inside."

I went over to a window and looked out at Horatio Street. It was the most obvious suicide in the world, but I couldn't swallow it. Call it a hunch, a stubborn refusal to accept the fact that my client had managed to fool me. Whatever it was, I didn't believe the suicide theory. It just didn't sit right.

"I don't like it," I said. "I don't think he killed himself."

"You're wrong, Ed."

"Am I?" I went to Donahue's liquor cabinet and filled two glasses with cognac.

"I know nothing ever looked more like suicide," I admitted. "But the motives are still as messy as ever. Look at what we got here. We have a man who hired me to protect him from his former mistress—and as soon as he did, he only managed to call attention to the fact that he was involved with her. He received threatening phone calls from her. She didn't want him married. But her best friend swears that the Price girl didn't give a damn about Donahue, that he was only another man in her collection."

"Look, Ed—"

"Let me finish. We can suppose for a minute that he was lying for reasons of his own that don't make much sense, that he had some crazy reason for calling me in on things before he knocked off the girl. Maybe he thought that would alibi him—"

"That's just what I was going to say," Jerry interjected.

"I thought of it. It doesn't make a hell of a lot of sense, but it's possible, I guess. Still, where in hell is his motive? Not blackmail. She wasn't the blackmailing type to begin with, as far as I can see. But there's more to it than that. Lynn Farwell wouldn't care who Mark slept with before they were married. Or after, for that matter. It wasn't a love match. She wanted a respectable husband and he wanted a rich wife, and they both figured to get what they wanted. Love wasn't part of it."

"Maybe he wasn't respectable," Jerry said. "Maybe Karen knew something he didn't want known. There's plenty of room here for a hidden motive, Ed."

"Maybe. Still I wish you'd keep the case open, Jerry."

"You know I won't."

"You'll write it off as suicide and close the file?"

"But I have to. All the evidence points that way. Murder and then suicide, with Donahue tagged for killing the Price girl and then killing himself."

"I guess it makes your bookkeeping easier."

"You know better than that, Ed." He almost sounded hurt. "If I could see it any other way I'd keep on it. I can't. As far as we're concerned it's a closed book."

I walked over to the window again. "I'm going to stay with it," I said.

"Without a client?"

"Without a client."

A maid answered the phone in the Farwell home. I asked to speak to Lynn.

"Miss Farwell's not home," she said. "Who's calling, please?"
I gave her my name.

"Oh, yes, Mr. London. "Miss Farwell left a message for you to call her at—" I took down a number with a Regency exchange, thanked her and hung up.

I was tired, unhappy and confused. I didn't want the role of bearer of evil tidings. I wished now that I had let Jerry tell her himself. I was in my apartment, it was a hot day for the time of the year, and my air conditioner wasn't working right. I dialed the number the maid had given me. A girl answered, not Lynn. I asked to speak to Miss Farwell.

She came on the line almost immediately, "Ed?"

"Yes—I."

"I wondered if you'd call. I hope I wasn't horrid last night. I was very drunk."

"You were all right."

"Just all right?" I didn't say anything. She giggled softly and whispered, "I had a good time, Ed. Thank you for a lovely evening."

"Lynn—"

"Is something the matter?"

I've never been good at breaking news. I took a deep breath and blurted out, "Mark is dead. I just came from his apartment. The police think he killed himself."

Silence.

"Can I meet you somewhere, Lynn? I'd like to talk to you."

More silence. Then, when she did speak, her voice was flat as week-old beer. "Are you at your apartment?"

"Yes."

"Stay there. I'll be right over. I'll take a cab."

The line went dead.

9

WHILE I WAITED FOR LYNN I THOUGHT ABOUT JOE CONN. IF ONE person murdered both Karen Price and Mark Donahue, Conn seemed the logical suspect. Karen was blackmailing him, I reasoned, holding him up for hush money that he had to pay if he wanted to keep wife and job. He found out Karen was going to be at the stag, jumping out of the cake, and he took a gun along and shot her.

Then Mark got arrested and Conn felt safe. Just when he was most pleased with himself, the police released Mark. Conn started to worry. If the case dragged out he was in trouble. Even if they didn't get to him, a lengthy investigation would turn up the fact that he had been sleeping with Karen. And he had to keep that fact hidden.

So he went to Donahue's apartment with another gun. He hit Mark over the head, propped him up in the chair, shot him through the mouth and replaced his own prints with Mark's. Then he dashed off a quick suicide note and got out of there. The blow on the head wouldn't show, if that was how he did it. Not after the bullet did things to Mark's skull.

But then why in hell did Conn throw a fit at the ad agency when I tried to ruffle him? It didn't make sense. If he had killed Mark on Sunday afternoon, he would know that it would be only a matter of time until the body was found and the case closed. He wouldn't blow up if I called him a murderer, not when he had already taken so much trouble to cover his tracks.

Unless he was being subtle, anticipating my whole line of reasoning. And when you start taking a suspect's possible subtlety into consideration, you find yourself on a treadmill marked confusion. All at once the possibilities become endless.

I got off the treadmill, though. The doorbell rang and Lynn Farwell stepped into my apartment for the third time in two days. And it occurred to me, suddenly, just how different each of those three visits had been.

This one was slightly weird. She walked slowly to the same leather chair in which she had curled up Saturday morning. She did not wax kittenish this time.

"I don't feel a thing," she said.

"Shock."

"No," she admitted. "I don't even feel shock, Ed. I just don't feel a thing.

"I wasn't in love with him," she said. "You knew that, of course."

"I gathered as much."

"It wasn't a well-kept secret, was it? I told you that much before I told you my name, almost. Of course I was on the make for you at the time. That may have had something to do with it."

She looked at her drink but didn't touch it. Slowly, softly she said, "After the first death there is no other."

There was a minute of silence. Just as I was about to prompt her into speaking, she repeated, "After the first death there is no other." She sighed. "When one death affects you completely, then the deaths that come after it don't have their full effect. Do you follow me?"

I nodded. "When did it happen?" I asked.

"Four years ago. I was in college then."

"A boy?"

"Yes."

She looked at her drink, then drained it.

"I was 19 then. Pure and innocent. A popular girl who dated all the best boys and had a fine time. Then I met him. Ray Powell introduced us. You probably met Ray. He worked in the same office as Mark."

I nodded. That explained one contradiction — Ray's referring to Lynn as the pure type, the one-man woman. When he had known her, the shoe fit. Since then she had outgrown it.

"I started going out with John and all at once I was in love. I had never been in love before. I've never been in love since. It was something." For a shadow of an instant a smile crossed her face, then disappeared. "I can't honestly remember what it was like. Being in love, that is. I'm not the same person. That girl could love; I can't.

"He was going to pick me up and something went wrong with his car. The steering wheel or something like that. He was going around a turn and the wheels wouldn't straighten out and —

"I changed after that. At first I just hurt. All over. And then the callous formed, the emotional callous to keep me from going crazy, I suppose." She picked up the cigarette and puffed on it nervously then stubbed it out. "You know what bothered me most? We never slept together. We were going to wait until we were married. See what a corny little girl I was?

"But I changed, Ed. I thought that at least I could have given him that much before he died. And I thought about that, and maybe brooded about it, and something happened inside me." She almost smiled. "I'm afraid I became a little bit of a tramp, Ed. Not just now and then, like last night. A tramp. I went to Ray Powell and lost my virginity, and then I made myself a one-woman welcoming committee for visiting Yale boys."

Her face filled up with memories. "I'm not that bad any more. And I don't honestly feel John's death either, to be truthful. It happened a long time ago, and to a different girl."

"I don't think Mark Donahue killed himself," I said, "or the girl. I think he was framed and then murdered."

"It doesn't matter."

"Doesn't it?"

"No," she said, sadly, vacantly. "It should, I know. But it doesn't, Ed." She stood up. "Do you know why I really wanted to come here?"

"To talk."

"Yes. I've learned to pretend, you see. And I intend to pretend, too. I'll be the very shocked and saddened Miss Farwell now. That's the role I have to play." Another too-brief smile. "But I don't have to play that role with you, Ed. I wanted to say what I felt if only to one person. Or what I didn't feel." She rose to leave.

"And now I'll wear imitation widow's weeds for a while, and then I'll find some other bright young man to marry. Goodby, Ed London."

I almost forgot about the date with Ceil. I'd made it the night before instead of the pass I would have preferred to make. When I got there, she said she was tired and hot and didn't feel like dressing.

"The Brittania is right down the block," she said. "And I can go there like this."

She was wearing slacks and a man's shirt. She didn't look mannish, though. That would have been slightly impossible.

We walked down the block to a hole in the wall with a sign that said, appropriately, FISH AND CHIPS. There was half a dozen small tables in a room decorated with travel posters of

Trafalgar Square and Buckingham Palace and every major British tourist attraction with the possible exception of Diana Dors. We sat at a small table and ordered fish-and-chips and bottles of Guinness.

I said, "Donahue's dead."

"I know. I heard it on the radio."

"What did they say?"

"Suicide. He confessed to the murder and shot himself. Isn't that what happened?"

"I don't think so." I signaled the waiter for two more bottles of Guinness.

"It's possible that someone—probably Conn—killed Donahue," I added. "The door to his apartment was locked when the police got there, but it's one of those spring locks. The inside bolt wasn't turned. Conn could have gone there as soon as he learned Mark was released, then shot him and locked the door as he left."

"How could he know Mark was released?"

"A phone call to police headquarters, or a call to Mark. That's no problem."

"How about the time? Maybe Conn has an alibi."

"I'm going to check that tomorrow," I said. "That's why I would have liked to see Jerry Gunther keep the file open on the case. Then he could have questioned Conn. The guy threw punches at me once already. I don't know if I can take him a second time."

She grinned. Then her face sobered. "Are you sure it was Conn? You said Abeles had the same motive."

"He's also got an alibi."

"A good one?"

"Damn good. I'm his alibi. I was with him in Scarsdale that afternoon, and I called Donahue's apartment as soon as I got back to town, and by that time Donahue was dead. Phil Abeles would have needed a jet plane to pull it off. Besides, I can't see him as the killer."

"And you can see Conn?"

"That's the trouble," I said. "I can't. Not really."

We drank up. I paid our check and we left. We walked a block to Washington Square and sat on a bench. I started to smoke my pipe when I heard a sharp intake of breath and turned to stare at Ceil.

"Oh," she said. "I just had a grisly idea."

"What?"

"It's silly. Like an Alfred Hitchcock television show. I thought maybe Karen really did make those phone calls to him, not because she was jealous but just to tease him, thinking what a gag it would be when she popped out of the cake at his bachelor dinner. And then the gag backfires and he shoots her because he's scared she wants to kill him." She laughed. "I've got a cute imagination," she said. "But I'm not much of a help, am I?"

I didn't answer her. My mind was off on a limb somewhere. I closed my eyes and saw the waiters wheeling the cake out toward the center of the room. Stripper music playing on a phonograph. A girl bursting from the cake, nude and lovely. A wide smile on her face—

"Ed, what's the matter?"

Most of the time problems are solved by simple trial and error, a lot of legwork that pays off finally. Other times all the legwork in the world falls flat, and it's like a jigsaw puzzle where you suddenly catch the necessary piece and all the others leap into place. This was one of those times.

"You're a genius!" I told Ceil.

"You don't mean it happened that way? I—"

"Oh, no. Of course not. Donahue didn't kill Karen—" I stood.

"Hey, where are you going?" Ceil asked.

"Gotta run," I said. "Can't even walk you home. Tomorrow," I said. "We'll have dinner, okay?"

I didn't hear her answer. I didn't wait for it. I raced across the park and jumped into the nearest cab.

I called Lynn Farwell from my apartment. She was back in her North Shore home, and life had returned to her voice. "I didn't expect to hear from you," she said. "I suppose you're interested in my body, Ed. It wouldn't be decent so soon after Mark's death, you know. But you may be able to persuade me—"

"Not your body," I said. "Your memory. Can you talk now? Without being overheard?"

She giggled lewdly. "If I couldn't, I wouldn't have said what I did. Go ahead, Mr. Detective."

I asked questions. She gave me answers. They were the ones I wanted to hear.

I strapped on a shoulder holster and jammed a gun into it.

10

THE DOOR TO POWELL'S APARTMENT WAS LOCKED. I RANG THE bell once. No one answered. I waited a few minutes, then took out my pen knife and went to work on the lock. Like the locks in all decent buildings in New York, this was one of the burglar-proof models. And, like just 99 per cent of them, it wasn't burglar-proof. It took half a minute to open.

I turned the knob. Then I eased the gun from my shoulder holster and shoved the door open. I didn't need the gun just then. The room was empty.

But the apartment wasn't. I heard noises from another room, people-noises, sex-noises. A man's voice and a girl's voice. The man was saying he heard somebody in the living room. The girl was telling him he was crazy. He said he would check. Then there were footsteps, and he came through the doorway, and I pointed the gun at him.

I said, "Stay right there, Powell."

He looked a little ridiculous. He was wearing a bathrobe, his feet were bare, and it was fairly obvious that he had been interrupted somewhere in the middle of his favorite pastime. I kept the gun on him and watched his eyes. He was good—damned good. The eyes showed fear, outrage, surprise. Nothing else. Not the look of a man in a trap.

"If this is some kind of a joke—"

"It's no joke."

"Then what the hell is it?"

"The end of the line," I said. "You made a hell of a try. You almost got away with it."

"I don't know what you're driving at, London. But—"

"I think you do."

She picked that moment to wander into the room. She was a redhead with her hair messed. One of the buttons on her blouse was buttoned wrong. She walked into the room, wondering aloud what the interruption was about, and then she saw the gun and her mouth made a little O.

She said, "Maybe I should of stood in the other room."

"Maybe you should go home," I snapped.

"Oh," she said. "Yes, that's a very good idea." She moved to her left and sort of backed around me, as if she wanted to keep as much distance as possible between her well-constructed body and the gun in my hand. "I think you're right," she said. "I think I should go home . . . And you don't have to worry about me."

"Good."

"I should tell you I have no memory at all," she said. "I never came here, never met you, never saw your face, and I cannot possibly remember what you look like. It is terrible, my memory."

"Good," I said.

"Living I like very much better then remembering. Goodby, Mr. Nobody."

The door slammed, and Ray Powell and I were alone. He glared at me.

"What in hell do you want, exactly?"

"To talk to you."

"You need a gun for that?"

"Probably."

He grinned disarmingly. "Guns make me nervous."

"They never did before. You've got a knack for getting hold of unregistered guns, Powell. Is there another one in the bedroom?"

"I don't get it," he said. He scratched his head. "You must mean something, London. Spit it out."

"Don't play games."

"I—"

"Cut it," I said. "You killed Karen Price. You knew she was going to do the cake bit because you were the one who put the idea in Phil Abeles' head."

"Did he tell you that?"

"He's forgotten. But he'll remember with a little prompting. You set her up and then you killed her and tossed the gun on the floor. You figured the polce would arrest Donahue, and you were right. But you didn't think they would let him go. When they did, you went to his place with another gun. He let you in. You shot him, made it look like suicide, and let the one death cover the other."

He shook his head in wonder. "You really believe this?"

"I know it."

"I suppose I had a motive," he said musingly. "What, pray tell, did I have against the girl? She was good in bed, you know. I make it a rule never to kill a good bed partner if I can help it." He grinned. "So why did I kill her?"

"You didn't have a thing against her," I said.

"My point exactly. I—"

"You killed her to frame Donahue," I added. "You got to Karen Price while the bachelor dinner was still in the planning stage. You hired her to make a series of calls to Donahue, jealousy calls threatening to kill him or otherwise foul up his wedding. It was going to be a big joke—she would scare him silly; and then for a capper she would pop out of the cake as naked as the truth and tell him she was just pulling his leg.

"But you topped the gag. She popped out of the cake covered with a smile and you put a bullet in her and left Donahue looking like the killer. Then, when you thought he was getting off the hook, you killed him. Not to cover the first murder—you felt safe enough on that score . . . because you really didn't have a reason to kill the girl herself. You killed Donahue because he was the one you wanted dead all along."

Powell was still grinning. Only not so self-assuredly now. In the beginning, he hadn't been aware of how much I knew. Now he was learning and it wasn't making him happy.

"I'll play your game," he said. "I killed Karen, even though I didn't have any reason. Now why did I kill Mark? Did I have a reason for that one?"

"Sure."

"What?"

"For the same reason you hired Karen to bother Donahue," I said. "Maybe a psychiatrist could explain it better. He'd call it transference."

"Go on."

"You wanted Mark Donahue dead because he was going to marry Lynn Farwell. And you don't want anybody to marry Lynn Farwell. Powell, you'd kill anybody who tried."

"Keep talking," he said.

"How am I doing so far?"

"Oh, you're brilliant, London. I suppose I'm in love with Lynn?"

"In a way."

"That's why I've never asked her to marry me. And why I bed down anything else that gets close enough to jump."

"That's right."

"You're out of your mind, London."

"No," I said. "But you are." I took a breath. "You've been in love with Lynn for a long time. Four years, anyway. It's no normal love, Powell, because you're not a normal person. Lynn's part of a fixation of yours. She's sweet and pure and unattainable in your mind. You don't want to possess her completely because that would destroy the illusion. Instead you compensate by proving your virility with any available girl. But you can't let Lynn marry someone else. That would take her away from you. You don't want to have her — except for an occasional evening, maybe — but you won't let anyone else have her."

He was tottering on the edge now . . . trying to take a step toward me and then backing off. I had to push him over that edge. If he cracked, then he would crack wide open. If he held himself together he might wriggle free. I knew damn well he was guilty, but there wasn't enough evidence to present to a jury. I had to make him crack.

"First I'm a double murderer," Powell said. "Now I'm a mental case. I don't deny that I like Lynn. She's a sweet, clean, decent girl. But that's as far as it goes."

"Is it?"

"Yes."

"Donahue's the second man who almost married her. The first one was four years ago. Remember John? You introduced the two of them. That was a mistake, wasn't it?"

"He wouldn't have been good for her. But it didn't matter. I suppose you know he died in a car accident."

"In a car, yes. Not an accident. You gimmicked the steering wheel. Then you let him kill himself. You got away clean with that one, Powell."

I hadn't cracked him yet. I was close, but he was still able to compose himself.

"It was an accident," he exclaimed. "Besides, it happened a long time ago. I'm surprised you even bother mentioning it."

I ignored his words. "The death shook Lynn up a lot," I said. "It must have been tough for you to preserve your image of her. The sweet and innocent thing turned into a round-heeled little nymph for a while."

"That's a damned lie."

"It is like hell. And about that time you managed to have your cake and eat it, too. You kept on thinking of her as the unattainable ideal. But that didn't stop you from taking her virginity, did it? You ruined her, Powell!"

He was getting closer to the edge. His face was white and his hands were hard little fists. The muscles in his neck were drumtight.

"I never touched her!"

"Liar!" I was shouting now. "You ruined that girl, Powell!"

"Damn you, I never touched her! Nobody did, damn you! She's still a virgin! She's still a virgin!"

I took a breath. "The hell she is," I yelled. "I had her last night, Powell. She came to my room all hot to trot and I bedded her until she couldn't see straight."

His eyes were wild.

"Did you hear me, Powell? I had *your girl* last night. I had Lynn, Powell!"

And that cracked him.

He charged me like a wild man, his whole body coordinated in the spring. I stepped back, swung aside. He tried to turn and come toward me but his momentum kept him from pulling it off. By the time he got back on the right track, my hand had gone up and come down. The barrel of the gun caught him just behind the left ear. He took two more little steps, carried along by the sheer force of his rush. Then, he folded up and went out like an ebbing tide.

He wasn't out long. By the time Jerry Gunther got there, flanked by a pair of uniformed cops, Powell was babbling away a mile a minute, spending half the time confessing to the three murders and the other half telling anyone who would listen that Lynn Farwell was a saint.

They started to put handcuffs on him. Then they changed their minds and bundled him up in a straitjacket.

11

"I GUESS I MISSED MY CALLING," CEIL SAID. "I SHOULD HAVE BEEN a detective. I probably would have flopped there, too, but the end might have been different. We all know what girls become when they don't make it as actresses. What do lousy detectives turn to?"

"Cognac," I said. "Pass the bottle."

She passed and I poured. We were in her apartment on Sullivan Street. It was Tuesday night, Ray Powell had long since finished confessing, and Ceil Gorski had just proved to me that she could cook a good meal.

"You figured it out beautifully," she said. "But do I get an assist on the play?"

"Easily." I tucked tobacco into my pipe, lit up. "You managed to get my mind working. Powell was a genius at murder. A certifiable psychotic, but also a genius. He set things up beautifully. First of all, the frame couldn't have been neater. He very carefully set up Donahue with means, motive and opportunity. Then he shot the girl and left Donahue on the hook."

I worked on the cognac. "The neat thing was this — if Donahue managed to have an alibi, if by some chance somebody was watching him when the shot was fired, Powell was still in the clear. He himself was one of the few men in the room with no conceivable motive for wanting Karen Price dead."

Ceil moved a little closer on the couch. I put an arm around her. "Then the way he got rid of Donahue was sheer perfection," I continued. "He made it look enough like suicide to close the case as far as the police were concerned. And Jerry Gunther isn't an easy man to bulldoze. He's thorough. But Powell made it look good."

"You didn't swallow it."

"That's because I play hunches. Even so, I was up a tree by

then. Because the murder had a double edge to it. Even if he muffed it somehow, even if it didn't go over as suicide, Donahue would be dead and he would be in the clear. Because there was only one way to interpret it—Donahue had been killed by the man who killed Karen Price, obviously, and had been killed so that the original killing would go unsolved. That made me suspect Joe Conn and never let me guess at Powell, not even on speculation. Even with the second killing he hid the fact that Donahue and not Karen was the real target."

"And that's where I came in," she said happily.

"That's exactly where you came in," I agreed. "You and your active imagination. You thought how grim it would be if Karen had only been playing a joke with those phone calls. And that was the only explanation in the world for the calls. I had to believe Donahue was getting the calls, and that Karen was making them. A disguised voice might work once, but she'd called him a few times."

"That left two possibilities, really. She could be jealous—which seemed contrary to everything I had learned about her. Or it could be a gag. But if she was jealous, then why in hell would she take the job popping out of the cake? So it had to be a gag, and once it was a gag, I had to guess why someone would put her up to it. And from that point—"

"It was easy."

"Uh-huh. It was easy."

She snuggled closer. I liked her perfume. I liked the feel of her body beside me.

"It wasn't that easy," she said. "You know what? I think you're a hell of a good detective. And you know what else?"

"What?"

"I also think you're a rotten businessman."

I smiled. "Why?"

"Because you did all that work and didn't make a dime out of it. You got a retainer from Donahue, but that didn't even cover all the time you spent *before* Karen was killed, let alone the time since then. And you probably will never collect."

"I'm satisfied."

"Because justice has been done?"

"Partly. Also because I'll be rewarded."

She upped her eyebrows. "How? You won't make another nickel out of the case, will you?"

"No."

"Then—"

"I'll make something more important than money."

"What?"

She was soft and warm beside me. And it was our third evening together. Not even an amateur tramp could mind a pass on a third date.

"What are you going to make?" she asked, innocently.

I took her face between my hands and kissed her. She closed her eyes and purred like a happy cat.

"You," I said.

John D. MacDonald

COLLEGE-CUT KILL

John Dann MacDonald (1916–1986) was one of my heroes. I first read him in the early Fifties (Dead Low Tide; I was thirteen years old). I couldn't have articulated back then why the book was so special to me. But I reread it recently—it holds up marvelously—and now I can articulate it.

He was able to bring the working-class and the lower middle-class into the crime novel. As much as I love the paperback boys of that era—Day Keene, for example—their characters never exhibited much reality. Not that I could recognize anyway.

I grew up in the great years of America—great if you were white, your father gainfully employed and sober more often than not—a world of cars with fins, backyard barbeques, Jackie Gleason on Saturday nights, and girls even cuter than the ones on American Bandstand. Those were the days.

And it was this shared reality that MacDonald brought to his novels and short stories. He learned it gradually. Reading his earliest work, you see that his focus was as narrow as most other pulp writers. These were people in stories—not people you met in everyday life. But little by little, real people started showing up in his stories. And you coupled that with the best storytelling skills of his generation . . . well, fame and fortune weren't far away.

He was, in the best sense, an American who spoke for the middle-class and for his time. His people weren't all drifters and ex-cons and hoods, as they were in most crime novels. They were engineers and car salesmen and lawyers and housewives and high school students and doctors.

That's why his paperbacks sold by the millions. Because you were in his books. He was writing about your dad and mom and sister and neighbors. People you wanted to emulate, people you loved, people you hated, people who scared you.

But always people you knew. If you want a deft sociological por-

trait of America in 1955, read Cry Hard, Cry Fast. *Sinclair Lewis never wrote as well or intelligently.*

His Travis McGee novels made him world-famous. I like them but I never loved them the way I did One Monday We Killed Them All *or* Soft Touch *or* The Neon Jungle *or* The Damned *or* Who Killed Janice Gantry *or* The End of the Night *or so many other of his paperback originals. Buy them. I think you'll see what I mean.*

Here is John D. MacDonald from his pulp days. He was damned good even then.

E.G.

1

Brethern, Here's to Death!

IT WAS HALF PAST TWELVE ON ONE OF THOSE EARLY SEPTEMBER days in Manhattan when the streets are Dutch ovens and a girl who can look crisp is a treasure indeed. I was completing the last draft of the current three-part blast, with Dolly sitting at my elbow noting the changes I wanted.

Miss Riven came in simultaneously with her crisp rap at the door, and said, "Mr. Engelborg wishes to see you immediately, Mr. Arlin."

She did a Prussian drill-sergeant's about-face and went back through the door, shutting it with a crisp clack that only Miss Riven can seem to get out of a door.

"Her!" Dolly said. "Her!" She made it sound like a dirty name.

"She thinks I work here," I said. During the six weeks that I had been provided with office space and Dolly, she and I had become good friends. "Look, lovely. I can't see anything more we need. Type it up with three carbons and get one over to the legal eagles for checking."

I hesitated, decided against my coat, and went down through the offices full of common people to the shrine where Engelborg, the almighty, flings his weight around.

Miss Riven gave me a cool look, glanced at her watch and said, "You may go right in, Mr. Arlin."

I pushed the door open. Engelborg, who looks like a giant blond panda, said, "This is Arlin. Joe, meet Mr. Flynn."

Flynn merely nodded but he stared at me intently. He was a big, sagging man in his late fifties with an executive air about him. There was a bloodhound sadness about his eyes.

"Arlin," said Engelborg, "is just finishing up a hot series on real estate swindles."

"It's all done," I said. "Ought to be out of the typewriter tomorrow. That is, if the lawyers have no kick."

"Good," Engelborg grunted. "I want you to understand, Mr. Flynn, that Arlin isn't a part of this organization. He works on a free-lance basis and this particular job was so hot we wanted him right here so we could coordinate more closely. What are your plans, Joe?"

I didn't like the sound of that. I said, "I am going to wait until I get page proofs on the first installment and then I am going to go to Maine."

"I understand," Flynn said, "that you're out of college two years. The University of Wisconsin. You were a Gamma U there?"

"That's right." I couldn't smell which way this was going. Flynn looked at me as though he resented me in a tired way.

"He looks young enough, doesn't he?" Engleborg said.

Flynn nodded.

That has been a sore point with me. When I was twenty I looked fifteen. Now, at twenty-eight, I look twenty. Professionally that has its limitations. Emotionally it's all right. I play on their maternal instincts.

"So I look young," I said. "Gee, thanks."

"Take it easy, Joe," Engelborg said. "Real easy. Don't get upset. How'd you like to go to college?"

"Thanks, I've been."

Flynn spoke heavily. "Let me talk, Arlin. My son is dead. He died last June at the age of nineteen. Everyone says he hung himself. I went down there. He was at West Coast University in Florida. I cannot believe he hung himself. He was a Gamma U. Other boys in that house died last year. In different ways. Automobiles. One drowned. Too many died. I cannot get help from the police. A private investigation firm would be too heavy-handed.

"Mr. Engelborg has been my good friend for many years. Last night I talked to him about this. He mentioned you. We discussed it. I want to pay you to go down and register for this fall term which starts very soon. I have certain influence and so does Engelborg. It can be arranged. We have a friend at the University of Wisconsin. The first three years of your credits will be transferred so you can enter as a senior. I know the secretary of the national chapter of Gamma U. There will be no trouble from that end."

I sat down. I kept my voice as calm and logical as I could. "Mr. Flynn, I appreciate your problem. There are many inexplicable suicides among young people."

"Teddy did not kill himself. I know that. I must have it proven. I have two other boys, younger boys. I don't want this thing hanging over them."

"Which would be better? Suicide or murder? If it isn't one it's the other."

"Suicide is a sign of basic weakness. Teddy was not weak. I want you to go down there and live in that house and find out what happened." He was as positive and undeniable as an avalanche.

I appealed to Mr. Engelborg. "Look, that isn't my line. I find things out to write them up."

Engelborg said, "You've done some very slick investigatory work, Joe. Those dock gangs, the Bermuda dope setup."

"I'm my own man," I said. "I do what I please."

"That's right, Joe," Engelborg said.

"I don't want to go to college. I want to go to Maine. Brother, it's hot down there now. I'm tired. I want to go fishing."

"You'll wonder," Flynn said, "all the rest of your life. You'll wonder what kind of a thing you might have uncovered. What kind of a twisted, diseased thing it is that causes the deaths of fine young boys."

"I won't do it," I said.

"You will be paid all expenses, plus a thousand a month plus a bonus of five thousand when it is all over, no matter what your conclusion is."

"I hate Florida," I said.

* * *

The blue gulf sparkled on my right as I drove south. The sun glinted off the chrome of the convertible, needling through the dark glasses. My luggage was stacked in the back end and I had not had to change to kollege kut klothes because the veterans pretty much took that aspect out of higher education. I had been one myself, the navy taking out a four-year chunk so that I got out when I had turned twenty-six.

The town of Sandson where the university was located turned out to be half on the mainland and half on a long island connected to the mainland by a half-mile public causeway. The university was inland from the mainland half of the town, perched on a hill a hundred feet high — which made it a mountain in that locality.

The timing was good and I arrived on the last day of registration. I dumped cash and traveler's checks into the Sandson National Bank and drove east along the wide main drag. The university turn-off was to the right just beyond the city limits. A curving road led up to the haphazard collection of Moorish, Neo-Gothic, Spanish and Twentieth Century Lavatory construction. The bright young girls walked and cycled by in their thin dresses, brown legs flashing, eyes measuring me and the car for possible future reference.

I told myself this was a wild goose chase, a big mistake, a bunch of wasted time. I told myself again. Then I stopped telling myself. It was too much fun dropping back into the college frame of mind. But this time I was doing it the way I wished I had been able to do it at Wisconsin. At Wisconsin I had been knocking myself out, wondering how tough it would be to make a living later. Here I was getting paid for the deal.

Temporary cardboard signs were tacked up, pointing the way to Administration and Registration. I parked beside the indicated building, took the transcript of my three years out of the glove compartment and went in. There were tables with people working at them, filling out the desired schedules of classes. I took one of the catalogues and one of the blanks and went to work. I laid out six courses.

Literature IV (Creative Writing), Psychology VIII (Abnormal), Philosophy III (Ethics), Political Science VI (Ecology of nations) Modern History II (1914–1950). Lastly, I dipped for an elective into the Business School, Accounting I (Basic Methods), because

I have never been able to see quite eye to eye with the Collector of Internal Revenue.

Then I joined the line leading to the window titled A to K. The young lady was very crisp. I gave the name we had agreed on—Rodney J. Arlin. It's my name. The one my stuff has been published under is R. Joseph Arlin, and we thought the name might be just a shade too familiar to the reading public of one certain large magazine.

She checked her card file. "Arlin, Rodney J. We have you listed as a transfer. You have your transcript?" I handed it over. She checked it carefully.

"We can give you full credit for the hours shown here, and admit you as a senior. As a senior you are not restricted to living on the campus. Do you have a place to live yet?"

"Not yet."

"Advise us immediately when you have an address. Your schedule is approved. Tuition will be three eighty-five for each semester. Yes, a check is acceptable. Take one of the getting acquainted bulletins as you leave. They're on that far table. Class hours and rooms are posted on all bulletin boards. Compulsory meeting tomorrow morning at nine. As a senior you will attend the meeting in the Science Building auditorium. Next, please."

I found the cafeteria, had a quick lunch and went off in search of the brethren. I found them in a rambling Miami-type house of cinderblock, with a big overhang to kill the heat of the sun, sprinklers turning lazily on the green lawn. There was a parking area to the left of the house with a dozen cars lined up in it, eight of them convertibles of recent vintage. I parked and went around to the front. The door was open. The interior looked dim and invitingly cool.

I punched the bell and stepped inside. Two of the brethren came into the hallway and stared at me curiously, warily. One, with heavy bone-structure, I immediately type-cast as a working guard or tackle. The other was the smooth-dan type that inhabits all major fraternities. Careful, casual, a shade haughty and a bit too handsome.

I picked him to slip the grip to. "Brother Arlin," I announced. "Beta chapter at Wisconsin. Just transferred here as a senior."

He looked slightly pained. "Nice to see you, Arlin. I'm Bradley Carroll and this is Brother Siminik."

He was giving me the inch-by-inch survey—and I knew right then that it was a political house. By that I mean one with cliques, possibly two strong ones. Bradley was trying to decide whether I'd be any addition to his clique, or whether I might be permitted to join the other as dead weight. We were like a couple of dogs that circle each other, stiff-legged.

I sighed inwardly. The next move was too obvious. "I put my wagon in the parking area. Hope it's all right there." I took out a pack and offered him a cigarette. Siminik refused it. I lighted Bradley Carroll's with a gold lighter, wide-ribbed, a thing I would never buy for myself, but something that a girl named Ann thought I ought to have.

"You drove down?" he asked politely. "*Where from?*" is what he was trying to say.

"From New York. Three days on the road."

"Oh, you live in New York?"

"No, I just took a place there for the summer. Everybody says it's a hell of a place to spend a summer. Not me."

He was still wary, but warmer. "Say, we're being pretty inhospitable, Arlin. Come on back to my room."

It was an exceedingly pleasant room. The bottle on the coffee table was the very best bourbon. Siminik wasn't drinking. Carroll mixed me a stiff one. He kept his good-looking slightly bovine eyes on me during our casual talk. I let him know without saying as much that I had no financial worries, that I was neither an athlete nor a bookworm, that I intended to sandwich a very good series of very good times in between the necessary study.

We went through the slightly oriental ceremonies until it was time to come to the point. "Would you recommend living in the house?" I asked.

He hadn't expected the question that way. "It's . . . very pleasant. The food is good." He suddenly realized that he was on the defensive, an unthinkable position. "But of course," he said quickly, "I can't say whether there'd be room for you. I mean a private room, of course."

"The house is too small?"

"Not that. Seniors are entitled to private rooms if they wish to live in the house. Juniors go two to a room and sophomores bunk in the dorm. There are only eight private rooms and all those are spoken for this semester."

Siminik said, "Brad, the room that Flynn was going to—"

Brad Carroll said hastily, "Quent is taking that one, Al. I thought you knew."

"Somebody drop out?" I asked very casually.

"No," Siminik said, "he—"

"—won't be here this year," Carroll said.

I let it go. No point in pushing.

"You'll have to see Arthur Marris anyway," Brad Carroll said. "He's house president and he handles the quarters problem. You might care to bunk with one of the juniors. That's been done before and I think there's one vacancy."

I yawned. "I don't know as I want to stay in the house anyway. I want to look around first. Maybe I can get some sort of a layout on the beach."

On the beach," said Al Siminik, "it is like there's a river of oil under the pier."

Brad looked at him as though he had a rude noise in public. He gave me an apologetic glance that said, "*What else do you expect from knuckled-headed athletes?*"

As I was leaving, promising to be back for dinner, I met two more of the brethren, one a shy, blond likeable sophomore named Ben Charity with a Georgia accent, the other a lean, hot-eyed, dark-haired, less-likeable junior named Bill Armand. I got over to the beach part of Sandson at about three-thirty. I found a small rental office inhabited by a vast, saggy female with an acid tongue.

"How much can you go for?" she said without hesitation. "If you want it through the winter it'll come high. From now until Christmas I can find you something for peanuts."

We went in my car to three places. I went back and took the second one, mostly because of its isolation. Bedroom, bath and kitchen made one side of an L and the living room made the other side. The L enclosed a small stone patio overlooking the gulf. It was sparkling new, completely furnished, and though the gulf front lot was small, a high thick hedge on either side kept the neighbors out. The car port was at the rear and it was ample protection against salt mist off the gulf. Two-eighty a month until the end of December. Four hundred after that.

I paid my two months in advance, unpacked, raided a package

store for all the necessities, bought a typing table and still had time for a dip in the warm gulf before dressing to run back over to dine amid the brethren.

The house was noisy when I went in. In the lounge somebody had racked a bunch of very poor bop on the machine. There was laughing and shouting going on back in the bedroom wing. Suitcases were stacked in the hall. Through the doorway to the dining room I could see the waiters setting the big table in the middle, the smaller tables around the walls.

A little redheaded sophomore with the face of an angel collared me. "Are you Brother Arlin? Come on with me. Brother Carroll said to wait for you and take you back to his room."

I told him I could find it and went back by myself. Brother Carroll was being the merry host. He smiled at me with what I guessed was his nearest approach to friendliness and steered me over to a tall boy. I found myself liking him immediately. He had gauntness and deep-set eyes and a firm-lipped wide sensitive mouth. He was older than the others.

"I'm Arthur Marris," he said. "I'm glad to know you, Arlin. You do have a first name."

I swallowed hard and said it. "Rodney. Rod, usually."

Siminik was there, drinking gingerale, and another senior named Step Krindall, a bulging, pink, prematurely bald boy.

"Martini all right?" Brad asked. I nodded and took the cool cocktail glass he handed me.

"I think we'll be able to make you comfortable if you'd like to move into the house, Rod," Arthur Marris said.

"I can see you're pretty crowded and I'm an outsider," I said. "I've taken a place on the beach. Turn left at The Dunes. Right at the end of the road. I see no reason why it can't be the Gamma U annex."

Arthur Marris looked a little hurt. He glanced at his watch. "One more round and then we'd better go in," he said.

The names and faces were slightly blurred at dinner. I knew I'd get a chance to straighten them out later. The cliques began to straighten out in my mind. Brad Carroll, with Siminik as a stooge, ran the opposition to Arthur Marris. The controlling group in the fraternity during the past years had been composed of veterans. Marris was one of the last of them in school. Bald-headed Step Krindall and Marris were the only two left in the house.

Brad Carroll was the leader of the group trying to get the reins of authority back into the hands of the younger nonveteran group. His biggest following was among the sophomores. Better than half the seniors and almost half the juniors seemed allied with Marris. With enough voting strength, Brad Carroll could effectively grab the power from Marris this year, even though Marris would retain the title as president of the house.

I found that there were thirty-three members. Ten seniors, nine juniors and fourteen sophomores. They hoped to take in fifteen freshmen who would not be permitted to live in a house until their sophomore year. Of the active members living in the house, eight were seniors, seven were juniors and ten were sophomores. My presence brought the number of seniors up to eleven.

After dinner, much to Brad's poorly concealed concern, Arthur Marris took me off to his room. Daylight was fading. He lit his pipe, the match flare flickering on his strong features.

"How do you like the chapter?" he asked.

"Fine. Fine! Of course, I'm not acquainted yet, but everything seems—"

"You're not a kid, Rod. You don't handle yourself like a kid. You spoke of the navy at dinner. How old are you?"

"Twenty-six," I said, chopping off a couple of years.

"I'm twenty-five. I can talk to you as man to man. That sounds corny, doesn't it? I want to ask you if you've noticed the tension. I can feel it. It's all underneath, you know. I brought you in here to talk to you about it. Part of my job is to protect the reputation of the chapter. You'll make friends outside the house. They'll gossip. I prefer that you hear the bad things from me, not from outsiders."

I shrugged. "So the boys get a little rough sometimes. Is that serious?"

"This is something else. This is a jinxed house, Rod. I want to tell you a little about last year. I was a junior. The house president was a senior named Harv Lorr. In October, just as the rushing season was about to begin, two sophomores on their way back from Tampa rolled a car. Both of them were killed."

I whistled softly. "A tough break."

"That's what we all thought. Just before Christmas vacation one of my best friends went on a beach party. His body was washed up two days later."

"Accidents in a row like that aren't too unusual."

His voice was grim. "In March a boy, a senior, named Tod Sherman, was alone in his room. The guess is that he was cleaning his gun, an army .45. It was against the rules to have it in the house. His door wasn't locked. It went off and killed him."

"Maybe they come in threes."

"In June, during the last week of school, one of the most popular kids in the house hung himself. A boy named Teddy Flynn. He was a senior, a very bright boy. He was graduating a week before his twentieth birthday. He hung himself in this room. I took it for this term because no one else wanted it. He used heavy copper wire and fastened it to a pipe that runs across the ceiling of that clothes closet."

It bothered me to think that it had happened in this room. It made the whole situation less of an an academic problem. It made me realize that I had taken a smart-alec attitude from the beginning. Now that was gone. There was a tangible feeling of evil. I could taste it in the back of my throat.

"Let me get this straight, Arthur. Why are you telling me this?"

"One, two or three deaths might be written off as accident and coincidence. I think five can too, in this case. But outsiders don't see it that way. They think it's fishy."

"Do the police?"

"Oh, no. I didn't mean that responsible people consider it fishy. The kids in the other houses do. By next year, it will all be forgotten. The transient population will take care of that. But this year is going to be rough. It'll affect our pledge total. There'll be a lot of whispering. For those inside the group it'll mean a stronger unifying force, I suppose. I thought you, as a senior transfer, should know all this."

"Why did the Flynn boy kill himself?"

"We'll never really know, I guess. His gal was really broken up. She was a junior last year."

"Did she come back?"

"I saw her at registration. Her name is Mathilda Owen. Tilly. You'll probably run into her sooner or later. This is a big school, but she'll travel in our group, I imagine."

"The five boys that died, Arthur. Outside of their being members of the fraternity, is there anything else to tie the five of them together?"

"No. Nothing."

"Teddy Flynn hung, Tod Sherman shot, two sophomores killed in a car and one unnamed guy drowned."

"That's it. The boy who drowned was Rex Winniger. The sophomores were Harry Welly and Ban Forrith. It was . . . a pretty bad year here."

"I can imagine."

He leaned over and put on the desk lamp. Evil was thrust back into the far shadows. He smiled without humor and said, "There had better not be any accidents this term."

I made myself laugh. "Hell, all the accidents for the next ten years are used up now. We're over the quota."

2

Axes to Grind

THE CREATIVE WRITING DEAL MET ONCE A WEEK FOR A TWO-HOUR session, Friday from ten to twelve. It was taught by a dry but pompous little man who, the year before, had hit one of the book clubs with a novel that had little to recommend it but the incredible size of the heroine from the waist up and the frenzy with which she met all emotional experiences.

Tilly Owen was in the class. I located her at the first session, a tallish dark-haired girl, almost plain. Her face showed nothing and I was disappointed in her. She took notes meekly, her dark head bent over the notebook. But when she walked out, I did a quick revision. The tall body had an independent life of its own. Her face showed a clear and unspectacular intelligence, an aloofness—but the body was devious and complicated and intensely feminine, continually betraying the level eyes. She went off with a few other girls before I could make an intercept.

During the week leading to the next session when I saw her again, I enlarged my circle of friends inside the fraternity. Brad Carroll thawed a great deal, particularly after I had a few of them out to the beach house for cocktails. I began to learn more about the insides of the brethren.

Step Krindall, with the baby blue eyes and the pink head, was as uncomplicated and amiable as a dancing bear. Arthur Marris had too deep a streak of seriousness in him, verging on self-importance. His touch was thus a shade too heavy. The better house president knows when to use a light touch. Every house has its types. Bill Armand, the dark, vital junior was the house skeptic, the cynic, the scoffer. Ben Charity, the shy blond Georgia boy was the gullible one, the butt of most practical jokes. The angel-faced redheaded sophomore named Jay Bruce was the house clown. There was the usual sullen, heavy-drinking kid on his way off the rails—one Ralph Schumann, a senior.

The rest of them seemed to merge into one composite type, a bunch of well-washed young men in a stage in their development when clothes, women, snap courses and hard-boiled books had a bit too much importance. They talked easily and well, made perhaps a shade too confident by their acceptance into one of the most socially acceptable groups on the campus. And, in many ways, they were exceedingly silly, as the young of any species is likely to be.

Their silliness pointed up the vast gulf that my two years out of college had opened up. I could see that in their group mind I was becoming rated as one hell of a fellow, a quick guy with a buck, a citizen who could handle his liquor, keep his mouth shut.

I found that I had not lost the study habit. Necessary research during the two intervening years had kept me from losing the knack. The courses were amazingly stimulating. I had expected boredom, but found intellectual excitement.

On Friday came the second writing class. As per instructions, the entire class had done a short-short apiece and dropped it off on the previous Wednesday at the instructor's office.

He gave us a long beady stare and we became silent. "I should like to read one effort handed in," he said. He began to read. I flushed as I recognized my own masterwork. I had banged one out with an attempt to give him the amateur stuff he expected.

He finished it and put it carefully aside. "I shall not tell you who wrote that. I read it because you should all find it interesting. I do not care to be laughed at. That story had complete professional competence. No doubt of that. And it is a devilishly clever parody of the other stories that were turned in. It is a tongue-in-cheek attempt to cover the entire scope of the errors that beginners make.

"Yet the perpetrator of this—this fraud, could not conceal his ability, his very deft turn of phrase and control of emotion. I am mystified as to why he or she should be taking my course. I suggest to this unnamed person that he or she give me credit, next time, for a bit more intelligence."

I shot a wary look to either side. No one was watching me. I forced myself to relax. Another dumb stunt like that and I would destroy my purpose, if I hadn't done so already. . . .

At noon I elbowed my way through the mob and went down the steps behind Tilly Owen. I fell into step beside her and said, "My name is Rod Arlin, Miss Owen." I gave her the very best smile. "I offer lunch, an afternoon on the beach, early dinner in Tampa, and a few wagers on the canines at Derby Lane."

She quickened her pace. "Please, no."

"I come well-recommended. Arthur Marris will vouch for me."

"I have a date."

I caught her arm above the elbow and turned her around. Anger flashed clear in her gray eyes.

"And a Mr. Flynn in New York considers me to be a bright kid, if that means anything."

The anger faded abruptly and her eyes narrowed. "If this is some sort of a—"

"Come on. My car's parked over in the lot behind Administration." I gestured.

She sat demurely beside me in the car. I parked in front of her sorority house. She dropped off her books, changed to a pale green nylon dress beautifully fitted at the waist and across the lyre-shaped flare of her hips, and came back out to the car with swim suit and beach case in an astonishing twenty minutes. She even smiled at me as I held the door for her.

At lunch she said, "Now don't you think you ought to tell me why . . ."

"Not yet. Let's just get acquainted for now."

She smiled again, and I wondered how I had managed to think of her as plain. I got her talking about herself. She was twenty-two, orphaned when she was eighteen. A trust fund administered by an uncle was paying for the education. During the summer she had gone north to work at a resort hotel. She adored steaks, detested sea food, kept a diary, lived on a budget, hated the movies, adored walking, wore size eight quad A shoes and thought the fraternity and sorority system to be feudal and foul.

She gave me a surprised look. "I don't talk like this to strangers! Really, I'm usually very quiet. You have quite a knack, Rod. You're a listener. I never would have thought so to look at you."

"What do I look like?"

She cocked her head to the side and put one finger on the cleft in her chin. "Hmmm! Pretty self-satisfied. Someone who'd talk about himself rather than listen. And you're older than I thought. I never noticed until just now those little wrinkles at the corners of your eyes. Quite cold eyes, really. Surprisingly cold."

"Warm heart."

"Silly, that goes with hands not eyes."

We drove out to the beach. She was neither awed by nor indifferent to my layout. "You should be very comfortable here," she said.

The sun bounced off the white sand with a hard glare. I spread the blanket, fiddled with the portable radio until I found an afternoon jazz concert. The gulf was glassy. It looked as if it had been quieted with a thick coat of blue oil. Porpoise played lazily against the horizon and two cruisers trolled down the shore line. Down by the public beach the water was dotted with heads.

She came across the little terrace and down across the sand wearing a yellow print two-piece suit. Her body was halfway between the color of honey and toast, fair, smooth and unblemished. I rolled onto my elbows and stared at her. It put a little confusion into her walk, a very pleasing shyness—with the mind saying don't and the body saying look. That kind of a girl. That very precious kind of a girl.

"Well!" I said. She made a face at me.

She sat on the blanket, poured oil into the palm of her hand and coated herself. We lay back, the radio between us, our eyes shut, letting the frank Florida sun blast and stun and smother us with a glare that burned through closed lids with the redness of a steel mill at night.

"Now," she said sleepily. "Now tell me."

I reached over and closed the lid of the radio. "Have you made any guesses?"

"Just one. That was your story he read today, wasn't it?"

It startled me. "A very good guess indeed. Mind telling me how you made it?"

"Too simple, really. Somebody in the class had to be there on . . . false pretenses. I'm a senior here, you know. So I happened to know everybody else in the class except you."

I told her why I had come.

She didn't answer. When I glanced over I saw that she was sitting up, her forehead against her raised knees. She was weeping.

I patted her shoulder. It was a very ineffectual gesture. The oil she had used was sticky.

She talked without looking at me. "I didn't want to come back here. I wanted to go to some other school. Every day I see places where . . . we were together."

"Do you feel the way Mr. Flynn does?"

"That Ted didn't kill himself? Of course. We were going to be married. Almost everybody knew that. And now they look at me and I can see in their eyes that they are full of nasty pity. The girls won't talk to me about dates or marriage. I thought I'd die this summer. I worked every day until I was too exhausted to think about anything, just go to sleep."

"If he didn't kill himself, somebody else did."

"That's the horrible part." She turned and looked at me. Her eyes were red. "That's the awful part, having to accept that. And that's why I came back. I thought I would try to find out. The first thing is to find out why anyone should kill Ted, why anyone should want him dead."

I took her in on my reasoning thus far. "If you assume that he was killed, you have two choices. The other deaths in the house were either accidents or they were caused too. If they were accidents, somebody was after Ted as an individual. If they were not accidents, then you have two further choices. Were they linked, or were they separate crimes? If they were linked, there is no use looking in Ted's history for an enemy. If they were linked, he and the others were killed as symbols, not as individuals. Do you follow me?"

"Of course. I've been thinking the same way. But you've organized it better."

"That may be the reason I'm here. The use of orderly thought processes acquired through feature work now applied to murder. Do you think you would slip in public if you called me Joe?"

"No. I'm Tilly, of course. But let's get on with it. Five died. Sherman, Winniger, Welly, Forrith and Ted. Suppose they were killed as a symbol. It had to come from someone inside the house, or an outsider. Each guess leads to a different set of symbols, Joe."

"You are doing very nicely. Keep going."

"If they were all killed by a fraternity brother, it had to be because of jealousy, spite, house politics. . . . all that doesn't satisfy me, Joe. Those reasons seem too trivial somehow. And if it came from outside the house, you have to agree that it was a male who was willing to take the chance of being seen inside the house. There the risk is greater, but the motives become stronger. The fraternity system is based on a false set of values. Kids can be seriously and permanently hurt by the sort of cruelty that's permitted. A mind can become twisted. Real hate can be built up.

"When I was a freshman, one sorority gave my roommate a big rush. She wanted to join and so she turned down the teas and dances at the other houses. When the big day came she was all bright-eyed and eager. The stinkers never put a pledge pin on her. She offended somebody in the house and in the final voting she was blackballed. But she had no way to fight back."

"What happened to her, Tilly?"

"She left school before the year was over. She wrote once. The letter was very gay, very forced. But even though it hurt me to see what happened to her, I was too much of a moral coward to turn down my own bid that night she cried herself to sleep."

"Then." I said, "if this is a case of a twisted mind trying to 'get even' with Gamma U, we have to find out who took an emotional beating from the brethren in the pledge department, eh?"

"Doesn't it look that way to you? And you can find that out, you know. There are six thousand kids in the university. Two thousand belong to clubs and fraternities and sororities. Four thousand are what we so cutely call barbarians. Barbs. Outcasts. Spooks, creeps, dim ones. There, but for the grace of the Lord—"

"It can be narrowed down a little, Tilly," I said. "The first two were killed last year just before the rushing season started. That means that if the assumption we're making is correct, the jolt came the year before and the party brooded about it for almost an entire year before taking action. That would fit. He would be a junior.

"Assume, with the even split between male and female, there are seven hundred and fifty juniors. Five hundred of them are barbs. Out of that five hundred, probably fifty were on the Gamma U rush list two years ago. Out of that fifty, I would guess that fifteen to twenty were pledged. The rush list should be in the files. If we both work on it, we ought to be able to narrow it down pretty quickly."

She looked at me and her eyes filled again. "Joe, I . . . some day I want to tell you how much it means that you've come here to . . ."

"Last one in is a dirty name," I said.

She moved like I thought I was going to. As I reached the edge, she went flat out into a racing dive, cutting the water cleanly. She came up, shook her wet hair back out of her eyes and laughed at me.

We swam out, side by side. A hundred yards out we floated on the imperceptible swell. "Ted and I used to swim a lot," she said in a small voice. And then she was gone from me, her strong legs churning the water in a burst of speed. I swam slowly after her. When I caught up with her, she was all right again.

"It's clear today," she said, going under in a surface dive. I went down too, and with my eyes squinted against the water I could see the dance of the sunlight on the sandy bottom. I turned and saw her angling toward me, her hair streaming out in the water, half smiling, unutterably lovely. I caught her arm and, as we drifted up toward the surface, I kissed her.

We emerged into the air and stared at each other gravely. "I think we'd better forget that, Joe," she said.

"That might be easier said that done, Tilly."

"Don't say things you don't mean, Joe. Ever."

Only three to go. I parked in the shade and was glad of it when I found he hadn't come back yet. It was a tourist court and trailer park. The layout had been pasted together with spit and optimism. Neither ingredient had worked very well. Dirty pastel walls, a litter of papers and orange peels, a glare of sun off the few aluminum trailers, some harsh red flowers struggling up a broken trellice. I watched his doorway. The sign on it said *Manager*. A half hour later a blonde unlocked the door and went in.

I walked over and knocked. She came to the door, barefoot. In another year the disintegration would have removed the last traces of what must have once been a very lush and astonishing beauty. That is a sad thing to happen to a woman under thirty.

"Maybe you can't read where it says no vacancy," she said.

"I want to see Bob Toberly," I said.

"If it's business, you can talk to me. I'm his wife."

"It's personal."

She studied me for a few moments. "Okay, wait a sec. Then you can come in and wait. He's late now." Her voice had the thin fine edge that only a consistently evil disposition can create.

She disappeared. Soon she called, "Okay, come on in."

Her dress was thrown on the unmade bed. She had changed to a blue linen two-piece play suit that was two sizes too small for her.

"I gotta climb into something comferrable the minute I get in the house," she said defiantly. "This climate'll kill you. It's hell on a woman." She motioned to a chair. I sat down. She glared at me. "Sure I can't handle whatever it is you wanna see Bob about?"

"I'm positive."

She padded over to the sink, took a half bottle of gin out of the cabinet and sloshed a good two inches into a water tumbler. "Wanna touch?"

"Not right now, thanks."

She put an ice cube in it, swirled it a few times and then tilted it high. Her throat worked three times and it was gone. The room was full of a faint sour smell of sweat.

The room darkened as Bob Toberly cut off the sunlight. He came in, banging the screen door. He was half the size of a house, with hands like cinderblocks. He looked suspiciously at me and then at the bottle on the sink.

"Dammit, Clara, I told you to lay off that bottle."

"Shaddup!" she snapped. "I drink what I please when I please with no instructions from you."

He grabbed her arm and twisted it up behind her. He pushed her to the door, shoved her outside. "Wait out there until I tell you to come in."

He turned to me, ignoring her as she screamed at him. "Now what do you want?"

"I'm making a survey of local students who were turned down by the local chapter of Gamma U. It's for a magazine article condemning fraternities. I got my hands on the rush list for two years ago. Your name was on it."

He rocked back and forth, his lips pursed, staring down at me. Suddenly he grinned. "What do you want to know?"

"What was your reaction when you weren't pledged? How'd you take it?"

"I wanted to go bust those smart guys in the chops."

"Did you know why they turned you down?"

"Sure. They were rushing me because they figured me for eventual All-American here. But the timing was bad. In early practise I got a bad shoulder separation. It happened during rush week. They got the spy system operating and found out I was out for the year, probably out for good. From then on I was just another guy with muscles."

"Has it made any change in your life?"

He frowned. "I got stubborn. I decided I wanted to stay in school. But they dropped me off the athletic scholarship list. I married Clara. Her daddy had just died and left her this place. It brings in enough to swing the school bills." He turned and stared at the door. Clara stood outside looking in through the screen. "I didn't know at the time that she was no good."

Clara screamed more curses at him. He went over casually and spit through the screen at her. A charming little family scene. I got out as quickly and quietly as I could. As I drove out onto the road I could still hear her.

3

No Suicides Today

THE NEXT TO THE LAST WAS A WASHOUT, THE SAME AS TOBERLY. The last was a kid named Harley Reyont. I found him at his room in the dormitory and I took him down the street to a beer joint. I knew he had seen me around the campus so I had to use a different approach with him.

I said, "I'm a transfer and I've been thinking of whether or not to hook up with the local chapter of my fraternity. But I don't like some of the things I've seen around there. I thought the smart thing to do would be to find somebody they gave the dirty end of the stick to."

I saw his hand shake as he reached for his stein. He was a pale, thin, pleasant-looking boy. "What makes you think I got the dirty end of any stick, Arlin?"

"I saw the rush list. They didn't pledge you and neither did any other group."

"They did me a favor, that bunch."

"Just how do you mean that?"

His mouth curled bitterly. "I was just as wide-eyed and eager as any of the rest of them. Hell, I thought I'd die when I wasn't tapped on pledge night. I thought something was wrong with me, that maybe I was a second-class citizen. I've smartened up since that night, believe me. My clothes weren't right during rush week and my conversation wasn't smooth enough to suit those snobs. They could see I wasn't going to be an athlete. So I got passed over in the rush."

"Was that good?"

"Take a good look at them, Arlin. A good look. Then come back and tell me what you think of their set of values. It's a damn superficial life, fraternity life. If they'd take me in I'd be like the rest of them now. Cut out of the same pattern."

"But you resented them at the time. Maybe you still do."

He frowned down at his stein. "No, I don't think I still resent them. I feel a little bit sorry for them."

"Didn't you want to get even?"

He looked up quickly. "I see what you mean. I suppose so. I sublimated it. I hated them and I had to show them. I turned in straight A's for the freshman and sophomore years. I'll do it again this year. But not because I still resent them—because in the process of acquiring the high grades, I learned that I'm actually pretty bright. I enjoy the work." Again the bitter smile.

"You could say the brothers helped me find myself." He sighed. "Hell, Arlin I guess I still resent it. I'll resent it all my life. Sour grapes, I suppose. Only I went for a walk along fraternity row during one of the big weekends. I could see them through the windows, dancing with their tall cool women, all wearing that same satisfied smirk. I wanted to bust the windows with rocks. I wanted to be inside there, one of them.

"I wanted to be Brother Reyont, the Big Man on the Campus. I walked back to the dorm and read Kant. He always puts me to sleep in short order. It took twenty pages that night. But I don't blame Gamma U. Any other house would have done the same thing. I was a pretty dim little freshman, that I can assure you."

"Thanks for being so frank with me."

"You're buying the beer, aren't you? . . ."

When I drove in I saw that my lights were on, and I knew that Tilly had used the key I had given her. I parked quietly and stopped and looked through the window. She was in the big chair wearing that green dress I liked. Her legs were tucked up under her and she was reading a news magazine. The lamplight brought out the very fine line of her cheek and throat.

She looked good to me. Having her waiting there for me made me play too many mental games. It wasn't healthy. On a crap table the wise man plays the field. Anybody who bets all night on the same number loses his shirt.

I went in and she came up eagerly out of the chair.

"Aha!" I said. "So you are here about the mortgage! Heh, heh, heh."

"Please, sire! The night is cold. You will not throw me and my piteous child out into yon snow."

"Mind your tongue, girl, or I shall feed you both to the wolves."

We laughed together. Silly people. She stopped suddenly and said, "Oh, Joe, it seems so long since I could laugh like this."

"Easy, easy," I said warningly. "Go weepy on me and I'll turn you over to the dean of women. They'll hang you for—damn! I'm sorry, Till. Foot in the mouth disease."

"That's okay. How did you do?"

"Reyont is off the list. And he's the last one, that is if you covered your boy. Did you?"

"That's why I came, Joe. I saw him. He . . . he's very odd. He frightens me a little. His name is Luther Keyes."

"Do you think he's capable of—what happened?"

"I don't know. I just don't know. You'd better talk to him to-

morrow. He's in my nine o'clock class, room fourteen in the Arts
Building. I'll arrange to walk out with him. We'll come out the
west door."

"Done. What did you tell him? What sort of a story did you
give him?"

"I played the gossip. I asked him if he thought one of the
Gamma U men had been killing his fraternity brothers. You
know, dumb innocent questions. Baby stare. I won't tell you how
he reacted. You be the judge of that." She looked at her watch.
"Gosh, it's late."

"And a bright moon and a warm breeze. It just so happens that
I picked up a suit the other day that ought to fit you."

She stared hard at me. "No nonsense, Joe?"

"Promise."

I waited for her in the living room. She went out first. I turned
off the lights. There was a trace of phosphorescence in the waves
as they broke against the shore.

We went out too far. The fear came without warning. She was
surging along, ten feet ahead of me. All knowledge of the shore
line was gone. We were in the middle of an ocean.

"Tilly!" I called. "Till!" She didn't stop. I put on a burst of
speed that I knew would wind me completely if I had to continue
it for long. As I made a long stroke, my fingertips brushed her
foot. I reached and caught her by the ankle.

"No, Joe," she gasped. "Let me go! Oh, please let me go! Don't
stop me!"

She fought to get free but I wouldn't let her go. "What good
would it do? You're trying to run away from something."

Suddenly she was passive. "All right, Joe. I'm all right now."

"Come on, we'll get you in." That was easy to say. In the
struggle we had become turned around. I could get no clue as
to the direction of the swells. I could see no lights on shore.
I knew then that we we were out so far that the lights were
too close to the horizon for us to see them from our angle of
vision.

"Which way, Joe?" she asked, her voice tautening with panic.

Oh, fine, I thought. *This was your idea and now you don't care
for it much.*

Then, like a letter from home, I saw the pink on the sky, the reflected city lights of Sandson.

"That way," I said. "Come on. Take it easy."

After a long time I was able to correct our course by the lights of a familiar hotel. It seemed that we would never, never make it—and then my knee thumped sand. She stood up, swayed and fell forward. I tried to get her up. She was out cold. I got her over my shoulder and weaved up to the house. I dumped her, dripping wet, on the couch. I turned on the hooded desk light, got big towels,

Her lips were blue. Her eyes were opened and her teeth were chattering so badly she couldn't speak. It was a warm night. I poured a shot and held her head up while she drank it. She gagged but she kept it down, I got blankets, covered her. She cried for a long time, softly, as a tired child will cry. I sat beside her and rubbed her forehead with my fingertips until she went to sleep.

After she was asleep, I sat for a long, long time in the dark and I knew, without her telling me, just how it had happened. She had grieved for Ted. But not enough. She had been strongly attracted to me, as I was to her. With a person of her intense capacity for loyalty, it seemed an unthinkable deceit. It made a strong conflict within her. What she had done had seemed to her at the time to be the only solution.

I knew that when she awakened, her reaction would tell me whether or not I had guessed right about her feelings.

I sat there until the eastern sky was gray shot through with a pink threat of tomorrow's sun. She stirred in her sleep, opened her eyes and looked at me with no alarm or surprise. She held her arms up and I kissed her. It was as natural and expected and unsurprising and sweet as anything I'll ever know.

"I had a nightmare," she whispered.

"A long, long bad dream, darling. It's all over now. For good."

"Don't ever say anything to me that you don't mean, Joe. Ever."

"Promise."

"And Joe . . ."

"Yes, darling."

"Please. Go away from me for a little while. Way over there. I feel like a hussy. I don't want to be one." She grinned. "Not quite yet."

"We ought to get you back."

"Isn't today Saturday?"

"Don't ask me like that. I always look at my watch when anybody asks me too quickly what day it is. Yes, it's Saturday."

"No classes, Joe. I can cook. How do you like your eggs?"

"After a swim at dawn, of course."

"Then go on out and swim, dear. You're dressed for it. I'll call you when it's ready. How's the larder?"

"Full of ambrosia."

"Come here, Joe. Now go swimming. Quickly, Joe. Quickly."

I swam. She cooked. She called me. I ate. We kissed. We made silly talk. Words are no good. Ever.

That Ted had himself a girl, he did. I was glad he was dead. To be glad for a thing like that gave me a superstitious feeling of eternal damnation. Bad luck. It gave me a shiver. She saw it. We held hands. No more shivers. No more bad luck, I hoped.

During that week, after I rubbed Keyes off our list, we plotted. I could speak more freely because now I could talk about Ted without it rocking her as badly at it had in the beginning.

I said, "We tried one way. I have a hunch that guy you mistrust is just another zany. Now we go at it from the other direction. We forget motive and try opportunity. We back-track on the beach party, the return trip from Tampa, the gun-cleaning episode, Ted's apparent suicide. Now from the motive viewpoint you brought out that the case is stronger for an outsider.

"From the opportunity point of view, the case is stronger against one of the brethren. Two of the incidents happened inside the house. At the beach party most of the members were present. The car accident is the hard one to figure out. I suggest that we drop it for the time being. Maybe it was a legitimate accident. Maybe it just served to give the murderer his idea. Were you on the beach party? Yes, I know you were, because I know Ted was there. And it was all couples."

"You want me to tell you about it."

We were in deck chairs side by side on the little terrace, our heads in shade, our legs outstretched in the sun. She took a cigarette. I held the lighter for her.

She leaned back. "The beach party was just before Christmas

vacation started. It was a fraternity affair, but there were a few outsiders, guests. Rex Winniger, the boy who drowned, was with a casual date, a snakey little blonde that I disliked on sight. Rex had broken off with Bets, a girl in my house. It seemed too bad. He was very popular and a good athlete, but not much of a swimmer. He came from Kansas, I think."

"Where was the party?"

"On a long sand spit called Bonita Island. We used a big launch belonging to Harry Fellow's father. Harry graduated last year. We moored it on the mainland side of the island and we had to wade ashore. We got there in mid-afternoon. Everybody swam and toasted in the sun. The drinking started a little later. Nearly everybody drank too much. The party got a little wild.

"The party broke up a little after midnight because some of the boys had passed out and their dates were yammering to be taken home. Somebody thought of counting noses. Rex and the little blonde were missing. Some of the group thought it would be a big gag to leave them marooned there. Then they went looking with flashlights. They found the little blonde asleep on the sand. They got her awake and she said she hadn't seen Rex in she couldn't remember when. You could feel people getting a little worried and a little soberer then.

"The boys made a line across Bonita holding hands—it's only about seventy feet wide. They went right from one end to the other. Quite a few of the other boys could have swum to the mainland as a joke. But Rex really couldn't swim that well. Then we all hoped that maybe he'd tried it and made it all right. But on the way back people were laughing in that funny nervous way that worried people do. Ted whispered to me that he didn't like the look of it at all. We girls were taken home.

"In the morning Ted met me and he looked haggard. He said that Rex hadn't showed up. They reported it early that same morning. Hundreds of people looked for the body. The papers made a big story of it and the blonde got her picture on the front page, looking tearful. Well, you know the rest. The beach party was on a Thursday night. They found his body on the beach on the mainland on Saturday afternoon, about three miles below Bonita Island."

"Did you notice if he got drunk at the party?"

"Everybody was drinking. Some of them got pretty sloppy. But

I don't remember that Rex was sloppy. We talked about that later. We compared notes. After dark everybody was in the water at one time or another, because the surf was coming in beautifully."

"Was there any incident, any trouble that caught your eye?"

She thought for a few moments. "No . . . I guess not. Nothing really unusual. When people drink they say things they normally wouldn't say. There were quarrels and poor jokes and some spiteful talk. Harv Lorr was president of the house. He saw that things weren't going too well. He tried to keep all the boys in line. Arthur Marris helped him, even though Arthur was only a junior then. Ted could have helped but he didn't want to leave me alone for as long as it would take."

"All in all, a bust party, eh?"

"Not a nice party, Joe. "Full of undercurrents."

4

Sweating Bullets

AT THAT MOMENT A CAR DROVE IN. I HEARD IT STOP. TILL GAVE me a quick look. I got up out of the chair. Bill Armand, the faintly vulpine junior, and Brad Carroll came around the side of the house, carrying suits and towels. One of Armand's dark eyebrows went high in surprise as he saw Tilly.

"Why, hello, Tilly!" Brad Carroll said in his careful voice. "Hi, Rod. I didn't know you two were acquainted. Rod, we decided this was the day to take you up on your standing invite."

"Hello, Brad," Tilly said, "And Bill. I met Rod in our writing class. The guy is persuasive."

"We've noticed that," Bill said. "Tilly, you're looking wonderful."

"Thank you," she said gravely.

There was a moment of awkwardness. I said, "The bar is the kitchen shelf, mates. Select your venom and some for us. Till's is rum and coke and I'm on bourbon and water if you feel industrious. You can change in the bedroom."

They went inside. Tilly reached over and touched my arm. "Joe, darling. This is going to give them a very choice bit of gossip."

"Do you really care?"

"Uh uh."

"That's my girl."

They came back out bearing drinks. Bill clowned it his towel over his arm like a waiter's napkin. He bowed low as he handed Tilly her drink, murmuring, "Madame." In trunks he was deeply tanned, whip-lean, with long smooth muscles. Brad was whiter, softer, thickening a bit in the waist, with a small roll of fat over the top of his yellow trunks.

Bill sat on the edge of the terrace turned toward us, with one eyebrow still high enough to give him a knowing look. Brad said, "We didn't do this right. We should have come armed with charming blondes and a couple of jugs to salve our conscience. We thought you hadn't had time yet to live dangerously, Rod."

"I keep telling you that we're underestimating the guy," Bill said.

"Where's Al Siminik, Brad?" I asked. It seemed odd to see Brad without his shadow.

"By the time we see him again, we'll have forgotten what he looks like. He's earning his keep, throwing his muscles around," Bill answered.

I eyed Bill. "What's your sport, Armand?"

He laughed. "Molly."

Tilly bristled. "That isn't a nice thing to say, Bill?"

"Protecting your sisters?" he jeered.

I was amazed at how cold Tilly's gray eyes could get. "The only thing I have against Molly is that she's stupid enough to find you attractive, Bill Armand."

He held up his hands in mock defense and ducked his head. "Hey! Take it easy."

Talk became more casual. After a while Bill drove to the main road and phoned Molly. He came back and said that Brad's girl, Laura, was coming out and bringing Molly with her. Shortly after that, Bill and Tilly went in for a swim. Brad moved over into the chair where Tilly had been.

His smile was very engaging. "Rod, you strike me as being a pretty canny guy."

"Oh, thank you, sir."

"No gag, Rod. I mean it. You're smart enough to see how things stand at the chapter. Arthur is one of the best friends I've got." He was working the knife out of the sheath very slowly and I knew why he'd decided to come out. Carroll, the tireless politician.

"But . . ." I said.

He gave me a quick look. "Oh, you see it too?"

"Better tell me what you see, Brad."

"I'll be frank. I wouldn't want this to go any further. I see a sweet guy who completely lacks the executive touch. He's too heavy-handed. Now take Harv Lorr. There was a great president. We used to have a penny-ante poker game going on weekends in his room. Will Arthur go for that? Not for a minute. It says in the book no gambling in the house. The boys resent that rule-book attitude, Rod. But a lot of the fellows figure it this way. They say that Arthur was elected and he'll graduate in June, so why not play along with him."

"And what do you say?"

"I say that this is a whole year out of our lives. Why let Arthur make it a poor fraternity year? Every member has a vote. Right now, because of some people's sense of duty, Arthur swings the majority. But if the rest of us who don't quite agree with some of his measures could consolidate our vote, we could do just about any thing we pleased."

"In other words, let Arthur have the title and let you have the real push."

"I didn't say that!" he said in a hurt tone.

"Doesn't it amount to the same thing?" I asked disarmingly.

He pretended to think it over. "Well, it would be one way to put it, Rod."

"Let's get it out in the open. You want me to vote with you."

"Only if you sincerely believe that it's the thing to do."

"Let's take the gloves off, Brad," I said. "I'm a transfer. I'm a senior. I'm not living in the house. As I see it, there's no reason for me to get messed up in local chapter politics. With either you or Arthur running things, the food is going to be good, the lounge is going to be comfortable, the dances are going to be fun. I don't care about anything else."

"That' " he said firmly, "is what I consider an irresponsible and selfish attitude."

"Consider it anything you want to."

"Then I may take it that you'll vote with Arthur?"

I saw I had hurt his feelings. Or at least he had decided that should be his attitude. "You may take it this way. I'm not for you or against you. When I attend chapter meetings I'll refrain from voting. Then you won't have to worry about a counterbalancing vote."

His smile was full of satisfaction. "I'm glad to hear you say that. Frankly, a lot of the younger boys would be willing to follow your lead in preference to mine, even. You've made quite an impression, Arlin. Quite an impression."

"Do you want some advice?"

"What do you mean?"

"Take it or leave it. You're creating tempests in teapots, Carroll. You're misdirecting a very strong itch for power. Find some new direction for it."

He dropped all expression. "Am I to judge from that that you consider the fraternity to be unimportant?"

"Take it any way you please."

"You damn veterans are all alike. Everything is a big joke. Arthur is the only one I ever saw who takes things seriously. Just because you fought a war, you've got this superior attitude. Frankly, Arlin, it makes me sick to my stomach."

"Vote for Carroll!" I said. "Vote for a square deal!"

"Go to hell!"

"Now you're being stupid. Offend me too much and I'll get interested enough to bust a few spokes out of your big wheel."

He chewed that around in his mind for a while. I was rewarded with his most charming smile, an outstretched hand. "Sorry, Rod. I get too worked up."

"Forget it," I said, yawning.

He stood up. "I'm glad to see Tilly dating, Rod. Poor girl. She needs a few good times."

"I'll tell her you said so."

He flushed. "You're damn difficut to talk to sometimes."

At that point a car stopped behind the house. We heard a girl's voice over the sound of the surf. They came around the side of the house. Bill and Tilly came out of the water to meet them. Molly had a trim little figure, chestnut hair, a set of large trusting eyes and a vulnerable mouth. Her eyes glowed as she watched Bill Armand walk toward her. Laura was as dark as Tilly, but taller, a shade leaner, with a face so patrician that it looked inbred. Her speech was a finishing-school drawl.

Molly was a giggler. Bill treated Molly with affectionate amusement. Brad treated Laura as a girl who had earned the right to share in his reflected glow as a large wheel around the university. Both girls tried without success to conceal an intense curiosity about Tilly and me and our current status.

Tilly turned feline on me, and in the process she was as cute as a bug. I saw her wondering how to handle the problem. Finally she gave me a meaningful stare and said, "Rod and I are so glad you could come out here. What are you drinking? Rod, fix them up, like a dear, will you?"

Laura gave Molly a meaningful look.

It was a complete essay, that look.

We swam, we loafed in the sun—three couples on a late Saturday afternoon. To any onlooker we were young and carefree and casual. Uncomplicated. I lay with Till sprinkling sand on the back of my arm and thought about us.

One vulnerable little girl heading for heartbreak, one icy maiden as ambitious as her grasping boy-friend, one young cynic complicated by a streak of ruthlessness, one lovely girl who had been persuaded the night before that this was not the time to die—and one pretender, a young man who had thought it possible to come to this place and solve a pretty problem without becoming emotionally involved, and who was slowly finding it impossible.

The police station of Sandson and the fire department shared the same building. It looked vaguely like a Moorish castle.

The man they steered me to was a Lieutenant Cord. He was an unlikely six foot six with a stoop that brought him to six three. He had a corded throat, heavy wrists, and a slack liver-spotted face.

"What can I do for you, Mr. Arlin?"

"I'm at the university, Lieutenant. I've been doing some work in psychology. One of the case histories assigned to me is the case of Tod Sherman, who was killed during March this year."

I made it pretty breezy. He leaned back in his chair and for the first time I noticed a very alert intelligence hiding behind his sleepy gray-green eyes.

"Let me get you straight. I remember Sherman. How does it

hook up with psychology when a lad had a bad accident like that?"

I took a deep breath. I had to make it better than I thought. "You know, of course, about accident-prone people and how they contribute the lion's share of motor vehicle accidents and accidents in the home. The study of such people is a legitimate part of modern psychology. I have reason to believe that Sherman was an accident-prone. Actually it is the death wish operating on a subconscious level, or else the result of a childish desire for attention."

"What do you want from me?"

"If it wouldn't be too much trouble, a summary of what happened. I've talked to the other members of the fraternity who were there at the time. Their reports are confusing."

He looked at the wall clock. "I guess it won't take too much time. We got the call on a Sunday afternoon. They don't operate the dining room at that house on Sundays and nearly everybody was out. A boy named Flynn, the one who hung himself three months later, was the one who heard the shot and traced it to Sherman's room. Flynn was in the lounge at the time, and it took him, he said, maybe ten minutes to find out who and what it was.

"One other lad, a sophomore named Armand, was in the house at the time. He was asleep and the shot didn't awaken him. Flynn was smart. He phoned the campus infirmary and then us. He didn't touch the body. He checked the time. We got there as the ambulance did. The doctor pronounced him dead. We were both there a little less than twenty minutes after the shot according to Flynn's watch. Sherman had been sitting at his desk by the window. There was an oily rag and a bottle of gun oil on top of the desk. The gun was a .45 Army Colt.

"The slug had caught him under the chin and gone up through the roof of his mouth, exploding out of the top of his head to lodge in the ceiling. He had fallen to his left between the chair and the window. The gun was under his desk. The ejected cartridge case was on the window sill. A full clip was on the desk blotter beside the oil bottle. It was the standard mistake. Ejecting the case and forgetting the one in the chamber.

"As I see it, he was holding it pointing up toward him, and he pulled the slide down so he could look through the barrel. His hand was oily and the slide got away from him. When it snapped up, it fired the shell in the chamber."

"Were you completely satisfied with the verdict of accidental death, Lieutenant?"

He smiled humorlessly. "Now what kind of a fool question is that, Arlin? If it wasn't accident it would screw up this psychology report, wouldn't it?"

I tried again. "Did you investigate to see if anyone said he was depressed?"

"Sure. Lots of guys are cagey enough to do a hell of a good job of faking an accident when they want to knock themselves off. But in that case there is an insurance angle, usually, and the guy himself is older. No, this Sherman was apparently a pretty popular guy in the house. He wasn't depressed. He'd busted up with his girl, but he had a new one pretty well lined up. He had enough dough, a good job after graduation, and his health."

"You've been very kind, Lieutenant." I stood up.

"Any time," he said.

I went to the door. As I turned the knob he said, "Just a minute." I looked back at him. He smiled. "Do me a favor, Arlin. Come around some time and tell me what the hell it was you really wanted."

"I don't think I know what you mean."

"See you around, Arlin."

I went out and sat in the car. There was a coldness at the nape of my neck. Up until the talk with Cord, I had been willing to go along with the theory of a chain of accidents. I had tried to be thorough for the sake of the pay I was getting. Mr. Flynn had just been a man pathetically anxious to prove his son was not a suicide. Tilly had been a girl who had not been able to understand how Ted Flynn's mind may have been unstable, along with his undeniable brilliance.

But now everything had a new flavor. It was something that Cord had said, and yet, going over his words again and again, I could not pick it out.

I knew, sitting there in the sun, as well as I knew my own name that the odds were in favor of someone else's finger pulling that trigger. I was sweating and yet I felt cold.

For the first time I realized that my operations were a bit transparent. If someone had killed Sherman—and I didn't know why

I was so sure they had—then that someone might still be in the house. If so, he was watching me. It would be natural for him to watch me. I was a stranger. I was an unknown factor.

I sensed a quiet and devious intelligence at work. A mind that could plan carefully and then move boldly.

I drove away. My hands were too tight on the wheel and my foot was shaky on the gas pedal.

5

Accidentally—On Purpose

I CUT THE HISTORY CLASS. TILLY CUT HER CLASS AT THE SAME hour and we drove down Route 19 through Clearwater to Largo and then turned left to Indian Rocks Beach. I found a place where we could park in the shade and watch the placid gulf. On the way I had told her of the talk with Cord.

She took my hand, looked into my eyes and said, "For the first time it's real to you, isn't it, Joe?"

"That's one way to put it."

"It's been real to me all along. You know how when people go with each other, they talk about everything under the sun. Once Ted and Step were arguing about suicide. It was after Sherman had died. Step couldn't see that it was wrong—but Ted told us that the only time he could see the remotest justification was when a person was painfully and incurably ill—that the world is too wide and wonderful a place to leave before the time you have is up. He wasn't just talking, Joe."

"I think I would have liked him, Till."

"You would have. I know it. When they told me he'd hung himself, I found out later that I'd screamed that he didn't do it, that someone had done it to him. I'm still just as certain of that as I was during the first moments. He was incapable of it. They were holding the last meeting of the year, the election of officers for the next year it was. They waited and waited and then they went looking for him.

"Brad cried like a baby. They cut him down and then he was shipped north for the funeral. I couldn't go to that. I couldn't even go to the memorial service for him in the chapel at school.

I was too sick. They had me in the infirmary. When I got out I went north and took that job."

"Up until now," I said, "I've been playing an intellectual game. Mental musical chairs. Now it isn't a game any more."

"For me it never has been." She bit her lip. "Joe, you'd better not let anything happen to you. You'd just better not."

I kissed her then, there in the cool shade with the warm wind touching our faces, and she came alive in my arms in a way I've never before experienced. Holding her was holding flame and purpose and a clean, wanting strength. It shook me, and shook her too. We sat apart from each other.

We said very little on the drive back. I left her off at the sorority house. I went to a bar and had a few. I arrived at Gamma U in time for dinner. I talked and I listened politely and the table conversation went over the surface of my mind while below the surface a tallish, faintly awkward girl walked, and her eyes were more than promise. . . .

I woke with a start at dawn. The bedroom had an outside door. I had left it open and latched the screen. A tall figure was silhouetted there.

"Rod," he said. "Rod, let me in."

I went to the door. "Oh, Arthur! Man, it's a little after six. I didn't know you boys were going to drop in at this time of day."

I unlatched the door. He brushed by me, walked to the bed and sat down, staring at his big hands. His faintly Lincolnesque appearance was more pronounced. The eyes had sunk deeper into his head. His cheeks were more hollow. I suddenly knew that this was no time for patter and laughter.

"I can't depend on anybody else," he said. "You've got to help me."

I sat beside him and reached over and took my cigarettes from the bedside table. I lit both cigarettes with my lighter. "What is it?"

"The most awful mess yet, Rod. The worst. Everybody's running around like headless chickens. I came out here to talk to somebody with sense. This time it has rattled me."

"Get to it, Arthur. What happened?"

"The police phoned the house at three this morning. It happened at the Onyx Court." I barely concealed my start of surprise. That was the court and trailer outfit owned by the Toberlys.

"They said that they had a body tentatively identified as Bradford Carroll. I dressed and went over along with Bill Armand. The place was swarming with police. Brad's throat had been cut. I told them that it was Brad all right. I still feel sick. There was blood all over. . . ."

"Take it easy, Arthur."

"They were still questioning Bob Toberly. He's a student too. We rushed him a couple of years ago and passed him over. He runs the place along with his wife. It's sort of a crummy place. Toberly said that Brad and his wife, a tall dark girl that he recognized as a student, had registered in at about ten for the night. He said they'd done it many times before. He said that they were secretly married.

"Well, Bill, standing beside me, said 'Laura!' They turned on Bill and made him admit that he thought it sounded like Laura Trainor. They got the name of the sorority house and two cops went to pick her up. They're holding her now. I've done all I could. I wired Brad's parents, and the sorority sisters phoned Laura's father. I heard he's on his way down. Rod, it would be bad enough without all that trouble last year, but this is absolutely the worst. I don't know what's going to happen."

I left him sitting there and made him a stiff drink. Laura was one of Tilly's sorority sisters, along with Molly. So Tilly would know already. I made a second stiff one for myself. He took his glass numbly and drank it as though it were water.

"The razor was right there," he said. "I saw it. A straight razor. He used them. I guess it was an affectation. I guess he had a kit with him so he could get cleaned up and go directly from the Onyx Court to class."

"Do you think Laura did it?"

He shuddered. "How do I know what to think? I don't think she's capable of a thing like that. But they could have quarreled."

"What will happen?"

"It was too late for the morning papers but the afternoon papers will give it a big play. They'll bring up all that stuff from last year. There were reporters there. Toberly's wife put on her best dress. To her it was like a party. They're giving Toberly a bad time. Brad voted against Toberly, of course, two years ago. Most of us did. They'll twist and turn until they make a motive out of it."

"How can I help?"

He gave me a tired smile. "You've helped by listening. I have to go back now. I have to get everybody together and tell them to keep their damn mouths shut. Then I have to pack Brad's things. A policeman is going to help me. He'll be looking for evidence. He's in the house now, sitting on a chair outside Brad's room. He was there when I left anyway."

"What about Brad's people?"

"They'll be down, I suppose. I ought to make a reservation for them at the hotel. Look, would you do that for me?"

"Sure thing."

He stood up and put the glass on the bedside table. "Thanks, Rod. That drink helped a lot."

"Let me dress. I'll go in with you."

"No, I'll go along. I'll be at the house. See you there."

Some of the brothers were having an early breakfast when I went in. The single waiter acted jittery. Lieutenant Cord was sitting in the lounge. He came over to me and said, "Is this another one of those accident-prone guys?"

I kept my voice low. "Do you think he cut his throat?"

Cord shrugged his big sloping shoulders. "He could have. The razor's in the right place. At least it was. But usually people that take a hack at their own throat, they're timid about it. This was a good try. He damn near slashed his head off—that is, if he did it. Now I got what the boys call an unhealthy interest in you. Want to talk right here?"

"It doesn't matter to me."

"You come in and give me a queer line of chatter and the next thing I know one of your friends is dead. I like to get all the loose ends pasted in or clipped off. Let's you stop trying to kid me."

"How do you mean?"

"I checked your schedule after you left and had a few words over the phone with your professor. I didn't mention your name. He told me somebody was kidding me and that the department wouldn't send a student out like that. So talk, Arlin."

"Suppose I tell you that my reason was good but that it's my business?"

"First let's see how you check out last night. You had dinner here and left. Where did you go?"

"Right back to my place on the beach. I studied until about eleven, wrote a few letters and went to bed at about quarter to one."

"No proof?"

"Not a shred."

"Now this Toberly tells me that somebody was around asking him questions about how Gamma U turned him down. The guy said it was for a magazine article on fraternities. He didn't give a name. Toberly gave me a description. It fits you pretty good, Arlin. Want to come on down to see if Toberly can make identification?"

"I give up. It was me."

"Now don't you think you better tell uncle?"

Two sophomores walked through into the dining room and stared at us curiously. "Someday I'll get smarter," I said. "Come on out and sit in my car for a little while."

The sun was climbing higher. Cord's face was drawn with fatigue. I told him my situation. He listened with a sour expression:

"What answer have you come to, Arlin?"

"I can't give reasons. It's just a very strong feeling. I say that four of them were murdered. Carroll is the fourth. I don't know about the automobile accident. We'll skip that one."

"And you think," he said bitterly, "that three murders took place right under our noses. You think we're that stupid!"

"It's not that you're stupid, Lieutenant. It's that the guy behind it is one clever operator. Take the beach party. No trick to get Winniger out into the surf and drown him. No special trick to take advantage of the empty house on a Sunday, start a conversation with Sherman and trick him. And if a guy were disarming enough, he could talk the Flynn boy up onto a chair in the closet on some pretext.

"And now Brad. This last one is bolder than the others. This last one was permitted to even look a little like murder. Was it hard to find out where Brad and Laura had a habit of going? Would it be difficult to wait until Laura left to go back to her sorority house? There was a moon last night. What time did it happen?" I asked Lieutenant Cord.

"Around two, I guess. The way it was discovered so fast, this Toberly couldn't sleep. He went for a walk around the place. He saw the light on and it bothered him. He took a quick look and phoned. We were there at quarter to three. Doesn't that spoil the moon angle?"

"Not completely. Sneak in there and find the razor and let him have it. Then snap on the light on the way out to make it look more like a suicide."

Cord studied me. "You talk a good game, Arlin. You almost get me believing it. Except for one thing. Why would anybody do all that? What the hell reason would he have?"

"Are you going to expose me, Lieutenant?"

He shrugged. "There's no point in that. Keep playing your little game if you want to, as long as you're getting paid for it. But stay out of my way. Don't foul up any of my work."

He got out of the car. He regarded me soberly. "And don't leave town. I'm taking a chance on believing you, but that doesn't mean I'm not going to do some checking to make sure."

I had no heart for the classes. I ate and went over to pick up Tilly. She came running out to the car. She climbed in beside me and her fingernails bit into my wrist. "Oh, Joe, I can't take it any more! All this horror! I keep seeing him the way he was out at your place. Smiling and happy."

"How did Laura take it?"

"They had to stop questioning her. She's in the Sandson General Hospital. Shock and hysteria. They're fools to bother her," she said hotly. "Laura goes all green if somebody steps on a bug."

"Have you eaten?"

"No, I couldn't. And I couldn't stand going to classes today, Joe. Start the car. Take me away from here. Drive fast, Joe."

We didn't get back until late afternoon. We bought a paper and read it together.

MYSTERY DEATH OF COLLEGE STUDENT.

That's the way they covered it, speaking neither of suicide nor murder, but hinting at murder.

Bradford Carroll, accompanied by a coed to whom he was secretly married, registered in at a local tourist court at ten o'clock last night. He was discovered shortly before three this morning by the proprietor of the court—who was attracted by the light which was left on. His throat had been cut with a straight razor which was found near his right hand.

Police took the coed into custody. She had returned to her sorority house some time before the body was discovered. Police report that before his wife collapsed, she testified that Carroll had been alive when she left, at approximately ten minutes of two.

Carrol, a senior at West Coast University, was a member of Gamma U, that same hard-luck fraternity which lost through suicide and accidental death, five members during the previous school year.

From there on the article went into his history and the school groups of which he was a member.

"It's a ghastly thing," Tilly said.

"The police," I said, "promise an early solution of Carroll's mysterious death."

A friend of Tilly's came over to the car. Tilly introduced us. The girl said, "How do you like the new ruling, kids?"

"Haven't seen it yet."

"No? It's on all the bulletin boards. Curfew for all students living on the campus in either houses or dorms. All special senior privileges rescinded. Now we stand a bed check just like the lower classes. All absences from living quarters after eleven are to be reported to the office of the dean until further notice. How do you like that?"

"I don't," Tilly said. "But what else can they do? Anxious parents will be giving the school a very bad time. They've got to have some sort of an answer."

I dropped Tilly with a promise to pick her up later, and went to the house. Step Krindall looked as glum as his round pink face permitted.

"Special meeting tonight," he said.

Bill Armand was standing in the lounge, staring out the windows toward the palms that bordered the drive. He gave me a crooked smile.

"Come to college for a liberal education," he said. "Where have you been all day?"

"Comforting the shaken."

"Tilly? When you need a stand-in, let me know."

I was surprised at the sudden feeling of jealousy. "Sure, Bill,"

I said easily. "What's the voting around here? Murder or suicide?"

"The dopes, which I might say covers about ninety percent of our membership, favor suicide. They overlook the very real argument that Brad was too selfish to kill himself. He wouldn't think of depriving the world of his presence for the next forty years."

"I thought he was your friend!"

"Is friendship blind, like love?"

"Armand, the adolescent cynic. Who stepped on you, Bill? And how hard?"

His lips tightened and his face turned chalk white. He turned on his heel and walked away.

I ate with placid Step Krindall, Arthur, Al Siminik and a quiet senior named Laybourne at a table for four. It was a very subdued meal. Once I went to a slaughterhouse. I saw the look in the eyes of the steer after that first brutal smack between the eyes. Siminik wore that look. Arthur ate doggedly, as though from a sense of duty.

After coffee, Arthur looked up at the dining-room clock. He rapped on his glass with a knife. "We'll go up to the meeting room in five minutes. You Step—you other latecomers—hurry it up."

We filed up to the meeting room. It was a meeting without ritual, the lights on full. Arthur took the chair. "We'll dispense with the minutes of the previous meeting and with the treasurer's report. This is a special meeting called for a special purpose. What happened last night was a severe shock to all of us. Brad was . . . our brother and our friend."

Siminik startled the group by sobbing once aloud. He knuckled his eyes like a small boy.

Arthur went on. "I have talked with the police, just before dinner. It begins to appear that the verdict of the coroner's jury will be death by his own hand."

"Nuts!" Bill Armand said loudly.

Arthur rapped for order. "That's enough, Armand. If you can't control yourself, I'll order you out of the meeting. Lieutenant Cord has made it clear to me that he anticipates that some of you will find a verdict of suicide hard to believe and will make some foolish, amateurish attempt to uncover evidence turning it into a crime. Murder. I have called this meeting to tell you that the police intend to deal with any such quixotic impulse very harshly. I will deal with it very harshly from this end. What happened is police business and will be handled by the police. I hope I've made myself clear.

"Now for my second point. The students will ask us Gamma U's innumerable questions. Was Brad depressed? Did we know about his marriage? It will be the duty of each and every one of you as a Gamma U to politely but firmly evade all such questions. It is our duty as Brad's friends to keep our mouths shut. By that I do not mean to go about with mysterious and knowing looks. Brad is dead. Nothing can alter that. The policy of this house will be to say that Brad had been troubled lately and that we did not know the cause. Any comment?"

"Yeah, what was he troubled about?" Armand asked.

"I consider that question impertinent, Armand. Any other comments?" He stared around the room. "All right, then. This meeting is adjourned. Wait. One more point. This is for you boys that live in the house. The bed check and curfew will be adhered to rigidly."

Chairs were shoved back. Arthur walked out first. I went down the stairs and out the door. Tilly was sitting in my car.

"I walked over," she said. "I didn't want to be stood up."

"How did you know I was going to?"

I turned on the lights and motor. She moved over close to me. "We're going to your place and talk, Joe. I can think more clearly now."

6

Shooting at Windmills

SHE WENT IN AHEAD OF ME AND PUT THE LIGHTS ON, AS I PUT THE top of the car up against the dew. The gulf was rough, the waves thundering hard against the beach. We dragged chairs out onto the terrace. I held her tightly against me for a moment. "Hey," she said, "I want to keep on thinking clearly for a while. Leggo!"

"Chilly woman."

"Hush!" She sat down and after three tries we got our cigarettes going. "This," she said, "is probably silly. You'll have to let me know. Remember when we talked about what the dead boys had in common except the fraternity?"

"I remember."

"Brad's death makes the pattern more clear, Joe. Can you guess what they had in common?"

I thought for a time. "No. Give."

"Rex Winniger, Tod Sherman, Ted and Brad were all very positive people. Strong personalities. They had influence in the fraternity. Every house has a certain quota of nonenities. But there was nothing wishy-washy about any one of that four. They had power in the house and on the campus. Is that going to help?"

I felt the excitement. "That *is* going to help. You are a lovely and intelligent gal. I was so close to it I didn't even see it. Wait a minute now. Let me think. It doesn't make motive any stronger from a sane person's point of view, but it does make it clearer. Jealousy. Lust for power. If the pattern is anything other than accidental, it means we have to look among the membership for our boy. And we said a long time ago that insiders would have the edge by far on opportunity."

I guess we got it both at the same time. She reached over and held my hand. Her hand was like ice. "It couldn't be, Joe. It just couldn't be."

"Come on inside. I want to read you something."

We went in and shut the terrace doors against the wind. I found my lecture notes from the abnormal psychology class. They were fragmentary, but I could piece them together.

"Listen, Tilly. One of the types of insanity least vulnerable to any known treatment is the true psychopath. It's as though the person were born with some essential part missing. Conscience. The psychopath has no understanding of right and wrong. To him, the only thing is not to get caught. Has reasonable-sounding motives for all his actions.

"This type of person, if displeased with service, will set fire to a hotel and think nothing of the consequences as long as he is not apprehended. Entirely blind to the other person's point of view. Many murderers caught and convicted and sentenced are true psychopaths. Motive for crime often absurdly minor. True psychopath shows high incidence of endowment of brains and charm of manner. Is often outstanding. Often basically arrogant.

"Delights in outwitting others. Capable of carrying on long-range planning. Constantly acts in the presence of others. Often a liar as well, with amazingly intricate and well-conceived fabric of untruth. Society has no good answer as yet to the true psychopath."

I put the notebook away. She frowned at me. "But Joe! He's such a sweet guy! Gentle, understanding. He was so nice to me after Ted . . . died."

"High endowment of charm of manner. Constantly acts in the presence of others. Delights in outwitting others."

"But with all he's got on the ball, he'd be almost as big without . . . going to such crazy lengths."

"Motive for crime often absurdly minor."

"But to kill . . . just for the sake of fraternity house politics. Joe, it's crazy!"

"A true psychopath is an insane person. He hides among us normal jokers because he looks and acts and talks just like one of us . . . up to a point."

"Will the police listen to you?" she finally asked.

"They'd laugh in my face. What proof have I got? We've got to show that each murder helped him, even though it helped him in a minor way."

She crossed the room. "Hold me tight, darling. I'm scared. I don't want to think about him. I wish it were Bill, or Step, or little Jay Bruce, or even Al Siminik. Anybody except Arthur Marris."

"We've got to get hold of Harv Lorr, the fellow who was president last year. He can help us straighten out the timing on those other deaths. He's probably in North Dakota or some equally handy place."

"He's a Tampa boy. He's working in the family cigar business. With luck, Joe, we can be talking to him in an hour or so."

Harv Lorr came across from the door to our booth. "There he is," Tilly said. I looked up and saw a tall man approaching. He was prematurely gray and there were deep lines bracketing his mouth. He wore a light sport coat and an open-collared shirt.

"It's nice to see you again, Tilly," he said. His smile was a white ash in his sun-darkened face.

I had slid out of the booth. "Meet Joe Arlin, Harv," she said. We shook hands and murmured the usual things. We all sat down.

Harv ordered beer. He sat beside Tilly. He turned so he could look at her. "You sounded a little ragged over the phone. What's up?"

"It's about Brad," she said.

Harv frowned. "I read it this evening. Terrible thing. How do I fit?"

Tilly looked appealingly at me. I took over. "Mr. Lorr, I want to ask you some pretty pointless-sounding questions. If you stop me to ask me why I'm asking them, it will just take that much longer. Believe me, there's a definite pattern in the questions. First. The two sophomores who were killed in that automobile accident. Were they of any particular importance in fraternity politics? Were they active?"

Harv looked puzzled. "They were two votes. At the election of officers the previous June they'd voted for me as house president for the next year, rather than Ted Flynn."

"We'll move on to the next question. We weren't particularly interested in those two sophomores anyway. The next guy we care about is Rex Winniger. Was he active?"

"He was the outstanding man in the junior class. If he'd lived, I don't think there was any doubt of his becoming house president during his last year. It was a blow to all of us."

"He died in December. Then in March of this year it was Tod Sherman. He was a classmate of yours, as Flynn was. Was he active in house politics?"

"Everybody is to a certain extent, Arlin. When I won out over Ted, Ted gave up having any pronounced opinions. There is usually a couple of strong groups in the house. Tod Sherman was my opposition. We fought each other tooth and nail, but it was good-natured. At the time he died, we were pretty well lined up for the June elections. I wanted Arthur Marris for president and it was understood that Tod Sherman was pushing Brad Carroll.

"In a house that size the cronies of the pres get the gravy. You know that. Tilly said over the phone you were in the fraternity up at Wisconsin. You know then how a president on the way out through the graduation route tries to get one of his boys in for the following year."

"And so after Sherman died, Ted Flynn took over the opposition."

"If you knew all that, why ask me?"

"I didn't. I just guessed."

"I don't see how you could guess a thing like that. Ted was quite a boy. He went to work on the membership. It began to look as though Brad was going to give Arthur a very close race or squeak in himself in Arthur's place. But, of course, it was all shot to hell when Ted killed himself. In fact, we had to vote by mail during July, after school was out. I handled it.

"Arthur made it by a good ten votes. If Ted had lived to give his little talk in favor of Brad, it might have been a different story. Probably would have been, as Arthur sometimes makes a pretty poor impression in spite of his ability."

I leaned toward him. "And what would you say if I told you that Brad had organized a pretty effective resistance to Arthur and was hamstringing him very neatly by having acquired a majority of the voting strength?"

Harv gave me a quizzical look. "Now wait a minute, Arlin, let's not go off—"

"Can't you see the picture? First Winniger, then Sherman, then Ted, and now Brad. Which did each death help. Which man? Arthur. Every time."

He gave me a long scornful look. "Now hold it up, Arlin. That's kid stuff and you know it. Sure, the boys play politics. It's a game. It's good training. But nobody—nobody *ever* took it that seriously! Man, are you trying to tell me that old Arthur goes around killing people so he can get to be house president and then so he can keep his authority." He turned to Tilly. "You ought to know better than that!"

Tilly counted it for him on her fingers. "Winniger, Sherman, Flynn, Carroll. All in the way, Harv. All dead, Harv. You know the law of averages. If you don't care for our answer, give us your answer."

I could see it shake him a little. But he kept trying. "People, you don't kill guys for that sort of thing. Look! It's a college fraternity."

Then Tilly carefully explained to him about psychopaths. I was surprised at how much she remembered. She told it well. When she was through, Harv Lorr knew what a psychopath was.

"It seems so incredible!" he complained. But I saw from his eyes that we had him.

"If it was credible," I said, "somebody would have found out a long time ago. If there'd been a million bucks at stake or something like that—some motive that everybody would be willing to accept, the whole thing would have looked fishy and friend Arthur would have been stopped in his tracks. But this way, for a goal that seems unimportant to the common man, he can hack away almost without interference."

"What do you want me to do?" he asked humbly. He had given up. He believed us.

"Just sit tight," I said. "Be ready to give over the facts when they're called for."

"What do you two plan to do?" he asked.

I looked at Tilly. I kept my eyes on hers. "We've got to give the guy a new reason," I said, "and then jump him when he jumps."

Her lips formed a soundless, "No!"

"There's no other way," I said. And there wasn't. I wanted her to talk me out of it. I was ready to be talked out of it. I wanted no part of it. But she saw the logic of it, the same as I did.

"Keep your guard up," Harv said.

"I'll make him be careful," Tilly said.

I looked at my watch. "If we can make fifty miles in fifty minutes, you stand a chance of not being expelled, Miss Owen."

We left. I got her back in time. I went out to my place on the beach and wished I was in Montreal. I wished I was in Maine looking at the girls in their swim suits. I wore myself out swimming in the dark, parallel and close to the shore. I had a shot. I tried to go to sleep. I had another shot. I went to sleep. I dreamed of Arthur Marris. He had his thumbs in my jugular . . .

***

I waited for the coroner's jury. I told myself it was the smart thing to do. They might force the issue. Then they returned a suicide verdict and sad-eyed people shipped Brad to his home state in a box. Laura went abroad. . . .

Call it a ten-day wonder. A small town might have yacked about it until the second generation. A college has a more transient sort of vitality. Life goes on. Classes change. New assignments. Next Saturday's date. Call it the low attention factor of the young. A week turns any college crisis into ancient history.

Tilly and I talked. We talked ourselves limp. The conversations were all alike.

"We've got to get him to make the first move, Tilly."

"But to do that, Joe, you've got to be a threat to his setup. You've got to take Brad's place."

"You don't think I can engineer a strong opposition move?"

"I know you can. That's the trouble."

"What's the trouble?"

"You fool! I don't want you being a target."

"The other boys didn't have their guard up. Not one of them knew until the very last moment. It must have been a horrid surprise. He won't be able to surprise me."

"How can you be sure?"

"By never being off guard."

"People have to sleep, don't they?"

"Now you're handing me quite a sales talk, Till."

We talked. At the drive-ins, between races at the dog tracks, on my small private beach, riding in the car, walking from class.

I didn't tell her, but I was already starting the program. I took over Brad's sales talk. I buttonholed the brethren and breathed sharp little words into their ears.

I racked up a big zero.

It was funny. When I had no axe to grind, I was Rod Arlin, a nice guy, a transfer, a credit to the house. As soon as I started to electioneer I became that Arlin guy, and what the hell does he know about this chapter, and why doesn't he go back to Wisconsin. . . .

Arthur tapped me on the shoulder after dinner. "Talk for a while, Rod?"

"Why, sure."

We went to his room. He closed the door. I glanced toward the closet. I sat down and the little men were using banjo pics on my nerves. But I worked up a casual smile. "What's on your mind, Arthur?"

I didn't like him any more. That warm face was a mask. The deep-set eyes looked out, play-acting, pretending, despising the ignorance of ordinary mortals.

He stood by his desk and tamped the tobacco into his pipe with his thumb. He sucked the match flame down into the packed tobacco with a small sound that went *paaa, paaa, paaa*. He shook the match out.

"It pleased me that you transfered here, Rod. I liked you when I first met you. I considered you to be a well-adjusted person with a pretty fair perspective."

"Thanks."

"Lately you've been disappointing me."

"Indeed!" I made it chilly.

"This job I have is fairly thankless. I try to do my best. I could understand Brad Carroll when he tried to block me in my job. Brad was a professional malcontent. Not mean—just eager. You know what I mean?" He was bold. He half sat on the edge of his desk.

"I know what you mean."

"When you try to operate in the same way, I fail to understand you, Rod. What have you got to gain? You're only spending one year in this school. I want this chapter to run smoothly. The least thing we can have is unity among the members."

"And you're the great white father who's going to give it to us."

"Sarcasm always depresses me a little, Arlin."

"Maybe you depress me a little. Maybe I think that if you can't run the house right, a voting coalition should take the lead away from you."

"Look, Arlin. You have your own place on the beach. You have a very pleasant girl to run around with. You have a full schedule of classes. If you still have too much energy left over, why don't you try taking on a competitive sport?"

"Is it against the house rules to buck the pres?"

He sighed. "I didn't want to say this. But you force me. You may have noticed that there is a certain coolness toward you among the membership."

I nodded. I had noticed it.

"The membership feels that you are stirring up needless conflict among the more susceptible boys. We had a small closed meeting of the seniors the other day. It was resolved that I speak to you and tell you to cease and desist. If you had any chance of being successful, I wouldn't speak to you this way. But you have no chance. You just do not have enough influence as a transfer."

"If I don't?"

"Then I can swing enough votes to deny the privileges of the house to you."

"That takes a three-fourths majority."

"I have more than that."

I knew that he did. It was no bluff. I made my tone very casual. "Well, you've taken care of me a lot easier than some of the others."

He took his pipe out of his mouth. "I don't think I quite understand that. Rod."

"Then we'll drop it right there." I stood up.

He put his hand out. "No hard feelings?"

I ignored his hand. "Isn't that a little trite?"

He was good. He actually looked as though he wanted to weep. "That isn't the Gamma U spirit, Arlin."

"You take your job pretty seriously, Marris."

"I do the best I know how."

"What man could do more!" I said breathlessly. I turned and walked out.

7

Setting Up the Kill

TILLY HAD STAYED UP UNTIL THREE, SHE SAID, FINISHING A STORY for our mutual Friday class. She wanted me to read it. She had brought her carbon with her, in her purse.

"Right here?"

"No. The atmosphere has to be better than this, Joe. Wine, soft music."

"At my place I can provide the wine and the soft music. Would you okay the background?"

"Look, I'm blushing about the story. I thought it was something I'd never try to put on paper. Maybe I don't want you to read it."

It was Friday afternoon. We went out to my place. I put on dark glasses and took the carbon out on the beach.

Tilly said, "One thing I'm not going to do is sit and watch you read it, Joe." She walked down the beach away from me. I watched her walk away from me. No other girl had such a perfect line of back, concavity of slim waist, with the straightest of lines dropping from the armpits down to the in-curve of waist, then flaring, descending in a slanted curve to the pinched-in place of the knee, then sleekly curving again down the calf to the delicacy of ankle bone and the princess-narrow foot.

She turned and looked back and read my mind. "Hey, read the story," she said.

I read it. She'd showed me other work and I'd been ruthless about too many adjectives, about stiltedness. This one was simple. A boy and a girl. The awkward poetry of a first love. The boy dies. Something in the girl dies. Forever, she thinks. She wants it to be forever. She never wants to feel again. But as she comes slowly back to life, she fights against it. In vain.

And one day she has flowered again into another love and she cannot fight any more—and then she knows that the bruised heart is the one that can feel the most pain and also the most joy. There was a sting at the corners of my eyes as I finished it.

"Come here," I called. My voice was hoarse.

She came running. I held her by her sun-warm shoulders and kissed her. We both wept and it was a silly and precious thing.

"I do the writing in this family," I said. "I thought I did. Now I don't know. Now I don't think so."

"In this family? That is a phrase I leap upon, darling. That is a bone I take in my teeth and run with."

"Trapped," I said.

"I release you. I open the trap."

"Hell no! I insist on being trapped. I want to be trapped. I am a guy who believed in a multiplicity of women. I still do. You're all of them. You'll keep well. You'll last. How will you look at sixty?"

"At you."

"I'll be six years older. I'll sit in the corner and crack my knuckles."

"With me on your lap it'll be tough."

"We'll manage."

"Is it good enough to hand in, my story?"

"Too good. We won't hand it in. We'll whip up something else for the class. This one we keep. Maybe someday we'll sell it." Something stirred at the back of my mind. She saw then the change in my expression.

"What is it, Joe? What are you thinking about?"

"Let me get organized." I got up and paced around. She watched me. I came back and sat beside her. "Look. I can't power Arthur into trying anything. It won't work. I can't become dangerous. But there's another way."

"How?"

I tapped her story with one finger. "This way."

"How do you mean?"

"I write it up. Other names, other places, but the same method of death in each case. I'll twist it a little. I'll make it a small business concern. The similarity will be like a slap in the face."

"You'll have to write an ending to it. How does it end, Joe?"

"I won't end it. I'll take it right up to a certain spot."

"Then what are you going to do with it?"

"Easy, my love. I'm going to leave it in Arthur's room and wait and see what happens. I am going to have it look like an accident. I am going to do it in such a way that he's going to have to give some thought to eliminating one Joe Arlin."

"No, Joe. Please, no!"

"I've got to finish it off. One way or another."

She looked at me for a long time. "I suppose you do," she said quietly.

"Be a good girl. Play in the sand. Build castles. I want to bang this out while it's hot."

Dust clouded the page in the typewriter and I put the desk lamp on. Tilly sat across the room reading a magazine. I could feel her eyes on the back of my head from time to time.

I had brought my bad guy up to the Sherman death.

". . . stood for a moment and took the risk of looking to see that nothing had been forgotten. The gun had slid under the desk. The

body was utterly still. He saw the full clip on the desk beside the bottle of gun oil and. . . ."

"Hey!" I said.

"What, darling?"

"I've got a slow leak in my head. So has Lieutenant Cord. So had the murderer."

She came up behind me and put her hand lightly on my shoulder. "How do you mean?" I pointed at the sentence I had partially finished. "I don't see anything."

"Angel," I said, "Lieutenant Cord spoke of a full clip. I do not think he meant seven or six. I think he meant eight. A clip will not hold nine. There was one shell in the chamber. So how did it get there? To load a .45 with nine you put in a full clip, jack one into the chamber, remove clip, add one more to the clip and slap it back into the grip. A guy loading with nine is not likely to forget he has done so. Let us go calling. . . ."

Lieutenant Cord was about to leave. He frowned at me, looked appreciatively at Tilly. I put the question to him.

"Yes, the clip was full, but what does that prove? Maybe that one had been in the chamber for months. It even makes the case stronger my way. The guy takes out the clip, counts eight through the holes, and forgets the nine load."

"Or somebody else palms another shell out of the box he had and puts it in the chamber."

"What kind of tea do you drink, Arlin?"

"Be frank with me, Lieutenant. Doesn't this make the whole thing just a little more dubious to you?"

"No," he said flatly.

"You," I said, "look at life through a peashooter. You can focus on one incident at a time. Don't you ever try to relate each incident to a whole series?"

"Not this time."

"Miss Owen and I know who did it, Lieutenant."

"She drinks tea too, eh?"

"You don't want to know?"

"Not interested. Go play games. Go play cop. Maybe it's a part of your education."

We left. "For a time there he seemed brighter than that," I said.

We got into the car. "Joe," she said. "Joe, why don't you go back to New York? Why don't you tell Mr. Flynn that in your opinion Arthur Marris did it? Why don't you let him take over? He could build a fire under the lieutenant. Why don't you go to New York and take me with you?"

"Shameless!"

"Determined. You're not getting out of my sight again, Joe."

"I propose and what do I get? A bloodhound yet."

"Take us home, Joe."

"Home! Haven't you ever heard the old adage about street cars?"

"Yes, but you a have a season ticket. Home, Joe."

What can you do? . . .

I finished the unfinished yarn, folded one copy carelessly and shoved it into my pocket. I finished it Saturday. Tilly, who'd driven down early, was singing in the small kitchen, banging the dishes around.

"I go to leave the epic," I said.

"Hurry back. And, Joe, bring two of the biggest steaks you can find. The biggest. I've never been so hungry."

I felt like a commuter going to work. Kissed in the living room. Kissed at the door. Waved to. Told to be careful, dear.

Although the brethren with Saturday morning classes were at them, the others were in bed, most of them, with a few others looking squinty-eyed at black coffee in the dining room. I had some coffee with Step Krindall. This morning his baby blue eyes were bleary.

He moaned at forty-second intervals, wiping his pink head. He said, "That wrist watch of yours, Rod. Could you wrap it in your handkerchief and put it in your pocket? The tick is killing me."

"A large evening?"

"I don't know. I haven't counted my money yet. I missed the curfew and the bed check and the last bus out here."

"Seen Arthur around this morning?"

"He was coming out of the communal shower as I went in. A ghastly memory. He smiled at me. He slammed the door."

I finished my coffee.

"You slurp a little, don't you?" he said weakly.

I gave him a hearty slap on the back and went back to the row of senior rooms. I tapped on Arthur's door.

"Come in!" He looked up from the desk. He was studying. He frowned and then forced a smile.

"I came in to tell you I was a little off the beam the other day, Arthur. I'm sorry. Must be the heat."

"You don't know how glad I am to hear that, Rod. Frankly, you had me puzzled. I was going to suggest a checkup at the infirmary. Sometimes the boys get working too hard. A lot of times you can catch them before they crack."

I looked at him blandly. "Too bad you didn't catch Ted Flynn in time."

He nodded. "I've felt bad about that ever since. Of course, it was Harv Lorr's responsibility then. But all upperclassmen should look out for all the other brothers, don't you think?"

"I certainly think so." I pushed myself up out of the chair, said good-by and left quickly before he could call my attention to the folded second-sheets I'd left tucked visibly between the cushion and the arm. I had written it up without my name so that anyone would naturally read it to find out whose it was. And I was depending on the narrative hook I'd inserted in the first sentence to keep the reader on the line until it broke off on page nine.

I went and bought two steaks as thick as my fist, frozen shrimp, cocktail sauce, an orchid with funny gray petals edged with green, a bandanna with a pattern of dice all adding up to seven or eleven, gin and vermouth, both imported, and a vast silly shoulder bag of woven green straw. I wanted to buy her the main street, two miles of waterfront beach and the Hope diamond, plus a brace of gray convertibles that would match her level eyes. But I had to save something to buy later.

When I got back, she was gone. I stowed the perishables in the freezing compartment and jittered around, cracking my knuckles, humming, pacing and mumbling until she came back at quarter to one.

"Just where do you think you've been?" I demanded.

"Hey, be domineering some more. I love it."

"Where did you go?"

"I took a bus to school and found Molly and talked her out of this." She took it out of her purse and handed it to me. It was ridiculously small. On the palm of her hand, it looked as vicious and unprincipled as a coral snake.

"Her father gave it to her," Tilly said.

I took it and broke it and looked at the six full chambers. I put out one load and snapped the cylinder shut and made certain the hammer was on the empty chamber.

"I thought we ought to have one," she said in a small voice.

"You're cute," I said. "You're lovable. Come here." I opened the bottom bureau drawer and took out the .357 Magnum. If the one she brought was a coral snake, this is a hooded cobra. "Now we've got an arsenal."

"How was I to know, Joe?"

"Look at me! Am I a bare-handed type hero? Am I a comic-book buccaneer? Uh uh, honey. At moments of danger you will find Arlin huddled behind the artillery. You should have seen me in the war. Safety-first Arlin, they called me. The only man in the navy who could crawl all the way into a battle helmet."

Suddenly she was in my arms and shivering. I laid the weapons on the corner of the bureau and paid attention. "I'm scared, scared, scared," she said.

"Hold on for twelve hours," I said. "To yourself—not to me. Junior will move fast. He has to. The chips are on the table. The mask has slipped. The hour is on the wing and the bird in the bush has become a rolling stone."

"You're not making sense."

"What do you expect? Get out from under my chin. Stand over there. Okay. This is the order of battle. Arthur will show. He has to. He will show in one of two ways, but first night must fall. He will either come in here playing house president looking for an opening, or he will sneak.

"We will have the daylight hours in which to be gay. Then, come night, we must be boy scouts. We must guard against the sneak play. The surf makes considerable racket. A sneak will come from the beach.

"Thus, the answer is to be invisible from the beach and to be brightly lighted. The south corner of the living room answers that purpose very neatly. We will move the couch there and sit pleasantly side by side with weapons available and wait. In that way we shall be facing the door at which he will knock, should he decide to come openly. Should he knock—you, in great silence, will dart into the living room closet.

"Either way, we shall have two witnesses, you and me. Should he come openly, you must rely on my reflexes and my glib tongue, darling."

"I love your reflexes."

"On the ice you will find two mastodon steaks, shrimp that need no cleaning and one wild flower. The wild flower is for you.

"If the steaks turn out poorly, due to the cooking thereof, I shall take away the flower."

Oh, we were glib and gay throughout that long afternoon. We swam, drank, ate, told jokes, sang, held hands. Nothing did very much good. Our laughter was too brittle and high, and our jokes were leaden.

There were ghosts lurking behind our eyes.

Violence belongs in damp city alleys and shabby tenements and sordid little bars. It doesn't fit into an environment of white sand and the blue-green gulf water, and the absurd and frantic running of the sand pipers, and the coquinas digging into the wash of wet sand. Murder doesn't go with the tilt of white gull-wings against the incredibly blue sky, or the honeyed shoulders of the girl you love.

From time to time during that afternoon I would almost forget, and then it would come back—the evil that hid behind the sun and under the sand, and under the water and around the corner of the house.

8

Booby-Trap

THE SUN SANK GOLDEN TOWARD THE GULF AND THEN TURNED A bank of clouds to a bloody fire that was five thousand miles long. Dusk was an odd stormy yellow, and then a pink-blue and then a deep dusty blue. A cool wind came from the north west, and we shivered and went in and changed. We were as subdued as children who have been promised punishment.

It was possible that he might listen. As night gathered its dark strength and the sea turned alien, we sat in the brightness in the corner and read silently together from the same book, but even that was not powerful enough to keep us from starting with each small night noise. The wind grew steadily. The Magnum was a hard lump by my leg. She had clowned possession of the .32, stuffing it under the bright woven belt she wore, but it did not look particularly humorous.

When the knock came, firm and steady, we looked at each other for a moment frozen forever in memory. Her face was sun-bronzed, but the healthy color ran out of it so that around her mouth there was a tiny greenish tint. I squeezed her hand hard and pointed to the closet. I waited until the door was closed so that a thin dark line showed.

"Come on in!" I called. I let my hand rest casually beside me so that in one quick movement I could slap my hand onto the grip inches away.

Arthur Marris came in. The wind caught the door and almost tore it out of his hand. He shut it. The wind had rumpled his hair so that strands fell across his forehead. It gave him a more secretive look.

He smiled. "The night's getting wild."

I made myself put the book aside very casually. "Sit down, Arthur. I wrenched my ankle in the surf. If you want a drink, you'll have to go out into the kitchen and make it yourself. I want to stay off the foot."

I admired his tailor-made concern. "Oh! Too bad. Can I fix you one too?"

"Sure thing. Bourbon and water. Plain water."

I sat tensely while he worked in the kitchen. He brought me a drink and I was relieved to see that he had a drink in each hand. I took my drink with my left hand and as I did so I braced myself and moved my fingers closer to the weapon. He turned away and went back to the chair nine feet away. He sat down as though he were very weary.

I lifted the drink to my lips and pretended to sip at it. I set it on the floor by my feet, but I did not take my eyes off him as I set it down. It made me think that this must be the way a trainer acts when he enters the cage for the first time with a new animal. Every motion planned, every muscle ready to respond, so much adrenalin in the blood that the pulse thuds and it is hard to keep breathing slow and steady.

"I'm troubled, Rod," he said.

"Yes?" Casual and polite.

"This is something I don't know how to handle."

"Then it must be pretty important."

He took the folder copy out of his pocket. "Did you leave this in my room by accident?"

"So that's what happened to it. No, don't bother bringing it over. Toss it on the desk. I can see from here that it's mine."

"I read it, Rod."

"Like it?"

"What do you intend to do with it?"

In the game of chess there is move and countermove, gambit and response. The most successful attacks are those, as in war, where power is brought to bear on one point to mask a more devastating attack in another quarter. But before actual attack, the opponents must study each other's responses to feints and counterfeints.

"It's an assignment for my Friday class. Due next week."

"I suppose you realize, Rod, that you've patterned your story, as far as it's gone, on the series of misfortunes we've had in the house. You've twisted it a bit, but not enough. The method of death and the chronology are the same."

"I still can't see how you're troubled."

He frowned. "Is that hard? I had two other people in the house read it this afternoon to see if their slant was the same as mine. You can't hand that in the way it is. Your instructor would really have to be a fool not to tie it up with what has happened, particularly because Brad Carroll's death is still fresh in everyone's mind."

"What if he does?"

"You've made an amazingly strong case, Arlin, whether you know it or not. Until I read your . . . story, I thought it was absurd to think of what has happened as anything except a series of tragic accidents and coincidences. No one can read your story, Rod, without getting, as I have, a strong suspicion that there is some human agency behind this whole affair. Absurd as the motives may seem, I have been wondering if . . ." He frowned down at the floor.

"What have you been wondering?"

"I took a long walk this afternoon. I tried to think clearly and without any prejudice. I want to ask you to hold up sending in that assignment for a time. Is the original copy here?"

"In that desk."

"Are there any other carbons?"

"No. You've seen the only one."

"I'd like to have you come back to the house with me, Rod. Right now. We might be able to clear this up."

I smiled and shook my head. "Not with this ankle."

He stood up and came two steps toward me. "I'll help you, Rod. You see I want you to come back there with me, because even though your reasoning might be right in that story, the conclusion is . . ."

Marris stopped short and stared at the leveled weapon. He licked his lips. "What's that for?"

"What do you think it's for? How do you like the end of the road."

He smiled crookedly. "Look, Arlin. You can't possibly believe that I . . ."

The room was gone as abruptly as though the house had exploded. Too late, I remembered the fuse box on the outside of the house, in typical Florida fashion. We were alone in the sighing darkness, in a night that was utterly black. The outside door banged open and the sea mist blew in, curling through the room, tasting of salt.

I moved to one side, toward the closet, as fast and as quietly as I could go. I took three steps when somebody ran into me hard. A heavy shoulder caught my chest and I slammed back against the closet door, banging it shut. The impact tore the gun out of my hand and I heard it skitter across onto the bare floor beyond the rug. I touched an arm, slid my hand down to the wrist and punched hard where the head should be.

I hit the empty air and the wrist twisted out of my grip. Something hard hit me above the ear and I stumbled, dazed and off balance. I fell and had sense enough to keep rolling until I ran up against a piece of furniture. I had gotten twisted in the darkness. I felt of it and found it was the desk. Tilly screamed at that moment and the scream was far away because of the closed closet door.

Crawling on my hands and knees, I patted the floor ahead of me, looking for the gun. Somebody rolled into me and there was a thick coughing sound. I slid away. There was a thumping noise. The shots came, fast and brittle against the sound of the sea. There was an angry tug at my wrist and then a liquid warmth across my hand.

The terrace doors we had locked splintered open and the white glare of flashlights caught me full in the face as I sat back on my heels.

Two figures tramped toward me and around me. I turned and saw that they had gone toward a moving mass in the center of the room. One of the figures who had come in towered over the other. I got to my feet and reached the closet door and opened the closet. At that moment the electricity came back on.

Tilly stared up at me and said, "I thought you were . . . I thought you were . . ." She leaned against the wall of the closet, closed her eyes and sank slowly toward the floor.

I turned and saw Lieutenant Cord pulling a man off Arthur Marris. Arthur lay on his back. His face was dark and the breath was whistling in his throat. His eyes were closed.

"Back up against that wall," Cord said quietly to the other man who had risen to his feet.

Step Krindall blinked his baby-blue eyes. Droplets of sweat stood on his pink bald head. He stared incredulously at Arthur. He said, "I thought I had my hands on Arlin! My heaven, I thought it was Arlin! I was strangling Arthur." He worked the fingers of his fat pink hands convulsively.

"You were trying to kill Arlin like you killed Carroll?" Cord asked, very casually.

"Sure," Krindall said. "And the other ones. My heaven, I have to take care of Arthur. He's not smart you know. He'd let them push him around, Arthur would. I've been watching out for Arthur now for a long time." He looked appealingly at Lieutenant Cord.

"He knew what you've been doing?"

"Oh, no! He wouldn't like it even though it helped him a lot. I never told him. He won't die, will he?"

Arthur stirred. He opened his eyes. He gagged and rubbed his throat as he sat up.

Krindall took a step forward, ignoring Cord. "Arthur, you're not sore at me, are you? I knew you wouldn't be sore. I was helping you. And then when you showed me that story today, I just thought Arlin would make trouble for both of us and it would be better if he was dead."

He reached down as though to touch Arthur's shoulder. Arthur pulled himself away, violently, hunching along the floor.

Step looked at Arthur for one incredulous moment and then began to blubber, his eyes streaming, his hands making helpless appealing flapping motions.

"Who was shooting?" Cord demanded.

That reminded me forcibly of Tilly. I turned back to her.

She was sitting on the closet floor staring at me. She wore a curious expression. "I felt myself fainting. I sort of expected to wake up on the couch. Only—I didn't."

Cord saw the punctured door, thin plywood splinters protruding. "You were shooting from inside the closet?" he asked incredulously.

"I was locked in," Tilly said with dignity as I helped her to her feet. "I thought Mr. Arlin was being killed. I wanted to create a diversion."

"Great diversion," Cord said dryly, staring at my hand. The blood was dripping from the tips of my index and middle fingers. Tilly looked down. This time I was ready. I caught her and put her on the couch.

Arthur stood up shakily. He said, "Rod, that's what I wanted to talk to you about. You built such a strong case you got me thinking about Krindall. Little things that I had half forgotten. I still couldn't believe it."

Krindall stood, weeping silently. But there was a gleam in his tear-damp blue eyes. I said,

"Look at him! Great emotion. Great acting. He's standing there trying to figure an angle. All this doesn't actually mean anything to him. This great devotion to Arthur is just a sham."

The tears stopped as abruptly as though they had been turned off with a pipe wrench. He looked like an evil, besotted child. "I could have got you, Arlin," he said. "I could have got you good. I rode Rex under the water and towed him out to where it was deep. I got Tod into an argument about guns and slipped a round into the chamber. The argument was whether you could see any glint of light down the barrel.

"I fixed the noose for Ted and got him on the chair to tell me if it was water pipes in the top of the closet. He didn't see the noose until I slipped it over his head and yanked the chair away. Then I had to keep pulling his hands off the pipe for a little while. I knew about Brad and his wife. When she left, I went in. It didn't take long. All of them were stupid. All of them. I've been smarter than any of you."

"Yeah, you're real bright," Cord said speculatively. "Real bright. We got some mind-doctors who can check on you."

"Doctors! You think I'm crazy!"

He made a dive to one side. Even as he moved, I saw the butt of the Magnum peeping out around the edge of the chair leg. I needn't have worried. Cord took one step and swung a fist that was like a bag of rocks on the end of the rope. The fist contacted Step Krindall in mid-flight. It made a sound like somebody dropping an over-ripe cantaloupe. Cord sucked his big knuckles and stared down at Krindall.

"Real bright," he murmured. He looked over at me. "You worried me, Arlin. I thought it wouldn't do any harm keeping an eye on this place."

Tilly revived and Krindall came to enough to be walked out. As I held my punctured epidermis under the cold water faucet, I apologized to a glum Marris.

We were alone again and the night wind still blew, but it was not alien. The sea sighed, but it was a domesticated beast.

Then we had a solemn nightcap together. Tilly said that she thought I ought to drive her back to the campus and I said why of course. We put the top up and I took her back as though we were returning from a very average date.

Ten days later I hit rain as I crossed into Georgia. I took the coast road and the rain stayed with me. The wipers clicked back and forth and the blacktop was the color of oiled sin.

I thought of facing one Mr. Flynn and telling him what had happened, what I had found out. He would have some of the details from the papers. There were others he should know, and other I would spare him. It wouldn't be pretty, but it was something that had to be done. Krindall would be institutionalized.

Tilly stirred and yawned and stretched like a sleepy cat and smiled at me. Depression went away as though the sun had come out.

"Hungry?" I asked.

"Mmm. Famished. Let's find a place to eat and then go find a nice court to stay in. We'll stay there until a sunny day comes along, huh?"

"What'll thinkle peep, honey? It's eleven o'clock in the morning."

"Who cares what they think, huh? Show 'em the license."

"Hunting, driving or marriage?"

"Hunting, of course. No, I'll tell 'em we had to get married."

"Then they'll ask why."

"Then I'll say because you got me expelled from junior high."

"You don't look old enough to have been in junior high."

She curled against me. "Just old enough to know better, hey?"

It was raining like crazy in Georgia and the sun was shinning bright.

Mickey Spillane

EVERYBODY'S WATCHING ME

Frank Morrison Spillane (1918–) created a literary stir in the Fifties that has never been equaled. Better known as "Mickey Spillane," he wrote six of the ten best-selling books of all time, much to the dismay of critics throughout the land.

His private-eye Mike Hammer set off the furor. Hammer was an unabashed vigilante, a one-man lynching party who swore to clean up the corruption that infested post-World War II America (like many men of his time, Spillane had served in the war).

The books were sexy, violent and dark. One of them made an excellent film, Kiss Me, Deadly. Robert Aldrich, the director, didn't appreciate the Spillane novels so he made Hammer a cynical divorce detective instead of a soiled hero.

What got lost in all the fuss—the books seemed to buy into every right-wing paranoid fantasy tearing the country apart—was that the guy could write. True page-turners. My generation of boys and young men read our first sex scenes in Spillane. Same with the violence.

I liked the atmospherics. Spillane claimed to be writing about American cities but he was actually writing about a version of hell. Nobody was to be trusted in this hell. And even in the daytime it was dark (read the opening of One Lonely Night if you're curious about how to evoke fear and dread and an almost exquisite sense of loneliness). And a lot of the time the good guys lost.

He could write very well. In personal interviews he was sardonic, self-deprecating, and appealing. People expected an ogre. Instead they got a guy who'd make a great neighbor.

He got wealth, he got security, and he got the fame that comes to only the few.

But not until the a few decades later did he get his due as a literary craftsman, when the Private Eye Writers of America gave him its coveted Lifetime Achievement Award.

Among those who leave footprints behind, Spillane's are some of the biggest.
Here's an especially good example of Spillane at his best.

E.G.

I HANDED THE GUY THE NOTE AND SHIVERED A LITTLE BIT BE-cause the guy was as big as they come, and even though he had a belly you couldn't get your arms around, you wouldn't want to be the one who figured you could sink your fist in it. The belly was as hard as the rest of him, but not quite as hard as his face.

Then I knew how hard the back of his hand was because he smashed it across my jaw and I could taste the blood where my teeth bit into my cheek.

Maybe the guy holding my arm knew I couldn't talk because he said, "A guy give him a fin to bring it, boss. He said that."

"Who, kid?"

I spit the blood out easy so it dribbled down my chin instead of going on the floor. "Gee, Mr. Renzo . . ."

His hand made a dull, soggy crack on my skin. The buzz got louder in my ears and there was a jagged, pounding pain in my skull.

"Maybe you didn't hear me the first time, kid. I said who."

The hand let go my arm and I slumped to the floor. I didn't want to, but I had to. There were no legs under me any more. My eyes were open, conscious of only the movement of ponderous things that got closer. Things that moved quickly and seemed to dent my side without causing any feeling at all.

That other voice said, "He's out, boss. He ain't saying a thing."

"I'll make him talk."

"Won't help none. So a guy gives him a fin to bring the note. He's not going into a song and dance with it. To the kid a fin's a lot of dough. He watches the fin, not the guy."

"You're getting too damn bright," Renzo said.

"That's what you pay me for being, boss."

"Then act bright. You think a guy hands a note like this to some kid? Any kid at all? You think a kid's gonna bull in here to deliver it when he can chuck it down a drain and take off with the fin?"

"So the kid's got morals."

"So the kid knows the guy or the guy knows him. He ain't letting no kid get away with his fin." The feet moved away from me, propped themselves against the dark blur of the desk. "You read this thing?" Renzo asked.

"No."

"Listen then. 'Cooley is dead. Now my fine fat louse, I'm going to spill your guts all over your own floor.' " Renzo's voice droned to a stop. He sucked hard on the cigar and said, "It's signed, *Vetter*."

You could hear the unspoken words in the silence. That hush that comes when the name was mentioned and the other's half-whispered "Son of a bitch, they were buddies, boss?"

"Who cares? If that crumb shows his face around here, I'll break his lousy back. Vetter, Vetter, Vetter. Everyplace you go that crumb's name you hear."

"Boss, look. You don't want to tangle with that guy. He's killed plenty of guys. He's . . ."

"He's different from me? You think he's a hard guy?"

"You ask around, boss. They'll tell you. That guy don't give a damn for nobody. He'll kill you for looking at him."

"Maybe in his own back yard he will. Not here, Johnny, not here. This is my city and my back yard. Here things go my way and Vetter'll get what Cooley got." He sucked on the cigar again and I began to smell the smoke. "Guys what pull a fastie on me get killed. Now Cooley don't work on my tables for no more smart plays. Pretty soon the cops can take Vetter off their list because he won't be around no more either."

"You going to take him, boss?" Johnny said.

"What do you think?"

"Anything you say, boss. I'll pass the word around. Somebody'll know what he looks like and'll finger him." He paused, then, "What about the kid?"

"He's our finger, Johnny."

"Him?"

"You ain't so bright as I thought. You should get your ears to the ground more. You should hear things about Vetter. He pays off for favors. The errand was worth a fin, but he's gonna look in to make sure the letter got here. Then he spots the kid for his busted up face. First time he makes contact we got him. You know what, Johnnie? To Vetter I'm going to do things slow. When they find him the cops get all excited but they don't do nothing. They're glad to see Vetter dead. But other places the word gets around, see? Anybody can bump Vetter gets to be pretty big and nobody pulls any more smart ones. You understand, Johnny?"

"Sure, boss. I get it. You're going to do it yourself?"

"Just me, kid, just me. Like Helen says, I got a passion to do something myself and I just got to do it. Vetter's for me. He better be plenty big, plenty fast and ready to start shooting the second we meet up."

It was like when Pop used to say he'd do something and we knew he'd do it sure. You look at him with your face showing the awe a kid gets when he knows fear and respect at the same time and that's how Johnny must have been looking at Renzo. I knew it because it was in his voice when he said, "You'll do it, boss. You'll own this town, lock, stock and gun butt yet."

"I own it now, Johnny. Never forget it. Now wake that kid up."

This time I had feeling and it hurt. The hand that slapped the full vision back to my eyes started the blood running in my mouth again and I could feel my lungs choking on a sob.

"What was he like, kid?" The hand came down again and this time Renzo took a step forward. His fingers grabbed my coat and jerked me to the floor.

"You got asked a question. What was he like?"

"He was . . . big," I said. The damn slob choked me again and I wanted to break something over his head.

"How big?"

"Like you. Bigger'n six. Heavy."

Renzo's mouth twisted into a sneer and he grinned at me. "More. What was his face like?"

"I don't know. It was dark. I couldn't see him good."

He threw me. Right across the room he threw me and my back smashed the wall and twisted and I could feel the tears rolling down my face from the pain.

"You don't lie to Renzo, kid. If you was older and bigger I'd break you up into little pieces until you talked. It ain't worth a fin. Now you start telling me what I want to hear and maybe I'll slip you something."

"I . . . I don't know. Honest, I . . . if I saw him again it'd be

different." The pain caught me again and I had to gag back my
voice.

"You'd know him again?"

"Yes."

Johnny said, "What's your name, kid?"

"Joe . . . Boyle."

"Where do you live?" It was Renzo this time.

"Gidney Street," I told him. "Number three."

"You work?"

"Gordon's. I . . . push."

"What'd he say?" Renzo's voice had a nasty tone to it.

"Gordon's a junkie," Johnny said for me. "Has a place on River
Street. The kid pushes a cart for him collecting metal scraps."

"Check on it," Renzo said, "then stick with him. You know
what to do."

"He won't get away, boss. He'll be around whenever we want
him. You think Vetter will do what you say?"

"Don't things always happen like I say? Now get him out of
here. Go over him again so he'll know we mean what we say.
That was a lousy fin he worked for."

After things hurt so much they begin to stop hurting completely.
I could feel the way I went through the air, knew my foot hit the
railing and could taste the cinders that ground in my mouth. I
lay there like I was passing out, waiting for the pain to come
swelling back, making sounds I didn't want to make. My stomach
wanted to break loose but couldn't find the strength and I just
lay there cursing guys like Renzo who could do anything they
wanted and get away with it.

Then the darkness came, went away briefly and came back
again. When it lost itself in the dawn of agony there were hands
brushing the dirt from my face and the smell of flowers from the
softness that was a woman who held me and said, "You poor kid,
you poor kid."

My eyes opened and looked at her. It was like something you
dream about because she was the kind of woman you always stare
at, knowing you can't have. She was beautiful, with yellow hair
that tumbled down her neck like a torch that lit up her whole

body. Her name was Helen Troy and I wanted to say, "Hello, Helen," but couldn't get the words out of my mouth.

Know her? Sure, everybody knew her. She was Renzo's feature attraction at his Hideaway Club. But I never thought I'd live to have my head in her lap.

There were feet coming up the path that turned into one of the men from the stop at the gate and Helen said, "Give me a hand, Finney. Something happened to the kid."

The guys she called Finney stood there with his hands on his hips shaking his head. "Something'll happen to you if you don't leave him be. The boss gives orders."

She tightened up all over, her fingers biting into my shoulder. It hurt but I didn't care a bit. "Renzo? The pig!" She spat it out with a hiss. She turned her head slowly and looked at me. "Did he do this, kid?"

I nodded. It was all I could do.

"Finney," she said, "go get my car. I'm taking the kid to a doctor."

"Helen, I'm telling you . . ."

"Suppose I told the cops . . . no, not the cops, the feds in this town that you have holes in your arms?"

I thought Finney was going to smack her. He reached down with his hand back but he stopped. When a dame looks at you that way you don't do anything except what she tells you to.

"I'll get the car," he said.

She got me on my feet and I had to lean on her to stay there. She was just as big as I was. Stronger at the moment. Faces as bad off as mine weren't new to her, so she smiled and I tried to smile back and we started off down the path.

We said it was a fight and the doctor did what he had to do. He laid on the tape and told me to rest a week then come back. I saw my face in his mirror, shuddered and turned away. No matter what I did I hurt all over and when I thought of Renzo all I could think of was that I hoped somebody would kill him. I hoped they'd kill him while I watched and I hoped it would take a long, long time for him to die.

Helen got me out to the car, closed the door after me and slid in behind the wheel. I told her where I lived and she drove up to the house. The garbage cans had been spilled all over the sidewalk and it stank.

She looked at me curiously. "Here?"

"That's right," I told her. "Thanks for everything."

Then she saw the sign on the door. It read, "ROOMS." "Your family live here too?"

"I don't have a family. It's a rooming house."

For a second I saw her teeth, white and even, as she pulled her mouth tight. "I can't leave you here. Somebody has to look after you."

"Lady, if . . ."

"Ease off, kid. What did you say your name was?"

"Joe."

"Okay, Joe. Let me do things my way. I'm not much good for anything but every once in awhile I come in handy for something decent."

"Gee, lady . . ."

"Helen."

"Well, you're the nicest person I've ever known."

I said she was beautiful. She had the beauty of the flashiest tramp you could find. That kind of beauty. She was like the dames in the big shows who are always tall and sleepy looking and who you'd always look at but wouldn't marry or take home to your folks. That's the kind of beauty she had. But for a long couple of seconds she seemed to grow a new kind of beauty that was entirely different and she smiled at me.

"Joe . . ." and her voice was warm and husky, "that's the nicest thing said in the nicest way I've heard in a very long time."

My mouth still hurt too much to smile back so I did it with my eyes. Then something happened to her face. It got all strange and curious, a little bit puzzled and she leaned forward and I could smell the flowers again as that impossible something happened when she barely touched her mouth to mine before drawing back with that searching movement of her eyes.

"You're a funny kid, Joe."

She shoved the car in to gear and let it roll away from the curb. I tried to sit upright, my hand on the door latch. "Look, I got to get out."

"I can't leave you here."

"Then where . . ."

"You're going back to my place. Damn it, Renzo did this to you and I feel partly responsible."

"That's all right. You only work for him."

"It doesn't matter. You can't stay there."

"You're going to get in trouble, Helen."

She turned and flashed me a smile. "I'm always in trouble."

"Not with him."

"I can handle that guy."

She must have felt the shudder that went through me.

"You'd be surprised how I can handle that fat slob," she said. Then added in an undertone I wasn't supposed to hear, "Sometimes."

It was a place that belonged to her like flowers belong in a rock garden. It was the top floor of an apartment hotel where the wheels all stayed in the best part of town with a private lawn twelve stories up where you could look out over the city and watch the lights wink back at you.

She made me take all my clothes off and while I soaked in a warm bath full of suds she scrounged up a decent suit that was a size too big, but still the cleanest thing I had worn in a long while. I put it on and came out in the living room feeling good and sat down in the big chair while she brought in tea.

Helen of Troy, I thought. So this is what she looked like. Somebody it would take a million bucks and a million years to get close to . . . and here I was with nothing in no time at all.

"Feel better, Joe?"

"A little."

"Want to talk? You don't have to if you don't want to."

"There's not much to say. He worked me over."

"How old are you, Joe?"

I didn't want to go too high. "Twenty-one," I said.

There it was again, that same curious expression. I was glad of the bandages across my face so she couldn't be sure if I was lying or not.

I said, "How old are you?" and grinned at her.

"Almost thirty, Joe. That's pretty old, isn't it?"

"Not so old."

She sipped at the tea in her hand. "How did you happen to cross Renzo?"

It hurt to think about it. "Tonight," I said, "it had just gotten dark. A guy asked me if I'd run a message to somebody for five bucks and I said I would. It was for Mr. Renzo and he told me to take it to the Hideaway Club. At first the guy at the gate wouldn't let me in, then he called down that other one, Johnny. He took me in, all right."

"Yes?"

"Renzo started giving it to me."

"Remember what the message said?"

Remember? I'd never forget it. I'd hope from now until I died that the guy who wrote it did everything he said he'd do.

"Somebody called Vetter said he'd kill Renzo," I told her.

Her smile was distant, hard. "He'll have to be a pretty tough guy," she said. What she said next was almost under her breath and she was staring into the night when she said it. "A guy like that I could go for."

"What?"

"Nothing, Joe." The hardness left her smile until she was a soft thing. "What else happened?"

Inside my chest my heart beat so fast it felt like it was going to smash my ribs loose. "I . . . heard them say . . . I would have to finger the man for them."

"You?"

I nodded, my hand feeling the soreness across my jaw.

She stood up slowly, the way a cat would. She was all mad and tense but you couldn't tell unless you saw her eyes. They were the same eyes that made the Finney guy jump. "Vetter," she said. "I've heard the name before."

"The note said something about a guy named Cooley who's dead."

I was watching her back and I saw the shock of the name make the muscles across her shoulders dance in the light. The tightness went down her body until she stood there stiff-legged, the flowing curves of her chest the only things that moved at all.

"Vetter," she said. "He was Cooley's friend."

"You knew Cooley?"

Her shoulders relaxed and she picked a cigarette out of a box and lit it. She turned around, smiling, the beauty I had seen in the car there again.

"Yes," Helen said softly, "I knew Cooley."

"Gee."

She wasn't talking to me anymore. She was speaking to somebody who wasn't there and each word stabbed her deeper until her eyes were wet. "I knew Cooley very well. He was . . . nice. He was a big man, broad in the shoulders with hands that could squeeze a woman . . ." She paused and took a slow pull on the cigarette. "His voice could make you laugh or cry. Sometimes both. He was an engineer with a quick mind. He figured how he could make money from Renzo's tables and did it. He even laughed at Renzo and told him crooked wheels could be taken by anybody who knew how."

The tears started in the corners of her eyes but didn't fall. They stayed there, held back by pride maybe.

"We met one night. I had never met anyone like him before. It was wonderful, but we were never meant for each other. It was one of those things. Cooley was engaged to a girl in town, a very prominent girl."

The smoke of the cigarette in her hand swirled up and blurred her face.

"But I loved him," she said. With a sudden flick of her fingers she snapped the butt on the rug and ground it out with her shoe. "I hope he kills him! I hope he kills him!"

Her eyes drew a line up the floor until they were on mine. They were clear again, steady, curious for another moment, then steady again. I said, "You don't . . . like Renzo very much?"

"How well do you know people, Joe?"

I didn't say anything.

"You know them too, don't you? You don't live in the nice section of town. You know the dirt and how people are underneath. In a way you're lucky. You know it now, not when you're too old. Look at me, Joe. You've seen women like me before? I'm not much good. I look like a million but I'm not worth a cent. A lot of names fit me and they belong. I didn't get that way because I wanted to. He did it, Renzo. I was doing fine until I met him.

"Sure, some young kids might think I'm on top, but they never get to peek behind the curtain. They never see what I'm forced into and the kind of people I have to know because others don't want to know me. If they do they don't want anybody to know about it."

"Don't say those things, Helen."

"Kid, in ten years I've met two decent people. Cooley was the first." She grinned and the hate left her face. "You're the other one. You don't give a hang what I'm like, do you?"

"I never met anybody like you before."

"Tell me more." Her grin got bigger.

"Well, you're beautiful. I mean real beautiful. And nice. You sure are built . . ."

"Good enough," she said and let the laugh come out. It was a deep, happy laugh and sounded just right for her. "Finish your tea."

I had almost forgotten about it. I drained it down, the heat of it biting into the cuts along my cheek. "Helen . . . I ought to go home. If Mr. Renzo finds out about this, he's going to burn up."

"He won't touch me, Joe."

I let out a grunt.

"You either. There's a bed in there. Crawl into it. You've had enough talk for the night."

I woke up before she did. My back hurt too much to sleep and the blood pounded in my head too hard to keep it on the pillow. The clock beside the bed said it was seven-twenty and I kicked off the covers and dragged my clothes on.

The telephone was in the living room and I took it off the cradle quietly. When I dialed the number I waited, said hello as softly as I could and asked for Nick.

He came on in a minute with a coarse, "Yeah?"

"This is Joe, Nick."

"Hey, where are you, boy? I been scrounging all over the dump for you. Gordon'll kick your tail if you don't get down here. Two other guys didn't show . . ."

"Shut up and listen. I'm in a spot."

"You ain't kidding. Gordon said . . ."

"Not that, jerk. You see anybody around the house this morning?"

I could almost hear him think. Finally he said, "Car parked across the street. Think there was a guy in it." Then, "Yeah, yeah, wait up. Somebody was giving the old lady some lip this morning. Guess I was still half asleep. Heard your name mentioned."

"Brother!"

"What's up, pal?"

"I can't tell you now. You tell Gordon I'm sick or something, okay?"

"Nuts. I'll tell him you're in the clink. He's tired of that sick business. You ain't been there long enough to get sick yet."

"Tell him what you please. Just tell him. I'll call you tonight."

I slipped the phone back and turned around. I hadn't been as quiet as I thought I'd been. Helen was standing there in the doorway of her bedroom, a lovely golden girl, a bright morning flower wrapped in a black stem like a bud ready to pop.

"What is it, Joe?"

There wasn't any use hiding things from her. "Somebody's watching the house. They were looking for me this morning."

"Scared, Joe?"

"Darn right I'm scared! I don't want to get laid out in some swamp with my neck broken. That guy Renzo is nuts. He'll do anything when he gets mad."

"I know," Helen said quietly. Her hand made an unconscious movement across her mouth. "Come on, let's get some breakfast."

We found out who Vetter was that morning. At least Helen found out. She didn't cut corners or make sly inquiries. She did an impossible thing and drove me into town, parked the car and took a cab to a big brownstone building that didn't look a bit different from any other building like it in the country. Across the door it said "PRECINCT NO. 4" and the cop at the desk said the captain would be more than pleased to see us.

The captain was more than pleased, all right. It started his day off right when she came in and he almost offered me a cigar. The nameplate said his name was Gerot and if I had to pick a cop out to talk to, I'd pick him. He was in his late thirties with a build like a wrestler and I'd hate to be in the guy's shoes who tried to bribe him.

It took him a minute to settle down. A gorgeous blonde in a dark green gabardine suit blossoming with curves didn't walk in every day. And when he did settle down, it was to look at me and say, "What can I do for you?" but looking like he already knew what happened.

Helen surprised him. "I'd like to know something about a man," she said. "His name is Vetter."

The scowl started in the middle of his forehead and spread to his hairline.

"Why?"

She surprised him again. "Because he promised to kill Mark Renzo."

You could watch his face change, see it grow intense, sharpen, notice the beginning of a caustic smile twitch at his lips. "Lady, do you know what you're talking about?"

"I think so."

"You think?"

"Look at me," she said. Captain Gerot's eyes met hers, narrowed and stayed that way. "What do you see, Captain?"

"Somebody who's been around. You know all the answers, don't you?"

"All of them, Captain. The questions, too."

I was forgotten. I was something that didn't matter and I was happy about it.

Helen said, "What do you think about Renzo, Captain?"

"He stinks. He operates outside city limits where the police have no jurisdiction and he has the county police sewed up. I think he has some of my men sewed up too. I can't be sure but I wish I were. He's got a record in two states, he's clean here. I'd like to pin a few jobs on that guy. There's no evidence, yet he pulled them. I know this . . . if I start investigating I'm going to have some wheels on my neck."

Helen nodded. "I could add more. It really doesn't matter. You know what happened to Jack Cooley?"

Gerot's face looked mean. "I know I've had the papers and the state attorney climb me for it."

"I don't mean that."

The captain dropped his face in his hands resignedly, wiped his eyes and looked up again. "His car was found with bullet holes in it. The quantity of blood in the car indicated that nobody could have spilled that much and kept on living. We never found the body."

"You know why he died?"

"Who knows? I can guess from what I heard. He crossed Renzo, some said. I even picked up some info that said he was in the narcotics racket. He had plenty of cash and no place to show where it came from."

"Even so, Captain, if it was murder, and Renzo's behind it, you'd like it to be paid for."

The light blue of Gerot's eyes softened dangerously. "One way or another . . . if you must know."

"It could happen. Who is Vetter?"

He leaned back in his chair and folded his hands behind his neck. "I could show you reams of copy written about this guy. I could show you transcripts of statements we've taken down and copies that the police in other cities have sent out. I could show you all that but I can't pull out a picture and I can't drop in a print number on the guy. The people who got to know him and who finally saw him, all seem to be dead."

My voice didn't sound right. "Dead?"

Gerot's hands came down and flattened on the desk. "The guy's a killer. He's wanted every place I could think of. Word has it that he's the one who bumped Tony Briggs in Chicago. When Birdie Cullen was going to sing to the grand jury, somebody was paid fifty thousand to cool him off and Vetter collected from the syndicate. Vetter was paid another ten to knock off the guy who paid him the first time so somebody could move into his spot."

"So far he's only a name, Captain?"

"Not quite. We have a few details on him but we can't give them out. That much you understand, of course."

"Of course. But I'm still interested."

"He's tough. He seems to know things and do things nobody else would touch. He's a professional gunman in the worst sense of the word and he'll sell that gun as long as the price is right."

Helen crossed her legs with a motion that brought her whole body into play. "Supposing, Captain, that this Vetter was a friend of Jack Cooley? Supposing he got mad at the thought of his friend being killed and wanted to do something about it?"

Gerot said, "Go on."

"What would you do, Captain?"

The smile went up one side of his face. "Most likely nothing." He sat back again. "Nothing at all . . . until it happened."

"Two birds with one stone, Captain? Let Vetter get Renzo . . . and you get Vetter?"

"The papers would like that," he mused.

"No doubt." Helen seemed to uncoil from the chair. I stood up too and that's when I found out just how shrewd the captain was. He didn't bother to look at Helen at all. His blue eyes were all on me and being very, very sleepy.

"Where do you come in, kid?" he asked me.

Helen said it for me. "Vetter gave him a warning note to hand to Renzo."

Gerot smiled silently and you could see that he had the whole picture in his mind. He had our faces, he knew who she was and all about her, he was thinking of me and wanted to know all about me. He would. He was that kind of cop. You could tell.

We stood on the steps of the building and the cops coming in gave her the kind of look every man on the street gave her. Appreciative. It made me feel good just to be with her. I said, "He's a smart cop."

"They're all smart. Some are just smarter than others." A look of impatience crossed her face. "He said something . . ."

"Reams of copy?" I suggested.

I was easy for her to smile at. She didn't have to look up or down. Just a turn of her head. "Bright boy."

She took my hand and this time I led the way. I took her to the street I knew. It was off the main drag and the people on it had a look in their eyes you don't see uptown. It was a place where the dames walked at night and followed you into bars if they thought you had an extra buck to pass out.

They're little joints, most of them. They don't have neon lights and padded stools, but when a guy talks he says something and doesn't play games. There's excitement there and always that feeling that something is going to happen.

One of those places was called The Clipper and the boys from the *News* made it their hangout. Cagey boys with the big think under their hats. Fast boys with a buck and always ready to pay off on something hot. Guys who took you like you were and didn't ask too many questions.

My kind of people.

Bucky Edwards was at his usual stool getting a little bit potted because it was his day off. I got the big stare and the exaggerated wink when he saw the blonde which meant I'd finally made good about dragging one in with me. I didn't feel like bragging, though. I brought Helen over, went to introduce her, but Bucky said, "Hi, Helen. Never thought I'd see you out in the daylight," before I could pass on her name.

"Okay, so you caught a show at the Hideaway," I said. "We have something to ask you."

"Come on, Joe. Let the lady ask me alone."

"Lay off. We want to know about Vetter."

The long eyebrows settled down low. He looked at me, then Helen, then back at me again. "You're making big sounds, boy."

I didn't want anyone else in on it. I leaned forward and said, "He's in town, Bucky. He's after Renzo."

He let out a long whistle. "Who else knows about it?"

"Gerot. Renzo. Us."

"There's going to be trouble, sure."

Helen said, "Only for Renzo."

Bucky's head made a slow negative. "You don't know. The rackets boys'll flip their lids at this. If Vetter moves in here there's going to be some mighty big trouble."

My face started working under the bandages. "Renzo's top dog, isn't he?"

Bucky's tongue made a swipe at his lips. "One of 'em. There's a few more. They're not going to like Renzo pulling in trouble like Vetter." For the first time Bucky seemed to really look at us hard. "Vetter is poison. He'll cut into everything and they'll pay off. Sure as shooting, if he sticks around they'll be piling the cabbage in his lap."

"Then everybody'll be after Vetter," I said.

Bucky's face furrowed in a frown. "Uh-uh. I wasn't thinking that." He polished off his drink and set the empty on the bar. "If Vetter's here after Renzo they'll do better nailing Renzo's hide to the wall. Maybe they can stop it before it starts."

It was trouble, all right. The kind I wasn't feeling too bad about.

Bucky stared into his empty glass and said, "They'll bury Renzo or he'll come out of it bigger than ever."

The bartender came down and filled his glass again. I shook my head when he wanted to know what we'd have. "Good story," Bucky said, "if it happens." Then he threw the drink down and Bucky was all finished. His eyes got frosty and he sat there grinning at himself in the mirror with his mind saying things to itself. I knew him too well to say anything else so I nudged Helen and we walked out.

Some days go fast and this was one of them. She was nice to be with and nice to talk to. I wasn't important enough to hide anything from so for one day she opened her life up and fed me pieces of it. She seemed to grow younger as the day wore on and when we reached her apartment the sun was gilding her hair with golden reddish streaks and I was gone, all gone. For one day I was king and there wasn't any trouble. The laughter poured out of us and people stopped to look and laugh back. It was a day to remember when all the days are done with and you're on your last.

I was tired, dead tired. I didn't try to refuse when she told me to come up and I didn't want to. She let me open the door for her and I followed her inside. She had almost started for the kitchen to cook up the bacon and eggs we had talked about when she stopped by the arch leading to the living room.

The voice from the chair said, "Come on in, sugar pie. You too, kid."

And there was Johnny, a nasty smile on his mouth, leering at us.

"How did you get in here?"

He laughed at her. "I do tricks with locks, remember?" His head moved with a short jerk. "Get in here!" There was a flat, nasal tone in his voice.

I moved in beside Helen. My hands kept opening and closing at my side and my breath was coming a little fast in my throat.

"You like kids now, Helen?"

"Shut up, you louse," she said.

His lips peeled back showing his teeth. "The mother type. Old fashioned type, you know." He leered again like it was funny. My chest started to hurt from the breathing. "Too big for a bottle, so . . ."

I grabbed the lamp and let it fly and if the cord hadn't caught in the wall it would have taken his head off. I was all set to go into him but all he had to do to stop me was bring his hand up. The rod was one of those Banker's Specials that were deadly as hell at close range and Johnny looked too much like he wanted to use it for me to move.

He said, "The boss don't like your little arrangement, Helen. It didn't take him long to catch on. Come over here, kid."

I took a half step.

"Closer.

"Now listen carefully, kid. You go home, see. Go home and do what you feel like doing, but stay home and away from this place. You do that and you'll pick up a few bucks from Mr. Renzo. Now after you had it so nice here, you might not want to go home, so just in case you don't, I'm going to show you what's going to happen to you."

I heard Helen's breath suck in with a harsh gasp and my own sounded the same way. You could see what Johnny was setting himself to do and he was letting me know all about it and there wasn't a thing I could do. The gun was pointing right at my belly even while he jammed his elbows into the arms of the chair to get the leverage for the kick that was going to maim me for the rest of my life. His shoe was hard and pointed, a deadly weight that swung like a gentle pendulum.

I saw it coming and thought there might be a chance even yet but I didn't have to take it. From the side of the room Helen said, "Don't move, Johnny. I've got a gun in my hand."

And she had.

The ugly grimace on Johnny's face turned into a snarl when he knew how stupid he'd been in taking his eyes off her to enjoy what he was doing to me.

"Make him drop it, Helen."

"You heard the kid, Johnny."

Johnny dropped the gun. It lay there on the floor and I hooked it with my toe. I picked it up, punched the shells out of the chambers and tossed them under the sofa. The gun followed them.

"Come here, Helen," I said.

I felt her come up behind me and reached around for the .25 automatic in her hand. For a second Johnny's face turned pale and when it did I grinned at him.

Then I threw the .25 under the sofa too.

They look funny when you do things like that. Their little brains don't get it right away and it stuns them or something. I let him get right in the middle of that surprised look before I slammed my fist into his face and felt his teeth rip loose under my knuckles.

Helen went down on her knees for the gun and I yelled for her to let it alone, then Johnny was on me. He thought he was on me. I had his arm over my shoulder, laid him into a hip roll and tumbled him easy.

I walked up. I took my time. He started to get up and I chopped down on his neck and watched his head bob. I got him twice more in the same place and Johnny simply fell back. His eyes were seeing, his brain thinking and feeling but he couldn't move. While he lay there, I chopped twice again and Johnny's face became blotched and swollen while his eyes screamed in agony.

I put him in a cab downstairs. I told the driver he was drunk and fell and gave him a ten spot from Johnny's own wallet with instructions to take him out to the Hideaway and deliver same to Mr. Renzo. The driver was very sympathetic and took him away.

Then I went back for Helen. She was sitting on the couch waiting for me, the strangeness back in her eyes. She said, "When he finished with you, he would have started on me."

"I know."

"Joe, you did pretty good for a kid."

"I was brought up tough."

"I've seen Johnny take some pretty big guys. He's awfully strong."

"You know what I do for a living, Helen? I push a junk cart, loaded with iron. There's competition and pretty soon you learn things. Those iron loaders are strong guys too. If they can tumble you, they lift your pay."

"You had a gun, Joe," she reminded me.

And her eyes mellowed into a strange softness that sent chills right through me. They were eyes that called me closer and I couldn't say no to them. I stood there looking at her, wondering what she saw under the bandages.

"Renzo's going after us for that," I said.

"That's right, Joe."

"We'll have to get out of here. You, anyway."

"Later we'll think about it."

"Now, damn it."

Her face seemed to laugh at me. A curious laugh. A strange laugh. A bewildered laugh. There was a sparkling dance to her eyes she kept half veiled and her mouth parted just a little bit. Her tongue touched the tip of her teeth, withdrew and she said, "Now is for something else, Joe. Now is for a woman going back a long time who sees somebody she could have loved then."

I looked at her and held my breath. She was so completely beautiful I ached and I didn't want to make a fool of myself. Not yet.

"Now is for you to kiss me, Joe," she said.

I tasted her.

I waited until midnight before I left. I looked in her room and saw her bathed in moonlight, her features softly relaxed into the faintest trace of a smile, a soft, golden halo around her head.

They should take your picture like you are now, Helen. It wouldn't need a retoucher and there would never be a man who saw it who would forget it. You're beautiful, baby. You're lovely as a woman could ever be and you don't know it. You've had it so rough you can't think of anything else and thinking of it puts the lines in your face and that chiseled granite in your eyes. But you've been around and so have I. There have been dozens of dames I've thought things about but not things like I'm thinking now. You don't care what or who a guy is; you just give him part of yourself as a favor and ask for nothing back.

Sorry, Helen, you have to take something back. Or at least keep what you have. For you I'll let Renzo push me around. For you I'll let him make me finger a guy. Maybe at the end I'll have a chance to make a break. Maybe not. At least it's for you and you'll know that much. If I stay around, Renzo'll squeeze you and do it so hard you'll never be the same. I'll leave, beautiful. I'm not much. You're not much either. It was a wonderful day.

I lay the note by the lamp on the night table where she couldn't miss it. I leaned over and blew a kiss into her hair, then turned and got out of there.

Nobody had to tell me to be careful. I made sure nobody saw me leave the building and double-checked on it when I got to the corner. The trip over the back fences wasn't easy, but it was quiet and dark and if anybody so much as breathed near me I would have heard it. Then when I stood in the shadows of the store at the intersection I was glad I had made the trip the hard way. Buried between the parked cars along the curb was a police cruiser. There were no markings. Just a trunk aerial and the red glow of a cigarette behind the wheel.

Captain Gerot wasn't taking any chances. It made me feel a

little better. Upstairs there Helen could go on sleeping and always be sure of waking up. I waited a few minutes longer then drifted back into the shadows toward the rooming house.

That's where they were waiting for me. I knew it a long time before I got there because I had seen them wait for other guys before. Things like that you don't miss when you live around the factories and near the waterfronts. Things like that you watch and remember so that when it happens to you, it's no surprise and you figure things out beforehand.

They saw me and as long as I kept on going in the right direction they didn't say anything. I knew they were where I couldn't see them and even if I made a break for it, it wouldn't do me any good at all.

You get a funny feeling after a while. Like a rabbit walking between rows of guns wondering which one is going to go off. Hoping that if it does you don't get to see it or feel it. Your stomach seems to get all loose inside you and your heart makes too much noise against your ribs. You try not to, but you sweat and the little muscles in your hands and thighs start to jump and twitch and all the while there's no sound at all, just a deep, startling silence with a voice that's there just the same. A statue, laughing with its mouth open. No sound, but you can hear the voice. You keep walking, and the breathing keeps time with your footsteps, sometimes trying to get ahead of them. You find yourself chewing on your lips because you already know the horrible impact of a fist against your flesh and the uncontrollable spasms that come after a pointed shoe bites into the muscle and bone of your side.

So much so that when you're almost there and a hand grabs your arm you don't do anything except look at the face above it and wait until it says, "Where you been, kid?"

I felt the hand tighten with a gentle pressure, pulling me in close. "Lay off me, I'm minding my own . . ."

"I said something, sonny."

"So I was out. What's it to you?"

His expression said he didn't give a hang at all. "Somebody wants to know. Feel like taking a little ride?"

"You asking?"

"I'm telling." The hand tightened again. "The car's over there, bud. Let's go get in it, huh?"

For a second I wondered if I could take him or not and I knew I couldn't. He was too big and too relaxed. He'd known trouble all his life, from little guys to big guys and he didn't fool easily. You can tell after you've seen a lot of them. They knew that some day they'd wind up holding their hands over a bullet hole or screaming through the bars of a cell, but until then they were trouble and too big to buck.

I got in the car and sat next to the guy in the back seat. I kept my mouth shut and my eyes open and when we started to head the wrong way, I looked at the guy next to me. "Where we going?"

He grinned on one side of his face and looked out the window again.

"Come on, come on, quit messing around! Where we going?"

"Shut up."

"Nuts, brother. If I'm getting knocked off I'm doing a lot of yelling first, starting right now. Where . . ."

"Shut up. You ain't getting knocked off." He rolled the window down, flipped the dead cigar butt out and cranked it back up again. He said it too easily not to mean it and the jumps in my hands quieted down a little.

No, they weren't going to bump me. Not with all the trouble they went to in finding me. You don't put a couple dozen men on a mug like me if all you wanted was a simple kill. One hopped up punk would do that for a week's supply of snow. . . .

We went back through town, turned west into the suburbs and kept right on going to where the suburbs turned into estates and when we came to the right one the car turned into a surfaced driveway that wound past a dozen flashy heaps parked bumper to bumper and stopped in front of the fieldstone mansion.

The guy beside me got out first. He jerked his head at me and stayed at my back when I got out too. The driver grinned, but it was the kind of face a dog makes when he sees you with a chunk of meat in your fist.

A flunky met us at the door. He didn't look comfortable in his monkey suit and his face had scar tissue it took a lot of leather-covered punches to produce. He waved us in, shut the door and led the way down the hall to a room cloudy with smoke, rumbling with the voices of a dozen men.

When we came in the rumble stopped and I could feel the eyes crawl over me. The guy who drove the car looked across the room at the one in the tux, said, "Here he is, boss," and gave me a gentle push into the middle of the room.

"Hi, kid." He finished pouring out of the decanter, stopped it and picked up his glass. He wasn't an inch bigger than me, but he had the walk of a cat and the eyes of something dead. He got up close to me, faked a smile and held out the glass. "In case the boys had you worried."

"I'm not worried."

He shrugged and sipped the top off the drink himself. "Sit down, kid. You're among friends here." He looked over my shoulder. "Haul a chair up, Rocco."

All over the room the others settled down and shifted into position. A chair seat hit the back of my legs and I sat. When I looked around everybody was sitting, which was the way the little guy wanted it. He didn't like to have to look up to anybody.

He made it real casual. He introduced the boys when they didn't have to be introduced because they were always in the papers and the kind of guys people point out when they go by in their cars. You heard their names mentioned even in the junk business and among the punks in the streets. These were the big boys. Top dogs. Fat fingers. Big rings. The little guy was biggest of all. He was Phil Carboy and he ran the West Side the way he wanted it run.

When everything quieted down just right, Carboy leaned on the back of a chair and said, "In case you're wondering why you're here, kid, I'm going to tell you."

"I got my own ideas," I said.

"Fine. That's just fine. Let's check your ideas with mine, okay? Now we hear a lot of things around here. Things like that note you delivered to Renzo and who gave it to you and what Renzo did to you." He finished his drink and smiled. "Like what you did to Johnny, too. That's all straight now, isn't it?"

"So far."

"Swell. Tell you what I want now. I want to give you a job. How'd you like to make a cool hundred a week, kid?"

"Peanuts."

Somebody grunted. Carboy smiled again, a little thinner. "The kid's in the know," he said. "That's what I like. Okay, kid. We'll make it five hundred per for a month. If it don't run a month you get it anyway. That's better than having Renzo slap you around, right?"

"Anything's better than that." My voice started getting chalky.

Carboy held out his hand and said, "Rocco . . ." Another hand slid a sheaf of bills into his. He counted it out, reached two thousand and tossed it into my lap. "Yours, kid."

"For what?"

His lips were a narrow gash between his cheekbones. "For a guy named Vetter. The guy who gave you a note. Describe him."

"Tall," I said. "Big shoulders. I didn't see his face. Deep voice that sounded tough. He had on a trench coat and a hat."

"That's not enough."

"A funny way of standing," I told him. "I saw Sling Herman when I was a kid before the cops got him. He stood like that. Always ready to go for something in his pocket the cops said."

"You saw more than that, kid."

The room was too quiet now. They were all hanging on, waiting for the word. They were sitting there without smoking, beady little eyes waiting for the finger to swing until it stopped and I was the one who could stop it.

My throat squeezed out the words. I went back into the night to remember a guy and drag up the little things that would bring him into the light. I said, "I'd know him again. He was a guy to be scared of. When he talks you get a cold feeling and you know what he's like." My tongue ran over my lips and I lifted my eyes up to Carboy. "I wouldn't want to mess with a guy like that. Nobody's ever going to be tougher."

"You'll know him again. You're sure?"

"I'm sure." I looked around the room at the faces. Any one of them a guy who could say a word and have me dead the next day. "He's tougher than any of you."

Carboy grinned and let his tiny white teeth show through. "Nobody's that tough, kid."

"He'll kill me," I said. "Maybe you too. I don't like this."

"You don't have to like it. You just do it. In a way you're lucky. I'm paying you cash. If I wanted I could just tell you and you'd do it. You know that?"

I nodded.

"Tonight starts it. From now on you'll have somebody close

by, see? In one pocket you'll carry a white handkerchief. If you gotta blow, use it. In the other one there'll be a red wiper. When you see him blow into that."

"That's all?"

"Just duck about then, kid," Phil Carboy said softly, "and maybe you'll get to spend that two grand. Try to use it for run-out money and you won't get past the bus station." He stared into his glass, looked up at Rocco expectantly and held it out for a refill. "Kid, let me tell you something. I'm an old hand in this racket. I can tell what a guy or a dame is like from a block away. You've been around. I can tell that. I'm giving you a break because you're the type who knows the score and will play on the right side. I don't have to warn you about anything, do I?"

"No. I got the pitch."

"Any questions?"

"Just one," I said. "Renzo wants me to finger Vetter too. He isn't putting out any two grand for it. He just wants it, see? Suppose he catches up with me? What then?"

Carboy shouldn't't've hesitated. He shouldn't have let that momentary look come into his eyes because it told me everything I wanted to know. Renzo was higher than the whole pack of them and they got the jumps just thinking about it. All by himself he held a fifty-one percent interest and they were moving slowly when they bucked him. The little guy threw down the fresh drink with a quick motion of his hand and brought the smile back again. *In that second he had done a lot of thinking and spilled the answer straight out.* "We'll take care of Mark Renzo," he said. "Rocco, you and Lou take the kid home."

So I went out to the car and we drove back to the slums again. In the rear the reflections from the headlights of another car showed and the killers in it would be waiting for me to show the red handkerchief Carboy had handed me. I didn't know them and unless I was on the ball every minute I'd never get to know them. But they'd always be there, shadows that had no substance until the red showed, then the ground would get sticky with an even brighter red and maybe some of it would be mine.

They let me out two blocks away. The other car didn't show at all and I didn't look for it. My feet made hollow sounds on the sidewalk, going faster and faster until I was running up the steps of the house and when I was inside I slammed the door and leaned against it, trying hard to stop the pain in my chest.

Three-fifteen, the clock said. It ticked monotonously in the stillness, trailing me upstairs to my room. I eased inside, shut the door and locked it, standing there in the darkness until my eyes could see things. Outside a truck clashed its gears as it pulled up the hill and off in the distance a horn sounded.

I listened to them; familiar sounds, my face tightening as a not-so-familiar sound echoed behind them. It was a soft thing, a whisper that came at regular intervals in a choked-up way. Then I knew it was a sob coming from the other room and I went back to the hall and knocked on Nick's door.

His feet hit the floor, stayed there and I could hear his breathing coming hard. "It's Joe—open up."

I heard the wheeze his breath made as he let it out. The bedsprings creaked, he fell once getting to the door and the bolt snapped back. I looked at the purple blotches on his face and the open cuts over his eyes and grabbed him before he fell again. "Nick! What happened to you?"

"I'm . . . okay." He steadied himself on me and I led him back to the bed. "You got . . . some friends, pal."

"Cut it out. What happened? Who ran you through? Damn it, who did it?"

Nick managed to show a smile. It wasn't much and it hurt, but he made it. "You . . . in pretty big trouble, Joe."

"Pretty big."

"I didn't say nothing. They were here . . . asking questions. They didn't . . . believe what I told them, I guess. They sure laced me."

"The miserable slobs! You recognized them?"

His smile got sort of twisted and he nodded his head. "Sure, Joe . . . I know 'em. The fat one sat in . . . the car while they did it." His mouth clamped together hard. "It hurt . . . brother, it hurt!"

"Look," I said. "We're . . ."

"Nothing doing. I got enough. I don't want no more. Maybe they figured it's enough. That Renzo feller . . . he got hard boys around. See what they did, Joe? One . . . used a gun on me. You shoulda stood with Gordon, Joe. What the hell got into you to mess with them guys?"

"It wasn't me, Nick. Something came up. We can square it. I'll nail that fat slob if it's the last thing I do."

"It'll be the last thing. They gimme a message for you, pal. You're to stick around, see? You get seen with any other big boys in this town . . . and that's all. You know?"

"I know. Renzo told me that himself. He didn't have to go through you."

"Joe . . ."

"Yeah?"

"He said for you to take a good look . . . at me. I'm an example. A little one. He says to do what he told you."

"He knows what he can do."

"Joe . . . for me. Lay off, huh? I don't feel so good. Now I can't work for a while."

I patted his arm, fished a hundred buck bill out of my pocket and squeezed it into his hand. "Don't worry about it," I told him.

He looked at the bill unbelievingly, then at me.

"Dough can't pay for . . . this, Joe. Kind of . . . stay away from me . . . for awhile anyway, okay?" He smiled again, lamely this time. "Thanks for the C anyway. We been pretty good buddies, huh?"

"Sure, Nick."

"Later we'll be again. Lemme knock off now. You take it easy." His hands came up to his face and covered it. I could hear the sobs starting again and cursed the whole damn system up and down and Renzo in particular. I swore at the filth men like to wade in and the things they do to other men. When I was done I got up off the bed and walked to the door.

Behind me Nick said, "Joey . . ."

"Right here."

"Something's crazy in this town. Stories are going around . . . there's gonna be a lot of trouble. Everybody is after . . . you. You'll . . . be careful?"

"Sure." I opened the door, shut it softly and went back to my room. I stripped off my clothes and lay down in the bed, my mind turning over fast until I had it straightened out, then I closed my eyes and fell asleep.

My landlady waited until a quarter to twelve before she gave it the business on my door. She didn't do it like she usually did it. No jarring smashes against the panels, just a light tapping that grew louder until I said, "Yeah?"

"Mrs. Stacey, Joe. You think you should get up? A man is downstairs to see you."

"What kind of a man?"

This time the knob twisted slowly and the door opened a crack. Her voice was a harsh whisper that sounded nervous. "He's got on old clothes and a city water truck is parked outside. He didn't come to look at my water."

I grinned at that one. "I'll be right down," I said. I splashed water over my face, shaved it close and worked the adhesive off the bridge of my nose. It was swollen on one side, the blue running down to my mouth. One eye was smudged with purple.

Before I pulled on my jacket I stuffed the wad of dough into the lining through the tear in the sleeve, then I took a look in Nick's room. There were traces of blood on his pillow and the place was pretty upset, but Nick had managed to get out somehow for a day's work.

The guy in the chair sitting by the window was short and wiry looking. There was dirt under his fingernails and a stubble on his chin. He had a couple of small wrenches in a leather holster on his belt that bulged his coat out but the stuff was pure camouflage. There was a gun further back and I saw the same thing Mrs. Stacey saw. The guy was pure copper with badges for eyes.

He looked at me, nodded and said, "Joe Boyle?"

"Suppose I said no?" I sat down opposite him with a grin that said I knew all about it and though I knew he got it nothing registered at all.

"Captain Gerot tells me you'll cooperate. That true?"

There was a laugh in his eyes, an attitude of being deliberately polite when he didn't have to be. "Why?" I asked him. "Everybody seems to think I'm pretty hot stuff all of a sudden."

"You are, junior, you are. You're the only guy who can put his finger on a million dollar baby that we want bad. So you'll cooperate."

"Like a good citizen?" I made it sound the same as he did. "How much rides on Vetter and how much do I get?"

The sarcasm in his eyes turned to a nasty sneer. "Thousands ride, junior . . . and you don't get any. You just cooperate. Too many cops have worked too damn long on Vetter to let a crummy kid cut into the cake. *Now I'll tell you why you'll cooperate. There's a dame, see? Helen Troy. There's ways of slapping that tomato with a fat conviction for various reasons and unless you want to see her slapped, you'll cooperate. Catch now?*"

I called him something that fitted him right down to his shoes. He didn't lose a bit of that grin at all. "Catch something else," he said. "Get smart and I'll make your other playmates look like school kids. I like tough guys. I have fun working 'em over because that's what they understand. What there is to know I know. Take last night for instance. The boys paid you off for a finger job. Mark Renzo pays but in his own way. Now I'm setting up a deal. Hell, you don't have to take it . . . you can do what you please. Three people are dickering for what you know. I'm the only one who can hit where it really hurts.

"Think it over, Joey boy. Think hard but do it fast. I'll be waiting for a call from you and wherever you are, I'll know about it. I get impatient sometimes, so let's hear from you soon. Maybe if you take too long I'll prod you a little bit." He got up, stretched and wiped his eyes like he was tired. "Just ask for Detective Sergeant Gonzales," he said. "That's me."

The cop patted the tools on his belt and stood by the door. I said, "It's stinking to be a little man, isn't it? You got to keep making up for it."

There was pure hate in his eyes for an answer. He gave me a long look that a snake would give a rabbit when he isn't too hungry yet. A look that said wait a little while, feller. Wait until I'm real hungry.

I watched the truck pull away, then sat there at the window looking at the street. I had to wait almost an hour before I spotted the first, then picked up the second one ten minutes later. If there were more I didn't see them. I went back to the kitchen and took a look through the curtains at the blank behinds of the warehouses across the alley. Mrs. Stacey didn't say anything. She sat there with her coffee, making clicking noises with her false teeth.

I said, "Somebody washed the windows upstairs in the wholesale house."

"A man. Early this morning."

"They haven't been washed since I've been here."

"Not for two years."

I turned around and she was looking at me as if something had scared her to death. *"How much are they paying you?"* I said.

She couldn't keep that greedy look out of her face even with all the phony indignation she tried to put on. Her mouth opened to say something when the phone rang and gave her the chance to cover up. She came back a few seconds later and said, "It's for you. Some man."

Then she stood there by the door where she always stood whenever somebody was on the phone. I said, "Joe Boyle speaking," and that was all. I let the other one speak his few words and when he was done I hung up.

I felt it starting to burn me. A nasty feeling that makes you want to slam something. Nobody asked me . . . they just told and I was supposed to jump. I was the low man on the totem pole, a lousy kid who happened to fit into things . . . just the right size to get pushed around.

Vetter, I kept saying to myself. They were all scared to death of Vetter. The guy had something they couldn't touch. He was tough. He was smart. He was moving in for a kill and if ever one was needed it was needed now. They were all after him and no matter how many people who didn't belong there stood in the way their bullets would go right through them to reach Vetter. Yeah, they wanted him bad. So bad they'd kill each other to make sure he died too.

Well, the whole pack of 'em knew what they could do.

I pulled my jacket on and got outside. I went up the corner, grabbed a downtown bus and sat there without bothering to look around. At Third and Main I hopped off, ducked into a cafeteria and had a combination lunch. I let Mrs. Stacey get her calls in, gave them time to keep me well under cover, then flagged down a roving cab and gave the driver Helen's address. On the way over I looked out the back window for the second time and the light blue Chevy was still in place, two cars behind and trailing steadily. In a way it didn't bother me if the boys inside were smart enough to check the black Caddie that rode behind it again.

I tapped the cabbie a block away, told him to let me out on the corner and paid him off. There wasn't a parking place along the street so the laddies in the cars were either going to cruise or double park, but it would keep them moving around so I could see what they were like anyway.

When I punched the bell I had to wait a full minute before the lobby door clicked open. I went up the stairs, jolted the apartment door a few times and walked right into those beautiful eyes that were even prettier than the last time because they were worried first, then relieved when they saw me. She grabbed my arm and gave me that quick grin then pulled me inside and stood with her back to the door.

"Joe, Joe, you little jughead," she laughed. "You had me scared silly. Don't do anything like that again."

"Had to Helen. I wasn't going to come back but I had to do that too."

Maybe it was the way I said it that made her frown. "You're a funny kid."

"Don't say that."

Something changed in her eyes. "No. Maybe I shouldn't, should I?" She looked at me hard, her eyes soft, but piercing. "I feel funny when I look at you. I don't know why. Sometimes I've thought it was because I had a brother who was always in trouble. Always getting hurt. I used to worry about him too."

"What happened to him?"

"He was killed on the Anzio beachhead."

"Sorry."

She shook her head. "He didn't join the army because he was patriotic. He and another kid held up a joint. The owner was shot. He was dead by the time they found out who did it."

"You've been running all your life too, haven't you?"

The eyes dropped a second. "You could put it that way."

"What ties you here?"

"Guess."

"If you had the dough you'd beat it? Some place where nobody knew you?"

She laughed, a short jerky laugh. It was answer enough. I reached in the jacket, got out the pack of bills and flipped off a couple for myself. I shoved the rest in her hand before she knew what it was. "Get going. Don't even bother to pack. Just move out of here and keep moving."

Her eyes were big and wide with an incredulous sort of wonder, then slightly misty when they came back to mine and she shook her head a little bit and said, "Joe . . . why? Why?

"It would sound silly if I said it."

"Say it."

"When I'm all grown up I'll tell you maybe."

"Now."

I could feel the ache starting in me and my tongue didn't want to move, but I said, "Sometimes even a kid can feel pretty hard about a woman. Sad, isn't it?"

Helen said, "Joe," softly and had my face in her hands and her mouth was a hot torch that played against mine with a crazy kind of fierceness and it was all I could do to keep from grabbing her instead of pushing her away. My hands squeezed her hard, then I yanked the door open and got out of there. Behind me there was a sob and I heard my name said again, softly.

I ran the rest of the way down with my face all screwed up tight.

The blue Chevy was down the street on the other side. It seemed to be empty and I didn't bother to poke around it. All I wanted was for whoever followed me to follow me away from there. So I gave it the full treatment. I made it look great. To them I must have seemed pretty jumpy and on the way to see somebody important. It took a full hour to reach The Clipper that way and the only important one around was Bucky Edwards and he wasn't drunk this time.

He nodded, said, "Beer?" and when I shook my head, called down the bar for a tall orange. "Figured you'd be in sooner or later."

"Yeah?"

That wise old face wrinkled a little. "How does it feel to be live bait, kiddo?"

"You got big ears, grandma."

"I get around." He toasted his beer against my orange, put it down and said, "You're in pretty big trouble, Joe. Maybe you don't know it."

"I know it."

"You don't know how big. You haven't been here that long. Those boys put on the big squeeze."

It was my turn to squint. His face was set as if he smelled something he didn't like and there was ice in his eyes. "How much do you know, Bucky?"

His shoulders made a quick shrug. "Phil Carboy didn't post the depot and the bus station for nothing. He's got cars cruising the highways too. Making sure, isn't he?"

He looked at me and I nodded.

"Renzo is kicking loose too. He's pulling the strings tight. The guys on his payroll are getting nervous but they can't do a thing. No, sir, not a thing. Like a war. Everybody's just waiting." The set mouth flashed me a quick grin. "You're the key, boy. *If there was a way out I'd tell you to take it.*"

"Suppose I went to the cops?"

"Gerot?" Bucky shook his head. "You'd get help as long as he could keep you in a cell. People'd like to see him dead too. He's got an awfully bad habit of being honest. Ask him to show you his scars someday. It wouldn't be so bad if he was just honest, but he's smart and mean as hell too."

I drank half the orange and set it down in the wet circle on the bar. "Funny how things work out. All because of Vetter. And he's here because of Jack Cooley."

"I was wondering when you were gonna get around to it, kid," Bucky said.

"What?"

He didn't look at me. "Who *are* you working for?"

I waited a pretty long time before he turned his head around. I let him look at my face another long time before I said anything. Then: "I was pushing a junk cart, friend. I was doing okay, too. I wasn't working for trouble. Now I'm getting pretty curious. In my own way I'm not so stupid, but now I want to find out the score. One way or another I'm finding out. So they paid me off but they aren't figuring on me spending much of that cabbage. After it's over I get chopped down and it starts all over again, whatever it is. That's what I'm finding out. Why I'm bait for whatever it is. Who do I see, Bucky? You're in the know. Where do I go to find out?"

"Cooley could have told you," he said quietly.

"Nuts. He's dead."

"Maybe he can still tell you."

My fingers were tight around the glass now. "The business about Cooley getting it because of the deal on Renzo's tables is out?"

"Might be."

"Talk straight unless you're scared silly of those punks too. Don't give me any puzzles if you know something."

Bucky's eyebrows went up, then down slowly over the grin in his eyes. "Talk may be cheap, son," he said, "but life comes pretty expensively." He nodded sagely and said, "I met Cooley in lotsa places. Places he shouldn't have been. He was a man looking around. He could have found something."

"Like why we have gangs in this formerly peaceful city of ours. Why we have paid-for politicians and clambakes with some big faces showing. They're not eating clams . . . they're talking."

"These places where you kept seeing Cooley . . ."

"River joints. Maybe he liked fish."

You could tell when Bucky was done talking. I went down to Main, found a show I hadn't seen and went in. There were a lot of things I wanted to think about.

At eleven-fifteen the feature wound up and I started back outside. In the glass reflection of the lobby door I saw somebody behind me but I didn't look back. There could have been one more in the crowd that was around the entrance outside. Maybe two. Nobody seemed to pay any attention to me and I didn't care if they did or not.

I waited for a Main Street bus, took it down about a half mile, got off at the darkened supermarket and started up the road. You get the creeps in places like that. It was an area where some optimist had started a factory and ran it until the swamp crept in. When the footings gave and the walls cracked, they moved out, and now the black skeletons of the buildings were all that were left, with gaping holes for eyes and a mouth that seemed to breathe out a fetid swamp odor. But there were still people there. The dozen or so company houses that were propped against the invading swamp showed dull yellow lights, and the garbage smell of unwanted humanity fought the swamp odor. You could hear them, too, knowing that they watched you from the shadows of their porches. You could feel them stirring in their jungle shacks and catch the pungency of the alcohol they brewed out of anything they could find.

There was a low moan of a train from the south side and its single eye picked out the trestle across the bay and followed it.

The freight lumbered up, slowed for the curve that ran through
the swamps and I heard the bindle stiffs yelling as they hopped
off, looking for the single hard topped road that took them to
their quarters for the night.

The circus sign was on the board fence. In the darkness it was
nothing but a bleached white square, but when I lit a cigarette I
could see the faint orange impressions that used to be supposedly
wild animals. The match went out and I lit another, got the
smoke fired up and stood there a minute in the dark.

*The voice was low. A soft, quiet voice more inaudible than a
whisper. "One is back at the corner. There's another a hundred
feet down."*

"I know," I said.

"You got nerve."

*"Let's not kid me. I got your message. Sorry I had to cut it short,
but a pair of paid-for ears were listening in."*

"Sorry Renzo gave you a hard time."

"So am I. The others did better by me."

*Somebody coughed down the road and I flattened against the
boards away from the white sign. It came again, farther away this
time and I felt better. I said, "What gives?"*

"You had a cop at your place this morning."

"I spotted him."

*"There's a regular parade behind you." A pause, then, "What
did you tell them?"*

*I dragged in on the smoke, watched it curl. "I told them he was
big. Tough. I didn't see his face too well. What did you expect me
to tell them?"*

I had a feeling like he smiled.

"They aren't happy," he said.

*I grinned too. "Vetter. They hate the name. It scares them." I
pulled on the butt again. "It scares me too when I think of it too
much."*

"You don't have anything to worry about."

"Thanks."

"Keep playing it smart. You know what they're after?"

*I nodded, even though he couldn't see me. "Cooley comes into
it someplace. It was something he knew."*

*"Smart lad. I knew you were a smart lad the first time I saw
you. Yes, it was Cooley."*

"Who was he?" I asked.

Nothing for a moment. I could hear him breathing and his feet moved but that was all. The red light on the tail of the caboose winked at me and I knew it would have to be short.

"An adventurer, son. A romantic adventurer who went where the hunting was profitable and the odds long. He liked long odds. He found how they were slipping narcotics in through a new door and tapped them for a sweet haul. They say four million. It was paid-for shipment and he got away with it. Now the boys have to make good."

The caboose was almost past now. He said, "I'll call you if I want you."

I flipped the butt away, watching it bounce sparks across the dirt. I went on a little bit farther where I could watch the fires from the jungles and when I had enough of it I started back.

At the tree the guy who had been waiting there said, "You weren't thinking of hopping that freight, were you kid?"

I didn't jump like I was supposed to. I said, "When I want to leave, I'll leave."

"Be sure to tell Mr. Carboy first, huh?"

"I'll tell him," I said.

He stayed there, not following me. I passed the buildings again, then felt better when I saw the single street light on the corner of Main. There was nobody there that I could see, but that didn't count. He was around someplace.

I had to wait ten minutes for a bus. It seemed longer than it was. I stayed drenched in the yellow light and thought of the voice behind the fence and what it had to say. When the bus pulled up I got on, stayed there until I reached the lights again and got off. By that time a lot of things were making sense, falling into a recognizable pattern. I walked down the street to an all-night drug store, had a drink at the counter then went back to the phone booth.

I dialed the police number and asked for Gonzales, Sergeant Gonzales. There was a series of clicks as the call was switched and the cop said, "Gonzales speaking."

"This is Joe, copper. Remember me?"

"Don't get too fresh, sonny," he said. His voice had a knife in it.

"Phil Carboy paid me some big money to finger Vetter. He's got men tailing me."

His pencil kept up a steady tapping against the side of the phone. Finally he said, "I was wondering when you'd call in. You were real lucky, Joe. For a while I thought I was going to have to persuade you a little to cooperate. You were real lucky. Keep me posted."

I heard the click in my ear as he hung up and I spat out the things into the dead phone I felt like telling him to his face. Then I fished out another coin, dropped it in and dialed the same number. This time I asked for Captain Gerot. The guy at the switchboard said he had left about six but that he could probably be reached at his club. He gave me the number and I checked it through. The attendant who answered said he had left about an hour ago but would probably call back to see if there were any messages for him and were there? I told him to get the number so I could put the call through myself and hung up.

It took me a little longer to find Bucky Edwards. He had stewed in his own juices too long and he was almost all gone. I said, "Bucky, I need something bad. I want Jack Cooley's last address. You remember that much?"

He hummed a little bit. "Rooming house. Between Wells and Capitol. It's all white, Joe. Only white house."

"Thanks, Bucky."

"You in trouble, Joe?"

"Not yet."

"You will be. Now you will be."

That was all. He put the phone back so easily I didn't hear it go. Damn, I thought, he knows the score but he won't talk. He's got all the scoop and he clams up.

I had another drink at the counter, picked up a deck of smokes and stood outside while I lit one. The street was quieting down. Both curbs were lined with parked heaps, dead things that rested until morning when they'd be whipped alive again.

Not all of them though. I was sure of that. I thought I caught a movement across the street in a doorway. It was hard to tell. I turned north and walked fast until I reached Benson Road, then cut down it to the used car lot.

Now was when they'd have a hard time. Now was when they were playing games in my back yard and if they didn't know every inch of the way somebody was going to get hurt. They weren't kids, these guys. They had played the game themselves and they'd know all the angles. Almost all, anyway. They'd know when I tried to get out of the noose and as soon as they did, they'd quit playing and start working. They wouldn't break their necks sticking to a trail when they could bottle me up.

All I had to do was keep them from knowing for a while.

I crossed the lot, cutting through the parked cars, picked up the alley going back of the houses and stuck to the hedgerows until I was well down it. By that time I had a lead. If I looked back I'd spoil it so I didn't look back. I picked up another block at the fork in the alley, standing deliberately under the lone light at the end, not hurrying, so they could see me. I made it seem as though I were trying to pick out one of the houses in the darkness, and when I made up my mind, went through the gate in the fence.

After that I hurried. I picked up the short-cuts, made the street and crossed it between lights. I reached Main again, grabbed a cruising cab in the middle of the block, had him haul me across town to the docks and got out. It took fifteen minutes longer to reach the white house Bucky told me about. I grinned to myself and wondered if the boys were still watching the place they thought I went into. Maybe it would be a little while before they figured the thing out.

It would be time enough.

The guy who answered the door was all wrapped up in a bathrobe, his hair stringing down his face. He squinted at me, reluctant to be polite, but not naturally tough enough to be anything else but. He said, "If you're looking for a room you'll have to come around in the morning. I'm sorry."

I showed him a bill with two numbers on it.

"Well . . ."

"I don't want a room."

He looked at the bill again, then a quick flash of terror crossed his face. His eyes rounded open, looked at me hard, then dissolved into curiosity. "Come . . . in."

The door closed and he stepped around me into a small sitting room and snapped on a shaded desk lamp. His eyes went back down to the bill. I handed it over and watched it disappear into the bathrobe. "Yes?"

"Jack Cooley."

The words did something to his face. It showed terror again, but not as much as before.

"I really don't . . ."

"Forget the act. I'm not working for anybody in town. I was a friend of his."

This time he scowled, not believing me.

I said, "Maybe I don't look it, but I was."

"So? What is it you want?" He licked his lips, seemed to tune his ears for some sound from upstairs. "Everybody's been here. Police, newspapers. Those . . . men from town. They all want something."

"Did Jack leave anything behind?"

"Sure. Clothes, letters, the usual junk. The police have all that."

"Did you get to see any of it?"

"Well . . . the letters were from dames. Nothing important."

I nodded, fished around for a question a second before I found one. "How about his habits?"

The guy shrugged. "He paid on time. Usually came in late and slept late. No dames in his room."

"That's all?"

He was getting edgy. "What else is there? I didn't go out with the guy. So now I know he spent plenty of nights in Renzo's joint. I hear talk. You want to know what kind of butts he smoked? Hobbies, maybe? Hell, what is there to tell? He goes out at night. Sometimes he goes fishing. Sometimes . . ."

"Where?" I interrupted.

"Where what?"

"Fishing."

"On one of his boats. He borrowed my stuff. He was fishing the day before he got bumped. Sometimes he'd slip me a ticket and I'd get away from the old lady."

"How do the boats operate?"

He shrugged again, pursing his mouth. "They go down the bay to the tip of the inlet, gas up, pick up beer at Gulley's and go about ten miles out. Coming back they stop at Gulley's for more beer and for the guys to dump the fish they don't want. Gulley sells it in town. Everybody is usually drunk and happy." He gave me another thoughtful look. "You writing a book about your friend?" he said sarcastically.

"Could be. Could be. I hate to see him dead."

"If you ask me, he never should've fooled around Renzo. You better go home and save your money from now on, sonny."

"I'll take your advice," I said, "and be handyman around a rooming house."

He gave me a dull stare as I stood up and didn't bother to go to the door with me. He still had his hand in his pocket wrapped around the bill I gave him.

The street was empty and dark enough to keep me wrapped in a blanket of shadows. I stayed close to the houses, stopping now and then to listen. When I was sure I was by myself I felt better and followed the water smell of the bay.

At River Road a single-pump gas station showed lights and the guy inside sat with his feet propped up on the desk. He opened one eye when I walked in, gave me the change I wanted for the phone, then went back to sleep again. I dialed the number of Gerot's club, got the attendant and told him what I wanted. He gave me another number and I punched it out on the dial. Two persons answered before a voice said, "Gerot speaking."

"Hello, Captain. This is Joe. I was . . ."

"I remember," he said.

"I called Sergeant Gonzales tonight. Phil Carboy paid me off to finger Vetter. Now I got two parties pushing me."

"Three. Don't forget us."

"I'm not forgetting."

"I hear those parties are excited. Where are you?"

I didn't think he'd bother to trace the call, so I said, "Some joint in town."

His voice sounded light this time. "About Vetter. Tell me."

"Nothing to tell."

"You had a call this morning." I felt the chills starting to run up my back. They had a tap on my line already. "The voice wasn't familiar and it said some peculiar things."

"I know. I didn't get it. I thought it was part of Renzo's outfit getting wise. They beat up a buddy of mine so I'd know what a real beat-up guy looks like. It was all double talk to me."

He was thinking it over. When he was ready he said, "Maybe so, kid. You hear about that dame you were with?"

I could hardly get the words out of my mouth. "Helen? No . . . What?"

"Somebody shot at her. Twice."

"Did . . ."

"Not this time. She was able to walk away from it this time."

"Who was it? Who shot at her?"

"That, little chum, is something we'd like to know too. She was waiting for a train out of town. The next time maybe we'll have better luck. There'll be a next time, in case you're interested."

"Yeah, I'm interested . . . and thanks. You know where she is now?"

"No, but we're looking around. *I hope we can find her first.*"

I put the phone back and tried to get the dry taste out of my mouth. When I thought I could talk again I dialed Helen's apartment, hung on while the phone rang endlessly, then held the receiver fork down until I got my coin back. I had to get Renzo's club number from the book and the gravelly voice that answered rasped that the feature attraction hadn't put in an appearance that night and for something's sake to cut off the chatter and wait until tomorrow because the club was closed.

So I stood there and said things to myself until I was all balled up into a knot. I could see the parade of faces I hated drifting past my mind and all I could think of was how bad I wanted to smash every one of them as they came by. Helen had tried to run for it. She didn't get far. Now where could she be? Where does a beautiful blonde go who is trying to hide? Who would take her in if they knew the score?

I could feel the sweat starting on my neck, soaking the back of my shirt. All of a sudden I felt washed out and wrung dry. Gone. All the way gone. Like there wasn't anything left of me any more except a big hate for a whole damn city, the mugs who ran it and the people who were afraid of the mugs. And it wasn't just one city either. There would be more of them scattered all over the states. For the people, by the people, Lincoln had said. Yeah. Great.

I turned around and walked out. I didn't even bother to look back and if they were there, let them come. I walked for a half hour, found a cab parked at a corner with the driver sacking it behind the wheel and woke him up. I gave him the boarding house address and climbed in the back.

He let me off at the corner, collected his dough and turned around.

Then I heard that voice again and I froze the butt halfway to my mouth and squashed the matches in the palm of my hand.

It said, "Go ahead and light it."

I breathed that first drag out with the words, "You nuts? They're all around this place."

"I know. Now be still and listen. The dame knows the score. They tried for her . . ."

We heard the feet at the same time. They were light as a cat, fast. Then he came out of the darkness and all I could see was the glint of the knife in his hand and the yell that was in my throat choked off when his fingers bit into my flesh. I had time to see that same hardened face that had looked into mine not so long ago, catch an expressionless grin from the hard boy, then the other shadows opened and the side of a palm smashed down against his neck. He pitched forward with his head at a queer, stiff angle, his mouth wrenched open and I knew it was only a reflex that kept it that way because the hard boy was dead. You could hear the knife chatter across the sidewalk and the sound of the body hitting, a sound that really wasn't much yet was a thunderous crash that split the night wide open.

The shadows the hand had reached out from seemed to open and close again, and for a short second I was alone. Just a short second. I heard the whisper that was said too loud. The snick of a gun somewhere, then I closed in against the building and ran for it.

At the third house I faded into the alley and listened. Back there I could hear them talking, then a car started up down the street. I cut around behind the houses, found the fences and stuck with them until I was at my place, then snaked into the cellar door.

When I got upstairs I slipped into the hall and reached for the phone. I asked for the police and got them. All I said was that somebody was being killed and gave the address. Then I grinned at the darkness, hung up without giving my name and went upstairs to my room. From way across town a siren wailed a lonely note, coming closer little by little. It was a pleasant sound at that. It would give my friend from the shadows plenty of warning too. He was quite a guy. Strong. Whoever owned the dead man was going to walk easy with Vetter after this.

I walked into my room, closed the door and was reaching for

the bolt when the chair moved in the corner. Then she said, "Hello, Joe," and the air in my lungs hissed out slowly between my teeth.

I said, "Helen." I don't know which of us moved. I like to think it was her. But suddenly she was there in my arms with her face buried in my shoulder, stifled sobs pouring out of her body while I tried to tell her that it was all right. Her body was pressed against me, a fire that seemed to dance as she trembled, fighting to stay close.

"Helen, Helen, take it easy. Nothing will hurt you now. You're okay." I lifted her head away and smoothed back her hair. "Listen, you're all right here."

Her mouth was too close. Her eyes too wet and my mind was thinking things that didn't belong there. My arms closed tighter and I found her mouth, warm and soft, a salty sweetness that clung desperately and talked to me soundlessly. But it stopped the trembling and when she pulled away she smiled and said my name softly.

"How'd you get here, Helen?"

Her smile tightened. "I was brought up in a place like this a long time ago. There are always ways. I found one."

"I heard what happened. Who was it?"

She tightened under my hands. "I don't know. I was waiting for a train when it happened. I just ran after that. When I got out on the street, it happened again."

"No cops?"

She shook her head. "Too fast. I kept running."

"They know it was you?"

"I was recognized in the station. Two men there had caught my show and said hello. You know how. They could have said something."

I could feel my eyes starting to squint. "Don't be so damn calm about it."

The tight smile twisted up at the corner. It was like she was reading my mind. She seemed to soften a moment and I felt her fingers brush my face. "I told you I wasn't like other girls, Joe. Not like the kind of girl you should know. Let's say it's all something I've seen before. After a bit you get used to it."

"Helen . . ."

"I'm sorry, Joe."

I shook my head slowly. "No . . . I'm the one who's sorry. People like you should never get like that. Not you."

"Thanks." She looked at me, something strange in her eyes that I could see even in the half light of the room. And this time it happened slowly, the way it should be. The fire was close again, and real this time, very real. Fire that could have burned deeply if the siren hadn't closed in and stopped outside.

I pushed her away and went to the window. The beams of the flashlights traced paths up the sidewalk. The two cops were cursing the cranks in the neighborhood until one stopped, grunted something and picked up a sliver of steel that lay by the curb. But there was nothing else. Then they got back in the cruiser and drove off.

Helen said, "What was it?"

"There was a dead man out there. Tomorrow there'll be some fun."

"Joe!"

"Don't worry about it. At least we know how we stand. It was one of their boys. He made a pass at me on the street and got taken."

"You do it?"

I shook my head. "Not me. A guy. A real big guy with hands that can kill."

"*Vetter.*" She said it breathlessly.

I shrugged.

Her voice was a whisper. "I hope he kills them all. Every one." Her hand touched my arm. "Somebody tried to kill Renzo earlier. They got one of his boys." Her teeth bit into her lip. "There were two of them so it wasn't Vetter. You know what that means?"

I nodded. "War. They want Renzo dead to get Vetter out of town. They don't want him around or he'll move into their racket sure."

"He already has." I looked at her sharply and she nodded. "I saw one of the boys in the band. Renzo's special car was hijacked as it was leaving the city. Renzo claimed they got nothing but he's pretty upset. I heard other things too. The whole town's tight."

"Where do you come in, Helen?"

"What?" Her voice seemed taut.

"You. Let's say you and Cooley. What string are you pulling?"

Her hand left my arm and hung down at her side. If I'd slapped her she would have had the same expression on her face. I said, "I'm sorry. I didn't mean it like that. You liked Jack Cooley, didn't you?"

"Yes." She said it quietly.

"You told me what he was like once. What was he really like?"

The hurt flashed in her face again. "Like them," she said. "Gay, charming, but like them. He wanted the same things. He just went after them differently, that's all."

"The guy I saw tonight said you know things."

Her breath caught a little bit. "I didn't know before, Joe."

"Tell me."

"When I packed to leave . . . then I found out. Jack . . . left certain things with me. One was an envelope. There were cancelled checks in it for thousands of dollars made out to Renzo. The one who wrote the checks is a racketeer in New York. There was a note pad too with dates and amounts that Renzo paid Cooley."

"Blackmail."

"I think so. What was more important was what was in the box he left with me. *Heroin.*"

I swung around slowly. "Where is it?"

"Down a sewer. I've seen what the stuff can do to a person."

"Much of it?"

"Maybe a quarter pound."

"We could have had him," I said. "We could have had him and you dumped the stuff!"

Her hand touched me again. "No . . . there wasn't that much of it. Don't you see, it's bigger than that. What Jack had was only a sample. Some place there's more of it, much more."

"Yeah," I said. I was beginning to see things now. They were starting to straighten themselves out and it made a pattern. The only trouble was that the pattern was so simple it didn't begin to look real.

"Tomorrow we start," I said. "We work by night. Roll into the sack and get some sleep. If I can keep the landlady out of here we'll be okay. You sure nobody saw you come in?"

"Nobody saw me."

"Good. Then they'll only be looking for me."

"Where will you sleep?"

I grinned at her. "In the chair."

I heard the bed creak as she eased back on it, then I slid into the chair. After a long time she said, "Who are you, Joe?"

I grunted something and closed my eyes. I wished I knew myself sometimes.

I woke up just past noon. Helen was still asleep, restlessly tossing in some dream. The sheet had slipped down to her waist, and everytime she moved, her body rippled with sinuous grace. I stood looking at her for a long time, my eyes devouring her, every muscle in my body wanting her. There were other things to do, and I cursed those other things and set out to do them.

When I knew the landlady was gone I made a trip downstairs to her ice box and lifted enough for a quick meal. I had to wake Helen up to eat, then sat back with an old magazine to let the rest of the day pass by. At seven we made the first move. It was a nice simple little thing that put the whole neighborhood in an uproar for a half hour but gave us a chance to get out without being spotted.

All I did was call the fire department and tell them there was a gas leak in one of the tenements. They did the rest. Besides holding everybody back from the area they evacuated a whole row of houses, including us and while they were trying to run down the false alarm we grabbed a cab and got out.

Helen asked, "Where to?"

"A place called Gulley's. It's a stop for the fishing boats. You know it?"

"I know it." She leaned back against the cushions. "It's a tough place to be. Jack took me out there a couple of times."

"He did? Why?"

"Oh, we ate, then he met some friends of his. We were there when the place was raided. Gulley was selling liquor after closing hours. Good thing Jack had a friend on the force."

"Who was that?"

"Some detective with a Mexican name."

"Gonzales," I said.

She looked at me. "That's right." She frowned. "I didn't like him."

That was a new angle. One that didn't fit in. Jack with a friend on the force. I handed Helen a cigarette, lit it and sat back with mine.

It took a good hour to reach the place and at first glance it didn't seem worth the ride. From the highway the road weaved out onto a sand spit and in the shadows you could see the parked cars and occasionally couples in them. Here and there along the road the lights of the car picked up the glint of beer cans and empty bottles. I gave the cabbie an extra five and told him to wait and when we went down the gravel path, he pulled it under the trees and switched off his lights. Gulley's was a huge shack built on the sand with a porch extending out over the water. There wasn't a speck of paint on the weather-racked framework and over the whole place the smell of fish hung like a blanket. It looked like a creep joint until you turned the corner and got a peek at the nice modern dock setup he had and the new addition on the side that probably made the place the yacht club's slumming section. If it didn't have anything else it had atmosphere. We were right on the tip of the peninsula that jutted out from the mainland and like the sign said, it was the last chance for the boats to fill up with the bottled stuff before heading out to deep water.

I told Helen to stick in the shadows of the hedge row that ran around the place while I took a look around, and though she didn't like it, she melted back into the brush. I could see a couple of figures on the porch, but they were talking too low for me to hear what was going on. Behind the bar that ran across the main room inside, a flat-faced guy leaned over reading the paper with his ears pinned inside a headset. Twice he reached back, frowning and fiddled with a radio under the counter. When the phone rang he scowled again, slipped off the headset and said, "Gulley speaking. Yeah. Okay. So long."

When he went back to his paper I crouched down under the rows of windows and eased around the side. The sand was a thick carpet that silenced all noise and the gentle lapping of the water against the docks covered any other racket I could make. I was glad to have it that way too. There were guys spotted around the place that you couldn't see until you looked hard and they were just lounging. Two were by the building and the other two at the foot of the docks, edgy birds who lit occasional cigarettes and shifted around as they smoked them. One of them said something and a pair of them swung around to watch the twin beams of a car coming up the highway. I looked too, saw them turn in a long arc then cut straight for the shack.

One of the boys started walking my way, his feet squeaking in the dry sand. I dropped back around the corner of the building, watched while he pulled a bottle out from under the brush, then started back the way I had come.

The car door slammed. A pair of voices mixed in an argument and another one cut them off. When I heard it I could feel my lips peel back and I knew that if I had a knife in my fist and Mark Renzo passed by me in the dark, whatever he had for supper would spill all over the ground. There was another voice swearing at something. Johnny. Nice, gentle Johnny who was going to cripple me for life.

I wasn't worrying about Helen because she wouldn't be sticking her neck out. I was hoping hard that my cabbie wasn't reading any paper by his dome light and when I heard the boys reach the porch and go in, I let my breath out hardly realizing that my chest hurt from holding it in so long.

You could hear their hellos from inside, muffled sounds that were barely audible. I had maybe a minute to do what I had to do and didn't waste any time doing it. I scuttled back under the window that was at one end of the bar, had time to see Gulley shaking hands with Renzo over by the door, watched him close and lock it and while they were still far enough away not to notice the movement, slid the window up an inch and flattened against the wall.

They did what I expected they'd do. I heard Gulley invite them to the bar for a drink and set out the glasses. Renzo said, "Good stuff."

"Only the best. You know that."

Johnny said, "Sure. You treat your best customers right."

Bottle and glasses clinked again for another round. Then the headset that was under the bar started clicking. I took a quick look, watched Gulley pick it up, slap one earpiece against his head and jot something down on a pad.

Renzo said, "She getting in without trouble?"

Gulley set the headset down and leaned across the bar. He looked soft, but he'd been around a long time and not even Renzo was playing any games with him. "Look," he said, "you got your end of the racket. Keep out of mine. You know?"

"Getting tough, Gulley?"

I could almost hear Gulley smile. "Yeah. Yeah, in case you want to know. You damn well better blow off to them city lads, not me."

"Ease off," Renzo told him. He didn't sound rough any more. "Heard a load was due in tonight."

"You hear too damn much."

"It didn't come easy. I put out a bundle for the information. You know why?" Gulley didn't say anything. Renzo said, "I'll tell you why. I need that stuff. You know why?"

"Tough. Too bad. You know. What you want is already paid for and is being delivered. You ought to get your head out of your whoosis."

"Gulley . . ." Johnny said really quiet. "We ain't kidding. We need that stuff. The big boys are getting jumpy. They think we pulled a fast one. They don't like it. They don't like it so bad maybe they'll send a crew down here to straighten everything out and you may get straightened too."

Inside Gulley's feet were nervous on the floorboards. He passed in front of me once, his hands busy wiping glasses. "You guys are nuts. Carboy paid for this load. So I should stand in the middle?"

"Maybe it's better than standing in front of us," Johnny said.

"You got rocks. Phil's out of the local stuff now. He's got a pretty big outfit."

"Just peanuts, Gulley, just peanuts."

"Not any more. He's moving in since you dumped the big deal."

Gulley's feet stopped moving. His voice had a whisper in it. "So you were big once. Now I see you sliding. The big boys are going for bargains and they don't like who can't deliver, especially when it's been paid for. That was one big load. It was special. So you dumped it. Phil's smart enough to pick it up from there and now he may be top dog. I'm not in the middle. Not without an answer to Phil and he'll need a good one."

"Vetter's in town, Gulley!" Renzo almost spat the words out. "You know how he is? He ain't a gang you bust up. He's got a nasty habit of killing people. Like always, he's moving in. So we pay you for the stuff and deliver what we lost. We make it look good and you tell Phil it was Vetter. He'll believe that."

I could hear Gulley breathing hard. "Jerks, you guys," he said. There was a hiss in his words. "I should string it on Vetter. Man, you're plain nuts. I seen that guy operate before. Who the hell you think edged into that Frisco deal? Who got Morgan in El Paso while he was packing a half million in cash and another half in powder? So a chowderhead hauls him in to cream some local fish and the guy walks away with the town. *Who the hell is that guy?*"

Johnny's laugh was bitter. Sharp. Gulley had said it all and it was like a knife sticking in and being twisted. "I'd like to meet him. Seems like he was a buddy of Jack Cooley. You remember Jack Cooley, Gulley? You were in on that. Cooley got off with your kick too. Maybe Vetter would like to know about that."

"Shut up."

"Not yet. We got business to talk about."

Gulley seemed out of breath. "Business be damned. I ain't tangling with Vetter."

"Scared?"

"Damn right, and so are you. So's everybody else."

"Okay," Johnny said. "So for one guy or a couple he's trouble. In a big town he can make his play and move fast. Thing is with enough guys in a burg like this he can get nailed."

"And how many guys get nailed with him? He's no dope. Who you trying to smoke?"

"Nuts, who cares who gets nailed as long as it ain't your own bunch? You think Phil Carboy'll go easy if he thinks Vetter jacked a load out from under him? Like you told us, Phil's an up and coming guy. He's growing. He figures on being the top kick around here and let Vetter give him the business and he goes all out to get the guy. So two birds are killed. Vetter and Carboy. Even if Carboy gets him, his load's gone. He's small peanuts again."

"Where does that get me?" Gulley asked.

"I was coming to that. You make yours. The percentage goes up ten. Good?"

Gulley must have been thinking greedy. He started moving again, his feet coming closer. He said, "Big talk. Where's the cabbage?"

"I got it on me," Renzo said.

"You know what Phil was paying for the junk?"

"The word said two million."

"It's gonna cost to take care of the boys on the boat."

"Not so much." Renzo's laugh had no humor in it. "They talk and either Carboy'll finish 'em or Vetter will. They stay shut up for free."

"How much for me?" Gulley asked.

"One hundred thousand for swinging the deal, plus the extra percentage. You think it's worth it?"

"I'll go it," Gulley said.

Nobody spoke for a second, then Gulley said, "I'll phone the boat to pull into the slipside docks. They can unload there. The stuff is packed in beer cans. It won't make a big package so look around for it. They'll probably shove it under one of the benches."

"Who gets the dough?"

"You row out to the last boat mooring. The thing is red with a white stripe around it. Unscrew the top and drop it in."

"Same as the way we used to work it?"

"Right. The boys on the boat won't like going in the harbor and they'll be plenty careful, so don't stick around to lift the dough and the stuff too. That 'breed on the ship got a lockerful of chatter guns he likes to hand out to his crew."

"It'll get played straight."

"I'm just telling you."

Renzo said, "What do you tell Phil?"

"You kidding? I don't say nothing. All I know is I lose contact with the boat. Next the word goes that Vetter is mixed up in it. I don't say nothing." He paused for a few seconds, his breath whistling in his throat, then, "But don't forget something . . . You take Carboy for a sucker and maybe even Vetter. Lay off me. I keep myself covered. Anything happens to me and the next day the cops get a letter naming names. Don't ever forget that."

Renzo must have wanted to say something. He didn't. Instead he rasped, "Go get the cash for this guy."

Somebody said, "Sure, boss," and walked across the room. I heard the lock snick open, then the door.

"This better work," Renzo said. He fiddled with his glass a while. "I'd sure like to know what that punk did with the other stuff."

"He ain't gonna sell it, that's for sure," Johnny told him. "You think maybe Cooley and Vetter were in business together?"

"I'm thinking maybe Cooley was in business with a lot of people. That lousy blonde. When I get her she'll talk plenty. I should've kept my damn eyes open."

"I tried to tell you, boss."

"Shut up," Renzo said. "You just see that she gets found."

I didn't wait to hear any more. I got down in the darkness and headed back to the path. Overhead the sky was starting to lighten as the moon came up, a red circle that did funny things to the night and started the long fingers of shadows drifting out from the scraggly brush. The trees seemed to be ponderous things that reached down with sharp claws, feeling around in the breeze for something to grab. I found the place where I had left Helen, found a couple of pebbles and tossed them back into the brush. I heard her gasp.

She came forward silently, said, "Joe?" in a hushed tone.

"Yeah. *Let's get out of here.*"

"What happened?"

"Later. I'll start back to the cab to make sure it's clear. If you don't hear anything, follow me. Got it?"

". . . Yes." She was hesitant and I couldn't blame her. I got off the gravel path into the sand, took it easy and tried to search out the shadows. I reached the clearing, stood there until I was sure the place was empty then hopped over to the cab.

I had to shake the driver awake and he came out of it stupidly. "Look, keep your lights off going back until you're on the highway, then keep 'em on low. There's enough moon to see by."

"Hey . . . I don't want trouble."

"You'll get it unless you do what I tell you."

"Well . . . okay."

"A dame's coming out in a minute. Soon as she comes start it up and try to keep it quiet."

I didn't have long to wait. I heard her feet on the gravel, walking fast but not hurrying. Then I heard something else that froze me a second. A long, low whistle of appreciation like the kind any blonde'll get from the pool hall boys. I hopped in the cab, held the door open. "Let's go feller," I said.

As soon as the engine ticked over Helen started to run. I yanked her inside as the car started moving and kept down under the windows. She said, "Somebody . . ."

"I heard it."

"I didn't see who it was."

"Maybe it'll pass. Enough cars came out here to park."

Her hand was tight in mine, the nails biting into my palm. She was half-turned on the seat, her dress pulled back over the glossy knees of her nylons, her breasts pressed against my arm. She stayed that way until we reached the highway then little by little eased up until she was sitting back against the cushions. I tapped my forefinger against my lips then pointed to the driver. Helen nodded, smiled, then squeezed my hand again. This time it was different. The squeeze went with the smile.

I paid off the driver at the edge of town. He got more than the meter said, a lot more. It was big enough to keep a man's mouth shut long enough to get him in trouble when he opened it too late. When he was out of sight we walked until we found another cab, told the driver to get us to a small hotel someplace. He gave the usual leer and blonde inspection, muttered the name of a joint and pulled away from the curb.

It was the kind of place where they don't ask questions and don't believe what you write in the register anyway. I signed *Mr. and Mrs. Valiscivitch,* paid the bill in advance for a week and when the clerk read the name I got a screwy look because the name was too screwballed to be anything but real to him. Maybe he figured his clientele was changing. When we got to the room I said, "You park here for a few days."

"Are you going to tell me anything?"

"Should I?"

"You're strange, Joe. A very strange boy."

"Stop calling me a boy."

Her face got all beautiful again and when she smiled there was a real grin in it. She stood there with her hands on her hips and her feet apart like she was going into some part of her routine and I could feel my body starting to burn at the sight of her. She could do things with herself by just breathing and she did them, the smile and her eyes getting deeper all the time. She saw what was happening to me and said, "You're not such a boy after all." She held out her hand and I took it, pulling her in close. "The first time you were a boy. All bloody, dirt ground into your face. When Renzo tore you apart I could have killed him. Nobody should do that to another one, especially a boy. But then there was Johnny and you seemed to grow up. I'll never forget what you did to him."

"He would have hurt you."

"You're even older now. Or should I say matured? I think you finished growing up last night, Joe, last night . . . with me. I saw you grow up, and *I* only hope I haven't hurt you in the process. I never was much good for anybody. That's why I left home, I guess. Everyone I was near seemed to get hurt. Even me."

"You're better than they are, Helen. The breaks were against you, that's all."

"Joe . . . do you know you're the first one who did anything nice for me without wanting . . . something?"

"Helen . . ."

"No, don't say anything. Just take a good look at me. See everything that I am? It shows. I know it shows. I was a lot of things that weren't nice. I'm the kind men want but who won't introduce to their families. I'm a beautiful piece of dirt, Joe." Her eyes were wet. I wanted to brush away the wetness but she wouldn't let my hands go. "You see what I'm telling you? You're young . . . don't brush up against me too close. You'll get dirty and you'll get hurt."

She tried to hide the sob in her throat but couldn't. It came up anyway and I made her let my hands go and when she did I wrapped them around her and held her tight against me. "Helen," I said. "Helen . . ."

She looked at me, grinned weakly. "We must make a funny pair," she said. "Run for it, Joe. Don't stay around any longer."

When I didn't answer right away her eyes looked at mine. I could see her starting to frown a little bit and the curious bewilderment crept across her face. Her mouth was red and moist, poised as if she were going to ask a question, but had forgotten what it was she wanted to say. I let her look and look and look and when she shook her head in a minute gesture of puzzlement

I said, "Helen . . . I've rubbed against you. No dirt came off.
Maybe it's because I'm no better than you think you are."

"Joe . . ."

"It never happened to me before, kid. When it happens I sure
pick a good one for it to happen with." I ran my fingers through
her hair. It was nice looking at her like that. Not down, not up,
but right into her eyes. "I don't have any family to introduce you
to, but if I had I would. Yellow head, don't worry about me
getting hurt."

Her eyes were wide now as if she had the answer. She wasn't
believing what she saw.

"I love you, Helen. It's not the way a boy would love anybody.
It's a peculiar kind of thing I never want to change."

"Joe . . ."

"But it's yours now. You have to decide. Look at me, kid. Then
say it."

Those lovely wide eyes grew misty again and the smile came
back slowly. It was a warm, radiant smile that told me more
than her words. "It can happen to us, can't it? Perhaps it's happened before to somebody else, but it can happen to *us*, can't
it? Joe . . . It seems so . . . I can't describe it. There's something . . ."

"Say it out."

"I love you, Joe. Maybe it's better that I should love a little
boy. Twenty . . . twenty-one you said? Oh, please, please don't let
it be wrong, please . . ." She pressed herself to me with a deep-
throated sob and clung there. My fingers rubbed her neck, ran
across the width of her shoulders than I pushed her away. I was
grinning a little bit now.

"In eighty years it won't make much difference," I said. Then
what else I had to say her mouth cut off like a burning torch that
tried to seek out the answer and when it was over it didn't seem
important enough to mention anyway.

I pushed her away gently, "Now, listen, there isn't much time.
I want you to stay here. Don't go out at all and if you want
anything, have it sent up. When I come back, I'll knock once.
Just once. Keep that door locked and stay out of sight. You got
that?"

"Yes, but . . ."

"Don't worry about me. I won't be long. Just remember to

make sure it's me and nobody else." I grinned at her. "You aren't
getting away from me any more, blondie. Now it's us for keeps,
together."

"All right, Joe."

I nudged her chin with my fist, held her face up and kissed it.
That curious look was back and she was trying to think of something again. I grinned, winked at her and got out before she could
keep me. I even grinned at the clerk downstairs, but he didn't
grin back. He probably thought anybody who'd leave a blonde
like that alone was nuts or married and he wasn't used to it.

But it sure felt good. You know how. You feel so good you
want to tear something apart or laugh and it may be a little crazy,
but that's all part of it. That's how I was feeling until I remembered the other things and knew what I had to do.

I found a gin mill down the street and changed a buck into a
handful of coins. Three of them got my party and I said, "Mr.
Carboy?"

"That's right. Who is this?"

"Joe Boyle."

Carboy told somebody to be quiet then, "What do you want,
kid?"

I got the pitch as soon as I caught the tone in his voice. "Your
boys haven't got me, if that's what you're thinking," I told him.

"Yeah?"

"I didn't take a powder. I was trying to get something done.
For once figure somebody else got brains too."

"You weren't supposed to do any thinking, kid."

"Well, if I don't, you lose a boatload of merchandise, friend."

"What?" It was a whisper that barely came through.

"Renzo's ticking you off. He and Gulley are pulling a switch.
Your stuff gets delivered to him."

"Knock it off, kid. What do you know?"

"*I know the boat's coming into the slipside docks with the load
and Renzo will be picking it up. You hold the bag, brother.*"

"Joe," he said. "You know what happens if you're queering
me."

"I know."

"Where'd you pick it up?"

"Let's say I sat in on Renzo's conference with Gulley."

"Okay, boy. I'll stick with it. You better be right. Hold on." He turned away from the phone and shouted muffled orders at some-one. There were more muffled shouts in the background then he got back on the line again. "Just one thing more. What about Vetter?"

"Not yet, Mr. Carboy. Not yet."

"You get some of my boys to stick with you. I don't like my plans interfered with. Where are you?"

"In a place called Patty's. A gin mill."

"I know it. Stay there ten minutes. I'll shoot a couple guys down. You got that handkerchief yet?"

"Still in my pocket."

"Good. Keep your eyes open."

He slapped the phone back and left me there. I checked the clock on the wall, went to the bar and had an orange, then when the ten minutes were up, drifted outside. I was half a block away when a car door slapped shut and I heard the steady tread of footsteps across the street.

Now it was set. Now the big blow. The show ought to be good when it happened and I wanted to see it happen. There was a cab stand at the end of the block and I hopped in the one on the end. He nodded when I gave him the address, looked at the bill in my hand and took off. In back of us the lights of another car prowled through the night, but always looking our way.

You smelt the place before you reached it. On one side the darkened store fronts were like sleeping drunks, little ones and big ones in a jumbled mass, but all smelling the same. There was the fish smell and on top that of wood the salt spray had started to rot. The bay stretched out endlessly on the other side, a few boats here and there marked with running lights, the rest just vague silhouettes against the sky. In the distance the moon turned the train trestle into a giant spidery hand. The white sign, "SLIP-SIDE," pointed on the dock area and I told the driver to turn up the street and keep right on going. He picked the bill from my fingers, slowed around the turn, then picked it up when I hopped out. In a few seconds the other car came by, made the turn and lost itself further up the street. When it was gone I stepped out of the shadows and crossed over. Maybe thirty seconds later the car came tearing back up the street again and I ducked back into a doorway. Phil Carboy was going to be pretty sore at those boys of his.

I stood still when I reached the corner again and listened. It was too quiet. You could hear the things that scurried around on the dock. The things were even bold enough to cross the street and one was dragging something in its mouth. Another, a curious elongated creature whose fur shone silvery in the street light pounched on it and the two fought and squealed until the raider had what it went after.

It happens even with rats, I thought. Who learns from who? Do the rats watch the men or the men watch the rats?

Another one of them ran into the gutter. It was going to cross, then stood on its hind legs in an attitude of attention, its face pointing toward the dock. I never saw it move, but it disappeared, then I heard what it had heard, carefully muffled sounds, then a curse.

It came too quick to say it had a starting point. First the quick stab of orange and the sharp thunder of the gun, then the others following and the screams of the slugs whining off across the water. They didn't try to be quiet now. There was a startled shout, a hoarse scream and the yell of somebody who was hit.

Somebody put out the street light and the darkness was a blanket that slid in. I could hear them running across the street, then the moon reached down before sliding behind a cloud again and I saw them, a dozen or so closing in on the dock from both sides.

Out on the water an engine barked into life, was gunned and a boat wheeled away down the channel. The car that had been cruising around suddenly dimmed its lights, turned off the street and stopped. I was right there with no place to duck into and feet started running my way. I couldn't go back and there was trouble ahead. The only other thing was to make a break for it across the street and hope nobody spotted me.

I'd pushed it too far. I was being a dope again. One of them yelled and started behind me at a long angle. I didn't stop at the rail. I went over the side into the water, kicked away from the concrete abutment and hoped I'd come up under the pier. I almost made it. I was a foot away from the piling but it wasn't enough. When I looked back the guy was there at the rail with a gun bucking in his hand and the bullets were walking up the water toward me. He must have still had half a load left and only a foot to go when another shot blasted out over my head and the guy grabbed at his face with a scream and fell back to the street.

The guy up above said, "Get the son . . ." and the last word had a whistle to it as something caught him in the belly. He was all doubled up when he hit the water and his tombstone was a tiny trail of bubbles that broke the surface a few seconds before stopping altogether.

I pulled myself further under the dock. From where I was I could hear the voices and now they had quieted down. Out on the street somebody yelled to stand back and before the words were out cut loose with a sharp blast of an automatic rifle. It gave the bunch on the street time to close in and those on the dock scurried back farther.

Right over my head the planks were warped away and when a voice said, "I found it," I could pick Johnny's voice out of the racket.

"Where?"

"Back ten feet on the pole. Better hop to it before they get wise and cut the wires."

Johnny moved fast and I tried to move with him. By the time I reached the next piling I could hear him dialing the phone. He talked fast, but kept his voice down. "*Renzo? Yeah, they bottled us. Somebody pulled the cork out of the deal. Yeah. The hell with that, you call the cops. Let them break it up.* Sure, sure. Move it. We can make it to one of the boats. They got Tommy and Balco. Two of the others were hit but not bad. Yeah, it's Carboy all right. He ain't here himself, but they're his guys. Yeah, I got the stuff. Shake it."

His feet pounded on the planking overhead and I could hear his voice without making out what he said. The next minute the blasting picked up and I knew they were trying for a standoff. Whatever they had for cover up there must have been pretty good because the guys on the street were swearing at it and yelling for somebody to spread out and get them from the sides. The only trouble was that there was no protection on the street and if the moon came out again they'd be nice easy targets.

It was the moan of the siren that stopped it. First one, then another joined in and I heard them running for their cars. A man screamed and yelled for them to take it easy. Something rattled over my head and when I looked up, a frame of black marred the flooring. Something was rolled to the edge, then crammed over. Another followed it. Men. Dead. They bobbed for a minute, then sank slowly. Somebody said, "Damn, I hate to do that. He was okay."

"Shut up and get out there." It was Johnny.

The voice said, "Yeah, come on, you," then they went over the side. I stayed back of the piling and watched them swim for the boats. The sirens were coming closer now. One had a lead as if it knew the way and the others didn't. Johnny didn't come down. I grinned to myself, reached for a cross-brace and swung up on it. From there it was easy to make the trapdoor.

And there was Johnny by the end of the pier squatting down behind a packing case that seemed to be built around some machinery, squatting with that tenseness of a guy about to run. He had a box in his arms about two feet square and when I said, "Hello, chum," he stood up so fast he dropped it, but he would have had to do that anyway the way he was reaching for his rod.

He almost had it when I belted him across the nose. I got him with another sharp hook and heard the breath hiss out of him. It spun him around until the packing case caught him and when I was coming in he let me have it with his foot. I skidded sidewise, took the toe of his shoe on my hip then had his arm in a lock that brought a scream tearing out of his throat. He was going for the rod again when the arm broke and in a crazy surge of pain he jerked loose, tripped me, and got the gun out with his good hand. I rolled into his feet as it coughed over my head, grabbed his wrist and turned it into his neck and he pulled the trigger for the last time in trying to get his hand loose. There was just one last, brief, horrified expression in his eyes as he looked at me, then they filmed over to start rotting away.

The siren that was screaming turned the corner with its wail dying out. Brakes squealed against the pavement and the car stopped, the red light on its hood snapping shut. The door opened opposite the driver, stayed open as if the one inside was listening. Then a guy crawled out, a little guy with a big gun in his hand. He said, "Johnny?"

Then he ran. Silently, like an Indian, I almost had Johnny's gun back in my hand when he reached me.

"You," Sergeant Gonzales said. He saw the package there, twisted his mouth into a smile and let me see the hole in the end of his gun. I still made one last try for Johnny's gun when the blast went off. I half expected the sickening smash of a bullet, but none came. When I looked up, Gonzales was still there. Something on the packing crate had hooked his coat and held him up.

I couldn't see into the shadows where the voice came from. But it was a familiar voice. It said, "You ought to be more careful son."

The gun the voice held slithered back into the leather.

"Thirty seconds. No more. You might even do the job right and beat it in his car. He was in on it. The cop . . . he was working with Cooley. Then Cooley ran out on him too so he played along with Renzo. Better move, kid."

The other sirens were almost there. I said, "Watch yourself. And thanks."

"Sure, kid. I hate crooked cops worse than crooks."

I ran for the car, hopped in and pulled the door shut. Behind me something splashed and a two foot square package floated on the water a moment, then turned over and sunk out of sight. I left the lights off, turned down the first street I reached and headed across town. At the main drag I pulled up, wiped the wheel and gearshift free of prints and got out.

There was dawn showing in the sky. It would be another hour yet before it was morning. I walked until I reached the junkyard in back of Gordon's office, found the wreck of a car that still had cushions in it, climbed in and went to sleep.

Morning, afternoon, then evening. I slept through the first two. The last one was harder. I sat there thinking things, keeping out of sight. My clothes were dry now, but the cigarettes had a lousy taste. There was a twinge in my stomach and my mouth was dry. I gave it another hour before I moved, then went back over the fence and down the street to a dirty little diner that everybody avoided except the boys who rode the rods into town. I knocked off a plate of bacon and eggs, paid for it with some of the change I had left, picked up a pack of butts and started out. That was when I saw the paper on the table.

It made quite a story. GANG WAR FLARES ON WATERFRONT, and under it a subhead that said, *Cop, Hoodlum, Slain in Gun Duel.* It was a masterpiece of writing that said nothing, intimated much and brought out the fact that though the place was bullet sprayed and though evidence of other wounded was found, there were no bodies to account for what had happened. One sentence mentioned the fact that Johnny was connected with Mark Renzo. The press hinted at police inefficiency. There was the usual statement from Captain Gerot.

The thing stunk. Even the press was afraid to talk out. How long would it take to find out Gonzales didn't die by a shot from Johnny's gun? Not very long. And Johnny . . . a cute little twist like that would usually get a big splash. There wasn't even any curiosity shown about Johnny. I let out a short laugh and threw the paper back again.

They were like rats, all right. They just went the rats one better. They dragged their bodies away with them so there wouldn't be any ties. Nice. Now find the doctor who patched them up. Find what they were after on the docks. Maybe they figured to heist ten tons or so of machinery. Yeah, try and find it.

No, they wouldn't say anything. Maybe they'd have to hit it a little harder when the big one broke. When the boys came in who paid a few million out for a package that was never delivered. Maybe when the big trouble came and the blood ran again some-body would crawl back out of his hole long enough to put it into print. Or it could be that Bucky Edwards was right. Life was too precious a thing to sell cheaply.

I thought about it, remembering everything he had told me. When I had it all back in my head again I turned toward the place where I knew Bucky would be and walked faster. Halfway there it started to drizzle. I turned up the collar of my coat.

It was a soft rain, one of those things that comes down at the end of a summer, making its own music like a dull concert you think will have no end. It drove people indoors until even the cabs didn't bother to cruise. The cars that went by had their windows steamed into opaque squares, the drivers peering through the hand-wiped panes.

I jumped a streetcar when one came along, took it downtown and got off again. And I was back with the people I knew and the places made for them. Bucky was on his usual stool and I wondered if it was a little too late. He had that all gone look in his face and his fingers were caressing a tall amber-colored glass.

When I sat down next to him his eyes moved, giving me a glassy stare. It was like the cars on the street, they were cloudy with mist, then a hand seemed to reach out and rub them clear.

They weren't glass any more. I could see the white in his fingers as they tightened around the glass and he said, "You did it fancy, kiddo. Get out of here."

"Scared, Bucky?"

His eyes went past me to the door, then came back again. "Yes. You said it right. I'm scared. Get out. I don't want to be around when they find you."

"For a guy who's crocked most of the time you seem to know a lot about what happens."

"I think a lot. I figure it out. There's only one answer."

"If you know it why don't you write it?"

"Living's not much fun any more, but what there is of it, I like. Beat it, kid."

This time I grinned at him, a big fat grin and told the bartender to get me an orange. Large. He shoved it down, picked up my dime and went back to his paper.

I said, "Let's hear about it, Bucky." I could feel my mouth changing the grin into something else. "I don't like to be a target either. I want to know the score."

Bucky's tongue made a pass over dry lips. He seemed to look back inside himself to something he had been a long time ago, dredging the memory up. He found himself in the mirror behind the back bar, twisted his mouth at it and looked back at me again.

"This used to be a good town."

"Not that," I said.

He didn't hear me. "Now anybody who knows anything is scared to death. To death, I said. Let them talk and that's what they get. Death. From one side or another. It was bad enough when Renzo took over, worse when Carboy came in. It's not over yet." His shoulders made an involuntary shudder and he pulled the drink halfway down the glass. "Friend Gulley had an accident this afternoon. He was leaving town and was run off the road. He's dead."

I whistled softly. "Who?"

For the first time a trace of humor put lines at the corner of his lips. "It wasn't Renzo. It wasn't Phil Carboy. They were all accounted for. The tire marks are very interesting. It looks like the guy wanted to stop friend Gulley for a chat but Gulley hit the ditch. You could call it a real accident without lying." He finished the rest of the drink, put it down and said, "The boys are scared stiff." He looked at me closely then. "Vetter," he said. "He's getting close."

Bucky didn't hear me. "I'm getting to like the guy. He does what should have been done a long time ago. By himself he does it. They know who killed Gonzales. One of Phil's boys saw it happen before he ran for it. There's a guy with a broken neck who was found out on the highway and they know who did that and how." He swirled the ice around in his glass. "He's taking good care of you, kiddo."

I didn't say anything.

"There's just one little catch to it, Joe. One little catch."

"What?"

"That boy who saw Gonzales get it saw something else. He saw you and Johnny tangle over the package. He figures you got it. Everybody knows and now they want you. It can't happen twice. Renzo wants it and Carboy wants it. You know who gets it?"

I shook my head.

"You get it. In the belly or in the head. Even the cops want you that bad. Captain Gerot even thinks that way. You better get out of here, Joe. Keep away from me. There's something about you that spooks me. Something in the way your eyes look. Something about your face. I wish I could see into that mind of yours. I always thought I knew people, but I don't know you at all. You spook me. You should see your own eyes. I've seen eyes like yours before but I can't remember where. They're familiar as hell, but I can't place them. They don't belong in a kid's face at all. Go on, Joe, beat it. The boys are all over town. They got orders to do just one thing. Find you. When they do I don't want you sitting next to me."

"When do you write the big story, Bucky?"

"You tell me."

My teeth were tight together with the smile moving around them. "It won't be long."

"No . . . maybe just a short obit. They're tracking you fast. That hotel was no cover at all. Do it smarter the next time."

The ice seemed to pour down all over me. It went down over my shoulders, ate through my skin until it was in the blood that pounded through my body. I grabbed his arm and damn near jerked him off the stool. "What about the hotel?"

All he did was shrug. Bucky was gone again.

I cursed silently, ran back into the rain again and down the block to the cab stand.

The clerk said he was sorry, he didn't know anything about room 612. The night man had taken a week off. I grabbed the key from his hand and pounded up the stairs. All I could feel was that mad frenzy of hate swelling in me and I kept saying her name over and over to myself. I threw the door open, stood there breathing fast while I called myself a dozen different kinds of fool.

She wasn't there. It was empty.

A note lay beside the telephone. All it said was, *"Bring it where you brought the first one."*

I laid the note down again and stared out the window into the night. There was sweat on the backs of my hands. Bucky had called it. They thought I had the package and they were forcing a trade. Then Mark Renzo would kill us both. He thought.

I brought the laugh up from way down in my throat. It didn't sound much like me at all. I looked at my hands and watched them open and close into fists. There were callouses across the palms, huge things that came from Gordon's junk carts. A year and a half of it, I thought. Eighteen months of pushing loads of scrap iron for pennies then all of a sudden I was part of a multimillion dollar operation. The critical part of it. I was the enigma. Me, Joey the junk pusher. Not even Vetter now. Just me. Vetter would come after me.

For a while I stared at the street. That tiny piece of luck that chased me caught up again and I saw the car stop and the men jump out. One was Phil Carboy's right hand man. In a way it was funny. Renzo was always a step ahead of the challenger, but Phil was coming up fast. He'd caught on too and was ready to pull the same deal. He didn't know it had already been pulled.

But that was all right too.

I reached for the pen on the desk, lifted a sheet of cheap stationery out of the drawer and scrawled across it, *"Joe . . . be back in a few hours. Stay here with the package until I return. I'll have the car ready."* I signed it, *Helen*, put it by the phone and picked up the receiver.

The clerk said, "Yes?"

I said, "In a minute some men will come in looking for the

blonde and me. You think the room is empty, but let them come up. You haven't seen me at all yet. Understand?"

"Say . . ."

"Mister, if you want to walk out of here tonight you'll do what you're told. You're liable to get killed otherwise. Understand that?"

I hung up and let him think about it. I'd seen his type before and I wasn't worried a bit. I got out, locked the door and started up the stairs to the roof. It didn't take me longer than five minutes to reach the street and when I turned the corner the light was back on in the room I had just left. I gave it another five minutes and the tall guy came out again, spoke to the driver of the car and the fellow reached in and shut off the engine. It had worked. The light in the window went out. The vigil had started and the boys could afford to be pretty patient. They thought.

The rain was a steady thing coming down just a little bit harder than it had. It was cool and fresh with the slightest nip in it. I walked, putting the pieces together in my head. I did it slowly, replacing the fury that had been there, deliberately wiping out the gnawing worry that tried to grow. I reached the deserted square of the park and picked out a bench under a tree and sat there letting the rain drip down around me. When I looked at my hands they were shaking.

I was thinking wrong. I should have been thinking about fat, ugly faces; rat faces with deep voices and whining faces. I should have been thinking about the splashes of orange a rod makes when it cuts a man down and blood on the street. Cops who want the big payoff. Thinking of a town where even the press was cut off and the big boys came from the city to pick up the stuff that started more people on the long slide down to the grave.

Those were the things I should have thought of.

All I could think of was Helen. Lovely Helen who had been all things to many men and hated it. Beautiful Helen who didn't want me to be hurt, who was afraid the dirt would rub off. Helen who found love for the first time . . . and me. The beauty in her face when I told her. Beauty that waited to be kicked and wasn't because I loved her too much and didn't give a damn what she had been. She was different now. Maybe I was too. She didn't know it, but she was the good one, not me. She was the child that needed taking care of, not me. Now she was hours away from being dead and so was I. The thing they wanted, the thing that could buy her life I saw floating in the water beside the dock. It was like having a yacht with no fuel aboard.

The police? No, not them. They'd want me. They'd think it was a phony. That wasn't the answer. Not Phil Carboy either. He was after the same thing Renzo was.

I started to laugh, it was so damn, pathetically funny. I had it all in my hand and couldn't turn it around. What the devil does a guy have to do? How many times does he have to kill himself? The answer. It was right there but wouldn't come through. It wasn't the same answer I had started with, but a better one.

So I said it all out to myself. Out loud, with words. I started with the night I brought the note to Renzo, the one that promised him Vetter would cut his guts out. I even described their faces to myself when Vetter's name was mentioned. One name, that's all it took, and you could see the fear creep in because Vetter was deadly and unknown. He was the shadow that stood there, the one they couldn't trust, the one they all knew in the society that stayed outside the law. He was a high-priced killer who never missed and always got more than he was paid to take. So deadly they'd give anything to keep him out of town, even to doing the job he was there for. So deadly they'd could throw me or anybody else to the wolves just to finger him. So damn deadly they put an army on him, yet so deadly he could move behind their lines without any trouble at all.

Vetter.

I cursed the name. I said Helen's. Vetter wasn't important any more.

The rain lashed at my face as I looked up into it. The things I knew fell into place and I knew what the answer was. I remembered something I didn't know was there, a sign on the docks by the fishing fleet that said "SEASON LOCKERS."

Jack Cooley had been smart by playing it simple. He even left me the ransom.

I got up, walked to the corner and waited until a cab came by. I flagged him down, got it and gave the address of the white house where Cooley had lived.

The same guy answered the door. He took the bill from my hand and nodded me in. I said, "Did he leave any old clothes behind at all?"

"Some fishing stuff downstairs. It's behind the coal bin. You want that?"

"I want that," I said.

He got up and I followed him. He switched on the cellar light, took me downstairs and across the littered pile of refuse a cellar can collect. When he pointed to the old set of dungarees on the nail in the wall, I went over and felt through the pockets. The key was in the jacket. I said thanks and went back upstairs. The taxi was still waiting. He flipped his butt away when I got in, threw the heap into gear and headed toward the smell of the water.

I had to climb the fence to get on the pier. There wasn't much to it. The lockers were tall steel affairs, each with somebody's name scrawled across it in chalk. The number that matched the key didn't say Cooley, but it didn't matter any more either. I opened it up and saw the cardboard box that had been jammed in there so hard it had snapped one of the rods in the corner. Just to be sure I pulled one end open, tore through the other box inside and tasted the white powder.

Heroin.

They never expected Cooley to do it so simply. He had found a way to grab their load and stashed it without any trouble at all. Friend Jack was good at that sort of thing. Real clever. Walked away with a couple million bucks' worth of stuff and never lived to convert it. He wasn't quite smart enough. Not quite as smart as Carboy, Gerot, Renzo . . . or even a kid who pushed a junk cart. Smart enough to grab the load, but not smart enough to keep on living.

I closed the locker and went back over the fence with the box in my arms. The cabbie found me a phone in a gin mill and waited while I made my calls. The first one got me Gerot's home number. The second got me Captain Gerot himself, a very annoyed Gerot who had been pulled out of bed.

I said, "Captain, this is Joe Boyle and if you trace this call you're going to scramble the whole deal."

So the captain played it smart. "Go ahead," was all he told me.

"You can have them all. Every one on a platter. You know what I'm talking about?"

"I know."

"You want it that way?"

"I want you, Joe. Just you."

"I'll give you that chance. First you have to take the rest. There won't be any doubt this time. They won't be big enough to crawl out of it. There isn't enough money to buy them out either. You'll have every one of them cold."

"I'll still want you."

I laughed at him. "I said you'll get your chance. All you have to do is play it my way. You don't mind that, do you?"

"Not if I get you, Joe."

I laughed again. "You'll need a dozen men. Ones you can trust. Ones who can shoot straight and aren't afraid of what might come later."

"I can get them."

"Have them stand by. It won't be long. I'll call again."

I hung up, stared at the phone a second, then went back outside. The cabbie was working his way through another cigarette. I said, "I need a fast car. Where do I get one?"

"How fast for how much?"

"The limit."

"I got a friend with a souped-up Ford. Nothing can touch it. It'll cost you."

I showed him the thing in my hand. His eyes narrowed at the edges. "Maybe it won't cost you all that," he said. He looked at me the same way Helen had, then waved me in.

We made a stop at an out of the way rooming house. I kicked my clothes off and climbed into some fresh stuff, then tossed everything else into a bag and woke up the landlady of the place. I told her to mail it to the post office address on the label and gave her a few bucks for her trouble. She promised me she would, took the bag into her room and I went outside. I felt better in the suit. I patted it down to make sure everything was set. The cabbie shot me a half smile when he saw me and held the door open.

I got the Ford and it didn't cost me a thing unless I piled it up. The guy grinned when he handed me the keys and made a familiar gesture with his hand. I grinned back. I gave the cabbie his fare with a little extra and got in the Ford with my box. It was almost over.

A mile outside Mark Renzo's roadhouse I stopped at a gas station and while the attendant filled me up all around, I used his phone. I got Renzo on the first try and said, "This is Joe, fat boy."

His breath in the phone came louder than the words. "Where are you?"

"Never mind. I'll be there. Let me talk to Helen."

I heard him call and then there was Helen. Her voice was tired and all the hope was gone from it. She said, "Joe . . ."

It was enough. I'd know her voice any time. I said, "Honey . . . don't worry about it. You'll be okay."

She started to say something else, but Renzo must have grabbed the phone from her. "You got the stuff kid?"

"I got it."

"Let's go, sonny. You know what happens if you don't."

"I know," I said. "You better do something first. I want to see the place of yours empty in a hurry. I don't feel like being stopped going in. Tell them to drive out and keep on going. I'll deliver the stuff to you, that's all."

"Sure, kid, sure. You'll see the boys leave."

"I'll be watching," I said.

Joke.

I made the other call then. It went back to my hotel room and I did it smart. I heard the phone ring when the clerk hit the room number, heard the phone get picked up and said as though I were in one big hurry, *"Look, Helen, I'm hopping the stuff out to Renzo's. He's waiting for it. As soon as he pays off we'll blow. See you later."*

When I slapped the phone back I laughed again then got Gerot again. This time he was waiting. I said, "Captain . . . they'll all be at Renzo's place. There'll be plenty of fun for everybody. You'll even find a fortune in heroin."

"You're the one I want, Joe."

"Not even Vetter?"

"No, he comes next. First you." This time he hung up on me. So I laughed again as the joke got funnier and made my last call.

The next voice was the one I had come to know so well. I said, "Joe Boyle. I'm heading for Renzo's. Cooley had cached the stuff in a locker and I need it for a trade. I have a light blue Ford and need a quick way out. The trouble is going to start."

"There's a side entrance," the voice said. "They don't use it any more. If you're careful you can come in that way and if you stay careful you can make it to the big town without getting spotted."

"I heard about Gulley," I said.

"Saddening. He was a wealthy man."

"You'll be here?"

"Give me five minutes," the voice told me. "I'll be at the side entrance. I'll make sure nobody stops you."

"There'll be police. They won't be asking questions."

"Let me take care of that."

"Everybody wants Vetter," I said.

"Naturally. Do you think they'll find him?"

I grinned. "I doubt it."

The other voice chuckled as it hung up.

I saw them come out from where I stood in the bushes. They got into cars, eight of them and drove down the drive slowly. They turned back toward town and I waited until their lights were a mile away before I went up the steps of the club.

At that hour it was an eerie place, a dimly lit ghost house showing the signs of people that had been there earlier. I stood inside the door, stopped and listened. Up the stairs I heard a cough. It was like that first night, only this time I didn't have somebody dragging me. I could remember the stairs and the long, narrow corridor at the top, and the oak-panelled door at the end of it. Even the thin line of light that came from under the door. I snuggled the box under my arm and walked in.

Renzo was smiling from his chair behind the desk. It was a funny kind of smile like I was a sucker. Helen was huddled on the floor in a corner holding a hand to the side of her cheek. Her dress had been shredded down to the waist, and tendrils of tattered cloth clung to the high swell of her breasts, followed the smooth flow of her body. Her other hand tried desperately to hide her nakedness from Renzo's leer. She was trembling, and the terror in her eyes was an ungodly thing.

And Renzo grinned. Big, fat Renzo. Renzo the louse whose eyes were now on the package under my arm, with the grin turning to a slow sneer. Renzo the killer who found a lot of ways to get away with murder and was looking at me as if he were seeing me for the first time.

He said, "You got your going away clothes on, kid."

"Yeah."

"You won't be needing them." He made the sneer bigger, but I wasn't watching him. I was watching Helen, seeing the incredible thing that crossed her face.

"I'm different, Helen?"

She couldn't speak. All she could do was nod.

"I told you I wasn't such a kid. I just look that way. Twenty . . . twenty-one you thought?" I laughed and it had a funny sound. Renzo stopped sneering. "I got ten years on that, honey. Don't worry about being in love with a kid."

Renzo started to get up then. Slowly, a ponderous monster with hands spread apart to kill something. "You two did it. You damn near ruined me. You know what happens now?" He licked his lips and the muscles rolled under his shirt.

My face was changing shape and I nodded. Renzo never noticed. Helen saw it. I said, "A lot happens now, fat boy." I dropped the package on the floor and kicked it to one side. Renzo moved out from behind the desk. He wasn't thinking any more. He was just seeing me and thinking of his empire that had almost toppled. The package could set it up again. I said, "Listen, you can hear it happen."

Then he stopped to think. He turned his head and you could hear the whine of engines and the shots coming clear across the night through the rain. There was a frenzy about the way it was happening, the frenzy and madness that goes into a *banzai* charge and above it the moan of sirens that seemed to go ignored.

It was happening to Renzo too, the kill hate in his eyes, the saliva that made wet paths from the corners of his tight mouth. His whole body heaved and when his head turned back to me again, the eyes were bright with the lust of murder.

I said, "Come here, Helen," and she came to me. I took the envelope out of my pocket and gave it to her, and then I took off my jacket, slipping it over her shoulders. She pulled it closed over her breasts, the terror in her eyes fading. "Go out the side . . . the old road. The car is waiting there. You'll see a tall guy beside it, a big guy all around and if you happen to see his face, forget it. Tell him this. Tell him I said to give the report to the Chief. Tell him to wait until I contact him for the next assignment then start the car and wait for me. I'll be in a hurry. You got that?"

"Yes, Joe." The disbelief was still in her eyes.

Renzo moved slowly, the purpose plain in his face. His hands were out and he circled between me and the door. There was something fiendish about his face.

The sirens and the shooting were getting closer.

He said, "Vetter won't get you out of this, kid. I'm going to kill you and it'll be the best thing I ever did. Then the dame. The blonde. Weber told me he saw a blonde at Gulley's and I knew who did this to me. The both of you are going to die, kid. There ain't no Vetter here now."

I let him have a long look at me. I grinned. I said, "Remember what that note said? It said Vetter was going to spill your guts all over the floor. You remember that, Renzo?"

"Yeah," he said. "Now tell me you got a gun, kid. Tell me that and I'll tell you you're a liar. I can smell a rod a mile away. You had it, kid. There ain't no Vetter here now."

Maybe it was the way I let myself go. I could feel the loosening in my shoulders and my face was a picture only Renzo could see. "You killed too many men, Renzo, one too many. The ones you peddle the dope to die slowly, the ones who take it away die quick. It's still a lot of men. You killed them, Renzo, a whole lot of them. You know what happens to killers in this country? It's a funny law, but it works. Sometimes to get what it wants, it works in peculiar fashion. But it works.

"Remember the note. Remember hard what it said." I grinned and what was in it stopped him five feet away. What was in it made him frown, then his eyes opened wide, almost too wide and he had the expression Helen had the first time.

I said to her, "Don't wait, Helen," and heard the door open and close. Renzo was backing away, his feet shuffling on the carpet.

Two minutes at the most.

"I'm Vetter," I said. "Didn't you know? Couldn't you tell? Me . . . Vetter. The one everybody wonders about, even the cops. Vetter the puzzle. Vetter the one who's there but isn't there." The air was cold against my teeth. "Remember the note, Renzo. No, you can't smell a gun because I haven't got one. But look at my hand. You're big and strong . . . you're a killer, but look at my hand and find out who the specialist really is and you'll know that there was no lie in that note."

Renzo tried to scream, stumbled and fell. I laughed again and moved in on him. He was reaching for something in the desk drawer, knowing all the time that he wasn't going to make it and the knife in my hand made a nasty little snick and he screamed again so high it almost blended with the sirens.

Maybe one minute left, but it would be enough and the puzzle would always be there and the name when mentioned would start another ball rolling and the country would be a little cleaner and the report when the Chief read it would mean one more done with . . . done differently, but done.

Harry Whittington

SO DEAD MY LOVE

There's a reason that Harry Whittington (1915–1989) was known as "The King of The Paperbacks." He wrote more of them than anybody else—as many as 150. A lot of them were written in the Fifties, at the top of the paperback original boom. Is it necessary to point out that he wrote quickly?

Harry was a yarn spinner who started out in the pulps following World War II and then turned to the paperback original even before this new format had its sea legs. He wrote for virtually every publisher around. There were the upscale imprints of Gold Medal, Avon, Ballantine; and there were the downscale imprints of Phantom, Beacon and Phoenix Press.

And he worked in every category except science fiction—crime, western, nurse romance, war, slave plantation sagas and what passed for erotica in those days.

He wrote far more good ones than bad ones and a few of them are masterpieces of paperback original craft. Try Web of Murder, Brute in Brass, Backwoods Tramp, Fires That Destroy, A Night for Screaming.

Maybe if he'd had better agents and more dutiful editors, Harry could have been a major player. He had the stuff. But from what he told me over the last few years of his life, he was so successful early on he saw no reason to change his approach to writing books. Later in his career he had some hard times but then he came back steaming and enjoyed success again.

His work lives. There's a growing Whittington cult in the States now. France and England have always loved him, bless them. He was a snake-charmer of a storyteller and his short, somewhat primitive books still speak to us today. Yes, his best work is cast in a formulaic noir mold—but he brought his own interpretation to shaping his material and giving it life.

Here's a very nice short novel that ended up as half of one of the

old Ace Double Books. You're going to have a great time reading it.
I promise you.

E.G.

1

THERE WAS THIS FEELING OF ANXIETY. . . .
Talbot decided it came from returning to a place he hated, a town he'd run from in terror. A hot sweaty country that had haunted him for ten years. The last place in the world he should have come back to — the town and Nita. And the memory of Nita.

He stepped off the eight P.M. train and looked about the platform. The fifty-year-old station hadn't changed. He glanced up at the paint-scabbed sign: *Duval, Florida. Population 35,000.*

Talbot picked up his leather suitcase and started across the platform, searching for Mike Laynebeck.

He'd memorized Laynebeck's letter: *I know your memories of Duval and Florida — and Florida justice — must be steeped in bitterness, Jim. I know you own a successful investigating agency and you must be busy. But if an old friend in need can prevail upon you to come back to Duval, please do come. I've hesitated to ask you. But I do need you. You're the one man for this urgent business: you're an ace investigator and you know this part of the country. Devotedly, Mike.*

When he'd gotten the letter, Jim Talbot had crushed it in his fist and sworn he'd forget it. But he'd reread it a hundred times. And finally he'd bought a ticket on a streamliner south. And from the moment the wheels started turning twenty-five hours earlier, their clicking melody had had one jarring theme: *Nita. Nita. Nita. Nita.*

Talbot glanced through the waiting-room window. A small, well-stacked girl peered back at him. Talbot looked her over as he passed. She met his gaze and her eyes widened a trifle. Talbot kept walking.

At the parking area, he stopped and set down his suitcase. Laynebeck had promised to meet him. Laynebeck had insisted via long distance that he'd meet the eight o'clock train.

There was only one car parked at the curb. A black Plymouth with an aerial for two-way radio. Police car. A man was curled up under the steering wheel, watching Talbot.

Talbot heard a mewing at his heels. He turned and looked down.

A scrawny kitten spit at him, mewed again, and swiped at his cuff with a tiny claw.

Talbot smiled. "Your old lady know you're out?"

The kitten mewed again.

"Okay. Okay. I was hungry in this town once myself. I know what it's like, buddy. You don't have to sell me."

He pushed open the waiting-room door and walked to the candy concession. The girl made a production of going behind the counter. Hips, thighs and legs co-starred. Her eyes were bold prowlers. Her voice was as Southern as hominy grits for breakfast.

"What's foh yo'all, honey? . . . Uh, pahdon, Mistuh Honey."

Talbot grinned. Been a long time since he'd heard a voice like that. "Half-pint carton of milk, y'all."

"Milk? Foah yo'all? Yo'all just making a joke?"

"Saw you admiring my muscles. Where you think I got 'em?"

She handed him the carton, but she still didn't believe it. Her eyes wondered if that was all he wanted. He paid her and took the carton to the platform. The kitten was on its haunches, waiting.

Talbot tore the top off the carton. He hunkered down, setting the milk before the kitten. "Here, kid, drink this. I want you to grow up so you can get out of this town. A hell of a place to spend *nine* lives."

A pale blue Cadillac convertible skidded into the curb beyond the black Plymouth. Talbot straightened. He hefted his suitcase and started along the platform, staring at the man coming toward him from the sleek car.

Mike Laynebeck was taller even than Talbot remembered. Yard-wide shoulders in tailored gabardine. Shoulders that had looked good on long-ago football fields and made Laynebeck seem a giant in a courtroom. It gave you a hell of a lift to know such a man was on your side when your life was at stake. Talbot knew.

Talbot watched Laynebeck hurrying toward him. Mike sure had inherited the Laynebeck look of arrogance. Head erected, tilted, always looking down, making him seem even taller than he was.

Talbot began to see the changes. Ten years had been a long time for Mike Laynebeck. They'd been hell on him. He was bald except for a few slicked-down strands and the close-cropped hair on his temples was iron gray. He looked old, haggard.

They shook hands.

"Welcome home, Jim. I can never repay you for coming. Believe me, I'd never have brought you back. But it was important. To me, at least."

"I'm glad you called on me." Talbot glanced heavenward, expecting a thunderbolt to strike him dead for lying.

They started toward Laynebeck's Cadillac. The occupant of the Plymouth had emerged and was now draped against the front fender, picking at his fingernails with a penknife. Tall as Laynebeck, he was so thin that he looked as if he were standing on stilts.

He was looking Jim over, remembering him. He spoke to Laynebeck. "Evening, Senator."

Laynebeck inclined his head. "Hello, Clemmons."

Clemmons straightened. "Nice night." Clemmons was barring their way. "Real nice night." His gaze included Talbot. "Ain't it, mistuh?"

"All right, Clemmons." Laynebeck's voice held anger. "This is my friend Jim Talbot. Mr. Talbot, Deputy Sheriff Clemmons."

Talbot felt a constriction in his belly. Here was a man he remembered. Strick Clemmons shoved out his thin hand.

Talbot hated to touch it. He shook hands, managing to smile. "Goin' to be heah in town long, Mr. Talbot?"

"I don't know yet."

"We better push along," Laynebeck said. "I left a highball sitting at home."

Clemmons smiled again. "Remember me to the missus, Senator."

Laynebeck glanced at Talbot, nodded briefly at Clemmons. Clemmons stepped back, watching them. They got in the Cadillac. Clemmons backed his cruiser out. He went south on Main Street in a cloud of exhaust smoke.

Laynebeck laughed without mirth. "Sheriff Roberts' boy. Running to report."

"Report what?"

"That you're in town. That I met you at the train. That your name is Jim Talbot. That's enough for them to start on. They'll pick and worry at it until they get themselves in a stew."

"But why?"

Laynebeck sighed. "We're going through a political war right now, Jim. I've pretty well run the Party here in Marvel County as my old man did when he lived. But Sheriff Roberts is an ambitious man. He wants to run the county. Sometimes I think he wants to run the state. Nights I wake up in a sweat thinking what might happen if he ever did run Florida. He is just about taken over here—on a *reform* platform. It would be funny if it weren't so desperate. Things are getting rough now—so rough that Governor Reeves has threatened to move in personally at the next outburst of trouble. Roberts knows I'll make a last-ditch fight, so he has his boys report on everything I do. You've come to town. Roberts won't sleep until he knows why."

Talbot's hands clenched. "That's not why you brought me back?"

Laynebeck shook his head. "No. The job I have for you is in your line." His hand gestured expansively. "Duval has grown in ten years, Jim. We have one-way streets now."

"Doesn't matter which way the streets go in this town. Just so they all lead out of it."

Talbot watched the town slide past Senator Laynebeck's car. Narrow red brick streets. Old houses. Looking older and shabbier than ever.

"If you hate it that bad, why did you come back?"

"You sent for me."

"I told you I only hoped you'd come. I didn't really believe you would come."

"You knew I'd come." Talbot's voice was cold. "Without mentioning it, you let me know I owed my freedom to you."

"Come now. I hinted nothing. I said nothing."

"You didn't have to. You knew you didn't have to. Ten years ago I was in jail. Didn't have a chance in hell. You got me out. I owe everything I've got to you." He smiled. "It's all right. I knew you must need me all to hell, Mike, or you'd never have stooped to blackmail—even polite blackmail—to get me back to this garden spot."

"I do need you, Jim. There's no use pretending I don't."

"What's the job?"

"You remember Dan Calvert?"

"Yeah. He was in school with me."

"I took him in my law firm, Jim. Dan's smart. I made him a partner. A partner in everything. And Dan Calvert has disappeared. I don't know if he's been — murdered. I don't know anything. Only that he's gone. Almost two weeks and no trace of him. That's why I brought you back here, Jim. I want you to find Dan Calvert."

2

"Any reason to think Dan might have been murdered?"

Laynebeck said no. Not unless his being a partner of Laynebeck's was a reason. It didn't sound like a reason to Talbot. But Mike reminded him he'd been away a long time.

"What will you do with him when you find him?"

Laynebeck's foot came off the accelerator. The car slowed. He wanted to know what Jim meant by that.

"It's plain enough. If I'm going to look for Dan Calvert, I'll have to know the angles. One angle is obvious. He might have skipped out on you."

"He didn't." Laynebeck had checked their finances, those Calvert could have got his hands on. He had faith in Dan, but he'd checked all the angles. And Calvert had never suggested he was dissatisfied.

Laynebeck tooled the car off Fort Queen into a drive that curved into the Laynebeck place.

The house was a symbol of everything that Duval stood for. Old homes, old families, old hates, old wrongs.

There were lights in the sun room. Light splayed out on the columned veranda through floor-to-ceiling windows. A woman was wandering around in there with a highball glass in her hand.

Talbot smiled. He'd come a long way. He'd looked up at this old house many times. This was the first time he'd ever been invited inside.

Laynebeck parked under the east portico. He slid out from

under the wheel and started toward the front door. Talbot followed, lugging his suitcase.

Laynebeck opened the front door. Talbot entered the two-storied foyer.

"Leave your suitcase there." Laynebeck motioned toward the foyer closet. Another question answered. Talbot had been invited in. But he hadn't been invited to stay. He hadn't come that far.

Laynebeck glanced toward the sun room, frowning. He strode across the foyer and opened the library door. Talbot strolled through. Laynebeck followed, closing the door after him.

The library looked older than Laynebeck himself, though the furnishings were new. Shelves of books were ceiling high. But nothing helped. It was a tired room. Laynebeck seemed at home in it. He flopped into a leather-covered chair, waved Talbot into another. "You want a drink?"

"Sure."

Laynebeck dragged himself from the chair. *My God*, Talbot thought, *nobody is that old*.

Laynebeck poured two stiff drinks of bourbon, adding ice and water. He gave one to Jim and returned to his chair. He sagged into it with a sigh and regarded Talbot.

"I have no idea how you go about finding missing persons, Jim. I tried to get you right away so the trail—if he has disappeared and if he left a trail—wouldn't be too cold."

"It doesn't matter too much," Jim said. He finished his drink. "I've found the best thing you can do when you're tracing a missing person is to find out all you can about why he wanted to go."

"I can't help you there. I thought everything was fine. Dan was smart and I trusted him. Matter of fact, he was coming here to dinner the night he disappeared. I reminded him at noon that we were expecting him at seven. That was on a Tuesday. He said sure he'd be here. I was out of town that afternoon, selling some dairy property. Got home about five-thirty. I dressed for dinner. And Dan didn't show up."

Laynebeck had checked with Dan's friends. Unless they lied, they were astonished to learn that Dan had gone. There was no argument between them, personal or professional. Dan was a bachelor. He had plenty of women. Some of them were married. But he had stayed out of trouble. He owed nothing. He made around sixty thousand after taxes on their investments alone. Jim wanted to know if Calvert gambled. Laynebeck smiled. Sure. But not to the tune of sixty grand a year.

"Was he afraid of anybody?"

"He never told me if he was."

"Maybe he wouldn't. The hell of it is, none of us ever really knows anybody else. You can't ever know what the person before you is really thinking, really wanting. Their smiles don't mean a damned thing. I'll try to find Dan Calvert, Mike, but I'll have to ask a lot of people a lot of questions. You may not like all the answers."

"I brought you back here because I wanted him found."

"Right. You have a picture of him? A late picture. This year?"

"I'm sure we do." Laynebeck got up and went to the foyer door. He opened it. He called, "Nita."

Nita.

Talbot felt the breath in his lungs stop. Nita. He hadn't known how he would find her. Nita Barwell. He'd been aware that she might have moved away from Duval, married, divorced, died. And yet the simple answer hadn't occurred to him. The obvious angle. The merger of the Barwell money and the Laynebeck money.

What if there was over fifteen years' difference in their ages? Hell, now that it had happened, it was as though it had been destined to happen all along.

Nita Barwell, with all her boy friends, her crushes and summer romances. They hadn't meant a thing. All along, their families, the people who mattered, had been taking it for granted. Laynebeck had been adding to his fortune and his prestige. Nita had been growing up. Talbot felt his throat muscles tighten. What a growing up that had been!

She must have come across the foyer. Laynebeck spoke to her, his voice lowered. "Will you get the latest picture we have of Dan, my dear? The latest one."

Jim strained to hear her voice. He heard nothing. Maybe the pound of his own heart. The lazy night sounds beyond the windows. The steady throb of the clock. He set his glass on the table and looked at his hands. They were trembling.

Laynebeck returned to his chair. That odd frown was on his face again.

Talbot said, "I didn't know you'd married Nita. You should have told me when you wrote."

Laynebeck spread his hands. "I would have, Jim. It never occurred to me you didn't know."

I didn't know, Talbot thought. *Ten years away. I heard nothing of this town and didn't want to. If I'd known, nothing would have brought me back here.*

The door opened. Laynebeck pulled himself to his feet. Talbot stood, turning slowly. He was more aware of the throb of his heart than of anything else. He looked at Nita, wondering what he was trying to see, wondering what he was looking for in her face.

She was thirty. He knew how old she was. He knew all about her. Her full breasts swelled at the plunging line of her black evening dress. Her stomach was still flat. Her hips were fuller than he remembered and her thighs strained against the fabric of her gown. They'd always been like that.

She stood with the framed portrait of Dan Calvert in her hand. It pleased her that he was staring at her.

Talbot's gaze moved to her face. The slightly squared jaw, stubborn and arrogant—that was Nita. Stubborn, arrogant as hell. Her mouth was full and sensuous. Her nose was almost Greek classic. That was Nita, too, the goddess with the sensuous mouth. Her eyes were black and her hair was black. Then he saw the streak of gray.

It swept back from her widow's peak like a dove's soft wing. And it was the finishing touch. The gray wing in the crown of her black hair was what she had always needed. That wing of gray made her beautiful. Before, she'd been pretty and now she was beautiful.

Talbot felt the breath sigh out of him.

"He'o, Jim," Nita said.

Mike tried to laugh. "Remember the shaker of cocktails I mentioned? Now you see who drank it."

"I drank it," Nita said. She moved forward and placed her hand in Jim's. It was like ice. "Courage. Needed courage."

"Nita!" Laynebeck's voice was sharp. Nita withdrew her hand from Jim's and gave him the framed portrait.

"It's not a very good picture," she said. "He doesn't take a very good picture. He worries. Worries about how he'll look. Never take a good picture if you worry how you'll look."

"Something you never had to worry about," Jim said.

Nita looked at him. "Well, thank you. I can tell you, Jim, I've been looking forward to this moment with dread. Unaccustomed as I am to dreading old lovers. I wondered what you would say the first time we met. Funny, I never thought it would be a compliment."

"Funny," Talbot said. "Neither did I."

Her eyes widened, showing fear deep inside. She stared at him. Her lips moved, but she said nothing.

3

LAYNEBECK SAID, "IF YOU'RE GOING TO MAKE IT TO YOUR BED-room under your own power, Nita, it might be wise if you started now."

Nita heeled around. "It would have been wise if I'd started two hours ago. This is a very odd moment, Mike, and I wish you wouldn't spoil it."

"Tomorrow your perceptions will be keener, my dear. You'll appreciate the odd moment all the more."

"There never was an odder moment than this one, Mike, my love," Nita said. "I had to drink to be able to face it. I think Jim is being very fine about it. I was afraid he wouldn't be. I can tell you something else. I wouldn't have been fine about it." She turned again. "Did you ever forgive me, Jim?"

"Nita." Laynebeck's voice was chilled. "If you don't mind, Jim and I have a lot to discuss. It's getting late."

Nita stood looking at Jim. Her eyes squinted as though she were trying to find him through a haze that clouded her memory. She held out her hands, palms upward. They were trembling.

"I'm going to bed now," she said. "But one thing, Jim. When Mike said he was sending for you, I begged him not to. I made quite a scene. But he sent for you anyway. I just want you to know. Part of why I didn't want him to send for you was for you, Jim. I didn't think he had any right to bring you back to it."

She spun about on her high heels and walked from the room. They stood watching her. Talbot's gaze moved to Laynebeck's haggard face. What Mike felt for Nita was in his eyes.

"So you really love her?" Talbot said when the door was closed.

"There it is," Laynebeck agreed. "The beginning and the end. I grew up with her and never loved her. I married her and during the ceremony I thought that maybe I was fond of her. Now it's like a disease."

Yes, Talbot thought. *It is a disease. Loving Nita is a disease.*

"I control this town, this county. If I worked at it, I could control this state, or the men who control it would be working with me, which is the same thing. But I can't work at it any more."

"Nita."

"What do you mean?"

"Nothing. I just said her name."

"I heard you. And you're right. She's all that matters to me. And the hell of it is the more I let her see that I care, the worse she makes it for me. I can make everybody in this town dance except Nita. And she goes right on dancing if I tell her to stop."

Mike Laynebeck saw that he was talking too much. He tried to laugh, tried to make a joke of it. But he was too tired. He mixed drinks for them and returned to his chair.

"Did you ever marry, Jim?"

Talbot shook his head. "I tried to. Carrying the memory of a woman around inside you is foolish and unnatural. I've heard a man can't do it, anyway. He'll forget her. That's what I've heard."

Laynebeck tried to smile. "I'm sorry you were hurt. Sorry she hurt you. But I'm sure that Nita loved me, Jim. When I got you out of prison, I was a knight to her. I'd rescued you."

"That's God's truth."

"I think it meant as much to Nita as it did to you."

Talbot scowled. "It meant I was out of prison. I was free. If you hadn't gotten me a new trial—complete exoneration—I'd never have got an investigator's license in New York. That's what it meant to me. What could it have meant to Nita, except that a dirty matter was ended?"

"Don't you think it was a prison sentence for Nita? If she had put you in prison, do you think she was free as long as you were penned?"

Talbot laughed coldly. He thought, *you're defending her to me. What about what she's doing to you? You say Sheriff Roberts is trying to take over political control of this county. Isn't it possible only because your mind is on Nita?* He said, "Could Sheriff Roberts have bought out Dan Calvert?"

Laynebeck stood up. "Roberts is dirty. Dan isn't. Dan believes as I do in decent government. Roberts makes his on dirty little rackets."

"What kind of rackets?"

"All kinds. They were in existence in this town when my father was young, but now they're all owned by Roberts. He dares me to bring it out in the open. Everything from petty protection to gambling. The smell of it is another reason Governor Reaves has threatened to crack down here. Why, even women who dance publicly pay Roberts a tax—"

"What for?"

"To be safe. So his goons won't pick them up as common prostitutes. So they won't be put out of business. Mostly because it's another graft."

Talbot smiled. "No wonder he thinks he can take over. Are you sure Roberts isn't the answer to Calvert's disappearance?"

"Why should Dan Calvert fear Roberts?"

"Maybe things are getting too hot?"

"But if things got too hot, Dan wouldn't leave without money. He'd try to salvage something."

"Maybe. Depends on how scared he was."

"If he was that scared, Jim, some of it would have rubbed off on me. He was my partner, you know."

"But as you say, your mind was on something else." Talbot nodded toward the door through which Nita had gone. "If Dan had his eyes open, he might have seen things that scared hell out of him."

"Are you afraid already, Talbot?"

"No. But I thought this town was rotten when I ran away from it. It was a Sunday School picnic then."

"Yes. Things were simpler. They're not simple now."

"Are you afraid to look for Calvert?"

"Afraid?"

"Why else would you send for me? You control this county. Or you did. Until Roberts started taking over. You could find out all about Calvert if you wanted to dig. But you don't want to. You'd rather hire me. You're afraid to dig, Laynebeck. You're afraid of what you might find."

"That's not true. If I were afraid, I wouldn't have brought you back. You were the first man Nita ever loved. She told me. She told me when she was begging me not to bring you back to look for Dan."

"There's another kind of fear, Laynebeck. The fear of the muck you might get all over you. Maybe you're more afraid of that than of a love that's ten years dead."

Laynebeck finished off his drink. "All right, Jim, I'm going on looking for Dan. Just as I have been looking. I searched before I gave up and sent that special delivery to you. But so you won't believe I'm afraid, I promise you I'm going on looking."

Jim smiled, admiring the big man. "All right. That's good enough for me, Mike. Sorry my temper got the best of me. I'll find Dan Calvert for you."

He poured himself another drink, wondering what he was going to do about Nita. It had been clear in his mind before. He had known what he would do about her if he found her when he got back here. But now it was different. She was Mike Laynebeck's wife. Maybe the word wife didn't mean so much anymore. But it meant everything to the tired man, Mike Laynebeck. Nita was Mike's wife. Mike loved Nita more than life. Hell, life was cheap. Nita was everything.

Talbot shook his head. He had been so certain before. He was no longer sure. He didn't know what he could do about her now. . . .

Laynebeck picked up the house phone and told the chauffeur to bring the Buick coupé to the west drive. "I'm turning over one of my cars to you, Jim. If you like it and do a good job, I'll make it a bonus."

Talbot was studying the picture of Calvert. "Thanks, Mike."

Laynebeck looked over his shoulder at the picture. "About your age, Jim. His eyes are blue, though that picture shows them as brown. His hair is brown and is receding slightly, though not as alarmingly as mine, of course. As Nita pointed out, Dan looks worried. It's an habitual expression."

"He hasn't changed much. Nice looking. I didn't know him too well at school. But I'll know him when I see him."

"You think you're going to find him?"

"That's what you hired me for, isn't it?"

The chauffeur opened the library door and told Laynebeck the

Buick was in the west drive. A dark-faced man, he withdrew at once, closing the door.

"I won't walk out with you, Jim. I consciously avoid doing anything I can get out of."

"Sure. I'll take Dan's picture with me. It might frighten the goblins in my hotel room."

"By the way, I reserved your rooms for you. At the Duval House. That's the best, and I told them I wanted their best for you."

"Thanks, Mike. It's good to see you again. Not the town, but you. I don't forget what I owe you and I'll find Calvert for you."

They shook hands. Talbot got his suitcase, went through the front door and let it close behind him.

For a moment he stood on the veranda. The front porch light was snapped off. Somebody had allowed him just time to walk to the Buick in the west drive. The wind was rising. It dried the sweat across his forehead. He'd drunk too much in there. He'd been hired to find Dan Calvert, but that wasn't what made him keep refilling his drink. It was finding Nita. Finding her married to Mike Laynebeck. And wondering what he was going to be able to do about Nita now.

He strode across the veranda to the coupé, opened the door. A shadowy figure was slumped down on the far side of the seat. Nita laughed throatily. "Get in," she said. "Come on, Jimmy Talbot. Get in and tell me you're glad to see me."

4

TALBOT LOOKED AT HER. SHE'D TOSSED A SHEER GREEN WRAP about her bare shoulders. Its hood was draped over her dark hair so only the wing of gray winked at him in the dark.

He put his suitcase behind the seat, got in and sat with his hands on the steering wheel. "Where do you think you're going?"

"I don't know. Where are you going to take me?"

"Mike sent you to bed."

"Mike would always send me to bed. He's afraid I might see someone to think about besides Mike Laynebeck."

"Just the same, I'm working for him. You're his wife. This isn't starting things off on a fine plane."

"To hell with a fine plane. Start the car."

He started it. They moved along the drive, swung east on Fort Queen.

"I'm more than Mike Laynebeck's wife. I'm also the girl who let you go to prison. I played a rotten trick on you. Because you loved me, and I knew you loved me, I let you pay for something I did and didn't have the guts to face."

The light from the dash glowed on their faces. Talbot could feel Nita's eyes on him. The scent of her assailed him. The feel of her shoulder against his shoulder was fire.

"Faster, Jim. Drive faster." He pressed harder on the accelerator. The car lunged forward, its bright lights illuminating the road. He heard her whispered approval.

Forks in the road loomed ahead. Left was a huge sign: *Golden Springs—Nature's Underwater Fairyland*. To the right, the road was narrow and dark. Talbot swung the Buick right.

Memories swarmed in upon him on the whistling wind. They'd been on this road the first time he had her. He wondered if she would remember, and told himself she wouldn't.

His voice was bitter. "We had a fine love, Nita. I was a poor kid who rode the county bus to high school. You had your own car and more spending money than my family had for a week's groceries. But that didn't matter. You told me you loved me and if I liked, you wouldn't even speak to any one else but me, just to prove it."

Nita's voice was soft. "I meant it too. And I hated you in a way. I wanted to be able to laugh at you. The way my friends did—"

"You don't have to tell me."

"But I couldn't laugh. I found out I couldn't stay away from you. We'd fight and I'd make you beg me to come back, and all the time I knew I'd die if I didn't have you."

"Sure. You put me through hell."

"You were a fool to let me, Jim."

"No." His sardonic voice broke across hers. "I loved you. Nothing else mattered."

"You have the bitterest voice in the world."

"I'm the bitterest guy in the world."

"I didn't mean to hurt you. I got mixed up in a robbery for thrills. I was drinking. When I sobered up, I was with this boy, and the police were after us. All I could think was I had to get to you. If I could get to you, I'd be safe."

I remember, Talbot thought. Nita had broken a date. Another one. He'd been too miserable to sleep. At about eleven-thirty, he got out of bed, dressed and slipped from the house. He was sitting near the dark road when Nita's car came tearing along it. He still remembered how wonderful it had been to see her.

But it hadn't been wonderful. She'd told him all about it. She and a boy robbing a filling station just for the hell of it. Only the boy hadn't been drunk enough. He'd lost his nerves. Dressed as a man, Nita had done the thrill robbery alone. The station lights were already out. The operator's face was to the wall. She said she was sure he never saw her clearly.

The police were tracing her car. Nita begged him to help her. Sure, her family was rich enough to get her out of it, but she'd die before she'd let them find out. Jim was the only one who could help. She was hysterical. He told the cops he'd borrowed her car, gone alone, robbed alone. It wasn't until later that he learned that Nita had been armed.

It was too late then. The police believed every word of his first confession. He was poor, he'd borrowed Nita's car, he'd robbed in order to get money to date her. His family remembered he'd dressed, left the house. They couldn't say at what hour he left, and he hadn't returned that night.

A nightmare of jail and waiting. Nita didn't come near him. At the trial she attended only as a spectator. She stood by, hearing the Florida law read: *Armed Robbery. At the discretion of the court, a term of years equal to the natural life of the convicted.*

He'd believed until after the trial that Nita was going to come forward and tell the truth. Afterwards, he broke down and told the truth because he was scared and hopeless. And nobody believed him. . . .

He slowed the car abruptly and whipped it off the highway into a shell-paved road that ended on a bluff overlooking Cypress River. Headlights illumined oak and sweet bay matting the far bank of the black stream. This had been their bluff once.

He cut off the engine and sat watching the soft glow of light across her face, and the old emptiness hit him, hard.

"You know where you are?" His mouth twisted when he asked her.

She sat up and looked around. She shrugged.

She fumbled in her purse and found a cigarette. White fingers unsteady, she placed it between her lips. She dug again and came up with a gaudy book of matches.

He read the red letters on the yellow cover. *Bonny Williams' Golden Club. On the Golden Springs Road.*"

"No gold engraved cigarette lighter?" Talbot taunted.

She lighted her cigarette and tossed the dead match through the window.

"Can't keep 'em. I bet I've had three dozen and I've lost 'em all. Mike says he won't let me have any more." She laughed. "He says it's embarrassing where some of 'em are found. Once he told some friends that one had been found in the Y.M.C.A. men's room."

"Still careless. You haven't changed much."

She dragged a long nervous breath of smoke. The cigarette glowed cherry red. "Oh, I've changed. Don't think I haven't."

She slapped down on the door handle. The door swung open. Nita slid her legs around and stepped out of the car. Talbot watched her for a moment. His gaze moved to the seat. Her handkerchief was there, fragile and scented. He opened his mouth to taunt her that she'd dropped her handkerchief. But he said nothing.

He picked up the handkerchief, shoved it in his coat pocket. He got out of the car then and followed her to the edge of the bluff.

5

SHE FACED HIM IN THE DARKNESS. HE STOOD WITH HIS HANDS IN his coat pockets. The rising wind billowed the diaphonous wrap about her head.

"Cigarette lighters aren't the only things I lose, Jim. I lose everything. I'm hexed. Jinxed. I always lose everything I want."

"Maybe you just don't know what you want."

"You know me better than that. I know exactly what I want."

"Sure you do. And every day it's something different."

"I haven't been happy, Jim."

He couldn't see why not, he said, She had everything. Money.

Position. Marriage to Laynebeck. More money. Anyway, he hadn't talked to Laynebeck very long before he'd found out she wasn't spending a hell of a lot of effort to keep Mike happy.

She was silent a long time. Finally she whispered, her voice tense, "I can't help it, Jim! I'm in love with someone else."

He could see the outline of her face. Hazy, the way the memory had been through the years. Indistinct, and yet he could never lose it, no matter how hard he tried.

"That's why I had to see you, Jim. It's about Dan."

"Your husband's missing partner." His voice hardened. "You're in love with Dan Calvert? How long?"

"What does it matter how long? I've known him all my life. We were kids together. Maybe I always loved him."

"Nice to tell yourself that anyway. If you change men the way you do your pants, you begin to see yourself for what you are. But if you can remember you *always* loved the newest one, it changes it."

She flicked her cigarette out into the dark. "I thought I could talk to you."

"You can. In fact, I think you better. Anything you can tell me about Calvert might help me to find him."

She swore she could add nothing to that. She told him the same story Mike had, except she added that she and Calvert had laughed, planning to put sleeping pills in Mike's coffee so they could be alone all evening. But Calvert never showed up.

He asked her the same question he'd asked Mike. What would she do about Calvert if he found him? She didn't know. She'd tried to make Mike divorce her, but he'd refused. Very definitely.

She asked for a cigarette. He lit one for her and stuck it in her mouth with a short jabbing motion. He suggested that maybe Calvert was scared, and didn't want to come back. The kids had called Calvert the gutless wonder even in high school.

"I've only been here a few hours, but I already know plenty of reasons why Calvert might have run. Partners with a man losing his grip. In love with that man's wife. In the middle of a political scrap that he can't win. Nothing but trouble ahead. . . ."

"Dan loves me."

"Mike is sure Dan is still his loyal partner, too. Looks like both of you have faith in a man who might be fooling both of you."

"He might be deceiving Mike. I know he wants me." There was a chilled edge to Nita's voice.

He shrugged. "Shall we start back?"

She followed him, walking very slowly. When she reached the car, she flipped the cigarette away and slid inside. He slammed the door, went around and got in under the wheel.

She asked him not to hate her. It was ten years. He told her to forget it. On the highway, he shoved his foot to the floorboard and held it there. He heard Nita sigh, felt her relax against the seat. She broke the silence to ask if he disapproved of her because of his idol, dear Mike. His answer was short. Mike was the only person who'd given him a thought while he was in hell. She laughed and said nothing more. A block from her home on Fort Queen, she nodded toward a dark curb. He pulled into the curb, opened the door. She sat looking at him.

"We could have been happy. Only it took me ten years to get sense enough to know it. I'm sorry, Jim. Sorry as hell."

He said nothing. She slid out of the car, then reached back in for her purse. Their eyes met. She smiled ruefully. She stepped back on the curb. He moved away, looking for her in the rearview mirror. She was already lost in the darkness.

He parked the Buick across the street from the Duval House. Carrying his suitcase, he started toward the hotel entrance.

Almost at the curb, he noticed the black Plymouth. The police car with the two-way radio. The door opened. He watched Strick Clemmons get out.

Clemmons said, "Hey, fellow. You."

Talbot stopped at the doorway. He could feel his heart race. Anxiety. He'd been a scared kid in this town. No matter what he'd become, he still had the habit of fear, here.

He said, "All right. What you want?"

"How about coming along with me."

"You crazy? I'm going to bed. Maybe tomorrow."

"Look, mister. Don't make trouble. I ain't asking you. I'm telling you."

"And I just told you. Forget it." He hefted the suitcase and started walking again.

Clemmons took three steps on his pole-like legs. He caught Talbot's shoulder, trying to stop him and turn him at the same time.

Talbot dropped the suitcase. He turned on the balls of his feet. With a quick movement he drove his left wrist deep into the thin man's belly.

Clemmons jackknifed forward. Talbot gave him credit. The deputy sheriff recovered quickly. He didn't hit the walk face first. He went backwards, striking on the sharp knobs of his tail bones.

Talbot watched the police positive appear in the bony hands. Clemmons sat on the walk, the gun fixed on Talbot's belt buckle.

With his left hand, Clemmons wiped his long chin. His eyes were slits. "All right now, fellow. We're through playin'. You want to get in my car, or you want me to shoot you?"

"I want you to shoot me," Talbot said. His voice was cold. "First, I'd like you to tell me why you're doing it just this way."

"Resistin' an officer," Clemmons said.

"An officer!" Talbot's voice mocked. The thin man stood up. "I remember you, Clemmons. The time you took Crazy Perkins ten miles out on the Lake Ware road and made him walk home barefoot. The time you rolled the drunk after a football game. When they caught you, you swore he was a queer that had got fresh with you."

Clemmons stared. "Talbot! Now I remember. Used to live out on the Addison farm. Got you for armed robbery, didn't they?"

"Yeah. Only I didn't do it. So now we've covered old times. Put up that cannon and let me alone."

The gun didn't waver. "You might as well make up your mind, Talbot. You ain't walkin' back in here and takin' a poke at me."

"All right. I'll make a deal with you. Don't you ever grab me, Clemmons. And I'll never hit you."

"Still a wise guy, ain't you? Well, wise guy, Sheriff Roberts wants to see you. He's waitin' in his office for you. Get in my car. And get in it now."

6

CLEMMONS PARKED THE PLYMOUTH IN AN "OFFICIAL CARS" PARKing space on the courthouse square.

Talbot stepped out, looking around. Most of the stores were dark at this hour. Only a few cars lined the square.

Clemmons prodded Talbot in the side and they started across

the courtyard. There was a huge sign perched atop a building across the street. An arrow pointing east: *See Golden Springs. Six Miles. Nature's Underwater Fairyland.*

They walked together up the wide steps of the courthouse. They turned left in a musty, dim-lit corridor. Talbot listened to the echo of their heels. At the end of the corridor there was a lighted door with gold-leaf lettering: *Sheriff's Office. Marvel County, Florida.*

Clemmons pushed the door open, motioning Talbot in ahead of him. The room was large, sparsely furnished. It was divided in the middle by a wood railing. A man in his shirt sleeves sat at a blond-wood desk behind the railing. He wore a shoulder holster. It was empty. He looked up.

"What you got, Strick?"

"They guy Roberts wanted to talk to."

The deputy looked up at Talbot. His name was Ballard. A big man, broad-shouldered and thick-chested. His blue eyes were set like pig-eyes in sweaty sockets of fat. And yet Talbot saw that the eyes were the same as those in Clemmons' thin horse face. It was the hate that made them the same. He was a stranger and they mistrusted him. Though they were totally unlike, they saw him with the same suspicious eyes.

Ballard pressed a button on his desk.

The door marked *Sheriff L. F. M. Roberts, Private,* opened.

The Sheriff came through it. Take a man six-feet tall and stuff him tallow fat, give him more money than he can spend and more power than he has intelligence to wield, re-elect him to an office he should never have had in the first place, shake well and add high blood pressure, sloth and ambition. That was L. F. M. Roberts. Even his black wavy hair was oily. He was wearing an expensively tailored gray suit and hand-tooled brown leather boots. He was carrying a ten-gallon gray Stetson.

"Well now," he said in a thick drawl, "what's this?"

Ballard swiveled around. "The guy you wanted to talk to, Sheriff. Talbot."

The Sheriff plodded across to the railing and peered at Talbot. "Youah face is familiar, suh. You live around here?"

"I used to."

"Jim Talbot," Clemmons said. "He used to live out on the Addison farm."

"That's right. You were a deputy then, Sheriff." Talbot said.

"He did time," Clemmons said. "Two years. Armed robbery."

Roberts frowned. "Armed robbery is good for a life term in this state."

"Sure. And that's what this guy's sentence was, too. Don't you remember, Sheriff? Laynebeck got him a new trial and sprung him."

Robert's mouth tightened. "Laynebeck. . . . Yeah. Now I remember." He faced Talbot. "And now you've come back to town and Laynebeck meets you at the station, eh? Still good friends with him?"

"Which criminal statute does that violate, Sheriff?"

"I'm asking you a question," Roberts said. "It won't avail you a lot to make an enemy of me in this town, Talbot."

Talbot tried to keep his temper, knowing all the time he wasn't going to. His voice was cold. "Stop shoving, Sheriff. I came back here on business. I don't want trouble. But I don't want to be pushed around, either."

The Sheriff leaned forward across the railing. His eyes glistened in their sockets of fat.

"Listen to me, Talbot. You been away a long time. So I'll explain to you. I been sheriff in this county eight years. Don't make trouble with me. Don't think being Mike Laynebeck's boy will save you. Not this time. I want to know why you're here. You'll be smart to play along with me. There's something about Laynebeck you better know. He's got troubles. He's running down. His grip on this county is going and mine is tightening. Get it?"

"Go on."

"That's it. If you came back here thinking that maybe you were going to last as Mike Layneback's muscleman—you better forget that right now. In fact if you came here to help Laynebeck at all, you'd be wise to get out of town. Tonight. Laynebeck can't help you. Like I said, he's got his own troubles."

Talbot studied the sweating man. "I'm in this town to do a job, Sheriff. I'm going to do it."

"Then you're a damned fool."

"I don't think so. I came back here to work for Mike Laynebeck. It doesn't have anything to do with you—or your politics. I thought I'd forgotten all about you. But I know now I haven't.

When I was a kid you came out with a furniture company truck to the Addison farm where we lived. Deputy Sheriff Roberts! You helped them repossess some furniture my mother had been paying for on instalments. We owed only twenty dollars more but you took it all back. Beds, chairs, everything."

A flush crawled across Robert's beefy face. "That's the law, Talbot. You miss an installment, the whole bill comes due."

"Even the furniture company was willing to let Mom keep part of it. I'll never forget the look on her face. You took everything she'd worked so hard for. When the driver wanted to leave part of the furniture because he couldn't stand the hurt look in her eyes, you wouldn't let him."

Roberts' jaw was thrust out. "Why did you come back here, Talbot?"

"I told you. Mike Laynebeck hired me to do a job for him."

"Is that all?"

"That's all."

"If I was you, I wouldn't take that job."

"I've already taken it."

"Why?"

"For money."

"Maybe you didn't know what you'd run up against trying to buck me in this town, Talbot. So I'm telling you. I don't know what job you're supposed to do for Laynebeck, but you're going to find out you got plenty of opposition. I'm a big man in this town. Stay here, Talbot, and you'll find just how big a puddle I do make."

Talbot walked across the square, carrying his suitcase. Panic and anger were stirring up his insides. He entered the Duval House and went through the silent lobby.

He had to wait at the desk. A woman was there ahead of him. She'd evidently just arrived in town. She was tired and washed-out looking. Looking at her, Talbot remembered that not even the nights were cool here in summer. This near to hell, he thought, how could it be cool?

"I'd like a room, please," the woman said to the clerk. Talbot yawned, waiting.

"Yes, m'am. Single or double?" The clerk rang for a bellhop

while the woman signed a registration card. The bellhop took her bags and the tired woman followed him toward the elevator.

Talbot took her place at the desk.

"I'm James Talbot," he said. "I think you have a room reservation for me."

"Yes, Mr. Talbot."

The clerk turned to the files. Jim watched the man's face pale. He came back to the desk, shaking his head.

"I'm sorry, sir. I'm afraid there's a mistake. There was a reservation. But it's been canceled."

"What is this? I know —"

He stopped. He knew, all right. Roberts hadn't been kidding! In the few minutes it had taken Talbot to cross the square and walk one block north, Roberts had started making things tough for him. Sure, Roberts would know this was the hotel Talbot had intended staying in. Clemmons had picked him up outside it earlier.

The clerk looked miserable. He was shaking his head.

"I'm sorry, sir. There isn't a thing available. Not tonight."

Talbot stared at him. The man remained pale but adamant. Talbot nodded, his laugh was short. The clerk said again that he was sorry. Talbot hefted his suitcase. It seemed heavier than ever. He couldn't remember having ever been so tired.

He crossed the street, got in the Buick and drove up the street to the Marvel Hotel. His hopes were not very high. He parked in the loading zone and went across the deserted lobby.

The clerk was smiling and pushed a registration card across the desk to him. Talbot scrawled his name. The clerk turned the card around. The smile on his face froze.

"I'm dreadfully sorry, sir. But I let you sign without checking my files. There isn't a thing available tonight." And as Talbot started to protest, he said again, "Nothing."

Talbot returned to the street. There were other hotels here in town. But he was sure that Roberts had sent out the word. This was the beginning. Sheriff Roberts was showing his muscle pretty fast.

Talbot yawned as he crossed the walk and flung himself into the Buick. He knew it was useless to try the other hotels. He decided to drive out of town somewhere, park the Buick and sleep in it. He had slept in a hell of a lot less comfortable places.

Tomorrow he'd find a room. Tomorrow the magic name of Laynebeck would go to work. Meanwhile, the only important thing was sleep.

He drove slowly, more asleep than awake.

He was aware first of the blurred sound of movement on his right.

A car sped past him on the wrong side. Talbot swung his car left, slamming on his brakes.

The other car was a few feet ahead of him. Something blossomed red in its window. The sound of the pistol was like a cannon in the silent street.

The right-hand side of the windshield shattered, streaking out from the bullet hole.

In the second that Talbot stared at the shattered windshield, the other car roared ahead, whipped around the corner, tires squealing. There were no lights on it. There was a blink of red as the driver went chicken at the last minute and touched the brake pedal to keep from skidding into the curb of the narrow side street.

Talbot whipped the Buick around the corner. He drove with one hand, gripped his .32 automatic in the other.

The other car made another turn in the darkness. An alley or a drive. Talbot went three blocks before he admitted the sour truth. He had lost it.

He pulled in to a curb and stopped the car. He looked at the gun. His hand was shaking. Then he noticed he had snagged something else when he grabbed at the .32 in his pocket. There was Nita's fragile-scented handkerchief crushed in his fingers.

At Barnett's All-Night Drug Store on the west side of the Square, Talbot entered a telephone pay booth. He looked for a dial. There was none. When a woman's sleepy voice finally questioned him, he gave her Laynebeck's home telephone number. He could hear the telephone ringing across the lines a long time before Mike answered.

"Mike. Jim Talbot. I thought I better tell you. Somebody just took a shot at me."

"A hell of an hour to be out. I didn't expect you to start work tonight. Why don't you get some sleep?"

SO DEAD MY LOVE

SO DEAD MY LOVE

"It seems I can't get a hotel room. But the hell with that. Either Roberts has gone completely nuts ordering me shot at, or somebody was shooting at *your* car. I just want to make sure before I do anything."

"Why would they shoot at you?"

"Not more than three people knew I had that Buick tonight—until I got down to Roberts' office. You. Nita. And your chauffeur."

"Yes. I trust Fisher. Nita is in bed."

"Just maybe they weren't shooting at me. Do you use the Buick very often?"

"No. Very infrequently."

"Does Nita use it?"

"Sometimes."

"Anyone else?"

"Yes. Dan Calvert used it often, Jim."

Talbot breathed heavily. His hands were still shaking. He'd have to check with Roberts' office. But maybe Dan Calvert was the answer to the gunshot. If it was the answer, that meant somebody in that town was pretty sure Dan Calvert was still alive.

7

TALBOT LEFT THE BRIGHTLY LIGHTED ALL-NIGHT DRUG STORE. HE looked at the bullet-shattered windshield, glanced up at the lights burning in the windows of the Sheriff's suite of offices in the courthouse.

He crossed the deserted street. Street sweepers were grooming the curbs with large brooms. He went up the short walk and entered the courthouse. There was an eerie silence in the dim corridors.

Ballard was dozing in his swivel chair with his big feet crossed on the blond-wood desk. Talbot entered the office, went through the swinging gate at the railing and shoved Ballard's feet off the desk.

The fat deputy sat up, blinking.

For a moment, neither spoke. Ballard relaxed, straightened up in his chair. "The tough guy," he said.

Talbot looked around the bare room. "Where is Clemmons?" he said. "Out doing more errands for the boss?"

Ballard shrugged. "He might be."

Talbot looked at him. "Some day you're going to talk yourself to death. . . . Is Roberts still here?"

"Maybe. You want to see him?"

"I want to talk to him."

"What about?"

"I'd like to report a shooting."

Ballard's pig-eyes narrowed. "All right," he said. "Just a minute."

He got up and knocked on the Sheriff's door. Talbot heard Roberts' thick drawl. "All right, Ballard. What is it?"

Ballard opened the door and spoke through the opening. "Jim Talbot is back. Says he wants to talk to you."

"Come to say good-bye, eh?" Roberts' voice boomed. He appeared in the doorway. "Well, suh," he said. "You want to come in my office, Mistuh Talbot?"

Talbot nodded and entered the private office. He heard Roberts closing the door behind him. He looked about. There were expensive furnishings in this room, a sleek new desk, steel filing cabinets, leather-covered chairs and couches. There was a Silex coffee-maker behind Roberts' desk, with coffee brewing. On all the desks and cabinets and tables were enlarged photos of Roberts and his large family. All daughters. In every picture Roberts was beaming in the center of them, his arms about as many of them as he could encompass.

Roberts went around and slopped down behind his desk. He nodded toward a chair facing him. Talbot sat down.

"Well, suh, what can I do for you?"

"I don't know. I can't get a room in any hotel in town. I suppose you wouldn't know anything about that. But I came here because I was shot at tonight. I thought I'd report it to you."

The Sheriff's face darkened. He sat forward.

"When did it happen?"

"Less than thirty minutes ago."

"Did you get a look at the man who did it?"

"No. A car pulled up on the wrong side of me. I slammed on my brakes. Whoever was driving took a shot at me. It shattered the windshield on Laynebeck's new blue Buick."

Roberts made a sound of sympathy. "And you didn't get a look at the man?"

"Like I said, it all happened in a hurry. They took off like a bat out of hell. I tried to catch them and I couldn't. They had no lights burning, and I didn't have a chance to see the license."

Roberts took a deep breath. "That's why I hate to see men like you coming back to town, Talbot. Bad guys. With reps. It always means trouble. And I hate trouble in my county."

"I didn't ask for trouble. Looks like the only trouble I've had so far has been with you and your boys."

"Are you intimatin'—"

"That you warned the hotels not to take me? Yes. As to the shots. I didn't see Strick Clemmons when I came in the office. The driver of that car could have been alone—"

"You really want trouble, don't you?" The Sheriff's voice was hoarse. "Comin' back heah. Makin' accusations . . ."

"Strick Clemmons may be in a beer parlor for all I know. I came here to report an attempt on my life. Are you going to do anything about it, or not?"

Roberts spread his fat hands. "What can I do? Like you said, it was dark, the car got away, you got no chance to see who shot at you. What do you want me to do?"

Talbot brought a smashed-nosed bullet slug from his pocket. He held it out in the palm of his hand.

"Where'd you get that?" Roberts said.

"It's the slug that was shot at me," Talbot replied. "I picked it up off the floor of the car. I want a ballistics report on it."

"What good will that do? You got a gun for comparison?"

Talbot smiled. "I might find one. Later. I want a complete report. Model gun, calibre. Grooves, bullet markings. Everything. Your office can handle a thing like this?"

Roberts' florid face paled. He stared at Talbot for a silent moment. He got up and poured himself a half cup of coffee. He drank it black.

He nodded. "We can make the tests," he said. "I'll have the report for you tomorrow. If you're still in town."

"I'll be here," Talbot said. He tossed over the slug.

The Sheriff caught it and placed it on a pad of white paper at the edge of his desk. "Now maybe you'll answer a question for me?"

"Why not?"

"Why are you here?"

"I told you. Mike Laynebeck hired me."

"We've found out about you, Talbot. You run a successful private investigating agency in New York City. Why would Laynebeck brink you back here? To spy on me? I want to know! Why would you give up good paying accounts to come back here?"

"Sheriff, Laynebeck saved me from hell. I'll do whatever I can for him. I came here without even knowing exactly what he wanted. Now I know. And I'm willing to tell you. Maybe it'll pull you off my neck for a little while. He hired me to find his partner, Dan Calvert."

"Oh, for God's sake! That! I've tried to tell Laynebeck that Calvert probably just took off on some business of his own. He's a queer duck. Don't like to be told nothing. Don't like to have to explain. He just wanted to go. He went."

"Maybe. Maybe not. That might hold up for a week-end, or even a week. He's been gone three weeks now."

"And you're going to find him?"

"I'm going to try. In spite of you. How about it, Sheriff? Maybe you can help me on that? Did Calvert have enemies here? Weren't things getting pretty hot for Laynebeck and him? Maybe Calvert got scared."

"I wouldn't know."

"Would you know that Calvert often drove Laynebeck's blue Buick? The one I was driving tonight when somebody took a shot at me? Maybe they weren't shooting at me. Maybe they thought Dan Calvert was back in town."

"That's an interesting theory. But I'm afraid I wouldn't know anything about it either way."

"Wouldn't you? What have you found out about Calvert's disappearance, Sheriff? He couldn't disappear and your office do nothing about it, could he?"

"I've assigned a deputy to the case, Mr. Talbot. When the time comes to make a report, I'm sure he'll have one."

"Calvert's a big man in this town. Yet you're not very upset about his disappearance, are you?"

"No, suh, I'm not. I'm surprised that Mike Laynebeck is takin' it seriously enough to bring you all the way here from New York to look for him." He leaned over the desk. His voice was hard.

"As a matter of fact, I'm beginning to think maybe your lookin' for Calvert is just a cover-up for your real reason for being here."

Talbot met his eyes evenly. "That's why Laynebeck hired me."

"Is it? Or did he hire you to see what I'm doing? Maybe to keep some of his boys in line? Boys that are losing their faith in him and would like to break off—"

Talbot laughed. "If you investigated me, Sheriff, you know I'm no muscle and rod man."

"Like you said, you owe your freedom to Laynebeck—"

A scream broke across the Sheriff's words. A scream that cut across Talbot's raw nerves, sending a tingle along his spine.

For a moment the two men stared at each other. The Sheriff looked slightly ill. The door behind Talbot burst open. Ballard bolted into the room, his eyes still red-rimmed with sleep.

"Get out of here." The Sheriff's low voice was hard.

It stopped Ballard like a blow in the chest. "Yes, sir." He stood looking foolishly from one to the other. He backed out, closing the door after him.

The Sheriff tried to pick up the unraveled ends of the conversation. "Now, like I was saying—"

"Who's your company, Sheriff?" Talbot was standing up. "Who's the woman in that room?"

"That's none of your business. We have our prisoners. We have our way of handling them. Now, if you got no more to discuss with me—"

"I have, though." Talbot went around the desk. Roberts sprang to his feet. Talbot brushed past him.

"Don't open that door." Roberts' voice was a tense whisper. "Workin' for Laynebeck don't give you the right to interfere—"

Talbot was looking over his shoulder. His mouth twisted. "A scream like that gives any human being the right to interfere."

He turned the knob. The door was locked but the key was in it. He unlocked the door and swung it open.

A jail matron stood just inside the door. She had a short leather belt in her fat hand. Her graying hair was awry and her face perspiring. She stared at Talbot a moment and then her gaze moved on to Sheriff Roberts just behind him.

Strick Clemmons was standing over the blonde girl who was tied in a straight chair. Talbot's mouth formed a dry smile. Another question answered. Clemmons hadn't been the man who took a shot at him from the darkened car on Fort Queen. Strick had been busy with other matters.

Talbot stepped into the small, hot room. The air was heavy with the odor of sweat.

The blonde girl was sprawled half out of the chair. Her arms were handcuffed together behind the chair back and they were twisted, pulled so tightly that her full breasts strained against the torn bodice of her white shirtwaist. Her head sagged on her shoulder. Her thick creamy-colored hair hung down loose. She had screamed only once. She appeared to be unconscious.

"What's the matter with her?"

Strick Clemmons turned slowly and stared at Talbot. He wiped a mist of spittle from his twisted mouth. His shoulders moved in an effeminate gesture of disgust.

"Why, she's drunk," Clemmons said.

The girl moaned, her eyelids flickered, and slowly she straightened her head. Talbot saw the livid marks of Clemmons' hand across her bloodless cheeks. A thin thread of blood ran from her nostrils across her teeth-marked lips and chin. Spots of blood were on her torn shirt and her exposed body.

Talbot spoke to the matron. "Take off those handcuffs."

The matron glanced at Roberts. He nodded. She shrugged and removed the metal links. The girl almost fell from the chair.

"What are the charges, Sheriff?" Talbot said. He saw the girl was alert now, watching him closely.

The Sheriff was silent a moment. At last he said, "Common prostitute."

Talbot couldn't say why, but he knew this was a lie, that there was another reason why they'd beaten this girl in this back room. But it would do no good arguing with the Sheriff.

"Is there a fine?"

"Fifty dollars."

"And she couldn't pay it?"

"She wouldn't."

"It's a lie," the girl whispered.

"Shut up," the matron said. "If you know what's good for you, shut up."

"He brought me here," the girl jerked her head toward Clemmons. "He hit me. He—"

"It's all right," Talbot said. "The Sheriff will let me pay your fine. You're going to be all right."

"I'm willing to let her go," the Sheriff said. There was a short static pause. "If she gets out of town."

The girl stood up, staring at the Sheriff. She wiped the blood from under her nose with the back of her hand. Her bright mouth twisted. She staggered a little and caught herself against the back of the straight chair.

The matron brought a lightweight gray coat. She handed it to Talbot. The girl didn't look at him as he draped it over her shoulders. She couldn't seem to see Roberts well enough to please her. Her pale eyes were clouded with her hatred.

"I want to get out of here," she whispered. She began to tremble suddenly. She looked up at Talbot. "Will you take me out of here?"

"Sure." Talbot took out his wallet. He fished out a pair of twenty-dollar bills and two fives. He offered them to the Sheriff.

Roberts' face was cold. "Pay Ballard. Outside," he said. "He'll give you a Sheriff's Office receipt."

Talbot's lips pulled thin over his teeth. "I'll be pleased to have it, I'm sure."

He took the girl's arm and led her through the door and out into the Sheriff's private office. Her steps faltered and he led her to a chair and poured her a cup of coffee from the Sheriff's private container. Roberts, the matron and Clemmons followed them into the room. They stood silent, watching the girl sip the steaming liquid. Roberts seemed scarcely breathing. He didn't take his eyes from Talbot's face.

The girl finished the cup, and her whisper thanked Talbot for the coffee.

Talbot took her arm and led her from the office. Outside, Ballard wrote out a receipt for fifty dollars.

Talbot read it. "Don't you put down what the fine was paid for?"

Ballard just looked at him. "You make jokes," he said.

Talbot felt the girl leaning heavily against him as they left the office. He put his arm about her as they went along the darkened corridor. He heard her breath catch once in a stifled sob. She made no other sound. They went down the steps to the sidewalk.

He glanced at her in the street light. Why had they beat her? And why released her to him like this? Why had Roberts said casually that she'd been picked up as a common prostitute when obviously they'd been putting her through some kind of third degree?

He shook his head. He knew what the law in the wrong hands could do.

He took two twenty-dollar bills from his pocket, closed the girl's trembling hand over them. She tried to draw away, protesting.

"Don't be a fool," he said. "There's only one thing for you to do. Get out of town."

She looked at him. Finally she nodded. "All right. I'll leave tomorrow."

"Look. If you're smart you'll leave right now. There's the bus station, right across the street. That's the lovely thing about this town. You can get out of the place as soon as you've seen what it's like."

"I can't run off like this—without my clothes."

"If Roberts gets his hands on you again, your clothes won't seem important. You live here in town? Your folks live here?"

"No."

"Then show Roberts you're smarter than he is. Get out of town before he can get hold of you again."

"They've got to let me alone. They can't run me out!"

He shrugged. "All right. Go back up there and play some more games with Strick Clemmons."

"Thanks for what you've done. But—"

"Look, baby. Get smart. Either tell them what they want to know, or get out of town fast—"

He started away. She caught his arm. Her mouth was a taut line. "How do you know—they were asking me anything?"

She was looking up at him. Her eyes were filled with fright. Here was one scared girl, he knew. Afraid to trust anyone. Had it been ten years since he'd run in terror from this hot land of injustice? He doubted it. He shook his head, his teeth gritting hard together. Above her head he could see the bright neon sign, the red, green and yellow arrow: *See Golden Springs—Six Miles—Nature's Underwater Fairyland.*

He shivered.

8

"WHAT THE DEVIL'S THE MATTER WITH YOU?" TALBOT DEMANDED.

"Why can't you get out of this town? Don't you know when you've had enough?"

She held out her hand with his money in it. "Take your money back," she said. "I'll be all right. I've got a job, mister. And maybe they'll leave me alone."

"Sure they will. When you get smart enough to tell them what they want to know."

"Whether I like it or not, mister, I can't go. I've got to stay here."

He took her arm and started along the walk. She looked up at him. "Where are we going?"

"Since we're going to be in this lousy town together, we may as well be friends."

He steered her across the street into an all-night café. They sat in a booth at the rear of the brightly lighted restaurant. A drunk was sitting alone, his head bowed over a bowl of soup, at the counter that ran the length of the room. Two taxi drivers argued sleepily at a table up in front.

"What's your name?" Talbot said. She sat across the table from him, took powder and rouge from her pocketbook and began to repair the damage to her face.

He caught his breath, looking at her. She had the kind of beauty that hit you with the impact of a fist in the belly. She wasn't over twenty, that was certain. He watched her trace a lipstick over her full lips, watching her reflection in a hand mirror. Her intent eyes were the impossible blue of the sky on a sultry day. He let his eyes move over her. There was a sheen to her pathless skin. Her tinted flesh was flawless. It made you sad for her.

She wasn't ever going to be so perfect again. And she was wasting her beauty on this town. She was young and lovely tonight, even frightened and worked over as she was. He smiled appreciatively at her perfection, her shoulder-length blonde hair, and skin that was like hot liquid platinum.

She hesitated, watching herself in the tiny mirror for a moment, then she said, "My name is Dawson. Laura Dawson. I'm a dancer. When I dance I use a very gaudy name. But that's what they want. Luri Dusan. Isn't that a swell name?"

It would be swell, if he could overlook the hysteria under her voice.

"It didn't keep you from being picked up by the law."

She bit her lip. "It didn't have anything to do with my dancing."

He was watching her. "You want to tell me about it?"

She shook her head, breathing heavily.

The waitress came. Talbot ordered a two-inch steak with french fries, salad and coffee. He looked at Laura. She nodded. "That sounds good to me," she said. "I'll have the same."

Talbot smiled. "Well, at least you've got sense enough to eat. Why haven't you got sense enough to run?"

She shrugged. "I want to stay here," she said. "What I want is here."

He smiled. "A man," he said. "So you're in love with some jerk. Then why did he let the police get you tonight?"

Her face was pale. She opened her mouth to answer him and then closed it. She just met his eyes evenly.

Now he grinned. "Okay. So now we know you won't leave town because you're in love with some guy. Let an old man tell you something, baby. Love can make you do some damn fool things. Staying in this town is one of them."

"Whether there's anyone I love or not, I'm not going to let them run me out of town. I'm going to stay. I've got a job. I dance at Bonny Williams' Golden Club."

Talbot frowned, trying to remember where he'd heard that name. He remembered. He'd seen the red letters on the golden cover of the book matches that Nita had been carrying in her purse.

"What sort of place is it?" Jim said.

"The Golden Club? As good as there is in this town, I guess. But nothing to sing about. I've danced in a lot better places. But no little town has any decent night spots."

"Why did you come here? A pretty girl like you who can also dance rates a hell of a lot better place than this."

She looked at him sharply but said nothing.

Talbot laughed wryly. "She was dancing in a decent town. *He* comes along. Next thing she knows, she's dancing in a hell-hole just so she can be near him. Boy, would I like to meet a guy that can do that a pretty kid like you!"

She smiled. "You guess things pretty good."

"Hell, baby. I'm not guessing. I was in love once myself."

"Anyway, here I am. And here I'm going to stay."

"Why couldn't Bonny Williams keep the Sheriff off you?"

"He tried. But—well, he's scared of Roberts. There wasn't anybody who could help me."

"Not even the great lover?"

She bit her lip. "There wasn't anything he could do." Her eyes flashed appreciation. "I guess nobody could have stopped them but you. I—I'm glad you came along. Maybe I can repay you."

"Don't worry about it."

The waitress brought their meal. Talbot began to eat, realizing for the first time how hungry he really was. The girl was watching him.

"Who are you?"

"My name is Jim Talbot. I just got in town at eight o'clock tonight. From New York." He said it all hurriedly, a chunk of steaming steak waiting on his fork.

"And you walked into Sheriff Roberts' office and got me out of there? Are you magic?"

He chewed his steak. "Not quite. I've been hired by a man Roberts is afraid of, that's all. Don't worry, Roberts is having his innings. I've tried all night to get a hotel room. I can't get one. Roberts has given out the order. So they won't take me in. He's making it tough for me to stay in town."

"I have a hotel room. I'll share it with you—for what you've done for me—if you'll be smart enough to know that's all I'm offering."

He nodded. "I'd never take advantage of a girl who loves another guy enough to stay in this hell-hole."

She didn't smile. "All right, so I do love him. I just never heard of a thing like that stopping a man when he thought there was a chance."

Talbot's voice was cold. "Maybe I don't want the chance."

Her head snapped up, color crept up her cheeks. "I didn't think I was that bad."

"I'd like a room, baby. But that's all I want."

She frowned, then looked down at her coat, caught tightly across her torn dress. "What's the matter with me?"

"Nothing, baby. There's something the matter with me."

Her eyes widened, shocked. "I don't know if I like you, after all."

"Does it matter whether you like me or not?"

She nodded. "It does to me. I had a chance to repay you. I could offer you a place to sleep. But I'm afraid of people I don't understand. I was beginning to like you. I guess every woman likes a man who is strong enough to protect her. You're good looking. But you—don't talk very nice."

"Okay. So why don't you grab a bus out of this town and let that wonderful guy you're so crazy about come to find you. He will, if he really wants you."

"Maybe I want him too much to care whether he'd follow me or not. Maybe he didn't do anything when the Sheriff sent that Clemmons for me—but at least he's really a man."

Talbot laughed. "You sound like you're begging me to rape you."

"I'm not! But I saw one man like—like that Clemmons tonight. It gets me all sick."

He grinned. "Look, honey. I'm thirty. You're twenty. You're in love with some guy. I'm in love with nobody. That's the way I want it. I don't want to get tangled up with any dame. Isn't that clear enough? I'd like to sleep, but you don't have to share your room with me."

She pulled her plate toward her and began to eat again. "Well, all right," she said. "If you're sure that's all it is. I guess I can see it now. You've hated somebody for a long time, haven't you? It's all in your eyes. Hated her and loved her at the same time." She shook her head. Her blonde curls trembled over her shoulders. "I know what that is, all right."

"I'm not in love with anybody." His voice was cold. He sat back, rammed his hand into his coat pocket. His fingers closed over the fragile handkerchief. It was almost as if he could smell her in the room.

9

LAURA'S ROOM IN THE BROADWAY HOTEL WAS SHABBY. CHEAP BUT clean. The twin beds looked like paradise to Talbot. He yawned just looking at their inviting softness.

Laura gestured toward the bathroom. "You can undress in there," she said. "I'll wait."

Talbot agreed and took his suitcase into the bathroom. He turned to close the door. He saw Laura flop across one of the beds. She was lying on her back. Her eyes were fixed on the ceiling.

He closed the door and looked at his watch. It was two-thirty A.M. What a wonderful homecoming! Picked up by the Sheriff's office. Shot at on a dark street. And now sharing a bedroom with a blonde he had never heard of before. And against it all, the elusive scent of Nita. Her voice. Telling him that it was Dan Calvert she loved. He was her love. Her latest love.

He undressed, showered, brushed his teeth and shook out a pair of pajamas. He brought his suitcase with him from the bathroom. Laura was where he had left her, on her back across the bed.

"It's all yours," he said.

She pulled herself up on her elbows. "What?"

"The bathroom. It's all yours."

"Oh. Thanks."

He frowned. "What's on your mind?" He carried his suitcase to the closet, shoved it inside and stepped over to his bed. He sat on the edge, yawning. He could feel Laura's eyes fixed on him as he lay down. "What's troubling you?"

"Nothing." She was standing now. "All right, it was silly. Very. I was wishing you were—him. I was wishing he and I were together like this—I could hear you in the shower, and I was wishing it was him I was waiting for."

He lifted his head. "You've got it bad."

She came around the bed and sat on it facing him. "What was she like?"

"Who?"

"The girl you loved. The one that hurt you so bad."

"I'm sleepy. Go brush your teeth and hit the sack."

"I guess you and I just—aren't lucky." She shrugged, got up and trailed into the bathroom.

It grew silent in the room. Talbot closed his eyes. They burned. The light on the table between the beds was too bright. He wished Laura would hurry and turn it off. He lay with his eyes closed, waiting.

It was no good. He couldn't sleep. He couldn't get her out of his mind. The guy wasn't human who could be hit with that much beauty and then go to sleep. How long since a girl had affected him like that? Wouldn't it be wonderful if he could look at Laura—and get *her* completely out of his mind? God help him, that was all he needed.

His mouth tightened. But this kid had her own love, and it was all cluttered with heartbreak. A hell of a way to repay her kindness! Well, he was going to lie right here and go to sleep if it killed him. His heart began to pound heavily. The blonde hair about her shoulders. Her breasts, young and firm and high. The eyes so pale. What the hell was keeping her? Why the devil didn't she turn off that light and go to sleep?

He turned over and opened his eyes. She was standing there watching him.

She smiled somberly. He decided he was asleep and dreaming. Her tawny, lustrous hair was free about her shoulders as he had imagined it would be. It shimmered in the light. Her eyes were clear, the color of fresh water. Her sooty lashes were at half-mast over them.

Talbot looked at her, scarcely breathing.

There had never been a lovelier girl. She lifted her face, and Talbot watched the light moving on her translucent skin. Flawless milky flesh shining in the brightness.

"Why don't you go to bed?" he said.

She smiled. "I was just looking at you."

"Cut it out. Let's get some sleep."

"Do you really want to?"

He stared at her. "I thought you were in love with some noble character."

She was still smiling. "I am," she said. "But I also dance. The kind of dancing that ends up with everything off. I see men wanting me in the middle of a crowded room." She unzipped her skirt and stepped out of it. "And yet you sleep while I undress."

That was the first time he felt the chilling premonition of wrong. Maybe he'd been too tired. Maybe he had wanted a room so badly that he had been willing to believe she'd be ready to share hers because he had gotten her out of the Sheriff's back room and away from the Sheriff's goons. But there was something else.

This babe wanted something.

As he watched, Laura slid both her hands upwards from her hips moving them slowly over the roundness of her breasts to unbutton her white shirtwaist.

She was watching him for effect! She was trying to see in his face the effect of her young beauty on his senses.

He sat up. "Who are you, Laura? What do you want from me?"

He saw her eyes flicker, and then she was smiling again.

"I don't want anything. I'm trying to be nice to you."

"You're lying."

She came around the bed toward him. "Do you think I'm pretty?" she said.

"I think you're pretty, baby. But all of a sudden I don't care."

Her eyes narrowed. "What's the matter?"

"You were a girl so in love with a guy you couldn't leave town. Even if it meant trouble. Now all of a sudden, I'm the only guy in your mind. That doesn't add up, baby. Maybe you'd like to explain."

She started to draw back. He caught her wrist suddenly. He twisted, pulling her towards him. She fell heavily. He held her across him, her arm bent behind her back. Her face was inches from his.

"All right, baby, start talking. Is this business your own idea, or somebody else's?"

She said nothing. He twisted her arm. She gasped.

"Mine," she said. "My own idea."

"Why?"

"You—you said you'd been hired by a man that Sheriff Roberts is afraid of. There's just one man that he is even a little bit afraid of . . ."

"Go on."

"Senator Laynebeck."

He stared at her. "Laynebeck? What has he got to do with you?"

Her eyes were defiant. "I don't know. Maybe nothing."

"But that's what you're trying to find out."

"Yes. You're working for him, aren't you?"

"That's no secret. Sure, I'm working for Laynebeck. How does that tie in with you?"

The fear was deeper than ever in her eyes. She tried to smile, but failed.

"Please let me go," she said.

"Oh, no. You were trying to get close to me. Now you are close, baby. I like it like this. Besides, you've got a lot more to tell me. What is it to you if I work for Laynebeck or not?"

"It's nothing to me."

He twisted her arm. "Don't lie to me. Not any more."

"All I want to know is—why are you working for him?"

"What difference does it make to you?"

"Are you a detective?"

"Yes."

"You—" She watched his face, tensely silent for a long time. "You find missing people?"

"If I can."

All the life seemed to go out of her. He stared at her. His eyes widened. "Dan Calvert!" he whispered abruptly. "So that's the guy you're in love with. The missing Dan Calvert!"

She relaxed against him. He could feel the warmth of her body against his chest. He released her arm. She didn't move away.

"Why do you want to find him?" she whispered.

"So you *are* in love with him?"

"Is that so terrible?"

"I don't know. I don't know him. It's just that you're the second one tonight who has told me she loves Dan Calvert. He must be one hell of a guy."

"That's not true! There's nobody else." She sat up, her body suddenly taut, her eyes searched his.

Talbot shrugged. "Okay. Sure, if you say so."

She grabbed his arms, shaking him. "Tell me!" she cried. "It isn't true!"

He smiled. "Baby, I wish I were as young as you are. All right, it isn't true. But tell me one thing. Do you want me to find Dan Calvert?"

She was silent a long time. At last she shook her head. "Why don't you go away?" she said. "There's so much trouble here now. You'll only make more."

He caught her chin in his hand, turning her face to his. "That's why Roberts had you in that back room. You know something about Dan Calvert, don't you, baby? And Roberts was trying to beat it out of you?"

"No." Her breath came fast. "That isn't true."

"It's true, all right. Do you know where he is? Do you know what's happened to him?"

She shook her head. "No. I don't know!"

He smiled. "Well, I could hardly hope you'd tell me when Clemmons couldn't torture the facts out of you. . . . Okay, baby, let's call it a night and get some sleep."

She shook her head. "No. Listen to me, Jim. Tonight. Now. I'll give you anything you want. Do anything. Then tomorrow you'll tell Mr. Laynebeck that you can't take the job—you'll go back to New York."

"You're pretty wonderful, honey. It sounds very lovely. But I've got a job to do."

"Please, Jim. You won't be sorry."

"Look, baby. You get me in a sweat. Okay. I admit that. You're one beautiful little doll. And young. God, you're young. You're everything a guy could want. But it so happens I've promised to find Dan Calvert and—"

"You mustn't!" And before he could move, Laura had planted her mouth over his. He could feel the heat of her lips burning its way into him. "Anything," she whispered against his mouth. "Anything you want."

He tried to shove her away and found out he couldn't. Sweat broke out across his forehead. His hands began to move over her. She was like fire under his fingers. Her breath was hot against his face.

He pushed her away. Not too far. He could still feel the beat of her heart, the warmth of her body against his.

"I'd be lying to you, baby," he said. "No matter what I told you. No matter what we did. I'm still going to find Dan Calvert."

She moved away, got to her feet. She stood tall, her face flushed, looking down at him. He could see she was puzzled. She couldn't make him out. Every man she'd probably met made a big play for her. Nobody had ever resisted Laura Dawson before. That was clear enough in her troubled gaze. It was as though he had hit her. She, whose body exerted a lure that made men do handsprings—now when she was offering it for something she desperately wanted, it was no sale.

She backed away from him.

He sat looking at her, pitying this new look of defeat in her baffled eyes, and still wanting her, still feeling his heart racing.

He started to speak. He heard somebody at the door. The unmistakable sound of movement in the corridor. She stared at him, her eyes widening.

He got up cautiously. Laura sat there, watching him. He moved across the room toward the door.

As he touched the doorknob, he heard someone catch his breath on the other side of the panels.

Whoever it was leaped away from the door and began running down the corridor. Talbot fought the key in the lock and flung the door open. He stepped out in the hallway. It was silent and dimly lit. And deserted. The runner had disappeared, down the stairs, into some other room, or out the fire escape.

Talbot expelled his breath slowly. He stepped back inside the room and locked the door after him.

Laura had forgotten now that she had tried to seduce him and failed. The look he had first seen in her face was back now. Fear.

She was deathly afraid.

10

Talbot turned off the lights and lay down, sure he'd not sleep this night. He could hear the soft dry sobs from Laura's bed. Then the silence closed heavily on his eyelids and he fell asleep. Soundly.

When he awoke, sunlight was streaming in through the open windows. The mornings were hot early down here. For a moment he lay there, still groggy with sleep, and tried to remember where he was. A girl named Laura. A prowler. A cheap room in the Broadway Hotel. He turned over. She was not in her bed. He opened both eyes. She was applying lipstick at her mirror.

She was watching his reflection. She turned, looking at him over her shoulder.

"Hello," she said. "You were just too late for the morning performance."

His eyebrows rose. "You seem pretty gay this morning."

"I am. I did a lot of thinking last night after you went to sleep. You haven't found Dan. Maybe you won't."

"Don't bet on it."

"Well, anyway, I won't help you. The Sheriff won't help you. Looks like you won't get much help in this town."

He sat up in bed. "Look, kid," he said. "Don't waste your time. It doesn't make sense. A good-looking kid like you hanging around a town like this because of a guy like Calvert."

She turned from the mirror, her eyes mocking him. "Love doesn't make sense. If it did, you wouldn't still love that girl who hurt you so bad, would you?"

Maybe she had something there, he thought. "Where are you going?" he said.

"It's almost noon. I've got to get breakfast and report for rehearsal at one."

"Rehearsal? Where?"

"At the Golden Club. Luri Dusan. That's me. Remember? Very special."

"What about Clemmons and Roberts?"

"I can take care of myself."

"I hope so."

"If I didn't believe that, I wouldn't have dared stay here."

She gave him a mock salute and crossed the room. She unlocked the door, opened it. And as suddenly leaped back with a startled gasp.

Talbot grabbed his .32 automatic from under his pillow. He jumped off the bed and ran across the room. Laura was shaking her head at him. Warningly.

At the door was Sheriff Roberts.

Talbot's gaze moved from the obese lawman to the blonde Laura.

"Whatever your charge," he said coldly, "it's my doing, Sheriff. I came here. I couldn't get a room—as you damned well know. She had nothing to do with it."

Roberts moved into the room, his face blank. "I don't know what you're talking about." He turned to Laura and gave her one of his false, quick smiles. "You were going out, miss. Why don't you just go ahead?"

"Yes, Laura. Go." Talbot said. There was panic in his voice. He hated himself for it. It was a hell of a thing to allow this hick sheriff to see that he was afraid of him. But he half-shoved Laura from the room and locked the door after her.

The Sheriff was looking around the room. What he saw pleased him immensely. He shoved an undergarment off a chair and sat down. Talbot returned to the bed and sat on the side of it.

"I guess there's no use trying to hurry you, Sheriff, but I'd like to know what's on your mind."

The Sheriff smiled. There was no falseness about this smile. It was genuine. It meant trouble for someone else. That was the only real smile Roberts owned.

"I've got enough right here," he said affably. "If I wanted *anything*, this is it. This is all I need."

Talbot licked his tongue across dry lips. "Leave her alone. I couldn't get a room and you know why. That's the only reason I stayed here. Leave her out of it!"

"I may be able to. . . . If you're reasonable."

The breath sighed out of Talbot. "All right. What do you want?"

"I don't rightfully know—yet. Let's say right now I'll just take a promise from you that if I do want anything, you'll help me out?" His eyes went over the disarrayed room slowly, meaningfully.

"Like what?"

"Well, you say that Laynebeck hired you to find Dan Calvert. So if maybe you find there is some other reason Laynebeck hired you, or something else he wants, or you find out something about Calvert, you'll let me know what it is."

"In other words, you want to keep up with Laynebeck."

"That's right, suh. I do. With everything he does."

"And I'm to be another one of your stool pigeons?"

"You're calling yourself names, suh." Roberts looked around the room again. "What you call yourself, that's up to you. What happens to you and the little blonde lady—that's up to you, too."

Talbot stood up. "All right," he said. "You know where I am."

"You understand, Talbot. I don't like trouble in my county. Way to keep trouble down, suh, is to stay ahead of it."

"You want to get out of here now, and let me get dressed?"

"Well, if you want me to." The big man stood up, wiping a soiled handkerchief about the sweatband of his ten-gallon hat. "As long as we understand each other. And everything friendly."

"Isn't that a little too much, Sheriff?" Talbot said. "You and me. Friendly. When I know you for what you are, and you know I do?"

"A man in my position has to be friends with all kinds, suh. Now, frankly, I'm a church-going man. My whole family is. We go every Sunday. I don't particularly relish being friendly with a man who lives immorally like this." And his gaze went over Laura's rumpled bed. "But I'm willing to close my eyes to some things—just so I can be friendly."

Talbot's laugh was short. "My friend, the Sheriff."

They looked at each other.

Talbot said, "Tell me, friend, what sort of man is this Bonny Williams who owns the Golden Club?"

Roberts chewed that over for a moment. "All right, my friend," he said. "I believe I can tell you about him. Bonny Williams is trying to please everybody. Tries to please Senator Laynebeck and his friends on the one hand. Tries to please me and my friends on the other. It makes life pretty tough for him. You can't be friends with too many people with opposing ideas. That way you're trying hard to please everybody, but you ain't really pleasing nobody. You see?"

When the Sheriff was gone, Talbot showered and dressed. He drove the blue car down to the Buick agency garage and ordered a new windshield installed while he was at lunch.

He called Mike Laynebeck from the pay telephone booth in the Country Style Restaurant.

"I had a visit from the Sheriff this morning, Mike," Talbot reported. "He wants me to tell him everything you do while I'm working for you."

Laynebeck's laugh was sour. "You have my permission to report to him anything you see."

"I just wanted you to know what he said."

"I appreciate it, Jim. Did you find out anything about the attempt on your life?"

"Not yet. But I couldn't get a hotel room, either. Looks like nobody but you wants me in town. Somebody had canceled my reservation at the Duval House. I spent the night in a blonde's room. Roberts plans to hold it over my head to make me spy on you."

"Tell him what he wants to hear. I'll talk to those damned people at the Duval House. My God, I own a controlling interest in the place!"

"That's about all I have to report. Where did Dan Calvert live?"

"He has a suite at the Duval House. But we've looked through it."

"You don't mind if I have a look?"

"No. I want you to. By the time you get there, I'll have read the book to the bastards that work in the place. They'll treat you with respect."

Talbot laughed. "That's what I want."

"Don't worry. That's what you'll get."

Talbot hung up. He went to a table near the front window. He watched the people walk past on the sidewalk. There were no familiar faces among them. He didn't find the other thing he was seeking, either: there was no sign of anyone loitering out there, waiting.

If there was a spy on him from the Sheriff's office, the guy was playing it smart. Jim Talbot was unable to spot him yet.

He ordered orange juice and coffee and followed it with a lunch of roast beef, mashed potatoes and squash. When he had eaten, he walked back down to the garage, got the Buick and drove over to the Duval House.

The manager himself rode up with Talbot in the elevator and opened the door to Dan Calvert's suite.

Talbot thanked the manager and closed the door in his face. He stood there a moment with the key in his hand. He dropped it into his coat pocket. He remembered the fragile handkerchief that was in there. Nita's handkerchief. His smile was grim.

He wandered among the impersonal furnishings of the hotel living room. It was small and had been furnished for the transient. He wondered how many years Calvert had lived here without giving the place a lived-in look.

Talbot flopped on the divan, fixed a pillow under his head, crossed his feet on the divan arm and stared at the ceiling.

Reclining on the couch, he let his eyes move over each piece of furniture and picture and mirror that he could see without moving anything but his head.

Finally he got up and pulled open the drawer of the imitation mahogany secretary. There was a jumble of personal letters inside. He sat down in the straight chair and at his leisure read them all. There were a few bills: from the haberdashery, the laundry, the garage, the hotel. All were current, none overdue.

He looked again at the letters. All were boring, from stupid people with nothing to say and all the time in the world to say it.

Among the letters were several packages of book matches. All had gaudy yellow covers with red letterings: *Bonny Williams' Golden Club—On the Golden Springs Road.*" Now he saw that there was a bare dancer on the face of the folder. She was done in pink. She had a blue flower in her teeth.

He dropped a couple of the book matches in his pocket. This started his mind on a new train of thought. He moved every pillow in all the chairs and divans. This netted him a quarter and three bobby pins. He pocketed the quarter and decided that he had no more use for the bobby pins than Dan Calvert had.

He spent an hour in the room. When he was through, he had gone over it thoroughly. Almost no part remained untouched.

Then he went into the bedroom. He found whiskey in there and poured himself a drink. He had another drink while he was going through the drawers of the dresser. Dan Calvert loved clothes. He had dozens of pairs of underwear, one whole drawer of white handkerchiefs.

Talbot touched each shirt in every stack. He moved slowly, picking up every shirt, moving it and letting it fall back in place.

When he had gone through the clothes, the closets where Calvert kept his suits and shoes, Talbot pulled the sheets off the bed and wadded them in the middle of the mattress. Then he turned the mattress, dropping the sheets on the floor.

Behind the bed he found one of her cigarette lighters.

It was an ornate thing, with her initials in scroll upon its silver face. N. L. He looked at it and then dropped it into his left coat pocket.

"Very careless." That was all he said.

He went through the bathroom next, reading even the prescription labels on the bottles in the medicine chest. When he came out there was no place else to go in the small apartment.

He had another drink, went out the front door, locked it after him.

He rang for the elevator. He had spent almost three hours in that apartment.

The elevator man smiled at Talbot. Talbot could see the poor guy had his orders. Be nice to Mr. Talbot. Laynebeck must have stirred the place up with a nettled stick.

"Seen Mr. Calvert lately?" Talbot said.

"Oh, no, sir. Not in the last three weeks."

Talbot looked at him, nodding. He crossed the lobby. The manager was at the desk.

"Everything satisfactory, Mr. Talbot?" His voice was pleading.

"Fine. How long since Mr. Calvert was in that room?"

The manager swallowed hard. "It's been three weeks, sir. The whole town is upset about him. He's a great gentleman."

"I'm sure he is."

"I want to tell you again how sorry we are about the mistake in your reservations last night. If there is anything we can do. We find this morning that we have a suite—almost identical with Mr. Calvert's. With—with a better view. If you'd like it, it's available now."

"I'll sure keep you in mind," Talbot said.

"Please do." The manager wrung his hands. For a minute Talbot thought the fellow was going to cry.

The man at the haberdashery was sorry, but if he had heard a word on Mr. Calvert he would have notified the police immediately.

"You rendered him a bill, dated last month. Has that been taken care of?" Jim asked.

The clothier shook his head. "But we're not worrying about it. It'll be taken care of. We know that Mr. Calvert is good for any amount."

"And if something has happened to him?"

The man shook his head. "I hope nothing has. But if so, I'm sure his estate will take care of his debts."

The laundry was closed when Talbot got there. He sat outside it, smoking contentedly. He told himself he felt like a man who had accomplished a good day's work and was now ready to accomplish his night work.

He drove up the one-way street to the Duval House. He had supper in the Duval House restaurant. Afterwards he bought a Jacksonville paper at the cigar counter and sat in the Duval House lobby and read the news. When he had gone all the way through the newspaper, he folded it deliberately and looked over all the people in the room. None looked familiar. Not one of them had he seen before at all that day.

He got up, frowning. It was a hell of a thing. It irked him to think the Sheriff might be smarter than he was. Then he smiled, shrugging away that idea.

It was dark when he crossed the street and got into the Buick.

He drove west out of town, turned north at the deserted Fair Grounds. He crossed the Atlantic Coast Line railroad tracks and turned east on a shell-paved road. He followed this to the highway.

He turned north on the highway, drove for about a mile to Cypress Road. A neon arrow pointed east: *See Golden Springs.* With a wry smile, he followed the arrows, driving less than twenty-five miles an hour.

It was just nine o'clock when he drove into the dim-lit parking lot behind the Golden Club. There were plenty of other cars on the lot. It was still early. That meant the Golden Club was enjoying popularity. It was the spot at the moment.

Talbot killed the engine, slid down in the seat. He lit a cigarette and sat there puffing at it contentedly. About three minutes after he arrived, an old Plymouth pulled into the lot and parked near him. He sat up, tense, watching.

Two youngsters piled out, a boy laughing with his arm around his girl. Talbot sighed and relaxed. He sank down in the seat again.

He let his gaze rove over the big two-storied building. It was in good repair. Bonny Williams was making money. He was spending it, too, keeping the joint looking neat. Lights glowed in upstairs windows beyond drawn shades. Streaks of yellow showed where shades fit against sills.

A small door opened in the side of the building.

Talbot sat up, watching.

A woman came out of the door, closing it hurriedly behind her. She looked all around, then ran hurriedly toward a car parked in the shadows at the end of the club building.

It looked like Nita.

She was too far away for him to be sure. Maybe he just thought it was she. Anyhow, she was getting into her car before he could be positive.

Something flashed along her side as she stepped into the car. Talbot smiled. The woman had dropped something. He was pretty sure now that it was Nita.

She slammed the door, unaware that she had dropped anything.

The car backed a few feet out of the shadows. It was a gray Dodge. Late model. The woman didn't turn on her lights. She whipped the car around the side of the Golden Club and out onto the Golden Springs Road. She was headed into town before she cut on her lights.

Talbot stepped out, flipped the cigarette away and walked over to where the woman had parked her car. He took out one of the books of Golden Club matches. He struck one and from its fire, ignited all the matches in the book.

The flare made a nice torch. In the glare of the matchlight he saw a gold lipstick on the ground. It was what the woman had dropped. He had seen it flash when the light caught it as it fell.

Talbot picked it up. He sighed heavily and dropped the small cylinder in his coat pocket. It might not be Nita's. It might not have been Nita who came running out of the club. He shrugged. On the other hand, it might.

11

THE CROWD WENT WILD. THEY LOVED HER. THE DANCE SPACE darkened. The band began a rhythmic pattern. The spotlight blossomed out in the middle of the floor. And there she was. In the center of it.

It was the first show of the evening. The place was packed. Talbot had come through the ornate entrance of the Golden Club and he'd seen the displays of her. *Luri Dusan. Dances Extraordinary.* A headwaiter found him a small table near the wall.

The Golden Club had one thing in common with every night spot. It hated singles anywhere except at the bar. He ordered bourbon and sat down to wait for Luri Dusan. Last night she had been Laura Dawson and she had undressed for him alone. Now he was going to see the crowd in this room when she mixed her undressing with her dancing. He knew she wasn't going to fail here tonight. She'd have these yokels standing on their heads.

The m.c. was balding and his jokes were poor. But he had been coached in the proper adjectives to use to describe Bonny William's big attraction, Luri Dusan.

Talbot was mildly surprised to see that Laura's dancing was a matter of veils and was nothing more than an excuse for disrobing.

The lights were down about the crowded room. Smoke swirled in gray wisps above the heads of the spectators and hung like gossamer clouds in the brilliance of the spotlight. It was a good effect. The light moved with Laura, but the tenuous gray clouds were stationary and were always above her no matter where she danced on the oval floor.

Talbot smiled to himself. He was probably the only person in the place watching Laura's hands. But they were graceful and effective.

She kept them moving over her body. The effect was almost hypnotic.

The music reached a first crescendo, and Laura lost her first veil.

A long sigh went across the room.

You could almost feel the sweat on the foreheads of the men who were watching. You could see the intent expressions in the faces of the women.

Talbot saw that he was alone. Only the people who had ringside tables kept their seats during the floor show here at the Golden Club. Everybody crowded in around that first ring of tables.

Another loud "Ah" signalled the fact that Laura had discarded another veil. Talbot got up and moved in with the standees around the ringside tables. Laura's expressive hands were teasing the catch on the veil insecurely caught over the curvature of her right hip.

He grinned to himself. There was the devil himself in Laura's face now. She was teasing them. They were all one man and she was tantalizing them. Her eyes asked them if she dared let the veil fall away. Her expression taunted them because they weren't daring enough to say so. They were holding their breath.

Somebody a few inches away from Talbot spoke. Talbot looked down. Strick Clemmons was sitting alone at a ringside table. His drunken voice was loud: "Take it off, baby. Take it off!"

Laura seemed unaware of him. But her hands fluttered away from the veil and she danced again, making them wait, making them pant. Her body flashed on the floor, the remaining veil shimmered, and she bent low. Clemmons yelled at her again. She was only a few inches away from him. Her face didn't alter. Her whispered, "Drop dead," was absolutely devastating. It left Clemmons speechless, and almost no one else in the place heard it.

Before Clemmons could move, Laura was in the center of the floor again. And they were clapping, begging her to loosen that last veil. Their breaths were held, even the sweat showed clearly on their foreheads.

Talbot turned away. There was no need to worry about Laura any more. She was young, and there was a clean young innocence about Laura Dawson. But that other self, the dancing Luri Dusan was something else. Laura had not lied. Luri Dusan had been around. She knew how to take care of herself.

The applause and the cries were deafening as Talbot walked out of the room into the bar. It was deserted except for the bartender.

The bartender grinned at him. "What's the matter, mister? You don't like *that?*"

Talbot shrugged. "Why look at something like that, when you can't touch it?"

The bartender nodded. "You got something there. Only I can tell you, mister, there ain't a sweating guy in that room who hasn't been to bed with Luri Dusan in his mind already. It's her eyes. Mister, that girl is a devil. Her eyes make every man in the place think he's in there alone with her."

"I'll still take a double bourbon and water."

The bartender grinned again, shoving the drink across the bar. "Just hope I never get that old, that's all."

"Is Bonny Williams in there watching?" Talbot asked after he'd finished his drink.

"He may be, but he'll be back in his office as soon as Luri goes off. He gets a real charge out of that girl. You can't drag him out to see anything else that goes on in this place."

"Where's his office?"

"Across the room and down that corridor," the bartender said.

"Think he'd mind if I wait for him in his office?"

"I doubt it. Takes a lot to make Bonny mad. But why don't you just sit here until he goes back in his office? I'll give you the nod."

"Okay. Another bourbon. That the idea?"

"That's the idea."

"Have one with me before the crowd comes back."

"Never drink while I'm working, mister. I'm a guy that gets plastered on the smell of the stuff. If you feel friendly, drop the price on the bar. I'm saving for a new mink coat."

Talbot laughed and dropped a couple of bills on the bar. "Saving up for Luri Dusan, eh?"

The bartender nodded. "That and a rainy day, mister."

Talbot toasted him with his glass. "Hope it's a deluge that day."

The bartender nodded toward the corridor. "Dusan is off, mister. Bonny Williams just went back into his office."

Bonny Williams looked up when Talbot entered his office. Bonny Williams was a scared-looking fat man. He wore expensive clothes. His club was a success. But Bonny was pale and scared. He was sick in his gut with it. That was the first thing Talbot noticed about him. Next was his dark, balding head, the heavy brows and the clipped moustache over his full, nervous mouth.

Bonny Williams was an unhappy man.

It just never occurred to him that Talbot's presence in his office meant anything except more trouble. He nodded at a chair that Talbot was to sit in. His voice was heavy as he said, "What do you want?"

"I want to ask you some questions."

"My God. What now? Who you from, Internal Revenue, the Treasury, or are you another salesman with something I don't want?"

"I'm looking for Dan Calvert."

Bonny Williams seemed to melt like tallow in his chair behind his sleek desk.

"Oh." It was a whisper. A prayer. It was final defeat.

"Do you know him?"

"Yes. But I don't know you, mister."

"My name is James Talbot. I'm working for Mike Laynebeck. Maybe you'd like to call him and verify that?"

Bonny Williams licked his lips. "I think so."

He picked up the telephone and gave Laynebeck's house telephone number without even looking it up. He watched Talbot as he waited, sweating.

"Mr. Laynebeck, please," he said. And then, "Hello, Mr. Laynebeck. How are you, Senator? This is Bonny Williams. I run the Golden Club. You know? That's fine. Thank you, Senator. There's a—James Talbot here. He says he has been hired by you to look for Mr. Calvert. He is? Good. Oh, yes, I'll be more than happy to cooperate with Mr. Talbot."

He said he would be happy to cooperate. His voice sounded happy enough. But when Bonny Williams hung up, he looked sicker and paler than ever.

"You need more sun," Talbot said.

Bonny Williams' head jerked up. "Yeah." He tried to laugh. "I could stand a vacation, all right."

"What about Dan Calvert?"

"What about him?"

"Why don't *you* tell me? Dan Calvert needed help from somebody if he disappeared."

"I don't know anything about it."

"If he didn't disappear, somebody helped him."

"Why pick on me, mister?"

Talbot shrugged. "I've got to start somewhere. There are a lot of reasons for starting with you. First, you run the most successful night spot in the county—"

"Not if this trouble keeps up."

"Second, Dan Calvert was out here a lot."

"How do you know that?"

"You practically kept him supplied with book matches. You know the pink nude on the yellow cover? He was out here a lot.

Third, you're mixed up with Roberts and Laynebeck. That's two distinct crowds."

"I'm just trying to get along."

"Maybe. Anyhow, you're in a position to know a hell of a lot more than almost any other man in this county. Now, is that enough reasons?"

"Even if I knew a lot," Williams said, "how long would I last if I told anything I knew?"

Talbot just looked at him. "You talked to Laynebeck. How long do you think you'll last with him when he finds out that you held out on me?"

"Mister, for God's sake. I don't know you. You don't know me. You couldn't have any reason for wanting to ruin me. Yet that's surer than hell what you're doing—"

"I don't want anything except to find Dan Calvert."

"I don't know a thing about it, mister. I swear it."

"You look mighty sick."

"I am sick. The whole business scares hell out of me."

"Why? If you don't know anything about it, why?"

"My God, mister. Who believes me? Do you?"

Talbot stood up. "Sorry. I don't. I'm not going to say anything to Laynebeck for a while. I'm going to give you a chance to think it over. Maybe you'll want to get in touch with me—say, before tomorrow night?"

Williams seemed not to be breathing. He just licked his lips again and nodded. He sat, melted-down blubber behind his desk. Talbot got to the door with his hand on the knob.

"I won't say anything about seeing Nita Laynebeck sneaking out of here by a side door about an hour and a half ago, either."

For a minute Williams looked like he might faint.

Laura was waiting for Talbot at the entrance of the bar. She was wearing a white terrycloth wrap-around. Her face was freshly scrubbed and clean. It looked as clear and honest as her sun-bleached blue eyes. She had looked like a she-devil out on that floor. She looked twenty now.

"Hi," she said. Her eyes were studying him. "I saw you watching me dance."

"You're terrific."

She managed to smile through the fear in her eyes. "Was I really good?"

"You're wasted in a place like this."

She tried to go on smiling. "You didn't think I was so wonderful—last night."

"I don't like to be bought."

"It would have made things a lot easier."

"It would make it a lot easier if you'd tell me why you don't want me to find Dan Calvert."

"Maybe he had a reason for going away. Did you ever think of that?"

"Sure. I know he had a reason. Before I'm through I'll know the reason. Before I'm through, I'll have Dan Calvert."

"Please—don't meddle in something that—that you don't know anything about."

"Stop worrying. It wrinkles that pretty brow. Smile now and I'll see you later, baby. At home. Our own little room."

There was envy in the bartender's eyes as Talbot walked past him and out of the club to the parking lot.

When he stepped out in the darkness, he moved quickly into the deep shadows of a recess in the facade of the building. He pressed close against the wall, waiting.

After a moment a stocky man in a dark suit came out of the club. He stood for a moment on the steps looking around. He frowned when there was no sign of Talbot anywhere on the lot. He threw down his cigarette and broke into a run across the macadam toward the parked cars.

Talbot came out of the shadows and slid quietly around the side of the building. He walked swiftly past the kitchen entrance, ran across the lighted drive to the thick line of cars. With his gun in his hand, he moved in the darkness, keeping close to the automobiles.

Ahead of him he saw the man. He was standing there looking around, puzzled. Talbot went between the cars and walked up behind the man. With his left hand he reached out and tapped him on the shoulder.

As the man turned, Talbot brought the butt of his gun down across the side of his skull. There was the sharp sound of metal against bone. The man grunted once and crumpled to his knees.

Talbot stepped back and let him fall. He bent over, rolled him on his back. He went through his identification, finding nothing that linked the fellow either to the Sheriff or to anyone else.

He ran for his car, and got out of there as fast as he could.

12

TALBOT PARKED THE BUICK IN THE EAST DRIVE BESIDE THE BIG Laynebeck house. He was still breathing as though he had run all the way from the Golden Club and the man he'd left lying unconscious in the darkened parking lot.

He crossed the veranda, glancing in the open windows of the sun room as he went. Nita was in there, alone. He paused, involuntarily.

She was drinking. He hesitated outside, looking in from the darkness with that old feeling creeping over him.

There she was. The girl who belonged in the big house on Fort Queen. The goddess he had loved so hopelessly and so helplessly. She was really beautiful now. The years had given her a breathtaking kind of beauty.

Talbot clenched his fists inside his coat pockets. He stalked beyond the windows to the front door and rammed hard on the doorbell. He could hear it from within the house. Hear it echoing in the bottomless pit of his belly.

The butler opened the door.

"Talbot. I want to see Senator Laynebeck."

"Come in, Mr. Talbot. Senator Laynebeck is expecting you."

He crossed the foyer in the wake of the butler. He couldn't keep his eyes from the door of the sun room. Nita was standing there. After you saw how beautiful she was, you saw her eyes, you saw how drunk she was.

"Talbot," she said.

Jim and the butler stopped. She came out into the foyer, glanced at the butler. "That'll be all, Meffert."

She looked up at Talbot. He couldn't say what it was about her, but she had changed since last night. Now she seemed very pleased with herself.

"Have you found him yet?" she said.

"No."

"Do you think you will?"

"Nobody wants to cooperate. But I think I will."

She smiled. But behind her smile, Jim was sure she was laughing at him.

He tightened his sweaty fist over her handkerchief in his pocket.

"We better not keep our lord and master waiting," Nita said. She nodded toward the closed library door.

Jim stared at her for a moment longer. He heeled about and knocked on the library door.

"Come in," Laynebeck said.

He opened the door and stood aside. Nita preceded him into the room.

Laynebeck got up from behind his old desk and came around it. He tried to smile, but plainly he felt that none of it was worth the effort.

"Welcome, Jim," he said. He glanced at Nita. "You mind, my dear, Jim wants to make a report to me."

"I'm a big girl," Nita said. "I won't be shocked if your private operative announces he entered a whorehouse in this fair city—"

"Nita!" Laynebeck's voice was harsh.

"Sorry, master."

But her voice wasn't sorry. She was laughing at the tall man. She didn't even try to hide her laughter from Talbot.

Laynebeck sank against his desk. He was defeated.

"She may as well stay," Talbot said, trying to preserve the older man's feelings. "I'm afraid I haven't a lot to report. I looked over his apartment. Found out who his friends were, and what his habits were." He glanced at Nita. "For instance, Calvert has a half-dozen toothbrushes in his apartment but not one tube of toothpaste."

Laynebeck's smile was gray and preoccupied. But at least he smiled. At least he was listening.

"I made some progress. For instance, I think that Calvert hasn't run away at all."

Laynebeck's head jerked up. He stared at Talbot, his jaw taut. "What are you talking about?"

"That he might be right in this town. Alive."

"Impossible. How could he get away with it?"

"By being careful. By trusting only people who liked him, feared him, or wanted him to help them."

"Fantastic!"

"Is it? That's why I came here tonight. I want to know if you want me to go on with it."

"Why wouldn't I?"

"I told you last night. You might not like the answers."

Laynebeck dragged in a deep breath. "You believe that Calvert is crossing me?"

Talbot glanced at Nita before he answered. "Well, if you want to put it mildly and conservatively, yes, that's what I think."

"I've been in the same office with Calvert for years and I don't believe it. You came back to town last night, and you're positive he's crossing me. What do you base this belief on?"

Again Talbot glanced at Nita. His voice was flat. "Maybe people tell me things they wouldn't dare tell you."

Nita's face became suddenly stony.

"Maybe they do," Laynebeck said. "Who—who have you talked to?"

Talbot heard Nita's sharp intake of breath.

Talbot's lips twisted. "Do you know a dancer at Bonny Williams' Golden Club?"

Laynebeck was looking at him. "No. I've never been out there. Haven't had the time. Do you know her, Nita?"

Nita's voice was a whisper. "I've seen her."

Talbot spoke to Laynebeck, but he was watching Nita. "Her name is Luri Dusan. Her real name is Laura Dawson. She does a strip dance. She's Calvert's girl friend. His latest."

There was almost no change in Nita's face. Just a little color fading, just the slightest widening of her eyes. But Talbot knew. He'd hit her hard. She hadn't known about Dan's little love, either.

Her voice was carefully casual. "This is all very boring, Mike. I think I'll go back to the sun room. I left a drink there, unfinished. Unbelievable as that sounds."

She went slowly across the room. It seemed to Talbot that the room got chilled as she went out of it. The scent of her was gone, and the warmth. He remembered those two years in the chain gang. That had been the worst. The need for her then.

When the door closed behind her, Talbot turned to look at Laynebeck. The big man was still watching the door. He exhaled heavily and met Talbot's eyes.

"It's a hell of a thing you're telling me," Laynebeck said. "Maybe I've been stupid, not to suspect. But you want to believe in somebody—in something."

"Maybe I'm wrong. For your sake I hope so. But just now it looks like you put your money on the wrong horse." Talbot's mouth twisted, and to himself he added, *on a couple of wrong horses.*

"Do you think that Calvert is selling out to the Sheriff and his gang?"

"What would he have to offer them?"

"Oh, I suppose Dan could swing a lot of weight if he decided to. And of course he knows some explosive secrets. If you handle a stable of politicians for very long you find a hundred wrongs that you have to conceal. For the good of the Party—for the sake of votes. And sometimes even when a man is bad—he's better for his job than his opponent. It's a tough racket."

"All right. It may be that. I would think so except that the Sheriff had Calvert's girl friend, this Dusan babe, down at his office. They were beating hell out of her. She knows something the Sheriff wants to know—and he's not afraid of Dan when he mistreats her . . ."

Laynebeck's eyes were narrowed. "Or maybe—maybe Roberts is trying to get Dan to sell out. Maybe Dan's agreed. I don't know. I'm just guessing, of course. But if the Sheriff didn't trust Dan, he could try to check on him through the girl—and if Dan is selling me out, Dan's got nobody to holler to except the Sheriff." The big man's wide shoulders slumped. "That would leave Calvert in one hell of a spot all right. The Sheriff won't trust him until he delivers at election time."

"And then again, Dan might want out. Maybe he's trying to work out something on his own."

"But would he disappear? That focuses a lot of attention on him. He must have known I'd try to find him. Everybody is talking about him—"

Talbot slapped his fist into the palm of his hand. "That's it! Calvert has taken out life insurance by disappearing. Attention is on him. No matter what kind of switch he is plotting, he's safe as long as everybody is talking about him, thinking about him, looking for him."

Laynebeck nodded slowly.

Talbot strode over and poured himself a drink.

"There you are," Talbot said. "A pretty dirty picture. Do you want me to drop it?"

Laynebeck shook his head. "No. I want you to find Calvert. I've got to talk with him, anyway. There's a chance I might save the Party—and Calvert, if I can make him listen to reason."

Talbot shrugged. "Seems to me Calvert made up his mind to ditch you, Mike, a long time ago. Maybe one reason he decided to step out for a while was because he could no longer pretend that he was your loyal partner."

Laynebeck's head sank on his chest. His hands clenched at his sides.

"Anyway," he said. "Find him for me."

Talbot was almost at the front door before Nita stopped him.

She was standing in the sun-room doorway again. She smiled at him. "Come have a drink, Talbot. One for the road."

He looked at her, started to refuse. He shrugged and went past her into the sun room. She closed the door.

She poured drinks and then turned up the volume of the console radio. "Sit down," she said. She sat on the divan and looked at him. He went on standing, looking at her over the rim of his glass.

"I haven't been able to get you out of my mind," she said. Her voice was petulant. "I thought you were never going to get through talking in there."

"Your husband is pretty upset," he said, "about the man who is double-crossing him. A man he trusted. And he doesn't even know part of it."

She looked at him, her eyes slumbrous. "Are you going to tell him?"

"Maybe."

She leaned forward. "Why? Because I need someone to love me? Maybe you don't know what it is like to *need* to be loved."

His mouth twisted. "No. I wouldn't know anything about that."

Now she smiled. The tigress claws were hidden, sheathed beneath the silk and nylon that rustled when she moved on the divan. "Sit down, Jim. Talk to me. I'm lonely."

"Yes. Is that why you were at the Golden Club at nine o'clock tonight?"

He caught her unaware. Her lips parted, and her face colored a little. "Were you there?" she said at last. Her voice was casual now. "I didn't see you."

He sat down beside her. Waited.

"I went to see Bonny Williams," she said. "I thought maybe he'd heard something about Dan. . . . But I don't have to explain myself to you."

"That's right, you don't."

Her hand trailed across the short distance between them on the divan. "Let's not fight. I want you for my friend."

"Friend? Good lord!" He began to laugh.

"Stop laughing. I hate it. I won't have you laughing at me."

"Oh, I'm not laughing at you. It's that gag. Friendship. The two people I could never be friends with have offered me friendship today."

"Please, Jim. No matter what I've become—oh, I know what you think of me for falling in love with Dan, I know what you think when you watch me drink too much—but it's because I need someone. Maybe I wouldn't have been like this, Jim, if I'd had you."

Her trailing fingers had reached his hand. He brushed them away and stood up.

She jumped up too and closed the gap between them. "All right, I know. It was my fault. My fault you went to jail. My fault we weren't together—the way we should have been. My fault I'm like I am now. But I can't help it, Jim. I need help and you've got to help me."

She looked around nervously, picked up a cigarette from a pack on an end table. She searched helplessly then for a match. He took his cigarette lighter from his pocket, snapped it and held the flame out to her.

Her icy fingers closed over his. When she had lighted the cigarette, she inhaled deeply and blew a cloud of gray smoke at the ceiling. She took his lighter from his fingers.

She examined it. "Very nice," she said. "I'm glad you're able at last to afford nice things."

"And thanks to Mike Laynebeck," he told her. "I'm sorry, Nita. That kind of puts me on his side in this business."

"You can't desert me." There was no panic in her voice. She was an indulged child asserting a fact. People didn't turn their backs on Nita Laynebeck. Not when she needed them.

"I've got a job."

"I must talk to you. Not now. But later. Out by Cypress River. You know where you drove me last night. Please meet me. After Mike has gone to sleep. Be there at midnight. I'll be there as soon as I can."

He smiled and shook his head. "No."

"Jim. You won't be sorry. I've been mixed up. But I'm not mixed up now. Don't tease me. Don't make me beg. I'll make it up to you, Jim. I never forgot you, Jim. I wanted to. I tried to."

He inhaled deeply. "All right, Nita. This one time. I can't argue with you here. I'll be there. This time. No more. I'm not helping you keep a Dan Calvert. As far as I'm concerned you belong to Mike Laynebeck. As far as I'm concerned, you should have been mine."

"I should have been," she said. It was a whisper. But he heeled around and started across the room.

Her voice stopped him.

"Jim, your lighter."

At the door, he stopped. With his hand on the knob, he turned and looked at her over his shoulder. She was holding his lighter out in the palm of her hand. He looked at it, remembering the one in his coat pocket. Remembering where he had found it. The Duval House. Dan Calvert's apartment. Behind his bed.

His voice was hollow. "Keep it," he said. "I've got another one."

13

PETE MOSTELLA OWNED THE NEWSSTAND NEXT DOOR TO THE ENtrance of the Duval Professional building. Mostella didn't have a lot of space and sold only newspapers, magazines and pocket books. But he took his business seriously, met everybody with a grin and was a successful merchant.

He was just closing up for the night when Talbot pulled his car up in front of his stand. The whole town was almost dark.

Only a few lights burned in the windows of the courthouse on the square. Even the department store display windows were dimly lit.

Talbot came around the car and crossed the walk. Mostella stopped pushing news racks into the narrow room and looked up grinning. He was a dark-eyed little man with thick black hair.

"Yes, sir, friend. What can I get for you?"

Talbot bought a pocket book. A detective story with a lovely girl on the yellow cover. There was a green knife in her back. He also bought a Jacksonville newspaper. He started out of the tiny shop as though he intended leaving, although he had no intention of doing that.

"You do a lot of business with the people in the office buildings?"

Mostella grinned. "Why don't you ask me, mister? You're a detective. I heard all about it today. Mike Laynebeck hired you to find his partner Mr. Calvert."

Talbot laughed. "That's right. You should take up detection in case the news business falls off."

"Mister, the news business can't fall off. There ain't no place for it to fall to. Besides, I just keep my big ears open."

Talbot leaned against the bare wall of the building. "All right," he said. "I'd like to know. Calvert disappeared on a Tuesday, between noon and five o'clock. Did you see him that day at all?"

Mostella shoved the last news rack inside and pulled an iron grate across the front. He fixed a lock and snapped it. Then he reached inside and snapped off the lights. He loosened a canvas then. It slid down behind the grate and he secured it along the flooring. Then he straightened up, dusting off his hands.

He nodded at Talbot. "Sure, I seen him. I seen him every day. He bought magazines and papers from me. And I seen him that day. He left the office about four o'clock. Last time I seen him."

"How did he leave? Did someone meet him? Did he walk? Was he alone?"

"His car was parked at the curb. He must not have been in his office an hour because there are parking meters and hour limit parking. But I know I saw him get in his car and drive away. Yes sir, drove right off the face of the earth."

"Not quite," Talbot said. "He could drive a long way from Duval without doing that."

* * *

Talbot didn't leave the car on the street tonight. He drove around the rear of the Duval House and went down the ramp into the hotel garage.

The attendant was a two-headed man of about forty. He was wearing tan coveralls. His hands and clothes were smeared with grease. He had the look of a busy man, except for his eyes. They were red-rimmed, as though he'd been sitting in the warm garage office fast asleep.

"Yes, sir. Park your car for you, sir?"

"I don't know. Maybe. I may be going in the hotel to bed. That might depend on you."

The man looked puzzled.

"Dan Calvert lives in this hotel, doesn't he?"

Now, the attendant was worried.

"Well, yes sir. He did. That is, he did until he disappeared a few weeks ago."

"Three weeks," Jim said. "Did he leave his car in here nights?"

"Yes, sir. It's here now."

Talbot nodded, feeling the old pounding of his heart. He was moving along now.

"Let's look at it," he said.

Before the attendant could open his mouth to protest, Talbot showed him his badge and credentials.

"I'm trying to find Calvert," he said. "I was told he drove off in his car the day he disappeared."

"Well, he couldn't have done that. There it is, right over there." The attendant pointed to a blue Cadillac hard-top convertible.

Talbot strode across the drive. The attendant followed.

"How long has this car been in here?"

"It was here the night Mr. Calvert disappeared."

"Did you see him bring it in?"

"No, sir. It came in during the afternoon. I come to work at ten at night. It was here when I came to work that night. It's been here ever since."

Talbot got in under the wheel. The keys were in the ignition. He turned them, started the engine. It purred into life at once. He looked questioningly at the attendant.

"Oh, we keep it in condition," the attendant said. "We run it, check the tires. It's ready for use any time."

"Who told you to do that?"

The attendant shrugged. "I don't know. The hotel, I guess. Anyhow it's an order over in the office. And that's all I do, mister. Follow orders."

14

TALBOT DROVE OUT OF THE DUVAL HOUSE GARAGE. HE LOOKED at the timepiece on the dashboard. It was almost twelve o'clock.

He drove up to Cypress Road, turned east under the neon arrow. *See Golden Springs.* He shook his head. People came from all over the country to this hot hell-hole just to see that attraction. Well, if he got out this time, nothing would ever bring him back. Not even neon arrows.

He let the car purr along at forty. The streets were deserted. At intervals he watched the rear-view mirror. He wasn't taking chances on being shot at again.

Whoever that had been had wanted to kill him or scare him out of town. And whoever it was, Talbot was ready for him if he came again.

He knew he should hurry. Perversely he let the car slow down. If Nita got there first, let her wait. It would be the first time she ever waited for anyone in her life.

He had a lot to think about. There was only one way to find out why Dan Calvert had pretended to leave town. That was to find Dan Calvert. Duval wasn't a big town, but there were places in it where a man could hide.

He had made up his mind to move his clothes from Laura's room in the Broadway Hotel to the Duval House. He could get a room now. There was no longer any need to stay there.

He smiled grimly. But would Laura know that? Why couldn't he go on trading on the fact that he couldn't get another place to sleep? One thing he knew for sure. Laura knew a lot about Dan Calvert. Even better than Nita, Laura could lead him to Calvert. If he worked it right, if he was careful, he could find out from Laura what she knew about Calvert.

One thing was a fact. It would be a mistake to leave Laura as long as she knew something about Dan Calvert that he didn't. The Broadway Hotel didn't care who shared her room. And Sheriff Roberts didn't care, not as long as he thought it provided him with a weapon against Talbot.

He grinned, satisfied with himself.

It was twelve-thirty when he pulled the Buick into the narrow gravel road that ended on the bluff overlooking the Cypress River. As he turned the car out into the open space, the headlights raked holes across the darkness. There was no other car on the bluff.

He was not surprised. He had not expected Nita would get there ahead of him. Wait. How many hours had he spent waiting for her in that past when he had been her latest love? How sick he had been, wanting her and afraid she wasn't coming. Needing her, and being sure that she had found something "more amusing" to do. The emptiness in his belly that he couldn't will away. And then, how suddenly he was all right when she came at last.

He pulled the big car almost to the edge of the precipice and killed the engine.

When the car was silent, the night outside became raucous. The bullfrogs were wailing in the mud flats at the foot of the bluff. There were birds out there that never slept, that didn't know spring from winter, midnight from noon. Occasionally a bull alligator would croak somewhere down the black stream, or land with a splash in the water from a log.

After a few moments you became accustomed to the sounds and you could almost fool yourself into believing there was silence in this hideaway place. The silence beat at him, and he waited, listening for the sound of her car.

He got out of the Buick and walked to the edge of the sheer bluff. He stood there, looking out into the blackness, hearing the slap of the swift current, the caterwauling of the frogs.

He got a cigarette and reached for his cigarette lighter. He remembered he had traded it to Nita, in a perverse kind of swap for hers.

He took out her lighter and tried it. It would not ignite. He dropped it back into his pocket. He had quite a collection there now. Lipstick, lighter and a handkerchief.

He found a folder of matches from Bonny Williams' Golden Club and lighted up.

The folder reminded him of the liquid-platinum skin of Laura

Dawson. In love with Dan Calvert. He shook his head. One thing he had done, he had spoiled one of Dan Calvert's games already. Laura hadn't known that Dan was having an affair with the wife of Senator Laynebeck.

He remembered the way Nita had looked when she heard that Dan was in love with Bonny Williams' little dancer.

It was a dirty trick he had played on both Nita and Laura. But it was good strategy. The best thing he could do to flush Dan Calvert out of hiding was to set the two women who loved him against each other!

The one he pitied in the whole business was Mike Laynebeck. What good could come to that poor devil? Probably no man in Florida had been as much a force for good in the past fifteen years. They were paying him back beautifully, all right. His partner, double-crossing him. His wife, faithless. The Sheriff plotting to take over after a smear campaign that would cover the Laynebeck name with mud that could never be scraped off.

He struck another match and looked at his wrist watch. It was one o'clock.

He might as well go back. Nita wasn't coming. Maybe she couldn't get away. Maybe she had a more interesting date. Anyway, she wasn't here and he wasn't going to wait any more.

Well, the day had had a lousy beginning. Sheriff Roberts walking in, smirking and leering at Laura's underthings strewn about the hotel bedroom. And now it had a lousy ending.

Jim Talbot was right back where he had started more than ten years ago. Waiting for Nita—who never showed up. A lousy ending for a lousy night.

A stinking lousy night.

He drove slowly back to town. He didn't pass more than half a dozen cars all the way to the Broadway Hotel. But he looked each one over carefully.

He admitted it. He was still looking for Nita. Just like he used to, in the long-ago.

His mouth pulled into an angry sneer. Oh, brother, but he had had it bad. What a fool! He had thought that was the way God meant for two people to love each other. But he had found out all right. Love was for laughs. It wasn't important. It was a foolish thing.

Well, it had put him through hell all right. There had been

plenty of women after Nita. He hadn't lied to her about that. But what he hadn't told Nita about was the laughter. The laughter that roiled up inside him whenever he tried to tell some woman that he loved her.

Sometimes they even knew he was laughing. Bitter, rotten laughter. All of it inside. And not a damned bit funny. . . .

He walked up the stairs to Laura's room on the third floor of the Broadway Hotel. She had given him a key last night and he was fumbling in his pocket looking for it as he went along the musty corridor.

He heard her crying as he fitted the key in the lock.

He thrust the door open. He stepped inside and slammed it shut after him.

Laura was sprawled across a twin bed in her slip. She was hugging her face into a pillow, and she was still crying deep inside her when she propped herself on an elbow and turned looking at him. Her face was streaked with tears and her lips were trembling.

She pushed her platinum blonde hair back from her face.

"What the devil is the matter?" Jim demanded. He went across the room and sat down on the bed beside her.

"Oh, I'm so glad you came back!" she whispered. Her voice held a touch of fright.

"Sure I'm here." He put his arm around her and held her head against his shoulder. "Now tell me, what's the matter? What are you crying about?"

"What difference does it make why I'm crying?" she whispered. "I'm crying, that's all. But you've got to make me stop. Make me stop crying."

She began to quiver. He pulled her closer, feeling her hot tears against his face, feeling her swollen mouth damp against his neck.

"Tell me about it," he said.

But she wouldn't talk about it. He felt a sob rack her full body. Her arms went about him, misery making her strong. Her fingernails dug into his shoulders as she pulled herself closer against him. She spoke against his face, "Make me stop crying. Make me stop crying." He could feel the tear-hotness of her breath, the resilient pressure of her breasts. He knew what she wanted, but it made him sad. Sad that she found out what he had learned long ago. That because you love with abandon, it doesn't mean your love is always returned that way.

She didn't have to tell him why she wept. He knew. Dan Calvert had broken her heart. She had found out the truth about Dan and Nita Laynebeck. And now there was only one way to stop her crying. The old gag. Pain to counteract pain.

God help you, baby, he thought. *We both loved in this town — with all our sucker hearts. And we got it good, baby, you and I. The way suckers get it everywhere.*

He pushed her back, covering the warmth of her mouth with his. He was trying to make her forget that Dan Calvert had broken her heart. And all the time he was trying to forget, too.

Nita had broken another date.

15

HE WAS DRESSED AND OUT OF THE ROOM THE NEXT MORNING before Laura woke up.

There were four good reasons why he wanted to get out of there without talking to her after last night.

First, he awoke needing violence. There was nothing else that was going to satisfy him now. He had to move and keep moving. He wanted to break things. Smash them. Watch them smash.

Second, he meant to put in at least twenty hours looking for Dan Calvert. He was positive Calvert had never left Duval. At least not for any length of time that mattered. Calvert was in town. He was in the mood to find him.

Third, he felt that the kid was going to want to be alone when she woke up. Sure, he'd made her stop crying. And she had gone to sleep in his arms. He had lain there for hours staring at the swirling patterns of darkness on the chipped ceiling of the cheap hotel room. She didn't wake up again that night.

The fourth reason he didn't like to think about. Not only had he made her stop crying last night. It had hit him where he lived, loving her. There was no cynical laughter boiling around inside him as he'd held her and loved her.

The hellish truth was that he had run away from Duval to escape one love. A love that had thrown him in a Florida prison and abandoned him. And now he had come back and found a new one.

He knew. With Laura he could go the rest of the distance. He'd be really civilized. No more bitterness, no more wormwood insides laughing at anything decent. A respectable citizen. She'd made him feel clean and young and worthwhile. Hell, with Laura he'd be thinking about a home, a business, washing machines, clotheslines, mortgages. The works.

And what chance did he have? She was twenty. Just twenty. The fact that he was thirty was minor. He was a thousand, he stunk with age and bitterness. He was what loving Nita Laynebeck had made of him. Laura needed a decent young guy.

He shook his head. He'd been laughed at for the last time. He wasn't going to stick his neck out. She was a kid. He wasn't right for her. What a laugh it would hand her when he told her he loved her. Only he wasn't going to tell her.

He got the framed photograph of Dan Calvert and left the room. He was almost running as he went along the corridor. His hand gripped the picture so tightly that he heard the glass smash under his palm. He didn't even look down at it.

There was a woman on duty at the bus station. Talbot went up to the window. He shoved the picture of Calvert across the desk. For the first time he saw that a sliver of glass had been pushed into his hand. He pulled it out, wrapped his handkerchief around his palm.

All the time the woman was staring at him instead of at the picture.

"Look at it," he told her. "You know that man?"

She looked at the picture. "I know him," she said. "I've seen his picture in the *Duval Sun*, and I've seen him around town. That stuck-up rich so-and-so disappeared."

"Did he buy a bus ticket?"

"That guy? That rich snob ride on a bus? Mister, you're making jokes early in the morning. Before breakfast."

The same full-bloomed little doll was at work in the news concession at the depot. She smiled as Talbot entered the place. She had the kitten up on the glass counter. She was stroking its back. Talbot shook his head. Two days. It seemed more like a month since he'd been in this train station.

Talbot poked a finger at the kitten. He looked at the girl. "What kind of hours do you have around this place anyhow?"

She smiled. "Oh, ah couldn't date you'all anyhow, mistuh. Ah'm mayried. Mah little ol' husben is just about the most jealous crittuh you evuh saw."

Talbot smiled. "Well, honey, I don't blame him for that. It's just that you're here day and night—when are you home with him?"

"Why, honey, I'm only heah before trains leave and before they arrive. We close up except for an hour before every train time. That's why I'm here everytime they's anything doin' around heah."

He laid the picture of Calvert on the counter beside the kitten. The kitten spit at it.

"Maybe you saw him when he got on a train about three weeks ago? Can you remember?"

Talbot fished out a five-dollar bill and laid it across Calvert's eyes, thinking Calvert looked much better that way.

"I could have remembered without the money, honey, but—" Her little hand covered the bill. "Thank you'all so much."

"All right. All right. How about this guy?"

"Honey, that's Mistuh Dan Calvert. I went out with him one night. Was mah little ol' husben mad! Mad? Why, he was fit to be tied. Even when I told him what an impohtant man Mistuh Calvert was. He just didn't seem to care—"

"All right. All right. When did he leave town? What train did he take? Did he tell you where he was going?"

"Honey, take it easy. You'all will work up a real sweat heah so early in the mohnin'. Mistuh Calvert ain't left town, honey. Least not on any train he didn't . . ."

The young fellow in the gray uniform at the ticket office at the Duval Airport looked bored. Talbot smiled. The airlines catered to the sophisticated who could afford air travel so they evidently hired blasé clerks to create acceptable atmosphere.

He showed Calvert's picture.

"No. He hasn't been on any of our flights. Not recently. Not in the last six months. I would remember. He flies frequently to Tallahassee and Washington with Senator Laynebeck. But not lately at all. No. There's no other place in town where he could buy plane tickets, and no other airport. No. Mr. Calvert didn't leave Duval by plane."

Talbot was almost out of the air travel office when he remembered something. He stopped and looked around for the public pay telephone booths.

Inside one of the booths, he thumbed through the telephone directory to the yellow classified section.

Calvert definitely had not left town in his own car, or by bus, plane or train. He either left town walking or in transportation furnished privately. Talbot didn't believe Calvert had done any of these.

He turned the pages of the yellow section. If Calvert was still in Duval, where could he hole in and arouse least notice?

He found the classification "Motels."

The listing was not long, Talbot glanced over his shoulder and then tore the listing from the directory. What the hell, no one as blasé as that air clerk over there was going to need a motel. If the clerk didn't, the patrons wouldn't. Anyway, he needed that list worse than they did.

John Spexter came out on the small front stoop of the office-cabin at the Park-Here Motel. He was a thin man in white trousers and white undershirt. A spray of white hairs showed above the line of the undershirt. He was barefooted.

"The heat," he told Talbot. "A man has to be comfortable. Reason I went in the motel business. Most relaxed business in the world next to a trailer park. In a trailer park you're right down to bare living. A motel is a cut better, but still relaxed. Community bathrooms, showers, washtubs. People relax. That's what I like. Especially in this heat."

Talbot shoved the picture at him. "You know this fellow?"

The motel owner looked disappointed. "Say, I thought you wanted to rent a cabin. Is this all you want? Checking up on some poor guy might have stayed here. How do I know? People come, late at night, stay a few hours. How do I know who stays here?"

Talbot's voice was sharp. "Well, look at the picture anyway."

John Spexter looked at him petulantly. But he took the picture, holding it carefully so he didn't touch the broken place. He adjusted his spectacles and then looked over the top of them at the worried countenance of Dan Calvert.

"Well, all right. I believe I've seen him."

"When?"

Spexter thought. "One night, say a week and a half, two weeks ago."

Talbot grinned. "Wonderful. Did he rent a motel?"

"Yes. That's when I seen him. It was him all right."

"Has he still got the cabin?"

"No. Oh, no. He just hired it for the one night."

"Oh."

Spexter smiled. "Now if you had another picture. Of the lady, I might be able to tell you if it was her that was here with him."

"There was a woman with him?"

"Well, not when he hired the cabin. But about an hour after he'd taken it, a car parked half a block down the road. I was sittin' out here on the stoop, all the lights out that hour and all the cabins taken. Too hot to sleep. I see the lady walk back down the road and come in here. She walked right past my porch, almost close as you are to me. She never seen me at all.

"Well, she walks right along the roadway. Then this feller in the picture there, he comes out of a cabin. They sort of run together and hug tight, right out there in the drive. Then they went in his cabin."

"What did you do?"

"Why, I went on sittin' here. Maybe I ruminated a bit 'bout people and people's ideas about life."

"About them using your cabin?"

"What the devil? They paid for it, didn't they?"

"And so they left the next morning? In her car?"

"No. She left sometime during the night. I was settin' out here, seen her leave. She stopped down by the road there and lighted a cigarette. I looked at her. She looked tired."

"And the man?"

"When I went to clean the cabin the next morning he was gone. They were mighty neat folks, I'll say that. Hardly messed the place up at all. I changed the sheets, swept up, and that ended the matter, far as I was concerned. Nice, quiet, refined folk. Wish I could get rentals like that all the time."

"You didn't see him leave?"

"No, sir. I didn't. Didn't look for him. Cabin was paid for in advance. Ended the matter right there, far as I was concerned."

Talbot drove back slowly into Duval. He had found Calvert and lost him just like that. If the woman at the motel were Nita, that would mean that Calvert had pretended to be out of town, and had arranged to meet her there for one night.

If it had been Laura who had run out there to stay with Calvert, that would make a different picture. In that case, Calvert was playing it safe. He was having his fun with Laura. But he was holding on to Nita. The rich woman. The one who would do his career the most good—when Laynebeck was out of the way. . . .

He parked outside the courthouse and went up the wide sidewalk. Old men were sitting on benches in the sun. He remembered when he had been a kid here. There had been a bandstand, and concerts at night, with the crowds standing around on the wide sidewalks and spilling out into the quiet streets.

Ballard was sitting at the blond-wood desk.

"You still in town?" he said.

"You didn't expect me to run just because the fat man in there said boo, did you? How about running in there and telling him that Talbot is back here to see him again."

Ballard got up and went to the door of Roberts' private office. He knocked.

"All right," Roberts said. "What is it?"

"Talbot is back to see you."

"Send him in here."

Ballard jerked his head at Talbot. Jim crossed the room. Ballard held the door open for him.

Roberts pushed back in his swivel chair. He regarded Talbot across the top of a steaming coffee cup.

"Morning, friend. You been shot at again?"

"Not since the first night. The high cost of ammunition and all."

Roberts put down the coffee cup. He picked up a sheaf of papers. Yellow, blue and white sheets stapled together.

"Here's the ballistics report," he said. "I think you'll find it pretty complete."

Talbot took it. "Thank you, friend," he said. "This is mighty neighborly of you."

Roberts peered up at him. "Not at all," he said, his smile as false as G.I. teeth. "You scratch my back. I'll scratch yours."

Talbot grinned. "Yeah. But your back is so much bigger than mine."

"Well . . . that's the way it goes in life." Roberts motioned toward a chair.

Now it's my turn, Talbot thought. He remembered what Laynebeck had said. The Sheriff would take a sliver of fact and chew at it, until he'd gotten all the juice out of it. That's the way they had worked when Talbot hit town. Clemmons went running to Roberts with the news. They haggled over it, ripped at it until they worked themselves in a frenzy—and sent Clemmons out to bring Talbot in. A friend of Laynebeck. A dangerous man.

And that was why they had brought Laura in. She knew Calvert and—and. . . .

Suddenly the whole thing was as clear to Talbot as though it were a series of photographs laid out on the Sheriff's desk before him.

Certainly, Calvert had never left town.

Where was he staying?

It was laughably simple. He was staying at two places. And suddenly Talbot knew exactly where to find Dan Calvert this morning.

All this time the Sheriff had been talking, worrying at each subject about which Talbot might remotely be informed! Laynebeck's latest plans; anyone who had been to see Laynebeck; any phone calls.

Talbot could think only one thing. He had to get out of this office. And yet he knew he couldn't hurry the Sheriff. If the Sheriff suspected Talbot was anxious to get out, he'd fret about that until he found out why. Maybe if he'd give Roberts some harmless lie to mull over and shake to pieces, he'd get a chance to ease out.

"There is one thing," Talbot said, "that I didn't tell you. While

I was out at Laynebeck's place last night, he did have one phone call. Some guy named—let me see, Laynebeck called him Erskine—"

"Erskine? Great lord! Erskine Reeves. Governor Reeves! Telephone? He called Laynebeck? On the phone? Uh, look, Talbot, my boy, you've done me a great service. And I won't forget it. You'll see that I appreciate neighborly acts. I'm a man situated so he can repay a favor. But will you excuse me now? I'm pretty busy at the moment. I'll tell you what. Come back. Drop back in here to see me any time."

And so, Talbot told himself, *here I am, outside his office, still friendly.*

He tossed Ballard a salute and sauntered out into the corridor. Out there, with the door to the Sheriff's offices closed, Talbot moved faster.

He went out in the street and started toward his car. But before he reached it, he realized he could move faster on foot. The one-way streets of this swollen hick town would delay him.

He crossed Main Street and started along it, forcing himself to remember not to run.

Where was Calvert? He was at the Broadway Hotel.

Why else would Laura Dawson stay in such a dingy dump?

Why would Calvert stay there?

Because nobody would think to look for the rich snob in such a trap. Because the people who worked there were so poor or else so deep in trouble that Calvert could buy their loyalty.

Didn't that explain the prowler the first night Talbot had stayed in Laura's room?

The prowler had been Calvert, calling on Laura. Or checking. He had run, disappearing probably in some other room on the same floor. Maybe he'd seen Talbot come in with her.

Didn't that explain the look of fear on Laura's face? She'd been afraid Talbot would tumble to Calvert's little hideaway. Afraid he would catch Calvert in the hall. And that explained why Laura was in better spirits the next morning. By then she had warned Calvert. . . .

So that was one of the places Calvert had been using as a hide-out.

* * *

Talbot was almost running as he went through the double doors into the dusty lobby of the Broadway Hotel.

The clerk was a thin man with black hair, a prominent Adam's apple and a sharp, hooked nose. Talbot walked to the desk, pushed the cracked photograph of Calvert across it. He saw the clerk go pale, staring at the picture as though he couldn't take his eyes off it.

"Which room?" Talbot said.

The clerk looked up at him, his jaws sagging. He managed to squeak, "I don't know what you're talking about."

Talbot kept his voice low. "Look, Calvert's in this hotel. Either you tell me which room he's in, or I'll tear down every door in this dump until I find the right one."

"Please, mister! I don't want any trouble."

"Then let's don't have any. Give me a key to his room."

"I couldn't do that."

"That's up to you. I'm going in to see him. With a key or without it. Trouble or no trouble. That's up to you, fellow."

The clerk moaned low in his throat. "He'll kill me," he whimpered. "He's going to just kill me." But he fumbled under the desk and handed Talbot a key across the top of it. "He's in room 206, mister. And for God's sake don't tell him I told you."

Talbot took two steps at a time to the second floor. He didn't want the clerk to have time to call Calvert's room. Few rooms in this place were equipped with telephones. There were just pay phones in the corridors on each floor. But Calvert would very likely have had a telephone installed.

He came out of the stairwell on the second floor. The room across was 208. He decided the numbers would start at the elevator and he turned left. There it was. 206.

He shoved the key into the Yale inside lock, thinking he had been wrong in one thing. Calvert hadn't had a room on the same floor with Laura. Calvert was always the one to do a thing the safe way.

He turned the key and shoved the door open. He moved in fast then.

He could have saved the effort of hurry. There was a man in

the room all right. He was sprawled out in the middle of the floor. There was a pool of blood under his head.

Talbot closed the door, leaning against it. He stared at the body on the floor.

Without touching him, Talbot knew the man was dead. He had been dead for several hours.

Talbot could feel the sickness boiling up in him. The man on the floor was dead. But it wasn't Calvert. Talbot hadn't yet found Dan Calvert.

The dead man was Mike Laynebeck!

16

TALBOT WALKED WOODENLY TO THE BODY ON THE FLOOR. HE knelt beside it, touching Laynebeck's cheek with the back of his hand. It was cold. The cold of death.

He lifted Laynebeck slightly. Just enough to see where the bullet had gone in. High in his left chest. The pool of blood had formed from the hole.

Talbot swallowed back the wad of tears that choked his throat. If there was one good man in Duval, one decent politician in the state of Florida, one swell guy in the world, this was he. Mike Laynebeck. Dead on the unswept floor of a dingy room in a cheap hotel.

Talbot clenched his fists until his fingernails dug into the palms of his hand. "My God, Mike," he whispered. "Why didn't you let me handle it? Why, Mike? Why?"

He could feel the sting of tears. He blinked them away angrily. He felt horrible. He had accused Mike of being afraid. Afraid of the questions. Afraid of the answers. Afraid of the muck.

Well, that showed how wrong you could be about a decent guy. Mike had been sincerely worried about that rotten bastard Calvert. He had been afraid Calvert was in trouble and needed him. That was why he had brought Jim Talbot back to a town he knew Talbot hated. He wanted the best talent he could buy to help him find Calvert. Find him so he could aid him, if Calvert needed it.

Laynebeck hadn't been afraid of anything. He had promised

Talbot he was going on seeking Calvert. And he had. Sometime last night he must have gotten the answer. This morning he had come to see Calvert. And this was what he had gotten. A bullet in his chest.

Laynebeck, Talbot thought, *he could have been the biggest man this state ever had, the kind it needed all to hell. Except for one thing. He had loved Nita.*

Loving Nita is a disease.

He was still hunkered over Laynebeck's body when he heard them in the hall. He was thinking that but for Laynebeck, he would be in a Florida road gang when he heard Roberts' voice: "Room 206, Clemmons. That's where they said."

Someone had called to report a shooting. But the shooting had occurred hours ago. And the call had gone in since Talbot left his office thirty minutes ago!

Talbot stared at the door. He was thinking, Laynebeck got me out of the chain gang. His body could send me back there. Especially if Roberts came in and found him.

He sprang up, ran to the window. There was no fire escape outside. It was a long two-story drop to the alley. He stuck his head through the curtains, looked both ways. The building was brick. There were no ledges, nothing to hold to.

It wouldn't do him any good to drop from the window. The fall to the littered alley would probably break his leg. He'd never get away then.

He looked up. The building across the narrow court had a flat roof. It was a long jump from this window. It was a desperate chance. It was his only chance.

He was already climbing through the window. He heard Roberts' voice from the corridor: "All right, all right. Open that door. Or would you like me to break it down?"

Talbot jumped. His hands caught on the inside of the ledge. His knees cracked hard against the bricks of the wall. He didn't have time for pain. He chinned himself up to the ledge, caught with his arm and pulled himself over.

He scrambled away from the ledge. It was in plain sight from the window of room 206. By now, the clerk was going to be staring speechlessly. He'd sent a man up to 206, and that man was gone!

Talbot ran across the hot tar roof. There was a rusty fire escape on the other side of the building that led down to another refuse-cluttered alley.

Talbot swung his legs over the ledge and clambered down the fire escape. There was a six-foot drop into the alley. Talbot made it, landing on his feet.

He straightened up, brushing the dust from his aching knees. A woman crossed the alley on Main Street. She stared in at him. He bowed, smiling.

"Good morning, ma'am."

She tilted her head and strode on. Another drunk in an alley.

Talbot stepped out on Main Street. He walked with what he hoped was jauntiness toward the courthouse square. But he couldn't be sure. His knees hurt so much that it was agony to take one step after the other.

He longed to look over his shoulder toward the Broadway Hotel. He managed to resist. He had to resist. Even though he felt he was wearing the latest thing in pistol targets—right in the middle of his back.

At the square, he waited for the traffic signal to change, crossed the street and managed to get to the Buick before his knees made him yell with agony.

He was still waiting for the shrilling of police whistles. He started the car, backed out, drove around the square to Cypress Road. There was one place for him to go. He didn't know when he had decided it, but there was no doubt in his mind.

The big arrow above the bus station pointed east. And Talbot headed east, keeping barely within the speed limit. He didn't want to be picked up for speeding. But he wanted to get where he was going before the call went out for him.

There were only two cars baking in the sun of the huge macadam parking lot that surrounded the white building with its huge unlighted sign: *Bonny Williams' Golden Club. Dancing Nightly. Floor Show.*

Talbot parked in the rear of the Club. He banged on the front door. This was padded and he didn't even hear himself. He walked back around the building in the sun.

There were half a dozen garbage cans outside the kitchen door. He brushed past them, walking unsteadily and entered the kitchen. Three men were laughing and talking over by the stoves. They stopped talking and stared at him.

He nodded, trying to look as though he owned the joint.

"Bonny up front?" he said. He didn't wait for their answer.

He wondered how much longer his knees were going to support him. Long enough, he determined grimly, till he got to the right door.

Bonny Williams looked up when Talbot pushed open the door to his private office.

"Hi, Bonny."

The Club owner looked ill. "What you want this time?"

"You didn't decide to tell me where Calvert was?"

Bonny licked his tongue across his lips. He shook his head.

"No." It was just a whisper. But there was fear in it.

"You don't need to tell me any more," Talbot said. "Now I know. I figured it all out. All by myself, Bonny. Isn't that nice?"

"Yes. Swell." Bonny was sweating now.

"If I told Mike Laynebeck that you'd been hiding Dan Calvert out, you wouldn't last long, would you, Bonny?"

"My lord, mister! Please!"

"I can't tell him, Bonny. Laynebeck's dead."

Bonny Williams' mouth fell open. Talbot could almost read the man's thoughts. Bonny had been willing to cross Laynebeck. But Laynebeck had stood between this gross, sweating man and ruinous protection pay-offs to Roberts and his thugs. Bonny didn't mind seeing Laynebeck cheated, robbed and double-crossed. But he hadn't looked ahead to the time when he was going to have to try to stay in business in Marvel County, Florida, when Laynebeck was dead.

"I need a room, Bonny," Talbot said.

"I got nothing."

"I think you have. Upstairs. Or maybe you'd like me to go to the Sheriff and tell him you've been playing along with Dan Calvert, hoping he could save you from Roberts even when Calvert pulled his double-cross and Laynebeck was dumped?"

"Maybe I got one room. It ain't nothing extra. You may not like it."

"It'll have to do. Let's go up and see it."

As they came off the stairway to the second floor, Talbot could hear the music from a phonograph or radio. The volume was turned up loud. It came from a room directly across the hall from the stairs.

Talbot looked questioningly at Bonny. Williams pretended he didn't even hear it.

Talbot strode across the corridor. He put his hand on the doorknob. The door was locked.

Williams' voice was almost a sob. "Not that room. That ain't the room I got for you!"

"It's good enough," Talbot said. "It's the room I want."

"Oh, lord, mister!" Bonny was wringing his hands. "Please come away from that door!"

Talbot grabbed Williams' shirt front. "Unlock that door or I'll tear it down—and I'll use your greasy head for a battering ram."

He could feel Bonny Williams' shivering. The Sheriff had the man's number, all right. Bonny was shaking so badly he could hardly work the key into the Yale lock. He turned the key and tried to knock warningly as the door swung open.

Talbot caught Bonny's balled hand and thrust him into the room ahead of him.

The radio console blared louder than ever in this richly furnished room with the Venetian blinds drawn tight against the sunlight and heat of the outside world. This room with air-conditioning, with a table set for a banquet. With divans to lounge on, and mirrors to check your beauty from every angle.

Calvert was standing with a cocktail glass in his hand. He was wearing an expensive dressing gown, a wine-colored thing with woven pictures through it. His brown hair receded from his high forehead. His eyes were blue, his nose straight. For all his worried expression, you could see that here was a man who felt himself an exceptionally handsome dog. A man of consequence. A man who was going places. The man Talbot had come to find.

Dan Calvert. . . .

17

CALVERT LOOKED DOWN HIS PATRICIAN NOSE.

"Jim Talbot, I presume?"

"It's not Dr. Livingstone, anyhow," Talbot said. He looked around the room. Calvert had been living in elegance here.

Calvert smiled. "Like it?" he inquired.

Talbot matched his smile. "Sure. I think the Romans lived something like this just before the bottom fell out."

Calvert walked over to an occasional table and poured himself a liqueur. He stood up, sipping it, inhaling it, absorbing it.

"I suppose you're here to tell me the bottom has fallen out."

Bonny Williams' trembling voice broke across Calvert's. "Mike Laynebeck is dead," he quavered.

"Or is that a surprise to you?" Talbot inquired.

Either Calvert was a hell of an actor, or the news did hit him like a sharp jab under the belt. He set the dainty glass down on the table and then stood up. He straightened his shoulders as though pain constricted his chest. His face was rigid and white.

"I didn't know," he whispered. "When did it happen? Where?"

Bonny looked at Talbot questioningly. Talbot went on staring at the foppish Calvert.

"Room 206, the Broadway Hotel," Talbot said. "It happened either last night or early this morning."

"And you found the body?"

"That's right. But Laynebeck went there looking for you. He found out last night after I left him that you were hiding out here in town, that you had not really disappeared at all. Some of your friends aren't as loyal as you seemed to believe."

His face still pale and rigid, Calvert was staring across Talbot's shoulder at Bonny Williams. The stout man shook his head negatively.

"I didn't, Dan," he protested. "I didn't say anything to nobody."

Calvert waved his hand, dismissing him. "All right, Bonny. We'll see. Meanwhile, why don't you get back downstairs?"

Bonny nodded, his face flooding with relief. He almost ran from the room.

Talbot waited until the door was closed behind the owner of the Golden Club. He faced Calvert across the table.

"I've no doubt you have the neatest set of alibis for last night and this morning?"

Calvert nodded. "Naturally. However, I don't have to answer to you. And besides, I'm quite upset at the news of Mike's death. We were very close — "

"Not too close that you couldn't double-cross him."

"I'm too upset to talk with you. I'm afraid you'll have to excuse me—"

"That's where you're wrong, Calvert. I came here to talk to you. Your grief doesn't interest me. I know what you did to Laynebeck before he died—and you weren't fit for him to spit on."

"A matter of opinion. Naturally you'd think Laynebeck a great man. He got you out of prison, didn't he?"

"He sure as hell did. When everybody else in this state had forgotten me, he was working for me. That's the kind of guy he was."

"Oh, I know all about your loyalty. It's quite touching. I even heard that you left a lucrative business up North to come running the first time he called you. Mike must have loved that. He loved to have people jump when he spoke."

"He earned loyalty, brother. He didn't buy it."

"Highly commendable, I'm sure. But your loyalty is no longer required. You are no longer needed here—if you ever were. As you have said, Laynebeck is dead. He hired you to find me, isn't that true? Well, since he's dead, there's no longer anyone to employ you. There's nothing more for you here in Duval."

"That's what you think. There's no fee in this for me from now on, Calvert. But this one is on me. There's one more thing here in Duval for me—the guy who killed Mike Laynebeck. I'm going to find him. And then God help him!"

Calvert's small mouth tightened into a hard line. "Don't be a fool! You should never have come back here in the first place. Oh, I know why you came. Loyalty to Mike Laynebeck—and the tender memory of Laynebeck's wife. Well, I can tell you this. Laynebeck's wife never loved you. You can forget that part of it now. Do you know who was with Nita the night she robbed the filling station?"

Talbot stared. Calvert's mouth twisted. He hadn't known. But he might have if he'd thought about it. A gutless wonder who hadn't had nerve enough to go through with it at the last minute.

His whisper was hoarse. "You. You were with her."

"That's right. I was with her. And we started off that evening laughing about you. No seat in your pants and mooning around after Nita Barwell! What a fool you looked. And we've been laughing at you ever since!"

Talbot made a pretense of shrugging it off. His heart was pounding like a kettledrum, but Calvert didn't have to know that.

"No more than I've laughed at myself," he said. "After I found out the score. Love is a matter of economics. You fall for a man who can support you, or a woman who can do your career some good, isn't that true?"

"If you're smart."

"Oh, well, I'm smart now, Calvert. You never met a smarter guy than I am now. So that's why if you know anything about Mike's murder you'd better talk."

"If you were smart you'd have left town that first night."

Talbot shook his head. "Just because you hired some thug to take a shot at me? Just because somebody shooting at you would have scared *you* out of town, Calvert, that doesn't mean that it would run me out. Oh, it scared me. I'm smart enough to be scared of guns when they're owned by men like you. But I don't run every time I'm scared."

"Maybe you'll wish you'd run, before we're through here."

"Or maybe you'll wish you had talked." Talbot took a step forward. Calvert straightened his immaculate dressing gown on his shoulders. "Maybe you'll wish you'd talked about what happened in room 206 at the Broadway Hotel last night. Or was it this morning?

"Somebody talked to Laynebeck, didn't they? After I saw him and convinced him that you were double-crossing him, he got on the telephone and started using some of that force that you rats forgot he possessed. Force that he could have been using all the time—"

Calvert smiled his contempt. "Forget it. Mike was a tired old man. Why do you think I was quitting him?"

"Because he needed you. That's why. That's when rats desert any ship, Calvert. When it's sinking."

"Laynebeck was on his way out, Talbot. He had gone soft. He was ruined. All he could think about was Nita. She spent too much money and ran too wild. He was too busy for politics. He wouldn't have had a handful of votes left in the next election—"

"So you got out from under? You hid out while you sold out to the Sheriff and his gang? What was it, Calvert—some scandal that Laynebeck had covered up for some of your politicians? You were going to smear him, weren't you? Oh, not you. The Sheriff and his boys would do that. All you would do was furnish the ammunition."

"All right. That's a good enough guess. Roberts' men are going in on a reform platform in the next election. They needed plenty of facts against the opposition. And there were plenty of facts. I haven't done anything dishonest. There's a certain judge. Laynebeck backed him for years. This judge is in graft up to his ears. Well, he's going out. And a Congressman, padding his payroll, taking a kickback—"

Talbot snarled. "Sure. They weren't perfect. Laynebeck said that. They were just the best possible men that could be rounded up for their jobs with things the way they are. That was why Laynebeck backed them. If anything ever blinded him, it was friendship. Loyalty to rats like you. And love—"

Calvert's smile was ugly. "Is it my fault I'm the one Nita loves?"

"And Nita you'll get when Laynebeck is gone. Nita. The Barwell money. The Laynebeck fortune. Social position. Prestige. And what did the Sheriff offer you? You'd be the next Senator?"

"I would have accepted, if it were offered me."

"Sure. And it would have been."

Calvert shook his head. "You're wrong Talbot. It will be. Laynebeck's death doesn't change that. I'm an important man in this state."

"I don't think you're as big as you think. You got evidence against the Sheriff as well as that judge to protect yourself until you were sure you'd get what you wanted. That was why Roberts was beating Laura, wasn't it? He'd found out you were maybe crossing him too. So he dragged in Laura to try to smoke you out. And when Mike Laynebeck found out where you were and what you were doing, he came to your room in the Broadway Hotel—and you had to kill him."

He lunged at Calvert, almost upsetting the table. Calvert staggered back with a cry of terror. Calvert's only possible response when actually threatened. The gutless wonder. The guy who let Nita rob for him when he lost his nerve even on a lark. The guy who didn't move to help Laura when the Sheriff got her, knowing the Sheriff was trying to smoke him out. He cringed. Afraid of pain. Afraid he might be hurt.

"No! I wasn't there. I wasn't there. Listen to me, Talbot, for God's sake!"

"I came here to listen." He gathered up the front of Calvert's lounging robe. "I've nothing on you but the fact that murder was committed in your hideout room. You killed the last decent guy I know. And I'd as soon kill you as take the time to prove you guilty. Start talking."

"All right. I only kept that room so I could—could see Laura Dawson. The blonde girl. You know her. She fell for me. Thought I was a big shot. She came here to dance. I was afraid Nita would find out. You don't know what Nita can be like when she hates—"

"So you took a cheap hotel room where you could shack up with Laura so Nita would never find out."

"So I got tired of Dawson. She's a nice kid. But right now, I'm going places—"

"Sure. Laura clutters it up. Nita is pretty important to a man who wants to be Senator—"

"Okay. If you know all about it, why ask me? Last night Laura begged me to come in to the hotel. I went in. I told her we were through, washed up. She better get out of town before Roberts got her again. I wouldn't lift my hand to help her. *But I didn't stay in that hotel.* I left there. I came back here. That's God's truth. You can prove that by asking Bonny Williams."

18

TALBOT GAVE CALVERT A SHOVE, RELEASING HIM. CALVERT WENT backward and landed hard on the pastel-tinted covers of the divan.

"I'll ask him," Talbot said. His voice was hard.

He turned around and strode across the room. He watched Calvert in one of the mirrored walls. Calvert remained on the divan where he had landed, his pale face twisted.

Talbot slammed the door of the apartment behind him. He was glad to get out. The closed-in odors of the Golden Club were clean after Calvert's plush, air-conditioned boudoir.

As he came off the lower step, Talbot heard the music of the band from the dining room. The band and the voice of a singer. His heart did a nip-up. Laura was in there. Rehearsal. But he didn't look in. He turned toward Bonny's office.

"Jim!"

Her voice struck at him. He hunched his shoulders against the sound of it and kept walking.

He could hear her running after him, the sharp sound of her breath, her heels on the corridor floor. She caught his arm, her hand barely touching him. Not pulling him around at all. Just begging him to turn. And look at her.

"Jim."

He kept his green eyes narrowed and cold. It was difficult. Her beauty was like white hot radium, and like radium burned through his defenses.

"You left this morning without saying good-bye."

He kept his voice cold. "What was there to say?"

"You were nice to me last night—you were good to me—you—"

"All right. Forget it." He forced himself to laugh. "Any time at all."

"Please, Jim. Don't be like this. I'm trying to tell you. It—"

"I don't want to hear it, baby. See? If I did, I'd have hung around this morning, wouldn't I?"

She took his hand, opened the door of a private dining room, drew him inside. She closed the door and leaned against it.

"I've been waiting all day to talk to you. I've been looking for you. I wanted to see you."

He shook his head. "Look, baby. You're a big girl now. You can't run after a guy."

From somewhere she pulled up a smile. "You mean Dan, don't you?"

"Sure. He's upstairs, honey. The great Calvert. He's the one you want, remember? I'm still the guy I always was. I'm not getting tangled up with anybody—"

"She really hurt you, didn't she?"

"She really did."

"But you can't go on letting her ruin your life!"

"Okay. And here's my tip to you, baby. You're a nice kid. Made to love. God knows I know that—"

"Jim—"

"No. Listen to me. Find some kid your own age. To hell with guys like Calvert. And guys like me—"

"And what's wrong with you?"

"I'm old. You'll never know how old."

"Don't treat me like this. Look, I admit it. I was in love with Dan Calvert. Or I thought I was. Maybe I'd never met anyone like him before. Politics. Money. Society. He asked me to come here, and I did. All right—I was—his girl. I was—I was what he wanted. And he kicked me out. I—I'm not going to lie to you about it. I'm not going to try to lie. Because I think maybe I've been lucky. Last night when you came in my room I was ready to die. I wanted to die. And today I don't want to. I want to forget Dan Calvert. I want to forget he ever lived—"

"Okay. That's swell. That's a good idea."

She was staring at him. The color was draining from her cheeks. Her mouth was stiff. She looked as though she'd been struck.

"I get it." Her voice was a whisper. "Forget Dan Calvert. But you—you don't want me—"

Talbot felt the rapid thudding of his heart over his empty belly. Want her? Mortgages. Washing machines. Kids' clothes hanging on the lines. The works.

"Because Dan had me, you don't want me." There was horror in her voice.

"Don't be a fool."

It was as though she didn't even hear him. She walked past him, sank down on one of the straight chairs. Her arms hung limp at her sides.

"I—I was honest about it. I thought that was what mattered. I was—in love. I didn't try to hide it. He made me keep it a secret. I didn't want to. I wanted to tell everybody. Now I know why. Because I wasn't good enough for him. I was just one—one of those girls that—he went to at night. The only difference was he didn't leave ten dollars on the table in the morning!"

She began to giggle. "Why should he? I was for free. I loved him."

"Cut it out, kid."

He touched her shoulder. She shrugged his hand away. "Let

me alone! I'm not good enough for you. I'm a rotten cheap little slut. No wonder you don't want me. I wasn't good enough for Dan Calvert.

"Oh, the things I did for him. 'Entertain the Congressman, Laura. Be nice to Mr. Jones. He's rich. He can do me a lot of good.' Sure. So Laura entertained the Congressman. She was nice to Mr. Jones. And all the time she was in love with Dan Calvert. All the time she was doing everything for him. Only he didn't see it that way, did he? Oh, no. I was a tramp. Only he didn't pay me. Only he *forgot* to pay me."

She began to laugh. She let the sound pour out rackingly, sobs and laughter all mixed together.

Talbot reached for her. She stared up at him, her eyes distended with tears. She hit him. She struck with both fists full in his face.

She hit with all her strength. For a second, he stood immobilized. Laura shoved him and ran from the room. The door slammed behind her.

Talbot leaned against the table. *Go after her*, his mind said. *Go after her.*

He sat there, without moving.

Sure, he could talk her out of it. He could find her and he could keep talking, and keep kissing her until she forgot all about Dan Calvert.

He shook his head. She would forget the hell Calvert had put her through. He knew how Calvert must have used her. He really must have been riding high. *Entertain the Congressman, Laura.*

Talbot's fists tightened. He could fill in the other part. He could see Calvert smirking and whispering in the Congressman's ear. Telling him what a charmer the Dusan wench was. "She jumps when I tell her to," Calvert would leer. He could hear Calvert's suave voice inside his head. "We'll have to be careful, Laura. We won't tell anybody. Not for a while."

And so he had his luscious little blonde. All he had to do was keep Nita Laynebeck from finding out the truth.

But now it was too dangerous to play around with Laura. Calvert's smooth voice again. "It's all over, Laura. It's been swell. But you must have known it was all just for fun. It's been fine."

Calvert had put her through it all right. Talbot knew. He had

been in love once. The terrible, star-moving kind that most people never know about. The lucky people. Laura loved hard. The
way Talbot had loved — once.

He stood up, started for the door. But it wasn't too late with
Laura. Hell, he could talk her out of it. Wasn't that what he had
wanted this morning? A cottage, a mortgage, a job. The works.

He shook his head again. It wasn't too late for Laura, but for
him . . . ten years too late.

Talbot stepped out of the kitchen door and started toward the
Buick parked at the end of the building. He saw Clemmons. He
started, heeling around. It was too late.

Clemmons' drawling voice stopped him. "I got my gun fixed
on youah back, Talbot. I don't mind pulling the trigger. But if'n
you're real smart, you'll stop. Right there where you are."

Talbot stood perfectly still.

"Your hands," Clemmons said. "Lift 'em up. High."

Talbot raised his hands.

Clemmons chuckled, coming up to him. "The great Talbot.
That private eye from New York. Boy, you shore don't look very
tough to me. You come off back down heah and got yourself in
a passel of trouble, ain't you?"

Talbot's face was stony. "You always were trouble, Clemmons.
A queer without sense enough to know he's queer. A fag without
intelligence enough to know why he likes to beat women. You
should have been a prison guard, Clemmons. You'd have made
yourself a fortune."

"Shut up! Shut up talking to me like that."

Talbot turned around slowly. He kept his hands up. "Do I get
you all nervous, Strick?"

"You like a bullet in your belly?"

"Where we going this time, Clemmons?"

"You ain't going far, tough guy. Raiford. The hot squat. Talk
tough now. Cause you're really fixed this time. Suppose you just
climb in that Buick and let's drive in to the Sheriff's office. Real
slow-like. I don't like you, Talbot. I never have. I'll put a bullet
in your gut."

"You'd like to do that, wouldn't you, Strick? You'd get a real
charge?"

Clemmons' eyes wavered; he dampened his lips and swallowed. "Try to escape, Talbot. You'll see."

"Escape? I don't want to. I want to ride in town with you and find out what you came out here to arrest me for."

"You don't have to ride that far to find that out, Talbot. I can tell you. You're gonna burn. For murder. For the murder of Mike Laynebeck."

19

CLEMMONS PUSHED OPEN THE DOOR OF THE SHERIFF'S OFFICE. "All right, tough guy," he said. "Let's go in."

Talbot went ahead of him into the office. The place was bedlam. There were newspaper men from all over the state. Nobody in Duval had realized that Laynebeck was their great man until he was dead.

Pushed against the wall across the room, Sheriff Roberts was sweating. He was facing the reporters and attempting to answer a barrage of questions. His face was a caricature of grief.

"Yes, gentlemen. Yes. This town, this nation has suffered a great loss. I promise you the Sheriff's office of Marvel County won't sleep until the murderer of that stalwart leader, Mike Laynebeck is behind bars."

"How soon will you make an arrest, Sheriff?"

"Do you have any leads, Sheriff?"

"Yes. Indeed we do. We promise a speedy arrest."

"Is it true, Sheriff, that Governor Erskine Reaves may conduct a personal investigation into Laynebeck's death?"

"Why, no. I'm shore that's just a rumor. Why, I know Governor Reaves has every faith in me. He'll allow me to conduct this investigation. He knows that his will is mine. His wish to arrest and convict the murderer of our good friend is my wish. I'm sure the Governor will let me handle this matter."

Roberts saw Clemmons and Talbot then. He jerked his head toward his inner office. Talbot felt the stout Ballard press close behind him and the three of them wedged their way through the crowd to the private office.

Clemmons closed the door against the shouting of the reporters and the hoarse bull voice of the Sheriff.

He nodded toward a chair. "All right, Talbot. Sit down."

The door opened and the sweating Sheriff squeezed through it. He locked it and leaned against it a moment to catch his breath.

He stared at Ballard. "Sit right here, Ballard. Don't let nobody in this door."

Ballard nodded.

"Here he is, Sheriff," Clemmons said. "Shall we get started on him?" Clemmons' eyes were glittering.

"Not in here, you fool!" Roberts snorted. He looked at Talbot. "All right, Talbot, in that room back there. It's quieter."

Talbot got up. "You want to be mighty careful, Sheriff. You're in a tough spot. You better not start kicking me around. I'll start out right now admitting I was in that hotel room. I saw Laynebeck's body. But I didn't kill him."

Roberts smiled. "You'll wish you had before we're through with you, Talbot. You ain't got the high and mighty Laynebeck to save you now. Laynebeck is dead."

"That's right and I didn't kill him."

Talbot was amazed that Roberts could move so fast. The Sheriff was catlike on his feet. He didn't telegraph his punch.

Talbot saw it coming just in time to jerk his jaw aside. He got the blow on his shoulder. It sent him hard against Roberts' desk.

He came off the desk on the rebound. He drove his left at Roberts' face. It never landed. There was a blur of movement behind him. Clemmons brought the gun butt down across his skull. Roberts' face danced, skidded and whirled out in front of Talbot's eyes. Then it caught fire and exploded. It burned like a million Roman candles. And when the fire was gone, the whole world was dark.

He could hear their voices a long time before he could see their faces. He came out of it slowly. It was a long time before he realized where he was.

His hands were cuffed behind him. He was sitting in a straight chair. The back room. The same back room where he'd found Laura Dawson that first night in Duval. Hell, the same chair.

What a sucker he had been. Roberts had hit at him for just

one reason. To make him hit back, to jockey him around so that he'd be set up for Clemmons. Clemmons and the gun butt. Well, they'd suckered him in. Big town guy and he'd fallen for it like the dumbest rube.

"We know you killed him," Roberts said.

"You're crazy! I worshipped the guy. He was the only decent guy I knew! Why would I kill him?"

Clemmons' hand came hard across his face. "You better tell us, killer!"

Talbot spat at him. He turned to Roberts. "You won't make it stick. You can't."

Clemmons hit him again. "This ain't no frame, Talbot. You killed him."

Roberts' voice was soft. "Wait a minute, Strick. Maybe we can make it easier for Mr. Talbot." He drew something from his pocket, held it out in the palm of his hand.

"An initialed cigarette lighter. Pretty expensive. The initials are J. T. James Talbot? Or am I wrong?? You know where we found that, Talbot? Right where you dropped it—beside Laynebeck's body!"

Talbot felt the world wheel out from under him. He stared at the cigarette lighter. Sure it was his. It was the one Nita had kept.

And it had been found in room 206, Broadway Hotel. So Nita had been there. She was so careless, wasn't she? Always losing things? Or had she lost it?

He shook his head. This was the jackpot. They were going to hold him. They wanted a man to convict. Whether he was guilty or not wasn't important. He could be made to look guilty. They could prove that James Talbot had been in that room. They could show that he had lost his cigarette lighter there. Why would he kill his benefactor?

There would be plenty of time before the trial came up. They'd think of something. Hell, they'd invent something.

And this time there would be no Mike Laynebeck to save him.

Wasn't that a hell of a twist? Mike Laynebeck had saved him from prison once. Now, Mike Laynebeck's body was going to send him back there—one way!

He stirred in the chair. He wanted out of there. He had to get out of there.

Clemmons brought the back of his hand across Talbot's face so hard that his head rocked back on his neck. Stars careened out before his muddled eyes.

His head sank forward on his chest. "Wait," he whispered.

Clemmons wiped the flecks of spittle away with the back of his hand. He started to hit again. Roberts stopped him.

"What is it, Talbot?"

"Unlock me. There ain't any use fightin' this any more."

Roberts nodded at Clemmons. The deputy bent down behind the chair and removed the handcuffs. Talbot sighed heavily, rubbed his wrists.

Ballard knocked on the door. "Sheriff!"

"Get the hell away from there. You know I'm busy."

"Sheriff. Please. For the Lord's sake! It's the Governor. Governor Reaves. In the outside office. He's on his way into your office right now!"

Talbot looked up at Roberts. All the blood had drained from the Sheriff's beefy face. For the moment he stood perfectly rigid. He was paralyzed. Finally, he turned and marched woodenly toward the door to his plush office.

He unlocked it. He turned, his eyes still dazed. He spoke to Clemmons over his shoulder. "Keep him quiet in here. I'll be back. Soon as I can."

Talbot sat slumped in the straight chair. From the Sheriff's private office, he could hear the voices of Governor Reaves, sharp and angry against the bull tones of Roberts.

A hell of a lot of good it was going to do him, Talbot thought. He knew all about Marvel County justice, and Marvel County mercy.

The Governor was upset. He was violently angry. It was going to take the Sheriff some time. But Talbot was sure he knew how it was going to end. Roberts would sell the Governor a bill of goods. They had a man in the back room. He could be made to look guilty. A carnival of a trial—and everything was fine again.

"The worst thing that has ever happened in my career!" The Governor's voice was savage. "Killed. Shot in a cheap hotel room. And his killer walks out without a trace—"

"Not without a trace!" Roberts voice boomed. "Now, Governor Reaves, if you'll leave this matter to me—"

"I cannot, L. F.! They're after me. The opposition papers are ripping into me. They're saying that our group has degenerated until it is nothing more than a gang—and that the death of Senator Laynebeck is the latest gang killing—"

"Now, Governor, you know a thing like that ain't true!" Roberts' loud voice was persuasive, soothing.

"I'll tell you what I know, Roberts. The people of this state are howling about the gambling syndicate and the rackets that are going on right under my nose."

"We'll settle this matter, Governor."

"How?"

"Look, Governor. In the room back there is a man who *could* be guilty—"

Talbot heard Reaves' voice rise to a crescendo of anger and crack like a whip. "Could be guilty! And now a frame-up to cover a heinous murder! My God, Roberts! What are you trying to get away with?"

"I'm trying to settle this thing, Governor. As quietly and speedily as possible."

"I don't know how stupid you people are, but you must know how shaky our position is right now. You take an innocent man into court, they'll crucify you. I wouldn't care about that—but it'll ruin every politician in this state."

"He won't be innocent!"

The Governor's voice cracked again. "You meant there won't be a way to prove him innocent after you're through! No, Sheriff. You've got to do better than that. I'm bringing in my own investigators tonight. We're going to get the real murderer. I'm perfectly sincere when I tell you that Laynebeck was known and respected all over the country. The smell of this thing can very well ruin us all. And I'll tell you this, Roberts, I agree with the opposition. Laynebeck's death does smack of gang killing. I'm warning you. One more political death—or scandal—in Marvel County and I'll purge you. You're finished!"

Talbot went on massaging his wrists. But there was no longer any pain in them. His mind had raced far ahead, planning, thinking, discarding, choosing.

There was a chance that Roberts would release him. There was no mercy in Governor Reaves' voice. Roberts was in a hell of a predicament. Very likely he would be afraid to hold Talbot now without some kind of conclusive evidence of his guilt.

Talbot knew he had one thing in his favor: few people didn't know how Talbot felt about Laynebeck. Against that was the cigarette lighter found in room 206 beside Laynebeck's dead body.

But he didn't want to take a chance on the Sheriff's releasing him. He wanted out of there. Now.

He slumped forward on the chair, groaning. Clemmons leaped across the room on his stilt-like legs. Talbot waited until he was close beside the chair.

He came up fast. He slapped his left hand over Clemmons' mouth, squeezing his fingers with all his strength into the deputy's lantern jaws. Clemmons was unable to utter a sound.

As he came up, Talbot drove his knee into Clemmons' groin. The deputy gasped, folding.

Talbot released him then. As Clemmons crumpled, Talbot brought the side of his hand in a short chop against the nape of his neck. Clemmons hit the floor hard and didn't stir.

The Governor was still tongue-lashing the Sheriff as Talbot stepped through the window into the breathless Florida night.

20

TALBOT WALKED ACROSS THE COURTYARD TO MAIN STREET. There was a taxi driver napping in his cab outside the bus station. Talbot got in the rear of the car and tapped the sleeping man on the shoulder.

"The Golden Club," he said. "And step on it. I'm trying to make that first show. That blonde that dances. I don't want to miss her."

The cabbie had already put the car in motion.

"You mean the babe that dances wit' them veils?" The driver whistled. "Mister, she sends me, calls me back and spins me like a top. And me with five kids already!"

Talbot sat on the edge of the seat, alternately listening to the driver's chatter and waiting to hear the sound of sirens behind him.

The taxi was clipping along at fifty-five. Cypress Road had never seemed so long. Houses, trees, lawns seemed to inch past. It had never taken so long to get out of the city limits. It seemed twenty miles to the Golden Club. And yet Golden Springs was only six miles east of the bus station, and the Golden Club was almost three miles closer to town. Talbot felt he could have pushed the cab at a better rate of speed.

The driver whipped the car into the macadam parking lot. Brakes squealed as he skidded to a stop before the brightly-lighted entrance of the club.

Talbot tossed him a bill.

The driver looked at it and grinned. "Thanks, mister. You musta wanted to see her bad."

Talbot went through the entrance. The blaring music of the dance band struck him like a douse of cold water. But he didn't look into the dining room. He ran past the hat-check booth and turned along the corridor toward the stairs.

He went up the steps two at a time.

The door to Calvert's apartment was closed. There was no sound from within this time. Talbot hammered on the door.

There was no answer. A waiter came from one of the rooms down the corridor. He looked worriedly at Talbot.

"Send Bonny Williams up here," Talbot snapped at him. He pounded on the door again.

Bonny Williams came puffing and sweating up the steps almost immediately.

"A key," Talbot snarled. "Open this door."

"He's not in there," Bonny Williams whimpered. "He's been gone three hours."

Talbot's shoulders sagged. He felt the defeat all over like bone-weariness. He heeled around and started slowly down the steps.

"How about Laura Dawson?" he said. "Where is her dressing room?"

Bonny Williams looked as if he were about to cry. "She didn't work tonight," he moaned. "My big night of the week and she doesn't show up. Sure. I got her veils. What will I put in them? Some cow? They'd laugh them off the floor, right off the floor."

But Talbot wasn't listening. He was already on his way to the taxi stands outside the front doors.

***

Talbot got out of the cab at the end of the dark block below the Broadway Hotel. He walked past its dim-lit entrance and around to the service alley.

Inside the delivery door, he ran for the stairs. He kept running, feeling his heart slugging like a hot rivet in his chest.

He went along the corridor to 314. She had to be in there. He fished the room key out of his pocket and fitted it in the lock.

He pushed the door open and there she was. Laura was sitting on a straight chair, her body lax, arms at her side.

"Laura!"

She lifted her head, turned it toward the sound of his voice. But it seemed an eternity before her pale eyes focused on him.

"Jim," she said. "Hello, Jim."

"Laura. Snap out of it. I want you to do something for me —"

"Entertain the Congressman, Laura. Be nice to Mr. Jones." Her voice was a parrot's voice.

He grabbed her by the shoulders. Her head flopped back. She stared at him. Her face expressionless.

"Laura. You've got to find Dan Calvert for me. Do you hear? I've got to find him, Laura. I've got to have him. I haven't much time."

She shrugged his hands away and straightened up on the chair. She ran her slender hand through her tousled blonde hair. She searched his features for long moments before she spoke.

"All right, Jim. I'll find him. I'll find him for you." Her wan smile was inscrutable.

She got up and started to walk past him. She staggered and almost fell. He leaped to grab her.

She shook his hands away. "No. Don't touch me."

He let her go. She looked at him again, breathing heavily. She stumbled again and caught herself against the doorjamb of the bathroom.

"Here he is," she said. "Here's Dan Calvert."

He stared across her shoulder. Dan was sprawled on the bathroom floor. There was a knife in his throat. He was dead.

21

LAURA BEGAN TO LAUGH, A SICK SOBBING SOUND LOW IN HER throat. "There he is, Jim. There's Dan Calvert. You asked for him and here he is."

"Laura, why'd you do it?"

She looked at him, her mouth twisting. "He killed me, didn't he? He killed me. Look what he made me. Cheap hotel. Cheap room. 'Entertain the Congressman, Laura. Be nice. Get out of town, kid.' I wanted to dance. I loved to dance. He killed me. Do *you* want me? Oh, no. You were a slut, Laura. You fell in love and so you're a slut. You're rotten. So that's why I'm rotten. Right there on the floor with a knife in his neck. That's why I'm rotten. So I killed him, too. Like he killed me. Only he won. He's dead. It's over for him. But I'm still living."

She buried her face in her hands. He put his arm about her shoulder but she shrugged it away.

"I was smart about it, Jim. You want to hear how I was smart about it? I went up to his apartment over Bonny Williams' Golden Club. His stinking sweet apartment. I never thought it stunk until you and I were together here—" She sucked in a deep breath and went on talking rapidly, breathlessly. "I went in up there. I told him I would leave town. I would never see him again. But I had to see him one more time." She snarled suddenly.

"Oh, he fell for that. The irresistible Mr. Calvert. How he loved it to have me beg him to love me—one more time. What a fool! Oh, I made it good. I danced. I never danced on any club floor like I danced for him. Then he began to want me. I drove him crazy. I had him begging.

"Only I wouldn't. Not up there I wouldn't. I told him he had to come back here. Back to my room. I wanted it here again. For the last time. Oh, how he fell for it!

"I even took a taxi back here. On my way through the Golden Club kitchen, I picked up a knife. A sharp one. They cut turkeys with it and cheap, tough meat. Oh, but it was easy. Dan wasn't cheap and tough. He was so elegant. Oh, he was elegant, wasn't he? But he cried and looked scared when he had to die."

She began to sob then as though she would never stop crying.

"I didn't want to kill him," she moaned. "I didn't. I just wanted to be loved, Jim. . . . I just wanted you to love me."

He pulled her against him then. She buried her face against his shoulder. He held her for a long time without speaking. Her sobs died out, slowly, and her arms crept up his back.

He began to talk against her hair.

"Listen to me, Laura. There's a blue Buick parked in the courthouse square. The keys are in it. Clemmons made me leave them there. I want you to walk up to it—and get in. Then drive out of town. Just keep driving until morning." He looked at his watch. "You have time to get to Tampa. Or Jacksonville. By that time there may be a ticker on the car. Right now they're too busy to notice. They know I didn't take it when I ran away from the Sheriff's office. They won't think I'd come back and get it. You've got time to get away, Laura—"

"I killed him. I can't get away."

"You can. There's a good chance—a very good chance. But pay attention. When you get to Tampa—ditch the car. Just park it and walk away. Get a job, Laura, slinging hash, sweeping, cooking. Anything. Forget you ever saw this town."

She looked at him. There was a thin glimmer of hope in her tear-stained eyes. "Could I, Jim? Could I get away from here?"

"You can, Laura. You will. I did once. And you will."

"Can I come to you then—sometime? When this is over? Will you let me?" Her voice was pleading.

"You won't want to, baby. I'll remind you of Duval—and all this. You'll be happier if you don't."

Her body slumped, the hope was gone. Her voice was dead. "You don't want me."

He felt a downrush of cold through his veins. How could he have been such a fool? She might have made the effort if he'd been smart. He forced himself to laugh.

"I want you. Believe that, Laura. You're the first girl I've wanted in ten years. That's the truth. Even if you don't believe it now, you will later when you think back. You'll know. You'll know I was different with you. But I was thinking about you. Why should a pretty kid like you want a wreck of a guy like me?"

Her voice choked. "But if I do want you?"

He nodded. "I'm in the New York phone book, Laura. Man-

hattan. When you get there, I'll be there. If you decide to come
to me, I'll be there. Waiting."

He waited only until he was sure she was in the lobby of the
hotel. The Broadway Hotel. A cheap little hotel in a hot Florida
town. But for one moment in eternity, two people had had together what God intended. . . .

He went into the bathroom. The gash in Calvert's throat was
no longer bleeding. Talbot got a hotel towel and wrapped it se-
curely about the dead man's neck, without touching the knife.

He picked him up then in his arms. He crossed the room,
cracked open the door and peered along the hall. It was quiet
out there.

He stepped out into the corridor. He left the door standing
open. Carrying Calvert in his arms he went to the stairway and
started down the steps. On the second floor he stopped at the
landing. Supporting Calvert's body against the railing, he fished
out the key the clerk had given him to room 206.

There was no one in the hotel corridor. It was closer to 206
than 314 had been to the stairwell.

But Talbot was sweating. He had to fight a key into a lock,
holding a dead man in his arms.

His hand trembled so badly that he had to stop, hold his breath
and try again. As he pushed the door open another door down
the corridor was opened. He leaped through the doorway, heeled
around and slammed the door shut.

He carried Calvert over and dropped him on the bed. He went
back to the door, opened it. A small man stood there, frowning.

"Say, did I see you carrying some man in this room?"

Talbot forced himself to grin. "My wife, partner. She had a
little too much. You know?"

"Oh, yeah. Looked like a man, but there was a funny wrap
around her neck—"

"Scarf—"

"Oh. Oh, sure. By the way, I wouldn't want that room. Man
killed in there—"

Talbot's eyes widened. "That so?"

"Yeah. I sure wouldn't have taken that room."

"Well, I'm new in town. Didn't know anything about it. You can bet I'll raise hell with the management." He closed the door in the little man's face.

He went back across the room, pulled Calvert's body off the bed to the floor. Then he turned the bed so that Calvert's body was concealed, hidden under it.

He went out of the room then, locking it after him. Back in Laura's room, he scrubbed every trace of Calvert's blood from the tiled floor of the bathroom.

He went out in the bedroom then and went over it carefully. He picked up Calvert's hand-blocked hat, his gloves, his cane. He went to the door and looked at the room for the last time.

He crossed the corridor and went back down to room 206. Inside, he put Calvert's hat on the dresser, dropped the gloves on top of it. He tossed the cane on the bed.

He picked up the telephone. The operator said, "Number, please?"

He gave her the number of Mike Laynebeck's house.

A man answered.

"I'd like to speak to Mrs. Laynebeck, please."

"I'm sorry, sir. There has been a tragedy in the family. Mrs. Laynebeck is prostrated with grief. If you'd care to leave a message."

"This is Jim Talbot. You better ask her if she wants to talk to me."

There was a delay. Talbot stood there counting his slow, thudding heartbeats.

"Jim?"

"Hello, Nita."

"Where are you?"

"I'm in room 206, Nita, at the Broadway Hotel. Dan Calvert is here with me. I think you'd better come over."

He heard her sharp intake of breath. Finally, she said very softly, "All right, Jim. I'll be there. As soon as I can."

He sat down then in a chair beside the telephone table. It pleased him that Calvert had had a private extension installed in his room. Count on Calvert to do everything up right.

Even, Talbot thought, *he couldn't have chosen a more opportune moment to die.*

Time dragged. He smoked a dozen cigarettes. He didn't drop

his ashes in the ashtray, nor did he leave the butts in there. As he finished each cigarette he carried it in to the bathroom and flushed it down the drain, ashes and all.

It was almost an hour later when he heard the elevator door open and close at the end of the corridor.

He lifted the telephone receiver. The operator said, "Number, please?"

He said nothing.

"Number, please?"

There were footsteps in the hall. A firm, sure tread; but light. A woman's foot. The steps ceased outside the door.

"Number, please!"

Talbot held the mouthpiece close against his lips.

"The Sheriff's office," he said. "Hurry."

Sheriff Roberts answered almost at once. He must have ordered an open wire during the emergency.

There was a very soft knock on the door.

"Roberts? This is Talbot."

The knock again.

"Where are you?"

"Room 206. Broadway Hotel. And you better come yourself." The knock again. "Come in," Talbot said. "It isn't locked."

He replaced the receiver as Nita walked in the door.

22

HE WALKED PAST HER, CLOSED THE DOOR, LOCKED IT. THERE WAS a night latch. He secured it.

Nita was wearing a black dress, a mink jacket and a mink beanie. He shook his head. She never belonged in a place like this. She was like a flawless gem that had rolled out of its setting and fallen in a gutter somewhere.

She looked about, her face white. "Where's Dan?" she said.

He looked at her, smiled. "I want to talk to you first."

She caught her breath. "You tricked me. He's not here at all."

"He is here. See, his hat and gloves on the dresser. His cane on the bed. You'll see him. But first I want to know something, Nita. Why did you kill Mike?"

Her mouth fell open. "I? Why—why do you think I did it?"

"Because you planted a cigarette lighter in this room, baby. Still playing me for a sucker. Still letting me take your raps. An old, old habit you got into—ten years ago. Only this time it didn't work, baby."

She began to shake her head from side to side. "I didn't. Jim! I didn't!"

"Oh, yes you did. You told Mike where Dan was. You'd found out that night when I saw you at the Golden Club. I saw you running out. You made a date with me for the river bank. A date you never intended keeping. But it would put me out there at one o'clock in the morning—eight miles from the nearest alibi."

She was staring at him. She shook her head. Her eyes wallowed in the mire of terror.

"It's not true, Jim. It isn't. Listen to me. You must listen to me! I had your lighter. But Mike took it from me. He warned me not to start on you, as he called it. He told me to leave you alone. He said I had hurt you enough, and he'd beat me to keep me from hurting you any more. He was going to give the lighter back to you. It was in his vest pocket. I saw him put it there. It must have fallen out when he was killed—"

He took a step toward her. A scream worked its way up through her throat but died on her lips.

"All right, Jim! All right! I was here. You told me about Laura Dawson and Dan. I'd never even suspected. I brought a gun. I—I paid the night clerk to let me in. I hid in the dark. I—I shot when the door opened.

"I thought it was Dan, Jim! I went crazy. I was wild to think he had been cheating! I went crazy. I wanted to kill him. I can't stand to have people hurt me, Jim. I never could. They've no right—"

"All right," he said tiredly. "What did you do?"

"When I saw it was Mike, I came to my senses. I saw him stagger into the room and fall. I tried to touch him—to see if I could help him. I—I couldn't. I ran out, I went down the back stairs. I went home."

"All right, Nita. Just so we know. Now, you wanted to see Dan." He strode past her and shoved the bed back against the wall.

He heard her gasp.

He heeled around, faced her. His face was set and cold. His voice was deadly.

"There he is, Nita. He's dead. And you killed him."

She tried to scream, but couldn't. Her hand worked at her paralyzed throat. Her eyes were bulging.

"You're insane," she whispered. "You've gone crazy."

"No, Nita. I've *been* insane. For ten years. I came back here more for revenge against you even than to help Mike. I didn't know he had married you. When I saw he had married you and loved you, it changed everything. I gave up any idea of getting even—an eye for the eye you robbed me of.

"But then I found out the truth. You were faithless. You killed Mike, and then I was free to do what I had planned to do. Make you pay for the hell I've been through.

"I was going to be a lawyer, Nita. Remember? Maybe I wouldn't have been a good one. On the other hand, I might have been another Mike Laynebeck. We'll never know. Because of what you did to me, we'll never know."

She backed away from him, bumped the wall, slumped against it. She watched him, her gaze fixed on his cold and bitter face.

"No, you let me take the rap for an armed robbery. Dan Calvert was with you. The gutless wonder. You've been building him up ever since until he's decided he was wonderful. . . . I'd have rotted in the chain gang, Nita, except that Mike Laynebeck got me free. You killed Mike. Maybe there is no way for me to prove that. Just my word against yours. Your money and your influence. I wouldn't get very far.

"But when I'm through, nobody will doubt that you killed Dan Calvert. You're going to pay, baby. Maybe not for the right murder—but just the same you're going to pay for murder."

"Jim. How can you do this? You love me. You came back here loving me."

"Did I, baby? I came back hating you. I haven't loved you, Nita, since the day I went to the chain gang. I've never been able to love anybody else. Because all the time I hated you too terribly. I hated all women because of you."

"Jim. Please. I'll make it up to you! We can get away. I can love you as you've never been loved. We'll make up all those years. We can get away—"

"I can get away. I can get out of this room. I did it once before. I'll do it again. But you can't come with me. Anyhow, Nita, it's too late. You're not what I'd want any more. This time it's going to be a blonde—twenty—with hair like hot platinum . . ."

Her laughter stopped him. Nita came away from the wall then. She was no longer abject. Her shoulders straightened.

"The little blonde dancer, maybe? Laura Dawson? Dan's little slut? Oh, no. No matter what you do, Jim, you'll never have her!"

He grabbed her arms in his hands, squeezing.

"Where is she? What happened?"

"That was why I was so late. The State Highway patrol. They called. The blue Buick. It was registered in my name. They were reporting an accident. Some woman named Laura Dawson was driving it. Eighty miles an hour. She missed a turn, Talbot, six miles east of Duval. She crashed into one of the big neon arrows pointing to Golden Springs. The car was demolished. There was a lot of damage done to the sign. I think the car plowed a hundred feet before it stopped. And by the way, the woman, the Dawson woman. She was dead when they found her."

Jim stood silent, looking at her. He heard the elevator door clang shut at the end of the corridor. He shoved his hands into his coat pockets. He brought out the initialed cigarette lighter he'd found under Calvert's Duval House bed, the lipstick Nita had dropped on the parking lot of the Golden Club. The handkerchief she'd left on the seat of the Buick. He looked at them. His bitter mouth was twisted.

"My things," she said. "You did love me—you saved them . . ."

"I saved them. But not because I loved you. Because I hated you. I saved them for just some sort of setup like this. I didn't know it would be murder. But that's fine.

"I'll just salt them around in here. Careless Nita. Always losing things. When you go to trial, baby, the hotel clerk down there will know you came up here. Know you paid him. But he never saw you leave. You think the people at the Duval House won't testify to the hours you spent up in Calvert's suite? I found that cigarette lighter up there. Your bobby pins. People around this town who saw you together. It'll all add up. I'll make it add up."

His whisper was hoarse. "You're too rich, too influential to burn for Calvert's murder. Maybe a miracle will save you from more than five years. If maybe Calvert can be proved to have killed Laynebeck, you might have a motive for killing Calvert that would sway a jury. But not much.

"I'm a private eye, Nita, and I'll dig up such a case against you and Calvert that there is only one lawyer who might possibly save you. Think, Nita! Think who might be able to save your hide. Mike Laynebeck. But he's not here. He's dead. The only man in God's world who could save you from prison, and he's dead—and you killed him."

There was the sound of fists against the door. Nita stared at Talbot.

Sheriff Roberts' voice boomed. "Open up in there, or I'll break down the door."

Talbot laughed at that. He could still hear Governor Erskine Reaves' voice rasping in the Sheriff's office: "One more political death—or scandal—in Marvel County, and I'll purge you."

Talbot stood there waiting. It seemed Roberts couldn't get into Room 206 fast enough. The room where the next murder and scandal awaited him. The one that was going to ruin him.

Roberts broke the lock with a kick. The door swung slowly open. Nita fainted, slumping silently to the floor beside Talbot.

But Talbot didn't even look at her. He didn't want to miss the look on the Sheriff's face when he stalked in and saw the surprise that was waiting for him in Room 206.